P9-BZI-073

Praise for
Way of the Wolf:
Book One of *The Vampire Earth*

"A winner. If you're going to read only one more post-apocalyptic novel, make it this one."
—Fred Saberhagen, author of the *Berserker* series

"I have no doubt that E. E. Knight is going to be a household name in the genre." —Silver Oak Book Reviews

"[If] *The Red Badge of Courage* had been written by H. P. Lovecraft." —Paul Witcover, author of *Waking Beauty*

"E. E. Knight has managed to create a compelling new world out of the ruins of our existing one. It's a major undertaking for a new author. . . . I would highly recommend checking out the book as soon as you can."
—Creature Corner

"It was obvious to me within the first few pages that Knight knew how to write. . . . Valentine is a complex and interesting character, mixing innocence with a cold-hearted willingness to kill. . . . His world is well-constructed and holds together in a believable fashion. . . . Compelling."
—SFReader.com

"Powerful. . . . Readers will want to finish the tale in one sitting because it is so enthralling."
—*Midwest Book Review*

"Character-driven speculative fiction adventure at its very best." —*Black Gate*

CHOICE OF THE CAT

BOOK TWO OF *THE VAMPIRE EARTH*

E. E. Knight

A ROC BOOK

ROC
Published by New American Library, a division of
Penguin Group (USA) Inc., 375 Hudson Street,
New York, New York 10014, USA
Penguin Group (Canada), 90 Eglinton Avenue East, Suite 700, Toronto,
Ontario M4P 2Y3, Canada (a division of Pearson Penguin Canada Inc.)
Penguin Books Ltd., 80 Strand, London WC2R 0RL, England
Penguin Ireland, 25 St. Stephen's Green, Dublin 2,
Ireland (a division of Penguin Books Ltd.)
Penguin Group (Australia), 250 Camberwell Road, Camberwell, Victoria 3124,
Australia (a division of Pearson Australia Group Pty. Ltd.)
Penguin Books India Pvt. Ltd., 11 Community Centre, Panchsheel Park,
New Delhi - 110 017, India
Penguin Group (NZ), 67 Apollo Drive, Mairangi Bay,
Auckland 1311, New Zealand (a division of Pearson New Zealand Ltd.)
Penguin Books (South Africa) (Pty.) Ltd., 24 Sturdee Avenue,
Rosebank, Johannesburg 2196, South Africa

Penguin Books Ltd., Registered Offices:
80 Strand, London WC2R 0RL, England

First published by Roc, an imprint of New American Library,
a division of Penguin Group (USA) Inc.

First Printing, May 2004
20 19 18 17 16 15 14 13 12

To Paul, for opening the door

"Cat 'e no yoke. You no see 'im, you no 'ear 'im. Den yomp! 'E come."

—Richard Adams, *Watership Down*

One

The Great Plains Gulag, March of the forty-fifth year of the
Kurian Order: Only the bones of a civilization remain,
monuments to mankind's apogee. Nature and time gnaw
away the rest. Derricks still stand in this corner of oil country, giant iron insects surveying the countryside. Beneath
them, the pumps rust, scattered in the long yellowish grass
like metal herbivores, snouts thrust into the earth. The former wheat fields, fallow for generations and returned to
native forest or prairie, feed longhorns, deer, and canny
wild pigs. It is a land of receding horizons, a stopped
watch, timeless.

The soil under cultivation bears the turned over, tram-
pled look of spring plowing. The tools and methods used on
the stretches of farmland would make a twentieth-century
resident either stare in wonder or spit in disgust. Horse-
drawn plows, some with just a single blade, sit at the edges
of the fields, where they were abandoned at quitting time,
plots fertilized only by what comes out of the back end of an
animal.

The agricultural settlements at the center of the remaining fields, always near a road or rail line, look more like
chain-gang camps than family farms. Surrounded by
barbed wire and watchtowers, the clapboard barracks that
house the workers and their families cry out for a coat of
paint and a new roof to replace the flapping plastic tarps
covering assorted holes. Trash heaps and pit toilets deco-
rate the compounds among pitiful vegetable gardens. The
children playing amid the tight-packed buildings flirt with
nudity, so worn away are their clothes.

Near the gate of these camps a more substantial building usually stands at a respectful distance from the barracks, avoiding contact like a visitor to a leper colony. Often a sturdy pre-22 brick construct; the windows hold glass behind bars or shutters, and curtains behind the glass.

A few miles north of Oologah Lake along old State Route 60, one of these collective farms, known to its residents as the Rigyard, is nestled between gently rolling hills. Two rows of tall wire fencing encircle the camp. Barracks laid out foursquare sit in the shadow of two watchtowers, dwarfed in turn by two cavernous garages like enormous Quonset huts. The garages are patchworks of earthen wall, structural iron, and corrugated aluminum. On the other side of them, in a commanding position near the gate, an L-shaped cinder-block building dating to the 1950s folds itself protectively around a set of gasoline pumps. A water tower—a recent addition, judging from the new shine to the steel—leans slightly askew above, adding a jaunty top hat to the guardhouse. Behind the cinder-block building, a fine two-story house stands in splendid isolation at the farthest point upwind from the barracks, circled first by a porch and then a set of razor-wire fencing with padlocked gate.

Each watchtower contains a single sentinel dressed in green-brown-mottle camouflage fatigues and black leather hunting cap. The sentry to the south is the more alert; he occasionally crosses his little crow's nest to glance up and down the highway bordering the camp's southern fence. The one to the north chews a series of toothpicks in appropriately beaverish front teeth. He watches a trio of smock-clad women wash clothing in the community sink set between the barracks.

Were the other guard equipped with an excellent pair of binoculars (unlikely, but possible), perfect eyesight (still less likely, as guarding farmers and mechanics is reserved for older members of the Territorials), and intelligent initiative in carrying out his duty (the phrase "cold day in hell" springs to mind) he would have paid attention to the gully winding up the hill that shelters the Rigyard from the prevailing winds. The wooded cut in the hill offers ample concealment and a commanding view, whether for simple observation or an organized attack.

A figure possessing all those qualities lies on that hill, surrounded by the white and yellow and red wildflowers of an Oklahoma spring. He is a muscular, long-limbed young man with coppery skin and wary brown eyes. Dressed not so differently from his ancestors on the Sioux side of his family, he wears a uniform of buckskin, save for a thicker cowhide equipment belt and boots. Lustrous black hair is drawn back from his face into a ponytail, giving him the illusion of closely cropped hair from every direction but behind, where it dangles to his shoulders. He wears an intent expression as he examines the camp. A young cheetah watching a watering hole might exhibit such wariness, unsure whether the vegetation contains game or a lion ready to pounce. His eyes wander from point to point in the camp with the aid of a pair of black binoculars, lingering here and there while his forearm acts as a monopod. Like the bucktoothed guard in the southern tower, his mouth is also working, thoughtfully nibbling on the tender end of a blade of seed-topped grass.

His gaze returns to the wire-enclosed yard of the two-story house. In the grassy back lawn of the house, two T-shaped metal posts face each other, missing the clothesline that once joined them. Instead of wash drying in the afternoon sun, three men and a woman are painfully attached to the improvised gibbet. Their wrists are clasped behind them and tied to the metal crossbeam above, tight enough to dislocate a shoulder if they slump in their bonds.

He knows that death awaits the four—not from pained exhaustion or exposure—but from something quicker, more horrible, and as sure as the setting sun.

The senior lieutenant of Foxtrot Company set down his binoculars and focused his eyes a few feet in front of him on a flowering coral bean, its delicate red spindles inclining toward the sun. The diversion failed; though they were a good kilometer away, he could still see the agonized figures in the yard. His shoulders throbbed with sympathetic pain.

After four years' service to the Cause, his sensitivity to suffering had grown more acute, rather than less.

Lt. David Valentine looked back down into the gully. His platoon, numbering thirty-five in all, rested with backs up against leafing trees, using their packs to keep their backsides off the rain-soaked earth. They had covered a lot of ground since skirting the northern edge of Lake Oologah that morning, moving at a steady, mile-eating run. Rifles rested ready in their laps. They wore leather uniforms frilled in variegated styles to taste. Some still wore their winter beards, and no two hats matched. The only accoutrement his three squads shared were their short, broad-bladed machetes, known as parangs—though some wore them on their belts, some across their chests, and some sheathed them in their moccasin-leather puttees.

They didn't look like mixture of legend and alien science, part of a elite caste known as the Hunters.

Valentine signaled with two fingers to the men waiting in the gully, and Sergeant Stafford climbed up the wash to join him in the damp bracken. His platoon sergeant, known as Gator off-duty because of his leathery skin and wide, toothy grin, worked slowly to Valentine's overlook. Wordlessly, the lieutenant passed Stafford his binoculars. Stafford examined the compound as Valentine chewed another inch off the grass stalk clamped in his teeth.

"Looks like that last sprint was for nothing," Valentine said. "The tractor trailer pulled in here. We wouldn't have intercepted anyway—this must be a pretty good stretch of road."

"How do you figure that, sir?" Stafford said, searching the compound in vain for any sign of the tanker truck they'd spotted crawling through the rain that morning. The platoon dashed cross-country in order to ambush the tempting target. Thanks to the state of the roads in this part of the Kurian Zone, the rig couldn't move much faster than the Wolves could run.

"Look at the ruts by the gate, turning off the road. They've got to have been made by an eighteen-wheeler," Valentine said.

"Could have been from yesterday—even the day before, Lieutenant."

Valentine raised an eyebrow. "No puddles. Rain would have filled in something that deep. Those were made since the shower ended—what?—a half hour ago?"

"Err . . . okay, yeah . . . so the truck's in one of those big garages getting worked on. We get in touch with the captain, the rest of the company is here in a day or two, and we burn the compound. I figure fifteen or twenty guarding this place at most. Ten's more likely."

"I'd like nothing better, Staff. Time's a problem, though."

"Val, I know food's short, but what else is new? There's enough game and forage in these woods—"

"Sorry, Gator," Valentine said, taking the binoculars back. "I misspoke. I should have said time's running short for *them*."

Stafford's eyebrows arched in surprise. "What, those four tied up down there? Okay, it's ugly, but since when have we gotten dead over the punishments handed out by these little Territorial commandants?"

"I don't think it's just punishment," Valentine said, his eyes now on the two-story house.

"Hell, sir, you know these collaborator creeps. . . . They'll flog a woman for not getting the skid marks out of their skivvies. These four probably were last out of the barracks for roll call or something. God knows."

Valentine waited for a moment, wondering whether to give voice to a feeling. "I think they're breakfast. There's a Reaper in that house, maybe more than one."

Sgt. Tom Stafford blanched. "H-how d-do you figure that, sir?"

Valentine read the sergeant's fear with a species of relief. He wanted a subordinate in mortal fear of the Reapers. Any man who did not tremble at the thought of facing a couple of Hoods was either a fool or inexperienced, and there were far too many inexperienced Wolves in Foxtrot Company. Whether or not the whole lot, officers included, were fools was a question Valentine sometimes debated with himself on long winter nights.

"Look at the first story of the house, Sergeant," Valentine said, passing the binoculars back. "It's a nice day. Someone is letting in the spring air. But that second story now . . . shuttered. I think I even see a blanket stuffed in between the slats. And that little stovepipe coming out of the wall—that's got to be for a bedroom, not the kitchen. See the vapor? Someone has a fire going."

"Dark and warm. Hoods like it like that," Stafford agreed.

"My guess is that after the sun's down, the visitor will rise and go about its business. It won't feed till almost morning. It wouldn't risk taking them before it could sleep safe again—you know how dopey they get after feeding."

"Okay, sir, then that's the time to hit 'em. Tomorrow morning." Stafford couldn't keep the excitement out of his voice. "Maybe the captain could even get here by then. That refinery he's scouting can't be more than thirty miles away. They feed, dawn comes, and they button up in that house. We burn them out, even if it rains again, and have enough guns to knock 'em down, and keep 'em down till we can get in with the blades."

"That would be my plan exactly, Sergeant," Valentine agreed. "Except for one thing."

"What, you think that house won't burn if it rains again? Those phosphorous candles, I've seen them burn through tin, sir. They'll get the job done."

"You missed my point, Staff," he said, spitting out the thoroughly chewed blade of grass. "I'm not going to let the Hoods get their tongues into those poor bastards."

Valentine knew the word *incredulous* was probably not in his platoon sergeant's vocabulary, but Stafford's expression neatly illustrated the meaning of the word. "Errr . . . sir, I feel for them, too, but hell, it's too much of a risk."

"Having thirty Wolves within a mile of the Reapers is a risk, too. Even if we all concentrate on lowering lifesign, they still might pick up on us. Then we'd be faced with Reapers coming at us in the dark."

Stafford's left eye gave a twitch. The Reapers hunted not by sight or scent, but by sensing an energy created by living beings. Energy the Reapers' Masters desired.

"The sun isn't waiting," Valentine continued. "We're going to hit them now, while most of the guards are off in the fields. Keep an eye on things from up here—whistle if anything happens."

The lieutenant returned to his platoon, scooting backwards on his belly until he reached the cut in the hillside. He gathered his three squads around him.

"Heads up, Second Platoon. The captain detached us with orders to raise a little hell if we get the chance, and we just got it. There's a pretty big civvie compound on the other side of this hill. Looks like farmworkers and maybe some mechanics—there's a couple of big garages behind the wire. Two guard towers with a man in each. I figure most of the able-bodied are out in the fields to the north, and the garrison is keeping an eye on them. Chances are, there are only a few left in the compound, counting the two in the towers. Looks like there could be Hoods in there, too."

Valentine gave them a moment to digest this. Newer Wolves composed the majority of Foxtrot Company, rebuilt after being bled white in action east of Hazlett, Missouri, in the summer of '65. Each of his three squads had only one or two reliable veterans; most of the experienced men were with the captain or leading smaller patrols on this scouting foray into the Gulag lands north of Tulsa. While all had gone through the arduous training of Southern Command, the gulf between training and experience had been crossed by only a handful of his men. But the newbies were eager to prove themselves as true Wolves, and all had reason to hate the Reapers and the Quislings assisting them.

Valentine's eyes searched the expectant eyes for a pair of almost cherubic young faces. "Jenkins and Oliver, take a map and head south. Sergeant Stafford will show you where the captain's headquarters is supposed to be. If he's not there, go back to summer camp south of the Pensacola Dam and report. If you do find him, tell him we're about to hit some Reapers. I expect the Territorials'll react, and there'll be columns from all over converging on this spot. Maybe he can bushwhack one. We're going to run east and wait at camp. Got it?"

Marion Oliver held up her hand. "Sir, can't we be in on the attack, *then* go find the captain?"

Valentine shook his head. "Oliver, I could sure use you, but just in case this goes to hell, the captain would want to know what we found, where we were when we found it, and what we were going to do about it.

"Now when it was raining earlier, I saw a few of you with those new rain ponchos you lifted outta that storehouse we broke into a couple days ago. I need to borrow three of them, and two volunteers. . . ."

An hour later, Valentine walked down the empty road toward the camp, watching clouds build up again to the southwest. He hoped for more rain overnight. It would slow pursuit.

He wore a green rain slicker—an oily-smelling poncho borrowed from one of his men. Two of his best snapshooters trailed just behind, brisk and bold in the open daylight, also wearing the rain gear stolen from the Quisling Territorials. Valentine had his sleeves tucked together to hide his hands—and what was in his hands.

As the trio approached the camp, the guard in the south tower near the road waved lazily and called something down to the cinder-block guardhouse below. Valentine smelled concentrated humanity ahead, along with the odors of gasoline and oil.

Like all Wolves, he possessed sharpened senses of hearing and smell and a mule's endurance, gifts from the Lifeweavers, humanity's allies in the battle against their fallen brothers from the planet Kur. Valentine made use of that hearing as he approached the camp, concentrating on the two guards walking up to the gate.

"Guy in front looks Injun, if you ask me," one uniformed

figure commented to his associate. Valentine, still a hundred yards away, heard every word as if from ten feet. "Mebbe he's Osage or something."

"Didn't ask you, Gomez," the older of the two replied, scratching the stubble on his chin in thought. "Better go tell the looie, strangers comin' to the gate on foot."

"Franks is having a beer with that truck driver. They've been through six by now, prolly."

"You'd better tell him, or he'll have you stripped. He's jumpy what with the Visitors."

Valentine worked the safety on the pistol in his left hand. The gun in his right hand was a revolver; he covered the hammer with his thumb so it would not catch when he pulled it from the baggy coat sleeves. The seconds stretched as the Wolves approached the gate. The Territorial named Gomez returned with a tall thin man, who threw away a cigarette as he exited the gatehouse.

"Shit, four at the gate . . . ," Alpin, the young Wolf behind him muttered.

"Stick to the plan. I just want you two to get the guy in the tower," Valentine said, quickening his step. "Hi, there," he called. "I'm supposed to see a Lieutenant Franks. He's here, right? I got a message for him."

The bored guard at the southern tower leaned over to hear the exchange below, rifle held ready but pointed skyward. Valentine took a final glance around the compound. Back toward the barracks, a few women and children squatted on the steps or peered out of tiny windows at the visitors.

The tall lieutenant stepped forward and eyed Valentine through the wire, hand on his stiff canvas holster. "I don't know you, kid. Where's the message, and who sent you?"

"It's verbal, Lieutenant," Valentine answered. "Let me think. . . . It goes like this: You're a shit-eating, traitorous, murderous disgrace to the human race. That's about it."

The guards inside the gate froze.

"Uuh?" Franks grunted. Franks's hand seized his sidearm, the Velcro on the clasp making a tiny tearing sound, but Valentine had the two pistols out before the

Quisling's hand even got around the grip. Valentine squeezed off two shots from the automatic and one from the revolver into the lieutenant's chest, the officer's limbs jerking with the false nerve signals generated by the impacting bullets as he fell.

Behind him, the two Wolves raised their carbines. One had some trouble with his poncho, delaying him for a second, but Alpin put a bullet through the guard's chin while the sentry was still shouldering his rifle. The other Wolf got his gun clear in time to put another shot into the lurching figure even as the magazine-fed battle rifle fell out of the tower.

In the time it took the guard's rifle to smack into the wet dirt twenty feet below, Valentine emptied his two pistols into the other Quislings at the gate. The three Wolves dived for the roadside ditch, splashing into puddled rainwater. Valentine abandoned the empty revolver and slipped a fresh magazine into the automatic, sliding the action to chamber the first round. A shot fired from the northern tower whizzed overhead.

Alpin slithered along the ditch as Valentine popped his gun arm and one eye over the crest of the depression, gun following his gaze as he checked the door and windows of the old guardhouse. An unlatched metal screen door with the word WELCOME worked into the decor squeaked in the gusty breeze. Valentine rolled back into the ditch.

"Should I make a try at the gate, sir?" Baker asked, muddy water dripping from his face.

Valentine shook his head. "Stay put, and wait for the sarge."

Farther down the ditch, Alpin popped up to swap shots with the northern tower.

"Alpin, stay down!" Valentine yelled.

The Wolf brought his gun up again, and a bullet burrowed into the ground right in front of his face. Dirt flew, and with a pained cry, Alpin dropped his gun and covered his right eye. Valentine crawled toward the youth, swearing through clenched teeth, when he heard a wet smack followed by the report of the shot. Alpin toppled backwards into the ditch. Valentine risked a dash to his trooper, whose one good eye fluttered open and shut next to the bloody ruin of the other.

The challenging wail of a hand-cranked siren sounded through the camp as he pulled Alpin along the ditch, seeking to put the gatehouse between them and the rifleman. Stafford had the platoon attacking the northern fence. Valentine heard a shot and the sound of breaking glass, where his other gunman was shooting at God-knows-what in the guardhouse.

Valentine found the wound in Alpin's arm and pressed hard to stop the bleeding. Thankfully, the sticky flow welled up underneath his palm in a steady stream rather than short arterial bursts. He called the other Wolf over.

"Baker! Alpin's hit!"

"Someone came to a window there. . . . I missed," Baker gabbled.

"Keep your head down. C'mere and help me put a dressing on," Valentine barked.

Baker scuttled over, but seemed at a loss as soon as he looked at Alpin. First-aid training always took place in a quiet meadow, not stretched out in a wet ditch with no elbow room.

Valentine blew out an exasperated breath. "Never mind. Just put pressure right here," Valentine said, placing Baker's hand on the underside of Alpin's arm, just below the armpit. "Press hard. Don't worry—he's in shock. He doesn't feel anything."

Valentine popped his head up again—still no sign of the other Wolves, although no more shots came from the direction of the northern tower. The guard had either run or been shot. Baker seemed to catch on, and he took control of keeping tension on the tourniquet.

"Mister, mister!" someone yelled from the guardhouse. "We surrender. . . . I surrender, I mean. I'm coming out, no gun. I got a woman with me."

"I'm just a housekeeper. I ain't one of the Territorials!" a woman's voice added.

He cautiously looked out of the ditch. "Come on out, then!" Valentine called. "Hands up in the air!"

The WELCOME door opened, and a young man in camouflage fatigues emerged, followed by a woman in a simple smock. Valentine aimed the pistol at the Territorial. "You in the uniform—facedown on the ground—now!"

The Territorial complied. No more shots came from the other side of the compound, but Valentine could see Oklahomans running from the barracks toward the north fence. The Wolves must have reached the compound.

"Open the gate, please." The woman rushed to comply. The unlocked gate swung easily on its hinges, and Valentine entered the camp. He walked up to the Territorial, still on the ground, face turned sideways and fearfully eyeing Valentine.

"Terri, you better tell me who's in the house, unless you want to piss off the man with the gun aimed at your head."

"Mister, it's four Skulls, and some administrator guy out of Tulsa. And I ain't really a Territorial, I just wear the uniform because I'm in the transports. I drive trucks. I just drive trucks, I swear."

"Did you drive a tanker in here today?"

"Yes, sir . . . that was me. They got a pump for the road vehicles and tractor. I'm s'posed to spend the night here at the Rigyard, then—"

"I found the lieutenant," a voice called. A Wolf pointed his gun around the corner of the guardhouse, covering the door.

"Sarge, Lieutenant Valentine's here. He's okay," another added.

"Keep an eye on these two," Valentine ordered. "Sanchez, help Baker carry Alpin in." Baker's head and shoulders popped up like a curious prairie dog. Wolves rushed to help him with their wounded comrade.

Chaos in the compound. Oklahoman civvies, mostly women and children, milled everywhere, shouting and crying with excitement. Wolves had taken up positions around the two-story house, pointing their rifles at it from cover, but no one was eager to get any closer than absolutely necessary. A pair of Wolves had grabbed a horse, interposing it between themselves and the house while they cut down the four figures hanging from the old T-shaped metal clothesline. Sergeant Stafford directed this last among a cluster of riflemen with barrels trained on the back door of the house.

Valentine waved over a corporal. "Get some men in that south tower. I want to know if anything shows on the road." He glanced at the horizon—with the thick clouds, it would be dark in less than an hour. He had to work fast. If he even had the hour: should the Reapers feel sufficiently threatened, they would simply bolt. He doubted he could stop four from getting away. And once night returned, bringing the Reapers back to full use of their senses, the triumphant Wolves might become tempting sheep. The Rigyard could turn into a death trap.

Valentine watched the rescue of the four bound victims, and then he trotted back to his truck-driving prisoner. A pair of Wolves stood above him, forcing him to squat, face to the wall, with fingers laced behind his head. Valentine waved them off and lowered himself to his haunches, facing the man.

"Here's the deal, friend. Usually when we catch a man wearing the enemy uniform, we take care of it with a bullet, or a rope—time permitting. Do you know what the Ozark Free Territory is?"

"Yes, sir. It's you folks in the hills there in Southern Missouri and Arkansas."

"I can arrange to take you there," Valentine said.

The young man's eyes widened. "What, to hang?"

"No, as a free man. I just need you to drive your truck one more time."

"Let me guess: a suicide mission?"

Valentine grinned. "Maybe. But I'll be riding shotgun."

The engine started with a growling, mechanical *grrrrrr grrrrrr grrrrrrrrrrrrr*. The brakes lifted with a hydraulic shriek; the tractor and its trailer pulled out of the barnlike garage.

As the vehicle accelerated, a Wolf gave the drop hose beneath the tanker a final twist of the cap. Valentine watched gasoline spray as his man jumped out of the way of the truck. The tanker moved across the compound, leaving a rainbow-catching trail.

Jouncing in the cabin of the tractor, with a pump-action shotgun ready to keep the Reapers off, Valentine glanced at the driver. The trucker wore a smile that was more than half snarl. "What's your name, anyway?" Valentine asked, raising his voice over the unmuffled engine.

"Pete Ostlander. Always dreamed of plowing this rig into something. Yours?"

"David Valentine."

Ostlander angled for the spacious front porch of the house. "Brace yourself, Valentine!" he shouted, changing gears. The truck shuddered and picked up speed, churning the wet turf of the lawn. Valentine put his feet against the dashboard and pushed himself tightly into the seat back.

The ancient hauler barreled onto the porch, taking out decking, supports, and roof. The aged wood collapsed like cardboard under the force of the truck's impact. The side of the house caved in, and Valentine could see the homey furnishings through the driver's-side window.

As the truck ground to a halt, Valentine opened his door and launched himself out of the cab, holding the shotgun with his finger across the trigger guard. He tumbled, turned it into a bone-jarring shoulder roll, and came to his feet running for the cinder-block gatehouse. Valentine glanced over his shoulder and saw Ostlander struggling with his seat-belt hook, which had caught on his boot. The driver freed himself and slid to the passenger side.

"Light it! Light it!" Valentine shouted.

Back at the garage, a Wolf touched flame to the gasoline trail. Fire raced across the pooled gasoline. By the guardhouse, three more Wolves waited with grenades ready in case the fuel failed to ignite the tanker. They yelled and pointed behind Valentine, who read the alarm in their expressions. One fired his gun. Valentine turned around, body twisting and following his gun barrel like a sidewinder coiling to strike.

Ostlander jumped from the tanker. Death knelt on the top of the truck, long monklike hood covering its head. The black-caped figure lashed down and grabbed Ostlander by the neck. The driver gave a spasmodic jerk—Valentine's ears caught to snick of vertebrae separating—then sagged with his head flopping forward. Shots from the covering Wolves tore into black robes. The Reaper ignored them; the heavy cloth dampened their kinetic energy, and the Reaper's tough frame did the rest.

The Reaper probably heard the approaching flames, rather than seeing them. It dropped the dying Ostlander and sprang up and over the roof of the house in a gravity-defying jump. When Valentine saw his Wolves fling themselves to the earth, he followed suit. He dropped to the ground with hands at the sides of his head, covering his ears with his thumbs and closing his nose with his pinkies. The tanker exploded with a *whump*. Valentine felt a hot blast of air lick across his back before the concussion knocked him senseless.

He awoke, with vague memories of a delightful dream. The drifting, blissful feeling bled away as his eyes focused on Corporal Holloway, the junior NCO.

"Good news, Holloway," Valentine murmured, still half-awake. "I like the way you handle yourself and the men—I'm recommending you to the captain for promotion to lance. Want the job?"

Holloway started to smile; then his brows furrowed. "Tell the sarge the lieutenant's awake, Gregg. He's kinda groggy."

Grogs? Danger! Valentine returned to Oklahoma with a rush, a long slide back into reality. He smelled burning tires and charred flesh and realized he lay in the cold confines of the gatehouse. He looked around at the rough, bare furniture and sat up, feeling nauseated.

"Okay, Holloway . . . better now. Water, please," croaked a voice that he had to convince himself was his.

Holloway handed him a tin cup, and Valentine gulped it down. "How long was I out?"

"About fifteen minutes, sir. Closer to twenty now."

"The Reapers?"

"Better let the sarge explain, sir. But I don't think there's anything to worry about right now."

Stafford bounced in, a relieved smile on his face. "It's getting dark, sir. No sign of the work details or their guards. They probably saw the smoke and put two and two together. I've got everyone set to pull out. There are a couple high-clearance pickups we can use. I put Alpin in one. Big Jeff volunteered to drive it. We could get you out in the other. Holloway's good behind a wheel."

Valentine stood up, the dizziness fading. "No ambulance required, Staff. Anyone else hurt?"

"Not a one, sir."

"The Hoods?"

"Only one made it out of the house, the one that jumped over the roof. He was on fire, took off like a scalded cat. We chased him down, but the light was fading. Looked like he fell over—his robe was still burning. We put about twenty rounds into it and threw a couple of grenades. Turned out it was just his robe. He must have dropped it and scuttled off flat-assed. My guess is he probably can't see—he plowed right into the wire and had to claw through it. We shouldn't have to worry about him."

Valentine thought for a moment. "What about the dependents?"

"That's your decision, sir. We're feeding those poor bastards that were tied up outside the house. They're in pretty poor shape. Some of the women were asking me, but I played dumb. Gave them the keys to the storeroom, though. They're emptying it now."

"Okay, I'll talk to them. We're going to head for the Pensacola Dam. Put the prisoners in one of the pickups, and find a driver. I'm putting you in charge of the vehicles. Make sure you got food, water, and fuel, spare tires if you can find 'em. Drive slowly with your lights off; you'll make it. Cross country where you can, especially after the old expressway."

"Beats walking, sir."

"Get rolling before the Territorials can organize themselves."

Stafford nodded and started calling men to him. Valentine turned to a level-eyed NCO with a single stripe on his tunic. "Corporal Yamashiro, you're in charge of getting the men ready for a march. Pass out the weapons to the Oklahomans. Wreck any machinery except the two pickups. Were there any more Territorial prisoners?"

Yamashiro coughed meaningfully. "We found two more in uniform hiding in the garage, sir. They say they're just mechanics."

"I'll let the women decide what to do with them. We'll give them guns—they're welcome to shoot them."

"Yes, sir."

Valentine offered his hand. "Good luck, Staff. See you at the dam."

Stafford shook it, his face grave.

Night crept over the compound, the ramshackle barracks now illuminated by a bonfire of the flaming wreckage of the house. Valentine watched preparations on the two pickup trucks for a moment. Both trucks seemed well maintained, with heavy-duty tires and plenty of ground clearance. He nodded to Big Jeff, who was already behind the wheel of one and gunning the engine, listening to its harsh roar like a concerned doctor with a wheezy patient.

Valentine walked over to the barracks, where Wolves were handing out weapons. A grizzled oldster selected a rifle and pocketed two boxes of ammunition. He examined the sights, opened the receiver, and peered down the barrel. The man knew weapons. Valentine caught his eye and beckoned him over.

"Sorry we can't do more for you folks just now, sir. We have to move fast," Valentine explained.

The man worked the action on the rifle. "Don't give it another thought, feller. Best thing to happen around here in years, you taking a poke at the bastards."

"What are you and the others going to do?"

"Well, that ain't been decided yet. Most will sit tight—

the women want their men around. Even if something bad happens, they want it to happen to them together. I expect them Territorials'll move back in. A couple of the younger ones have already run for it, heading for your parts east, I expect."

"And that rifle in your hands?"

"I'm sixty-six. I just do odd jobs around the camp. I could feel my time coming. In fact, I bet I was on the menu for them Skulls you burnt out, if'n they were to hang around much longer. I've got a little spot picked out in the old junk pile back of the garage. Real nice view from there of the whole place. There's a certain sergeant in the Territorials stationed here. I'm hoping for a chance to get him in the sights of this here repeater. And one or two others after him, mebbe. I gotta thank you, Lieutenant. It'll be a good death. I'll go now with the biggest damn smile."

Valentine opened his mouth to argue, but read something in the hard set of the wrinkles around the man's eyes that closed off debate.

"Right." Valentine groped for words. It seemed inappropriate to wish him luck. "Shoot straight."

"Don't worry on my account, sonny." With a nod, the man slung his rifle, picked up a shotgun, and moved off into the shadows of the open garage, whistling. Valentine heard the tune long after the figure disappeared.

A woman tugged at his sleeve. "Sir, sir!" she implored.

Valentine turned.

She thrust a diapered baby into his arms, cocooned in a plaid blanket. "His name's Ryan. Ryan Werth. He's only eleven months. Just mash any old thing up real good, and he'll eat it," she said, tears streaming down her cheeks.

Valentine tried to give the baby back to her. "Sorry, ma'am . . . but . . ."

The woman refused to take back the child. She put her palms over her eyes and fled into the crowd.

"Mrs. Werth! Mrs. Werth, I'm sorry, but we can't do this," Valentine called, going after her. He looked down at the baby, which was now squalling lustily. He could understand the mother's motives. The Kurians might do anything in the camp as a reprisal if they thought the inhabitants had cooperated.

He looked around for someone, anyone in the camp to hand the baby to, but they'd disappeared. He couldn't just set it down. Feeling more than a little ridiculous, Valentine returned to the pickups, trying to comfort the child. Perhaps Stafford had room for a bawling baby.

"Lieutenant Valentine, sir?" A young Wolf named Poulos stepped forward, saluting smartly. Poulos was a thick-muscled, good-looking young man who tended to keep to himself. He was one of the few survivors of the old Foxtrot Company, and wasn't going out of his way to bond with the new recruits, or else he'd have been promoted by now. Valentine understood his reasons.

"Yes, Poulos. What is it? I've got my hands rather full at the moment."

Poulos smothered the beginnings of a smile. "Sir, I have to ask your permission to take a dependent with us. Corporal Holloway told me to ask you, sir." Poulos stepped aside to reveal a beautiful girl in her late teens, wrapped up in a long coat with a bag over her shoulder. "Sir, this is Linda Meyer. She wants to come with us. Her ma was one of the ones tied up behind the house. I'll feed her off my rations. She'll keep up, she's healthy, and she can run, sir."

Valentine shook his head. "A girl already, Poulos? How many hours have we been here? I'd have thought with the Hoods afoot and the perimeter being secured, you'd have other things to do."

"She was showing me where the Terris hid the supplies, and we started—"

"Never mind the story. You know that's against regulations. Dangerous for her to be seen talking to us." *Bad for discipline for soldiers to go sniffing around for companionship in the KZ*, Valentine added to himself silently. Then there was the chance that she could be a plant. Two years ago, his first command in the KZ was almost destroyed by a boy leaving notes to the Reapers.

Poulos and the girl exchanged desperate looks. "But sir,

company rules do allow wives along with the commander's permission." Miss Meyer let out a small, shocked gasp.

"Not on a patrol, Poulos. I'll listen to tent-pole lawyering in camp, but not in the KZ." Valentine wondered if he had really regained consciousness. The flame-lit compound was growing more and more surreal by the moment. Even the fussing baby seemed quieter in the orange-tinged drama of the scene.

"There's a preacher here, sir. He can marry us right now. We're heading back. It's not like we're going into action, we're coming back from it. Doesn't that make a difference?"

"I can keep up, Mr. Valentine," the woman said. They took each other's hands.

"I don't want to hear another word about it," Valentine said, avoiding the hopeful eyes of the young couple. Standing orders from Regiment, enforced by the captain to the letter, discouraged the practice colloquially known as "rounding up strays." The prisoners from the yard were one thing: the Kurians might have reasons for wanting them dead, for all he knew one or more were captured Southern Command soldiers. Aid and assistance were always offered to refugees who made it to the Free Territory on their own, but unless an operation went into a region supplied and equipped to bring out people, taking on stragglers led to innumerable problems. Valentine twisted in the opposing mental winds of his humanity and his duty. He suddenly thought of the girl's mother. While she probably wasn't an Ozark POW, she certainly needed medical attention and care. A loophole, perhaps big enough to squeeze a teenage girl through, opened before him. He could also get rid of the squalling baby.

"Okay, Poulos. You got yourself a wife—and child."

He passed the babe into the girl's arms, and little Ryan quieted. "Poulos, you take them and ride with Stafford and this woman's mother. Miss, take care of this baby. His name is Ryan . . . errr."

"Ryan Werth. Born April last, Mr. Valentine. Thank you, sir. I'll take good care of him."

"I'm sure you will. Hurry, or the trucks will leave without you."

The young couple hugged in as close an embrace as possible with the baby in her arms. They turned to run to the pickups even now crawling toward the gate in a chattering of diesel valves.

"Poulos!" Valentine called after them.

The Wolf about-faced smartly as the truck stopped for the Meyer girl to climb in. "Sir?"

"Congratulations."

TWO

On the banks of the Lake o' the Cherokees: Foxtrot Company waits in a forward camp. Tepees, tents, wagons, livestock, and a smokehouse cluster around a stream running down from the hills into what remains of the lake behind the breached dam. A few eagles fish beneath the ruined arches, lingering along the flight paths most have already followed north up the Mississippi Valley.

In this border country, the Wolves of Southern Command imitate the eagles, moving quickly here and there to survey the countryside and striking at prey small enough to take. Their duty is to scout the Kurian Zone, pick up information, and warn the Free Territory of any impending threat to the human settlements in the hills and dales of the Ozark Freehold. Similar military camps lie scattered in the foothills of the Ozarks and Ouachitas throughout Missouri, the eastern edge of Oklahoma, Texas, and Arkansas. Beyond this uninhabited ring broods the Night of the Kurian Order.

The Kurians on the other side of no-man's-land wait for a chance, perhaps some combination of weakness and error, to engulf the Free Territory and put an end to one of the last bastions of human civilization.

"Congratulations, Valentine," Captain Beck said, emerging from his tent to receive the report of his tired lieutenant. "I hear you got four Reapers. You're a credit to the Regiment." Beck held out his right hand, back straight as a telephone pole, smiling at Valentine through clenched teeth.

The young lieutenant shook the proffered hand. "Three, sir. The fourth was a little burned, but got away."

"Stafford said he was blinded. That's one less Reaper to worry about, in my opinion."

Valentine never stopped worrying about a Reaper until its corpse quit twitching.

"Could be, sir," Valentine said, massaging his aching neck. He was so tired, he had a hard time organizing his thoughts, but he had to snap to for this particular superior, fatigue or no. Captain Beck had a reputation as a man-driver and courageous fighter. After being promoted as the senior surviving officer after the Battle of Hazlett in the summer of '65, he'd pushed his company through training and once up to strength requested a forward posting.

"I got Stafford's report on the action at the Rigyard," he said, inviting Valentine into his tepee with an outstretched arm. Valentine entered; the shelter smelled of leather and cigars. Socks and underwear drying on a line added a hint of mustiness. "How was the trip back?"

Valentine collected his thoughts. "It rained after Stafford drove off. Slowed us up. The next day I sent out details to start some fires to the north, make them think we were moving across the flatlands for the Missouri border. We spotted a couple of patrol toward evening, one on horse and one in a truck. We lay low and cold-camped. The next—"

Beck held up a hand. "What's that, Lieutenant? A single truck? Sounds like a good opportunity for prisoners."

"It had a radio antenna. Even from ambush, they might have got off a message. We had been lucky with casualties. I didn't want to press it."

Beck frowned. "I'd like my officers more worried about what they are going to do to the enemy than what might get done to them. Your return would be easier if the Territorials were too scared of losing patrols to send them out."

"We'll have a hard time scaring them worse than the Reapers, sir."

The captain clucked his tongue against his teeth, and the tepee seemed to grow warmer. "I'm not questioning your judgment, just telling you how I might have handled it, had I been there."

"Thank you, sir. The next day, we really put on some mileage. By nightfall we passed the old interstate. When did you get back, sir?"

"Two days ago, morning. We scouted that refinery outside Tulsa. It's fortified, but I think the whole Company could hurt it, if we could bait a chunk of the garrison out somehow."

Valentine nodded. Months ago, he had learned the best way to change his captain's mind was to make any objections he had seem like Beck's own. "Certainly, sir. While we're trying to draw the garrison out, what orders would you give if a flying column comes up? Or Reapers? I'm sure we could take it, leading some Bears and a regiment of regulars as a reserve. That or have the help of a really good Cat, sir."

"Getting Southern Command to launch something like that isn't so easy to do," Beck said with a knowing chuckle. "That's enough for now. Take tonight off, get some food and sleep, then give me your full report tomorrow."

"Has anyone talked to the four Okies Stafford brought out, sir?"

"Stafford got their vitals. None of them were military. Feel free to interview them yourself. Add it on to your report if you get anything. Nice work out there, Valentine. Dismissed."

Valentine saluted. "Sir," he said quietly, and backed out of Beck's tepee.

A night off. Exhausted from the fight at the Rigyard and eight days in the Kurian Zone, he longed to fall into his cot, into oblivion. A hot bath first was tempting, but the platoon needed to be checked over, and he wanted to have a word with the liberated prisoners before they were taken east into the Ozarks.

He found Stafford with the platoon, engaged in an impromptu celebration for Poulos and his new bride. Someone had produced a jug, and Freeman, the company's oldest ranker, was pouring generous portions into the cluster of wooden cups held under the spout. The mugs were pieces of off-duty artistry: Free Territory hardwoods had been carved into wolf heads and fox ears. Some had handles chiseled to resemble curved tails. Even the rawest recruit in Foxtrot Company had his individual mug.

"Stafford, a word please." Valentine had to raise his voice over the ribald jests being directed at Poulos and his new bride.

The ruddy-skinned platoon sergeant left the guffaws and joined Valentine. They watched the festivities from the edge of the campfire light. Though himself a teetotaler, Stafford allowed his men to indulge after hard duty. The 120 miles covered on foot in the last seven days qualified.

"Poulos and the Meyer girl tied the knot, Gator?" Valentine asked.

"This morning, Val. They did it up right and proper. She's got her mom's wedding ring on now."

"It'll be a story for their grandkids. Hope nobody takes the hooch too close to the fire; I think Freeman adds a little turpentine to give it that woody, aged flavor."

Gator snorted, and Valentine returned to business. "I looked over your report on the drive back. Anything happen that you didn't want to put on paper?"

"No, sir. Except that I was cutting the engines about every fifteen minutes to listen. God, it was like I was driving around, setting off firecrackers. It's a wonder I didn't get every Territorial for fifty miles around me. But all we saw were a couple of deer we flushed. Came leaping at us in the headlights with glowing eyes and twelve-foot jumps. It took about two minutes for my heart to start beating again." His left eye twitched at the memory.

"I need to talk to that girl's mom and the others you brought out. Where can I find them?"

"The captain had to deal with that when we pulled in. Since they were your responsibility, he put them up in your tepee. Maybe he's sending a message about picking up strays. Lieutenant Caltagirone is still out on patrol with a chunk of third platoon, so Beck figured he might as well give that space to them. The little old guy, though—the one with the really long hair—you won't get much out of him. I think he's cracked. Hasn't said anything that makes much sense the whole ride."

"I don't even remember what they look like. Can I borrow you for a quick introduction?"

"Follow me, Val." Dodging dancers, they moved toward the ring of Company tepees at the center of the camp.

Valentine followed Stafford through the flap of the tepee he shared with Lieutenant Caltagirone. The refugees were relaxing. Their faces had been washed, and plates that looked as though they'd been licked clean were stacked by a washbasin.

"Here's the lieutenant; just a few more questions for you," Stafford said.

Valentine looked longingly at his cot. What was left of last night's charcoal was cold gray ash at the center. Caltagirone's cot and a tiny folding table paired up with a rickety stool completed the furnishings. A folding wood lattice stood behind the beds; spare equipment and clothing belonging to the Foxtrot's lieutenants hung from hooks.

As the prisoners sat up, Valentine walked over to his paperwork pouch bearing his stenciled name—months ago, someone had sewn a patch of a floating white cowl with two black eyes beneath the letters, a reference to his nickname, "the Ghost"—and extracted a clipboard. A new letter was clipped to the top of the assorted forms. He recognized Molly's hand by the deliberately printed black inscription, like a schoolchild's. Temptation to let the questions wait in order to peruse its contents almost overwhelmed him, but he stuck it back in the pouch.

Knowledge that a letter awaited him lifted the fatigue. He swung his leg over the little camp stool, sat, and awaited introductions. Stafford gave the names of the three men—Mrs. Meyer still being at the wedding celebration— and then returned to the platoon.

Their stories were the usual sad tale of refugees from the Kurian Zone. When they relayed the usual Kurian propaganda stories about life in the Ozarks—that a Rule Eleven existed condemning anyone who ever cooperated with the

Kurians to either execution or being worked to death, and further, Free Territory soldiers were allowed to rape any woman they wished—Valentine only shook his head and returned to the routine questions. He had taken hundreds of statements in his time from refugees, and the picture was always the same bleak snapshot: a hard, bland life of labor until the inevitable end in the draining embrace of a Reaper.

Only one statement stood out, and that was from the man Stafford had described as "cracked." He was a smallish man with a permanent squint that gave him a wizened look. His name was Whitey Cooper, no doubt a reference to his snow-white hair. He wore blue-striped ticking, a shirt in the last stages of decay. Not a button remained, and the collar and cuffs were gone, so his bony forearms and hands had a false appearance of unnatural length. It was trying work getting anything out of him. Valentine finally managed to learn that he worked in the main rail yards of Oklahoma City.

"And for better than thirty years, junior," Cooper pointed out, stabbing one of those fingers at Valentine as if threatening him with a dagger. "Nope, not a bird to change its tune, not me. So many came and went there. Ducks—the lot of them, quack-quack-quacking out their lives before flying south. I wasn't set to fly, though, not by a long shot."

"No?" Valentine said, having given up the fight to make sense out of the man after an inquiring glance or two exchanged with the others. He wondered what Molly had written, and if her mother's health had improved.

"Naw, I was quiet as a broke television. If you're up to your neck in shit, don't make waves. Kept me kicking these years. Till them Nazis showed up on their way north and spoilt it with that big train. They messed me up, but they'll get theirs. Now, I know my history, boy. I've read mor'n books than you got fingers. I know the Nazis got beat once, and we'll beat 'em again."

Valentine stirred from musings. "Nazis?"

"That's the problem today, nobody's got no schooling. Yeah, Nazis, Mr. Lootenan. They were the bad guys way back when the world had the old-time black-and-white life."

"How do you know they were Nazis?" he asked, picking up his pencil.

"First I thought they were just train men like me. Most of 'em weren't much to look at. Thin and sickly kinda, so I assumed they was just railroad men on short commons. What I call the old "gun to yer head" Railway Local Union Nine Em Em. See this good-sized train come through, not the biggest I've ever seen, not by a long shot, but armored engines and caboose and all. I see these guys drinking coffee when it's stopped between, relaxing between the cars on break like. So I figure I grab a cup while it's hot and say howdy, 'cause I had a spare cigarette to trade. I climb up, and they get all exhilarated. Haul me to the caboose, where this big shot fancied-up general starts giving me the once-over. I got thirty years' worth of work stamps in my ID book, but does that cut anything with him? Prick. No, sir. Says I'm spying, as if a bunch of closed boxcars are anything worth spying on. Everyone's all saluting and calling him Generalissimo Honcho or something. Then they take me when the train leaves and start all zapping me with this electric stick. Oh man, I cried, no no not a spy."

"This general, he was in charge of the Nazis? Did you see a name, perhaps on his uniform?"

Cooper winced, as if the memory slapped him. "Oldish, sir. Not oldish and healthy, oldish and dried out, skin like a wasp nest in winter. Thick, wiry gray hair, cut real luscious 'n' full. Little shorter'n me, and I'm only five seven. Pink-eyed, too, like he was hungover. Had a voice like an old wagon running on a gravel road. I've never heard a young man talk like that. Old and squeaky and tired."

"Could you tell from the way they talked where they were from? Did they mention any cities?" Valentine asked again, keeping his voice casual.

"No, if he said it, I forgot."

"What about his men—you said they were thin and sickly?"

"Jest the ones hanging round the wagons. The ones that

grabbed me, big burly fellows they were. Plenty of guns, high-quality iron from back then, or as good. Had somun'em oversize gorilla-men with him, too—tall, tall they were, those snaggletooth varmints. It was them that held me when they started in on me."

"I still don't see how they were Nazis," Valentine said.

The man rocked as he sat hunched over, eyes screwed shut. "No, I got a good record here. Check my book. Me a spy?" Cooper trailed off.

Valentine switched tactics. "I think you're wrong, Mr. Cooper. You probably just mistook them for Nazis when they were hurting you."

"I'm learned, I tell you. I can read, just don't get the opportunity. How could I tell? The flag, like they had by the millions in them pictures. On the uniforms, and on the flags in the caboose behind the General Honcho's desk. Wore it proud, the bastards. You'll show 'em, though, like you did at the house."

Valentine wrote something on his clipboard. "Like this?"

"That's it, Mr. Lootenan. That's it. I bet you beat on them tons of times before, right?"

Valentine just nodded, to himself rather than to the poor man's words, looking down at the clipboard. He had seen that design before, here and there, and wherever he had encountered it, there had been trouble.

Written in pencil on the slightly yellow paper was the backwards swastika he'd heard called "the Twisted Cross."

"You're sure you don't know where they come from?"

"Naw. Why you need to know that?"

"You said we had to beat them."

"Course you will, Mr. Lootenan. Of course. But you don't have to go looking for them. They're coming for you."

It took Valentine a moment to come up with, "How can you be sure of that?"

"All summer, new lines is goin' in. Labor and materials already arranged. I was supposed to second a section chief. A new north-south running Dallas–Tulsa–Kansas City, and after that then three branch lines."

"Branch lines? Where?"

"Pointing like a pitchfork right at these hills."

Valentine camped in an accommodating wagon that night among three other Wolves who had given up their tepee to Poulos and his new bride. As the final earthy taunts and wedding-night stories died down, Valentine reread Molly's letter by the cold light of the rising moon.

January 18, 2067

Dear David,

I hope this letter finds you well and doesn't take too long—you'd think they could find your unit in less than a month, wouldn't you? Everyone here in Weening is good the winter passed with hardly any sickness but the food is all starting to taste the same though I shouldn't complain as I am certain it is worse for you. I read your last letter out loud during Sunday Services and received many greetings and well wishes to pass on to you that are too numerous to list. Mr. Bourne has something he's going to send you as soon as he can find one of the Wolves passing through the area since he doesn't trust the post with it—the package is a box or trunk of some kind so be on the lookout for it. He was working on it all winter and made me promise not to tell—and he can be sure I'm not telling as he is helping me with this letter! As you know I am somewhat behind in my education, the 3 Rs not being taught in that part of Wisconsin where we met. Have you heard anything from Frat? I think he's still an Aspirant down by Louisiana, but you all move around so much my information is always out of date. I am told the mail is even slower to him and just collects until he can return to his camp.

Graf has been recommended for Lieutenant—I think he's going to ask me to marry him if he gets the promotion. It may mean leaving the village but Mom is doing much better. Mary is old enough now where she can take over a lot of the chores and the Hudson brothers help out with the hardest. My mom and dad pretty much handle everything to do with veterinary work for the town livestock, if someone's having trouble with a calving they run and get them. With Mom better Dad's going to take a larger place in the Village, there's talk of him becoming a Director. To think when he first got here the town gave him a cow and two piglets and some chickens, and now we've got eight good milkers. Of course, in a way our start here is because of you. I should just say it, we owe everything to you: getting out of the badness in Wisconsin and everything that happened in Chicago.

Your letters are very cheery and polite in the way you ask about Graf. But you always are very casual and polite when you are upset. David, you're one of the finest men I've ever known. I still love you in a way, but a different way than I feel about Graf. I think you have a Purpose. I know we talked that our futures were woven together at one time, but something in me associates all the badness back there with you and every time I see you I remember. I should not say it was all wrong, before Chicago our time was wonderful, and precious, but I've sealed up everything that happened with Chicago, it's kind of like a memory of an old nightmare, not very clear. You were so patient with me all that winter, God did I even talk at all while we were in Minnesota? I think you need to be free of me to become whatever it is you are going to become (as you are all bound up with the Lifeweavers and Mr. Bourne says it is a hard way and the choice to follow them doesn't make for a normal life) I need to be free of you to start here with a clean slate. We tried last spring and it was just bad, I was cold—God it was the last thing you deserve!— and you were distracted.

The way things are now is for the best, I'm sure of it. You've written that you think it's great that I have a

*man like Graf and those words meant a lot to me and
I hope they weren't painful to write. I suppose we
both have mixed feelings for each other. One thing is
certain though, you will always have a home among
the Carlsons in Weening no matter what happens to
you. You've been my friend, my love, my protector, my
healer, my guide, and now I hold you as a dear
brother in a Very Special Place in my heart. I look
toward your next letter, and pray that your duties will
allow you to visit soon.*

> *Yours truly and
> always,
> Molly*

Molly was a bright young woman, and painfully right about them. Valentine returned the letter to his dispatch bag. He played a mental slide show of the Molly he had known: from when he first met her in Wisconsin when her family hid him at great personal risk from the Kurians, to his trip to Chicago to rescue her from violent public death after she had killed a Quisling official. They'd escaped by ship to the Minnesota shore, near where Valentine had been born and grew up, and stayed a season at his adoptive father's house.

Valentine and the old priest sat up night after night, discussing what he'd learned of the Kurians. It was the Padre who'd first taught him about ancient civil war that divided the Lifeweavers and led to the Kurian Lords, who—through their vampiric Reapers—killed sentient beings to harvest the energies that sustained their endless lives. They'd been thrown off Earth long ago, the interstellar gateways sealed and destroyed, but they'd come again in 2022, and won.

Valentine made no attempt to renew the intimacy that had briefly existed between himself and Molly, concentrating instead on feeding everyone. Each night he read to Molly by the light of a single candle out of the Padre's collection of old books. Books that had become his family, in a way, after his orphaning. They'd taken him out of his misery, and he'd hoped they could do the same for Molly.

That spring, Valentine was determined to rejoin Molly with her family, although he had no idea if the Carlsons had even successfully escaped to the Ozarks with his fellow Wolf, Gonzalez.

Molly strengthened and blossomed on the journey in the spring sunshine of the north. Valentine had a good nose for trouble, and skirted wide around areas controlled by the Quisling servants of the Kurians. They reached the outskirts of Southern Command on the first day of May, and the young pair caught up to Molly's family at one of the small fortress posts in the hills watching the old roads and trails up from St. Louis. That reunion on the soil of the Ozark Free Territory was perhaps the proudest moment in his life. As if some silent bargain had been fulfilled, he and Molly renewed their intimacy that night, making love with giddy, laughing abandon.

But it was not the same. The desperation and danger of their situation in Wisconsin was absent, and Valentine felt the pull of duty. He had been posted missing and presumed dead, and upon hearing of his safe return to the Ozarks, Gonzalez and a few other Wolves of Zulu Company showed up to welcome him back. He settled the family with old friends in the little borderland settlement of Weening in northern Arkansas near the Saint Francis River and returned to his duties.

It was a frustrating return. Southern Command read, and promptly forgot, his report on the mysterious Kurian operations in the hills of southern Wisconsin he and Gonzalez had stumbled upon, and shrugged their shoulders at Valentine's suggestion of a new organization under a reversed-swastika symbol Valentine had heard called the Twisted Cross.

Zulu Company had replaced him, and Valentine was assigned to Captain Beck and Foxtrot Company, mostly freshly invoked Wolves who had never seen a live Reaper and knew Grogs—the variegated, semi-intelligent beasts bred to aid the Kur in their subjugation of humanity—only by their oversize footprints.

Constant training drained him, and he found it impossible to visit Molly in far-off Weening; they exchanged letters less and less frequently. Molly was young and beautiful, and soon found herself under the attentions of a sergeant in the regulars, the well-turned-out Guards who formed the main body of Southern Command's armed forces. Twinges of jealousy vied with genuine hope for her happiness on the unstable emotional teeter-totter that described his feelings for her.

Valentine shifted his weight on the hard boards of the wagon, causing the springs to squeak in complaint. That trail of thought led to a dead end. He returned to present problems, reviewing Cooper's ravings. He still knew little of the Twisted Cross. Only that its members were human, at least some of them, and that they were objects of dread in the Kurian Zone and on its borders. He had briefly met one in the bizarre garden of unholy entertainments of the Zoo in Chicago while searching for Molly. A man who talked like a soldier and acted like a Reaper, even to the extent that he thirsted for blood. And whoever they were, they were now somewhere just outside the no-man's-land separating the Free Territory from the KZ.

Despite that unsettling thought, he finally slept. Above his hard bed, the stars whirled away in the bright clear night.

"Grogs, Mr. Valentine. Hundreds of 'em. Five miles off and coming hard," a pubescent voice intruded on Valentine's deep predawn slumber.

Valentine woke like a startled animal, instantly alert, and the boy ceased shaking his shoulder. It was Tom Nishino, one of the teenage Aspirants who traveled with the Wolves and performed assorted camp duties in the hope of someday joining their ranks. The youth almost danced with excitement beside the wagon. Captain Beck had taken Nishino, the brightest of Foxtrot's teens, under his wing and used him as a messenger.

"Whose are they?"

Nishino looked puzzled at the question. He'd never served down south, where Governer Steiner had his unique and independent enclave of humans and Grogs. So far, Steiner had never let his militias off his lands, which formed a buffer in the south between Kurian Louisiana and the Free Territory. Valentine had always hoped to hear of closer cooperation—he'd played a small part in that alliance his first year as a Wolf.

"Don't know, sir. They're coming out of Oklahoma."

"Are we supposed to sound assembly?" Valentine asked, letting his ears play across the campsite for sounds of the tents being struck and men gathering.

"The captain asks that you have your platoon turn out with full weapons and equipment, and you're to report to his tent, sir," Nishino reported.

"Thank you, son. Please walk, *walk* mind you, back to the captain and tell him I'll be there in five minutes. Sprinting in the dark is a good way to turn an ankle, or have a sentry put a bullet into you. Take it easy, boy."

"Sir," the boy said, showing his best salute, and turned neatly to begin a stiff-spined walk back to the captain's tent. Valentine tried to remember if he'd acted like that when he'd first joined the Cause at seventeen.

The Wolves sharing the wagon with Valentine still lay in their bedrolls. The pose was deceptive—Valentine had seen them lay hands on their rifles at the first hint of action in the air.

Valentine pulled on his boots. "Benning, find Sergeant Stafford, please. Tell him to get the platoon together, ammunition and two days' rations. Gabriel, please go and get the draft animals together on a line. We may be moving fast without the wagons. Thank you."

He hopped out of the wagon as the men exchanged knowing looks. They'd already seen through his facade. Whenever their young lieutenant spoke in that crisp, politely affected manner, action was in the air.

Valentine walked to the command tepee, unconsciously registering the clatter and curses in the night air as the camp came to life. Grogs were significant. The battle-bred warriors of the Kurians were rare in Oklahoma; Kur relied on Quisling troops in the plains. Might be they'd been brought down from Northern Missouri, and that could mean an attempt to thrust into the vitals of the Free Territory. Valentine ticked off the possibilities in his brain: a raid, an attempt on the Fort Smith region, or perhaps a thrust northeast to link up with others pushing south into Missouri, catching the forces and populace in that corner of the Free Territory in a meat grinder. Or most likely of all, it was a rushed-up retribution for the recent raid by Foxtrot Company. If that was the case, the Wolves could do what they did best: skirmish and ambush. They'd lead the Grogs on a chase until they could be decoyed into the Ozarks and cut off.

Captain Beck stood outside his tepee in the pink dawn, his hands behind him in the at-ease position.

Valentine came up beside him. "What's the situation, sir?"

"Pickets spotted the Grogs crossing the lake about midnight, five kilometers north of here. Tango Company might have picked them up; that's getting up in their area. They turned south right away, moving along the banks of the river. I sent the camp squad out to keep an eye on them—they're freshest. They'll bushwhack any scouts if they can. That'll slow the Grogs some."

"Strength?"

"Probably won't have any idea of numbers until daylight, but they're on those legworms—it's how they crossed the river so quick and easy. Pickets said they spotted harpies above the treetops. No sign of them here, so I'm hoping it's just their imagination."

"Coming here or just trying to raid into the Ozarks?"

"They're after us, no doubt about that. Maybe some Kurian is down to his last Reaper thanks to you, Valentine. We're going to make them sorry they caught up to us."

"How's that, sir?" Valentine asked, adding a silent prayer. It wasn't what he thought.

"I've already tele'd to Decatur for reinforcements and put the sick and wounded in the trucks you captured. Oh, and the children. There's a cavalry regiment of Guards in the area, and more behind them. The Grogs have got to be planning to burn this camp and maybe catch us pulling back toward the Free Territory. They've moved fast, so it can't be a well-planned assault. If we pull up onto Little Timber Hill, we can hold out there for days. It would take more artillery than the Grogs have in Missouri to blast us out of those rocks." Beck reached for the waxed linen packet in which he kept his cigars. With his usual courtesy, he offered one. Valentine shook his head, gathering the right words.

"Sir, there's nothing here worth fighting for. There aren't any of our farms within twenty miles at least. Let the Grogs burn some wagons and barrels of pork. If they follow us toward Fort Smith, the farther they go, the fewer will get back alive."

Beck's dark brows dueled like bighorn sheep. "Dammit, Valentine, you know how I feel about that kind of crap. Until we start making those Jaspers more afraid of us than we are of them, they're going to keep pushing into us whenever they feel like it. Besides, you're forgetting Lt. Caltagirone. He's still out with his short platoon. I don't want him coming back to a camp crawling with Grogs."

"I know that sir, and I agree. But we're Wolves, not Guards. Even a couple of our men are worth more to us, worth more to Southern Command, than every Grog in that column is to the KZ."

"Are you suggesting I'd throw away men's lives? Because if you are—"

"No, sir, certainly not, sir."

"The toughest decisions are always where to fight. I appreciate you speaking your mind, Valentine. That takes a kind of courage, too. Just because we disagree, it won't be held against you."

He waited, as if expecting a thank-you, then continued. "Someday you'll get a company of your own. When you get it, command it. No councils of war. This is a screen of Grogs who are about to get their noses lopped off. And even if it isn't, we can hold them until the regulars arrive.

You know how long I held outside Hazlett, Val? Five days. By the second day we were low on ammunition, and by the third even the Grog guns were empty."

Valentine had heard the story of those five days several times. Versions from the senior surviving Wolves of Foxtrot Company did not match the commander's account exactly, but this was not the time to bring that up.

"Your orders, sir?"

"Your platoon is going to haul as many supplies as possible up Little Timber Hill. We've already got trees down all around the hill, we've been working on the fortifications since we got here. Fill a couple wagons, triple-team them if you have to, and get them up that hill to Rocky Crown. Water's not a problem this time of year, but I want food and ammo. And every hand grenade we have. Drive the livestock up, and make a pen."

Valentine took the orders like bitter medicine. Now he had to decide how to carry them out, quickly. Grogs on legworms ate miles, skirmishing pickets or no, and with daylight they would move even faster.

"Yes, sir."

"Good. Clear the camp as soon as you can."

"And the spouses?"

"Some left with their kids. The others have to get up the hill, too. Any further questions, Valentine?"

"No, sir," Valentine said, already wondering if he could even get the wagons up that slope, triple-teamed or no.

The whole camp was stirring now as the Wolves gathered their weapons and equipment. Valentine returned to his platoon to find Stafford sitting on top of a wagon, issuing orders and equipment to the assembling men.

"We'll be ready to pull out in fifteen minutes, sir," Gator reported. "If we aren't moving the wagons, some of the women can ride on the draft animals. We'll make good time, probably hit the outskirts of the Territory by sundown."

"Good work, Staff, but we're not leaving. We have to

hitch up some wagons and fill them from the stores. We've got to get the ammo and food up to the redoubt."

Stafford's face fell, lacking only an audible thud. "The captain wants to fight it out?"

Valentine hid his own misgivings with his best airy smile. "Gator, it's probably just a screen of Grogs to flush us. The Guards are already on their way if it's not. And besides, Caltagirone is still out with his men. We can't abandon them to the Grogs. Get the men moving; they've got fifteen minutes to get something in their stomachs—then we have to hitch up a couple of wagons, fill them with food and bullets, and haul up that trail. Minutes count, okay, Sergeant?"

"Yes, Lieutenant."

Gator turned and began bellowing orders. Poulos's new bride, her mother, and a few of the other camp casuals were already passing out ersatz coffee and the morning's biscuits. The men squatted around their NCOs, cramming food into their mouths while they discussed how best to get the supplies up that hill. The smell of bacon frying brought saliva to Valentine's mouth, and he moved over to the cooking fire. A seven-year-old girl, the daughter of Corporal Hart of First Platoon, scuttled past him in a flutter of tangled dark hair chasing a chicken.

Valentine swore under his breath. She should have left with the trucks. Hart and his wife must have decided to keep the family together despite the risks. The girl got the chicken and hurried off to the coops. Valentine tried to put her out of his mind. It was too easy to imagine a Grog loping after her.

By the time he had eaten two heels of bread dripping with bacon fat and a pair of still-sputtering strips of meat, the platoon had the outlines of a plan. Stafford and the other NCOs decided to run two wagons, one from the camp to the base of the steep hill that served as the Company redoubt, and a second double-teamed one to run light loads up the hill. Valentine watched the first group of men move off with axes and two small horses toward the hill. They would improve the trail and check for deadfalls, then improvise a corral at the rocky top of the hill. The camp dependents would follow, bringing a few necessities and driving the goats, geese, and cows that made up the Company's livestock.

In the early hours of the morning, Valentine left everything but the ordnance to Stafford. He personally supervised digging up the Company's reserve grenades and ammunition. Some of the explosives used black powder, and he wanted to make sure that in the rush, the volatile mixture was not mishandled.

"Mr. Valentine," said O'Neil, uncovering the last case of grenades from the shallow trench that had covered them, "gimme half an hour, and I'll set a little booby trap here. We leave behind a case, and the first Grog tries to shift it gets blowed into pieces that wouldn't fill a spoon."

"If we had time, we'd leave surprises everywhere, O'Neil. But they're going to be here any minute."

It promised to be a cloudy morning. As Valentine walked behind the load of ammunition, eyeing the balance of the load in the wagon bed as it ascended the first gentle slope toward the redoubt, a running Wolf broke cover from the tree line to the north. Valentine watched him disappear into the thick trees of Little Timber Hill, making for the new command post.

"Let's keep it moving, men. The Grogs are on their way. We want to have this load to shoot at them, not the other way round."

O'Neil quickened the pace of the four horses, and the last of Valentine's platoon soon disappeared into the trees at the base of the hill. Stafford waited there, with more horses ready to be hitched to the rest.

"Everything and everyone's up at the top, sir. The corral took no doing at all—there's a little hollow in the rocks that we just closed off at one end. The captain's going to use the other wagon to block the trail once we make it to the crest."

"Good work, Staff. Let's get a man at each wheel with a rock, ready to brace it up if the horses need a breather. Get a few hides between the crates, just in case the load shifts. I don't think even a bad bounce would set it off, but better safe than dead. Where's the platoon supposed to be once we get up?"

"We're to form a reserve. He wants the dependents armed, too. The rest of the platoon will cover the south and the saddle to the east where it joins the rest of the hills. First platoon is going to be on the main line, covering the trail. The captain figures if they'll come, they'll come up the trail, where the slope's gentle."

The newly double-teamed wagon ascended the hill, with men ready to prop the wheels with rocks when the horses could no longer take the strain. Even this, the "gentle" part of the hill, had an exhausting slope to the grade, running way up Little Timber Hill like a long ramp.

A little more than halfway up the hill, they came upon the fortifications. Whatever Valentine's other disagreements with the captain, he had to admire the planning and execution of the redoubt. Trees were felled at the crest of the steepest part of the slope, pointing outward with their branches shorn and sharpened into abatis. Earth-and-wood fortifications, complete with head-logs in many places, frowned down on the steep slope. If the Grogs wanted Little Timber, they would pay a steep price, as steep as the hill the wagon now climbed, exacted by the marksmen of Foxtrot Company. Valentine put himself in the enemy's canoe-like sandals at the base of the hill. How would he go about the assault to minimize the cost?

He knew his men would fight like cornered rats, but Valentine disliked being in a corner in the first place. The Wolves lived and fought through their mile-devouring mobility, striking where and when the Kurians were weak and disappearing once the enemy concentrated. He dreaded the coming hammer-and-tongs battle, but what could he do in the face of orders?

"C'mon, men, push!" he shouted, throwing his weight against the wagon when the horses began to shift sideways in exhaustion. His Wolves hurled themselves against the wheels, sides—anywhere on the wagon where they could get a grip. The wagon and men groaned on up.

At the line of fortifications, Valentine braced up the wheels and passed out cases of ammunition and hand-bombs. The slope from here was easier to the crown of the hill. A little above them a small boulder-strewn spur off the crown marked Beck's designated command post. He saw the captain moving down the slope toward the trail.

"Keep it moving, Sergeant. I'm going to talk to the captain for a moment."

He found Beck, legs stiff as though rooted among the rocks.

"Nice work, Lieutenant. That was a big load at last."

"The ammunition took a while to dig up, sir. What's the word on the Grogs?"

Beck looked grim. "It's in the hundreds, at least. The scouts marked a dozen legworms. There're men with them, too, but they were too far away to see if it was Quisling regulars or just the supply train."

"Grogs don't move with much in the way of supplies. I think they eat rocks if it comes to it."

"Valentine, you and I both know what they eat. Let's just try to stay off the menu for a few days. I want your platoon covering that ravine to the south and the saddle where the rocky crown meets the other hills. Keep your best squad as a reserve, back up wherever they decide to hit us first. I've put a squad in reserve, too, and we're going to shift them as needed. Twenty or so extra guns will make the difference wherever they come."

Valentine did some quick mental math. Beck's deployment put a man every ten feet or so in the tree-trunk fortifications on the crest of the little hill. Maybe a little more to the west and on the saddle, a few less at the steep ravine on the south side. Lt. Caltagirone and his twenty men would be a godsend, if they would just return. The two flying squads would be very busy.

He jogged up to the crown of the hill, a windswept expanse of rocks on the heavily timbered rise protruding from the trees like a callused spot on an ox's back. Stunted specimens of scrub pine grew among the rocks, in what looked like just a few handfuls of dirt. A goat bleated from a little depression in the hill's crown. The stock drank from a muddy pool of rainwater caught in a basinlike depression. The camp casuals stood by, armed. Everything seemed to be in place here. He found a moment to smile and nod at the Meyer girl—or rather Mrs. Poulos now, the baby still in her arms, and tried not to think about their fate if the Grogs overran the hilltop. He turned to the men taking their positions at the breastworks.

Sergeant Stafford had already arrayed the men, stretching them painfully thin at the ravine to the south, and clustered them in two groups on the saddle that connected Little Timber Hill to a larger ridge to the east. Beyond that line of hills to the southeast stood the comforting mass of the Ozarks, blue in the distance.

Valentine made only one improvement in the Sergeant's defenses. He had the men drape a few hides, hats, and bits of clothing over appropriately shaped saplings. The Grogs were remarkable long-range snipers, and a few extra targets to absorb potshots during an assault might save the life of a real soldier.

The Wolves took to making scarecrows with a will, even going so far as to naming them Fat Tom, the Hunchback, Mr. Greenshoots, and other colorful monikers. As a few aged felt hats were being fixed atop the faux Wolves, shots echoed up from the west side of the hill.

"Looks like they found us," Valentine announced, seeing his men stiffen at the sound. "Keep your heads down, gents. Let them shoot, and mark them. Then shoot when they reload their pieces. Or when they psyche themselves up for a charge."

Valentine fought the urge to go to the other side of the hill for a glimpse of the opposition. His place was with his men.

"Gator, I'm putting you in charge of the reserve squad at the top. That'll be the final line if this one goes. Get the ammunition in there with the stock, and fill every bucket and canteen with water. Understand?"

"Ahead of you, sir, at least as far as the ammunition

goes. I'll get first squad to work up there. Whistle if there's trouble?"

Valentine extracted a little silver whistle on a lanyard from beneath his buckskin jacket. Stafford winced at the sight; the whistle had belonged to Valentine's predecessor. It would have been buried with him, too, if Stafford hadn't rescued it from before sending the body on to the field morgue. "We might be in for a long fight. Work the men in shifts."

A leaping figure raced up the hill from Beck's spur. It was the Aspirant, Nishino.

Valentine checked his carbine and pistol while he waited for the racing teen.

"Lieutenant Valentine, sir," Nishino said, again out of breath. "The captain wants you in charge of the flying squads. He says to assemble them behind the command post. They found us, and it looks like they're coming up the hill!"

"Thank you, Nishino. Tell the captain I'll be there at once," he said, granting the boy the formality of a salute.

He turned to Stafford. "I guess that leaves you in charge here, Gator. Put Corporal Holloway in with the dependents and the livestock at the last line."

"Yes, sir."

"The Grogs should be a while probing the hill. If they come in your zone, it'll be across the saddle. Put two men with good ears on the other side of it, and tell them to make sure the Grogs don't get between them and the crown."

"Good luck, Val." Gator shook his hand, hung on for an extra moment.

"You, too, Gator."

"See you soon."

"Soon."

Valentine trotted up the hill, feeling liberated. He'd done all he could. The Wolves would do the fighting now. All he could do is offer to stop a bullet like the rest of them. The day might see him as a hero, a coward, a fool, or a corpse. Like a drunk anticipating a hangover, he knew that the fear would come later, leaving him shaking in a cold sweat and nauseated.

He stole over to the command post, crabbing carefully between the rocks. Grog snipers could already have a view of the spur, and he wanted to avoid a rendezvous with one of the fifty-caliber bullets fired from single-shot rifles they favored.

Beck was scanning the bottom of the slope with his binoculars, listening to the popping of sporadic rifle fire, turning his head at the shots like an owl following mouse scratches.

He glanced once at Valentine and returned to the binoculars.

"Lieutenant, scouts are back. The legworms will be up this slope in a few minutes. They're lining the damn things up now in the camp. We've counted only ten. They'll have to do some winding to get around these trees, so they can't come up at a rush. Take the flying squads, and reinforce at that wagon. If I want you to pull out for some reason, you'll hear three short blasts from my whistle."

"Three blasts—yes, sir," Valentine repeated.

Beck put down the binoculars. "Give 'em hell, Val. Captaincies grow from days like these."

"Yes, sir."

Valentine hurried up to Yamashiro and his squad, wondering what sort of stress Beck was under, to make him think his lieutenant would fight harder if he thought there was a set of captain's bars in it. He had served with Beck for nine months, and his superior still had no idea what kind of man his senior lieutenant was. It was a disturbing thought on a day that already had many other unsettling mental threads unraveling.

He gained the tree where Yamashiro waited with the most veteran of the squads of Second Platoon. The expectant, confident expressions on the men's faces were a tonic to Valentine.

"Here's the story, gentlemen. We're going to have about ten legworms in our laps in a few minutes. But this isn't the open prairie; those big bastards are going to have a tough time in the woods. Corporal, do you have two reliable cata-pult teams?"

"Sure, sir. Baker can hit the strike zone from center field, and Grub is pretty near as good."

"Very well. I want one team just below the CP."

"Just below the command post—yes, sir."

"There's a pair of boulders kind of leaning together above the line of fortifications on the south side of the road—the other team should be posted there. Take a sack of bombs, men, and make them count. Remember, the brain on a legworm is buried in the middle."

The Wolves began putting together the catapults. They were improvised weapons for hurling the baseball-size grenades of Southern Command. Essentially larger versions of the classic childhood slingshot, they consisted of a broad U of one-inch lead piping, with thick surgical tubing attached at the top. The grenade rested in a little hardened leather cup at the center of the tubing. Two men held the U while a third pulled and aimed the catapult, launching the grenade twice as far as it could be thrown, often with uncanny accuracy in the hands of a skilled puller.

Valentine took Corporal Yamashiro and the other four men down to the breastworks. He looked around the makeshift "gate" in the trail, made up of a wagon with rocks and timber piled around it.

"Sergeant Petrie, you in charge here?" Valentine looked up at a man kneeling with two others behind a long log stretched across the length of the wagon.

"Yes, Lieutenant Valentine."

"Nice job spacing the men. Pass the word, Wolves—we've got legworms coming. It does no good to shoot the damn things; they won't even feel it. Knock the Grogs off the top. And don't be afraid to use the grenades. We've got a whole summer's worth." The last was not quite true, but Valentine wanted to encourage their use. Explosions had been known to make legworms reverse themselves and creep away as quickly as they came forward.

A few of the men had bundled bunches of grenades around a hefty branch, making a throwable stick bomb.

Valentine moved up and down the line, checking the men's positions and equipment. Most gripped their rifles and stared down the hill with hard, alert faces.

Valentine let his hearing play all along the bottom of the hill. Muted light from the cloud-filled sky gave the woods an eerie, shadowless uniformity. A woodpecker beat a tattoo on a distant tree, as if drumming a warning of what was to come.

"C'mon, apes, if you're gonna bring it . . . let's get it over with," a Wolf said as he peered down the leaf sights of his rifle to the base of the hill.

The answer came: a distant horn sounded a hair-raising call of three blasts, each slightly louder and higher than the preceding: *awwwk Awwwwwk AWWWWWUUK!* It made Valentine think of trumpeter swans he had heard in his Minnesota youth. A few of the newer soldiers looked at each other, seeking reassurance from their comrades after hearing the otherworldly sound.

"Good of them to let us know they're on the way," Valentine said. "Let's return the favor." Then more loudly, "Stand to your posts, men, and let them know that Wolves are waiting!"

The men cheered and began howling, imitating the cries of the canine predators. The cries were picked up and amplified by other Wolves up and down the thinly held line until the hills echoed with them. Valentine spotted skinny young Nishino a little way above in the rocks of the command post, red-faced from yelling his lungs out.

A steady rustle, like a wind through dry fall leaves, came from the base of the hill. The cheers ceased. Valentine brought up his carbine, comforted by its reliable weight and smell of gun oil.

The pale-yellow legworms advanced, slinking up the hillside like gigantic centipedes. Each individual limb rippled one at a time along the thirty-foot length of their bodies, faster than the eye could follow. The motion fascinated Valentine; it reminded him of quickly falling dominoes. He tore his gaze away from the hypnotic sight of the legs. A probing maw ringed with catfish whiskers waved to and fro, finding the way for the rest of the creature between the tree trunks. Gray troll-like figures, proportioned like huge apes, sat astride the long, tubular legworms. They held metal shields in cordwood-thick arms, with long-barreled rifles resting in eyebolts projecting from the side. Each legworm in the assault carried six of these Grogs, already firing up into the Wolves' breastworks. Their shooting was worse than usual, owing to the unsteady motion of their sidewinding mounts.

A few shots rang out from the Wolves as bullets zipped overhead. Explosions tore through the trees when grenades fired from the catapults detonated on the hillside. One Wolf whirled a stick bomb on a short lanyard, sending the grenades bouncing down the hill and into the approaching line.

Between the legworms, Grogs on foot jumped from tree to tree, covering each other with steady rifle fire. A few shots told among the Wolves. But the infantry Grogs could not keep up with their mounted comrades.

A stick bomb rolled under a legworm's middle. The grenades detonated, sending black digits flying. The creature collapsed at the middle, dead, but both ends still writhed on reflex-driven legs.

Another grenade exploded close enough to one's nerve center to send it into convulsions, throwing or crushing its Grog riders and trees alike as it whipped and rolled like a scorpion stinging itself to death. A legworm on the northern end seemed confused, moving sideways, forward and back amongst the trees as if looking for an escape, giving the Wolves a chance to pick off its riders. Freed of their control, the legworm moved back down the hill away from the chaos. Two more followed it despite the frantic efforts to control it on the part of its simian riders.

"Pour it into them, men, pour it on," Petrie yelled above the din, blood spilling down his face from a gash across his temple. The bullet that nearly killed him had taken his hat. White bone glistened red under a ragged flap of skin.

Valentine squeezed off shot after shot at the lead Grog on the nearest legworm, but the bullets seemed either to miss or bounce off the piece of armored shield it held in its hand.

Vexed, he knelt to reload. Grog snipers put bullets where his head had been a moment before. He noticed the Wolf to his right had the whole right side of his head torn away, as if sawn off with a precision tool.

Carbine ready, Valentine rolled and came back up behind the breastworks at the dead man's notch. He squeezed off three shots into the same leading Grog from the shield's off side. This time his shots found their mark; the Grog toppled off its mount. Its fellows tried to grab the reins, but the leg-worm already began to arc off to the right. At the rate of a Grog a second, the Wolves dropped the other five riders like ducks in a shooting gallery.

Cordite filled Valentine's nostrils. Another legworm thrashed in tree-cracking pain, badly wounded by a grenade. But two more were atop the breastworks, forcing their way through the abatis, ignoring the sharpened branches, which first impaled, then broke off in their soft, puffy skin.

Valentine saw the flash of a fuse and heard a faint, wet *pop*. A legworm's mouth exploded, leaving a greenish-yellow wound open across the whole front of its body. The thing reeled and sped back downslope, shaking its riders like a bucking bronco. One of the catapults had managed to put a grenade right down its throat, using the basketball-hoop-size maw as a target. But the remaining legworm was up and over the head-logs in a flash, and the Grogs dropped off it and onto the men below, closely followed by a second yellow giant. As it climbed onto the logs, heavy and pulsing above Valentine's head, he ignored his own advice and fired shot after shot into its belly at the approximate mid-dle. The bullets left green-goo-dripping holes, but the thirty-caliber shells fired muzzle-to-skin found nerve gan-glia. The legworm collapsed; as it fell, he threw himself out of the way, but it still trapped him below the knees. A few legs hammered against his thighs as they twitched out their final spasm.

The Grogs fought hand to hand with the Wolves, tossing the smaller humans right and left, firing oversize pistols and swinging double-bladed battle-axes that gleamed red with blood. Volleys of fire from above cut them down: the grenade teams had dropped their catapults and turned their rifles on the Grogs fighting at the barricades.

He got one leg out from beneath the fleshy mass.

A Grog from the legworm Valentine shot hopped up onto the abatis. Valentine brought up his gun, but the carbine's hammer came down with an impotent click. A misfire, or he was empty. The Grog raised its battle-ax, and Valentine read death in its purple eyes just before two holes opened in its chest, throwing it backwards. Valentine had no time to look for his unseen marksman-savior; he pushed free of the dead legworm and brought his gun up and over the breastworks, only to see the Grogs retreating through the trees. Valentine looked one second too long; a bullet whizzed past close enough to feel the pressure of its passage against his ear.

He dropped to his knees, seeking safety in the thick comfort of the breastworks. To either side of him, Wolves were still shooting down the slope. A bloody-knuckled man helped another stop the flow from a head wound as Valentine counted the cost of the attack. Four dead. Many wounded.

Valentine looked down at a Grog pistol by his knee. The weapon looked like two revolvers joined at the bottom of the grip, with a thick trigger guard running between the two. A single lever cocked and fired both barrels.

"They're going," someone shouted. The survivors of the legworm assault sagged against the protecting logs, many with tears of relief running down their faces.

"They'll be back," Petrie said as another Wolf wrapped a bandage around his head. "They'll keep coming until they're all dead . . . or we are."

They came six more times that cool spring day. Each time, like a rising tide, the Grog wave crested farther. And when they receded, they left snipers among the rocks and trees, sappers who could be silenced only by grenades and concentrated rifle fire. The Grogs wrapped their lines around Little Timber Hill like a python coiling around its

prey, waiting for it to weaken and smother under its irre-
sistible pressure.

Noon came and went, and afternoon brought a two-hour
lull in the fighting. Valentine let the men leave the breastworks in small groups to steal away to the rocky crown for
food and water—even a brief washup if they could get it.
Although the last might be rendered moot: the rain clouds
were piling up on the horizon again.

A sniper wounded Captain Beck when the Grogs came,
thick and screaming, up the long slope at about three in the
afternoon. Tom Nishino, not knowing what else to do, blew
his captain's whistle. Valentine heard the trilling above the
shrieks of the Grogs and looked up to see the boy waving to
him. Valentine gestured back, outflung arm trying to motion Tom to keep down, when a slug took the youth, spinning him in one quick, 360-degree revolution to drop dead
among the rocks.

Valentine left Petrie in charge and scrambled up to the
command post. Two Wolves and one of the camp women
knelt around Beck. The captain's left shoulder was shattered, leaving his arm dangling.

"How are the men holding?" Beck asked through pain-
gritted teeth. The woman bound the wound with quick
strokes, ignoring Beck's gasps. Valentine paused a moment,
admiring the sure motions of her hands.

"They're holding good, sir. But I've got nine dead
around the trail, and a lot of wounded."

"I don't know how long I'll be conscious here, Valentine.
So I want you to take command. Hold this position; the
Guards are on their way. Bring the wounded up to the rocky
crown. They'll be safe there. Sooner or later they're going
to figure out that the easiest way to get at us is from across
the saddle, so you'd better reform your flying squads."

Valentine wished Beck would stop talking. If he was
going to relinquish command, he should quit giving orders.

"Yes, sir," he said. "Let's get you up into the basin."

The two Wolves helped Beck to his feet, supporting him
with his good arm. The captain's face contorted in pain as
he made his first halting steps toward the rocky crown, the

trio keeping hidden from the snipers at the bottom of the hill.

Valentine picked up Beck's dropped binoculars. The odor of the captain's cigars clung to their casing and strap. What had been Beck's was now his. Responsibility for Foxtrot Company's future put his stomach into a knot of Gordian proportions. He watched the ragged young woman who had bandaged the captain as she picked up Beck's bolt-action carbine, examining it. She had brassy red hair cut very short, freckles, and pretty, if angular, features. She looked like she had been on short rations for a week: her eyes had a wide, alert, and hungry look. Valentine suddenly realized he didn't know her.

"I'm sorry, who are you?" Valentine said. "I thought I knew everyone in camp."

"I've been in your camp for only a couple hours, Wolf. Are you missing about two dozen men?"

Valentine frowned. "My name is David Valentine, Second Wolf Regiment of Southern Command. I'm in charge of what's left of this company. I'd be obliged if you'd give me your name."

"I'd prefer not to be put in any official reports. My code name is Smoke, if you have to say something."

An occasional shot from below punctuated the conversation.

"Code name? You're a Cat?"

"Yes, Mr. Lieutenant. Since the age of sixteen. Normally I work the plains of here, but I'm on the trail of something."

"What was that you said about missing men? Some Wolves under a lieutenant named Caltagirone are missing."

She looked grim. "Don't expect them back. They got caught on the banks of the Verdigris. Slaughtered."

Valentine froze his features into immobility to hide his shock. *Another friend gone.* "Grogs?"

"No—Reapers, at least sorta." She licked her lips, like an animal that comes across an unpleasant smell.

The news sank in. Caltagirone was as canny as Father

Wolf made them. Not like him to get taken unaware. "What do you mean, sort of?"

"It's a little hard to explain. It's a band of about twelve Reapers. I've never come across a group that big just roaming before. They're also using guns, which is odd from what I've heard about them."

"I've never heard anything like that before." It didn't make sense to him. Reapers served as conduits for vital aura between the victim and their master Kurian. Unless they were close enough to touch, the psychic energies were lost. Even in battle, Reapers killed so their masters gained the aura they craved.

"Saying I don't know my own eyes, Wolf?"

"No. Not at all. Thank you for the news about . . . about the Wolves on the Verdigris."

The redhead sat, removed a high-laced boot and two sets of dirty socks, then rubbed the instep of her right foot. Her bony feet had the calluses of someone who'd done a lot of walking.

"Now's not the time to discuss what the Kur are up to. Whatever or whoever these Reapers are, they still rest during the daylight hours. But I'm pretty sure they're headed here. If they wake at dusk, they'll be on you by midnight, maybe before. I about killed a horse getting here. I think the Grogs are just flypaper to stick you in place. The Reapers will be the ones to swat you."

She smelled of horse lather and swamp water.

"They might get their chance. The Grogs are all around us."

"Lieutenant, if I find a hole in their line, do you think you could raise a little hell somewhere else? It looks like you have enough horseflesh to drag your wounded out."

Valentine did not need any convincing to abandon the hill, as long at they could put some distance in between themselves and their gathering enemy.

"Night still comes early this time of year. Let me get my sergeants up here, and we'll talk."

The first mortar shell hit the rocky crown as they moved up the spur, and the pair threw themselves to the ground together. "This day just keeps getting better and better," Valentine said, spitting dirt.

Valentine had to raise his voice to be heard over the animals and gunfire sputtering below. The Grogs lobbed sporadic mortar shells into the hill, but they didn't make much more of a bang than the Wolves' hand grenades. The Grog column either did not pack much ammunition or lacked the ability to fire their piece very often. Maybe technology, maybe training.

The sun settled. Darkness crept up the hill, engulfing the wooded slope like a rising flood.

"One more time, Wolves. Stafford, you are with me on the diversion." Valentine had his best NCOs—save Hart at the breastworks—all around him, and he rotated like the second hand on a watch, issuing orders. "We're going to give the Grogs something to think about on the west side while everyone else pulls out east. Yamashiro, you cover the litters for the wounded. Make sure the drags stay attached to the draft horses and the wounded are ready to go."

Yamashiro nodded.

"I don't want to hear anything about some of them being too bad to move. We're not shooting anybody, and we're not going to leave anyone behind. Petrie, if you're still feeling up to it, I need you to handle the rear guard. I want the shell in the line ready to collapse as soon as the diversion gets going."

"Hell of a headache, sir. Not your instructions, the Grog's little tap, I mean."

Valentine looked into the sergeant's eyes; the pupils were normal, though he had a black eye worthy of a medical book forming on the left side of his face near the wound. He turned to the next man.

"Holloway, you take five good Wolves and go with our Cat here. She's going to pick the trail. Your job will be to make sure everyone gets on it. Avoid gunplay if you can."

The Cat in question shoveled hot beans and rice into her mouth as she listened. The pockets in her ratty overcoat bulged with bread, and she had more food wrapped up in her blanket roll.

"Sure the Grogs won't smell you coming now?" Valentine ventured.

A few snickers broke out among the Wolves, but the young woman just eyed Valentine coldly. "Not a chance. You just make some noise this side of the hill, and keep everyone moving hard for at least an hour. Can you handle that, Lieutenant?"

Valentine suppressed the urge to shrug his shoulders. In an hour he could be dead. "We'll see what we can do." He reviewed the faces of his NCOs, reassured by their self-reliant expressions. "Questions, gentlemen? No? Then let's saddle up, please. I want to be very far from here by morning."

As he slid down to the breastworks with Stafford and the other four crack riflemen, Valentine considered the fact that he was ignoring Captain Beck's final orders. But Beck was in a drag-litter now, unconscious from shock or pain. Even if the Cat's guess that these mysterious Reapers were on the way was wrong, Valentine doubted he could hold Little Timber for the problematical arrival of the Guard Cavalry. If the Grogs were reinforced at all, they could sweep over the top of the hill by making one more effort that matched the first legworm assault.

His team approached the wagon. The darkening sky was turning the woods to shadow.

Sergeant Hart had modified the wagon for a one-way trip down the slope. Each wheel now had its own hand brake with a new leather shoe at the end of the lever. Some Wolf who had read *Ben-Hur* had fixed knives, blades outward, on the hubs of each of the four wheels. The sides and front had small tree trunks added, interwoven and lashed together around sandbags for added protection. A case of grenades and a box of phosphorus candles were secured to the reinforced sides.

The volunteers climbed in, rifles, pistols, and sawed-off shotguns at the ready. "Be pretty funny if a mortar shell dropped in here after all this work," Stafford commented, helping Valentine up into the wagon bed.

"I've heard of toboggan rides to Hell, but I never expected to sit in one," another Wolf said, putting two rounds of buckshot into a scattergun. He snapped the breech closed with a grin.

Valentine picked up a captured Grog rifle. Another like it lay in the bed of the wagon, loaded and ready. It was heavy and unwieldy; he decided he could aim and shoot it properly if he could rest it on the side of the wagon. The bolt and trigger were oversize and strange to work—the bolt was drawn all the way up and across the gun to the other side to eject the expended shell, like a large switch. Even the lever looked odd, until Valentine remembered the strange head jerk of the Grogs after they shot—they opened the chamber and popped the shell with their chins. He placed one of the Grog fifty-caliber shells in the weapon. The bullets were as long as his hand and thicker than his index finger.

As the shadows deepened, Wolves slunk away from their positions, leaving Petrie's picked few to hold the breastworks.

Valentine assigned a man to each brake, taking the right front one himself. The shadows turned slowly purple in the growing night as the minutes ticked by.

Darkness.

"Okay, let's have a little covering fire, men. Give us a shove back there! Heave!" Valentine yelled over his shoulder at the waiting Wolves.

The wagon began to roll down the long, straight slope. The ruts in the trail would serve to guide the wheels in the absence of horses, as long as they didn't pick up too much speed.

"Keep on those brakes, there," Valentine called to the other three men at the levers. He wanted to be moving fast enough to be a difficult target, but not so fast that the wagon got outside of the brakes' ability to halt it. Bullets from both sides whistled and zipped around them. "Stop before we get out of the trees."

Stafford and the other free Wolf threw grenades to either side, for all the world like parade dignitaries tossing taffy to children lining the road. A Grog jumped out onto the trail in front of them, rifle raised to its shoulder. Valentine had an instant flash of his life ending in the bed of the wagon, thirsty boards absorbing his blood, but the report of the gun was not accompanied by the impact of a slug. The Grog threw down his rifle and drew a knife the size of a machete. It ran up to the wagon's side, throwing its arm across the side logs in an attempt to climb in. Its fierce snarl turned into wide-eyed surprise as the knives on the hub rotated their way across its belly. The eviscerated Grog dropped off the side as quickly as it had leapt on and fell writhing on the trail behind them.

Snap! The Wolf at the rear brake looked down in stupid amazement at the broken handle—or more precisely, the piece of wood that had attached the handle to the body of the wagon.

"Keep the pressure on—we're almost to the bottom," Valentine said. The grade lessened. They would be out of the trees in a few seconds. "Okay, hard brake, everyone. Stop this thing!"

Damn, damn, double damn! The wagon was slowing, but not stopping. It rumbled out of the trees to the tune of squealing wood: the leather pads had peeled off the brakes.

Gun flashes peppered the night around them. A Wolf fell, gripping a shattered arm and thrashing in the bottom of the wagon. The others fired back. Grogs ran forward, throwing themselves prone to shoot at the wagon.

"Stafford, the candles," Valentine yelled. He picked up a pair of flares and handed some to Gator, who coolly threw a grenade into the night.

Valentine and Stafford ignited the fireworks on a glowing piece of slow match. They burst into eye-cutting, blue-white light. Squinting against the glare, Valentine flung his as far into the night as he could. Grog shooters appeared in the pool of light where it landed, giving the riflemen in the truck a mark. Stafford threw two more off to the left.

"More! If we can't shoot 'em, let's blind 'em!" Valentine shouted. A form appeared out of the dark into the blue light of one of the candles, cloaked and hooded.

Reaper!

Valentine pulled up a Grog gun, balancing its overlong barrel on the log in front of him. The Reaper went into a defensive crouch as the Wolves fired at it, inhuman joints bent like a spider's and ready to spring.

The Grog gun roared like a cannon, flipping the Reaper neatly onto its back, feet twitching. Grog iron packed a kick at both ends: Valentine's shoulder felt as though he'd been shot, as well. But it was worth the pain; the bullet went through the Reaper's protective cloak. He reached for the second gun, but by the time he brought it up, the Reaper had already fled.

Splinters flew as Grog bullets pounded into the sand-bagged logs the Wolves used for cover. The distance between the wagon and the trees at the base of Little Timber was a dark, deadly chasm. They had to try for it before the Grogs clustered too thickly around the wagon.

"Now! Break for the woods!"

The firing men seemed not to hear him. "Move it!" Stafford barked, shocking the men out of their firing with his field-filling bellow and slaps on the back of the neck. The sergeant pulled the wounded Wolf to the rear as the men jumped out of the wagon.

At the sight of the Wolves abandoning their mobile fort, the surrounding Grogs came running, hooting to each other. Valentine dropped one of the chargers with the other Grog gun and rolled off the wagon.

Stafford suddenly sagged, gripping his stomach. "Go, go!" he gasped at the Wolves, folding and falling.

Valentine caught Gator as he fell, reflexes in top gear.

"Go . . . go," Stafford repeated, though whether he was still calling out his final order or encouraging his officer to leave him, Valentine couldn't say.

Valentine hoisted him on his shoulders in a fireman's carry. "Uh-uh. Not getting out of Foxtrot that easy," he puffed as he lumbered toward the woods. The howls and shots of the Grogs in pursuit spurred him on.

Another Wolf fell, sprawling dead on the field, a mere ten yards shy of the trees. The flash of a shotgun illuminated a Grog leaping at them from the woods, gray skin ghostly in the glare of the flares. It toppled, almost cut in two by the blast. Some acoustical trick made the shot seem as though from a great distance.

Valentine started up the slope, Stafford's hot, sticky blood running down his back. Nothing mattered but getting the sergeant to the top of that hill. Valentine forgot the Grogs, the other Wolves still hurrying beside him, covering him as best they could. The flaming agony in his legs, the thick, coppery-tasting burn in his chest—they were the here and now, all else faded into the noise and confusion of the running fight. He felt Stafford go limp. . . . *Please God let it be unconsciousness.*

"Get . . . to . . . the . . . wagon," Valentine gasped. The Wolves would be up the hill already, if they would only quit covering him and Stafford.

One worked the lever of his rifle. "After you, sir," he said, kneeling to shoot back down the hill. Valentine heard an inhuman scream of pain.

He found the strength and breath to keep moving.

"Lieutenant, get down!" Sergeant Petrie called from somewhere above.

Valentine sank to his knees, dropping one arm from Stafford to hold himself up.

A volley crashed out from the breastworks. A second ragged one followed as the Wolves worked the actions on their rifles.

"Now, sir!" Petrie called out. A tiny red dot, the fuse on a grenade, flew overhead.

The seconds of respite worked wonders on his legs. He struggled to his feet, still burdened by Stafford, and reached the breastworks at a run. Wolves squeezed off shots from a twenty-yard stretch of the breastworks.

"The rear guard should be off this hill already, Petrie," Valentine admonished his savior. "But I'm damn glad to see you."

"The feeling is mutual, sir. Shall I light the fuses?" the sergeant asked.

"Be my guest."

The second wagon, like the first, was lined up in the ruts leading down the hill. Only this one was filled with tinder, ammunition, black powder, and grenades, and manned by four smiley-face scarecrows pulled from the hill. Petrie nodded to a pair of Wolves who kicked out the rocks bracing up the wheels, and as the wagon began to roll, Petrie lit a spaghetti tangle of black fuse cord dangling off the end. Six individual threads hissed as they burned down toward the explosives.

The cart picked up speed.

"Let's not stay for the fireworks. Gavin, Richards, help Sergeant Stafford. Put him in that stretcher. I've got another man hit in the arm. Where's Holbrooke?"

"He didn't make it," one of the volunteers said. "He fell on the trail."

Valentine pushed Holbrooke, a newly invoked Wolf with the makings of a good officer, out of his mind. "Let's catch up to the others."

The Wolves fell back as explosions rumbled from the base of the hill. The small-arms ammunition and grenades cooked off, as well, adding their own notes to the destructive symphony.

The escape route Smoke scouted wound through the deep ravine on the south side of Little Timber Hill. Valentine and his weary men moved as quickly as they could along the crown of the hill to the Wolf posted at the point in the breastworks where the line of retreat began.

"Lieutenant Valentine," said the soldier, tears of relief in his eyes, "I'm to get you caught up with the rear of the column. That Cat sure knows her stuff, sir. We found two dead Grogs at the break in the ravine. Two others farther up, too. Did it without firing a shot."

With four men on Stafford's stretcher, they caught up to the rear guard in a matter of minutes. The Cat lingered at the back of the column, waiting for them.

"And they say we have nine lives," she said, eyes sparkling in the darkness. She twitched and turned at tiny sounds, pure nervous energy beneath her freckled skin. Her face was coated with black greasepaint, and she had turned her overcoat inside out to reveal a black shell on the reverse side. "Good to see you made it, Lieutenant. That was some stunt."

"Thank you, thank you for finding us a bolt-hole, that is. From everyone in Foxtrot Company." Valentine favored her with a little bow. "If there's anything the Wolves can do—"

"Sure. I'll take a carbine like the one I saw you with and a scattergun. A revolver would come in handy, too."

"Of course. Tomorrow morning you can have your pick."

"No, sir—now, if you don't mind. I'm going back to the hill."

Valentine stopped in his tracks, causing the Wolf behind to plow into him. Other men swore as the file sorted itself out. "What's that?" he asked, stepping aside and gesturing to the Wolf to keep moving.

"Look, Lieutenant, someone should keep the campfires going there. Fire an occasional shot at the Grogs. Tie up the stock so the lifesign fools them—at a distance, anyway.

"We already used some wounded Grogs for that," Hart cut in.

She flashed a smile before turning back to Valentine. "Besides, I think those Reapers we spoke of are going to hit your camp sometime tonight. I want another look at them."

Valentine was startled into an unguarded comment: "You're crazy."

"Mmmm. I'm not trying to take heads. Just a look and a listen. I'm pretty slippery; they won't get their tongues into me. If I stay back there, it improves your chances of getting away about a hundred percent. When I do leave, I'll leave noisy. I'll try to lure the Grogs down toward Fort Smith."

"It's your aura. Take whatever you want with my gratitude."

She grabbed weapons from the astonished Wolves. She moved lightly, making no more sound on the forest floor than a breath of wind. "Thanks. Maybe we'll meet again, Lieutenant," she said, throwing her new carbine over one shoulder and cradling a shotgun.

"Hope so. Let me know what you find out. You can get

in touch with me through the Miskatonic. I drop in there whenever I can."

"Those ghouls? They always want me to bring in Reaper blood bladders. Fresh ones. Like I walk around with a jar of formaldehyde."

"I've got friends there." He offered his hand, and the woman took it.

"You don't look like an egghead, Valentine. Until a better day."

"Better days," he agreed.

She disappeared into the darkness as quietly as she came, and Valentine was left with a grease-stained hand.

They buried Stafford at dawn the next day.

Foxtrot Company laid him to rest on a forested ridge overlooking a little ruined roadside town from the Old World.

The sound of the occasional shot from Little Timber Hill faded once they put the first ridge between themselves and the Grogs. With a couple of miles between him and the hill, Valentine relaxed into his after-action jitters, sticking his hands in his side pockets to keep them still. The news that Stafford had died barely registered through the worry and fatigue; he had been half expecting it. When he was told that Poulos, the handsome new bridegroom from his platoon, had succumbed to shrapnel wounds from the Grog mortars, he felt more of a shock. Poulos had been bleeding a little, but insisted on walking one of the litter horses instead of riding.

They paused to rest, eat, and bury the dead. Rain turned the dirt into wet lead for the diggers and as the little clusters of miserable people stood over the freshly covered mounds, saying the final good-byes of the graveside.

Good men and mediocre men, veterans and youths—all in all, Foxtrot Company had lost twenty-two Wolves, without counting Lieutenant Caltagirone and his short platoon. Adding in the wounded brought the casualty rate up and over 70 percent. A disaster. And he'd been in command.

Three

Fort Smith on the Arkansas River, March: HELL ON THE BOR-
DER *reads the sign hung just beneath the foot-tall stencils of
the post's official marker. The slogan goes back to Fort
Smith's days as a station at the edge of the Indian Territory,
when prisoners brought in from the Nations waited in a
dank series of cells for their turn before the Honorable
Judge Parker, U. S. Grant's "hanging judge."*

*Now the buildings around the Reynolds Bell Tower—the
bell still serves as the post's alarm system; it last rang in
the fall of '66 during an air raid by harpies—still see their
share of prisoners. Runaways from the Gulag, deserters,
captured Quislings, and troublemakers from the western
half of the Free Territory are brought here to be interrogated, and either sent downriver into the Free Territory or
brought up before a military court.*

*Fort Smith is the responsibility of the Guards, the uni-
formed defenders of the Free Territory. It marks the end of
the commercial line on the Arkansas River and four eastern
roads. There is a civilian presence supporting the soldiery
and schools and a hospital to accommodate them. It is a
hard-duty station. Only the posts south of St. Louis on the
Free Territory's border see more alerts and action. Hardly
a month goes by without the departure of a regiment or two
of Guard infantry with their supports to cover some portion
of the border against a real or threatened attack out of the
Kurian Zone. Lesser patrols depart and return at reports of
everything from Reapers to horse thieves, downed telephone wires and hayloft arsonists.*

The graveyard south of Belle Point is filled with the Guards who came back in the morgue wagons.

Duty at Fort Smith is not without its diversions. Traveling performers entertain at the Best Center—singing groups and acting companies inevitably called the "Worst Enters" by the sarcastic soldiers. The women at Miss Laura's, the most opulent of Fort Smith's brothels, provide assorted horizontal refreshments, but unlike the free Best Center, it takes a week's pay to enjoy a few hours of diversion. The local beer, Smith-Knoble, is well thought of throughout the Territory, and entrepreneurs who don't mind the occasional sound of artillery fire operate restaurants and pubs.

Hunters in from the KZ stick to a few boarding houses and pubs that welcome their kind. Neither civilians nor Guards, they are nominally subordinated to the Officer Commanding Fort Smith while within the broad boundaries of the post. But something about the Hunters, even in civilian dress, makes the civilians wary and Guard hackles rise. Perhaps it is the intense stares or the too-quick-for-the-eye flinches at unexpected movement or the tribal clannishness that sets them apart. But when word comes that a Reaper is on the border, Hell on the Border is glad to have them there.

The orders in Valentine's dispatch pouch that read "Survivors leave ending 9MAY2067" amounted to an epitaph to Foxtrot Company.

It meant the Second Wolf Regiment considered the company destroyed as a fighting force; even those still unwounded after Little Timber would be distributed to other units. If they decided to rebuild the company, he'd get a second set of orders soon enough. As the senior unwounded officer, he might even be selected for command. If so, he'd try to get a few of the veteran NCOs, perhaps arguing that "third time's the charm" for ill-fated Foxtrot, now decimated twice in three years.

After getting the flimsy, Valentine decided to spend his leave in Fort Smith. It would be easy for orders and mail to find him there; he could visit the library; perhaps he'd even be able to spend a few days fishing in the river or one of the lakes around the post if he could obtain a skiff, rod, and reel. He needed quiet and solitude to help the memories of Little Timber settle.

He'd thought about spending his leave in Weening. Molly had invited him to visit in her letter, but she was no doubt enmeshed in a celebration of her engagement or wedding plans—he'd seen in the spring issue of the *Service Bulletin* that her swain had been promoted. Molly didn't need Valentine hanging around like the proverbial skeleton at the feast. Her beau might even consider it an insult.

The part of him that wanted to get away was strong enough that he considered fleeing to Hal Steiner's enclave in the Arkansas bayou country. Frat had written that Steiner's unusual community of man and Grog had thrived since he'd first visited it years ago. But Steiner's independent land wasn't part of Southern Command's communication system. He'd have to journey to the nearest post to check for orders.

So he settled on Fort Smith. Besides, he had another report to make. This time he'd do it in person.

The afternoon he arrived he first went to the communications office on the old university grounds. There he reported his presence in person to the duty officer, and by phone to Second Wolf Regiment Headquarters. With that done, he drew a portion of his accumulated pay and was a free Wolf.

He asked about the town at the civilian liaison officer's station, but the sergeant behind the open, circular desk spoke with such enthusiasm about the food and beds at a particular boarding house that Valentine decided he was getting a kickback. He just picked up a mimeographed map and walked toward town.

Blue-steel storm clouds rolled in the distance, so he decided to look around town while the weather held. There were Guards in their charcoal-gray uniforms everywhere. Those on duty moved about under camouflage ponchos, rifles slung and helmets bumping from their hooks on their belts. As he got farther away from the fort, he met more off-duty soldiers, undershirts white in the spring overcast, thumbs hooked in their suspenders, hats pushed back to reveal close-cropped hair. The men and women of the Guards clustered about the pubs and markets in groups, laughing and talking with animated energy. Valentine with his dirty buckskins, mud-crusted ponytail, and meager possessions rolled in his hammock felt like a country hare wandering amongst hyperactive city squirrels.

Constant war had not been kind to Fort Smith. Every other lot was a reclaimed "rubble garden" with neat shelves of ruined masonry supporting wildflowers and surrounded by bushes. A few old homes were still standing in a section of town the map called the Grove. One of them, Donna's Den, was listed on the map as a boarding house. He'd heard the name from one of the Foxtrot Wolves. After getting his bearings off the Immaculate Conception Church, he found it.

Donna's Den was a white two-story house with an antique iron railing running around the roof. There was a chicken run and a garden in back. The front had a flower garden, with a pair of wooden sofas and a lounge chair sitting among the blossoms. The outdoor furniture supported domestic animals. Cats snoozed, and a dog twitched an ear as he passed. He smelled pies baking.

His knock on the screen door summoned a shirtless boy who thundered down the stairs. The boy had modified a laden tool belt with shoulder straps so it would go around his tiny waist. "Lieutenant Valentine, Second Regiment, Foxtrot Company," the boy said, looking at Valentine's collar tabs and sewn-in nameplate. "But the tunic is cut Zulu Company style, Lieutenant, sir. What's the story?" The boy sounded bored.

"David is fine, to a veteran like you." That got a brief smile out of him. "Do I speak to you about a room?"

"Mom!" the boy bellowed over his shoulder before vanishing back upstairs. "One of Dad's kind."

Donna Walbrook had flour in her hair and on her overalls. Valentine's nose picked up the scent of strawberries. She wiped her hands on a towel as she came to the door, showing more enthusiasm for Valentine's presence than the boy had.

"Brian has no manners," she apologized. She had a nice, though practiced, smile and a good deal of ragged beauty. "He's got his teeth into building armoires. Can I offer you a room?"

"Until the second week of May, if it's not inconvenient."

"No such thing for a boy in buckskin. Come into the parlor—just leave your bundle at the foot of the stairs."

It turned out the parlor had a small shrine to Hank Walbrook under a framed commendation letter. Valentine looked over a photograph; it showed a Wolf with an old United States Army beret set at a jaunty angle on his head. Walbrook's belt and parang lay in a case, a few rifles—Valentine noted that they smelled of gun oil and appeared well cared for—hung over the fireplace. She poured Valentine water out of a pitcher and presented him with a glass.

"Your husband?" he asked, feeling he already knew all the answers.

"Yes. A sergeant, First Regiment. Captain Hollis was his commanding officer, but I understand he's retired."

Valentine had never heard of him.

"My husband was killed in February of '55."

"I'm sorry."

She saw him glance upstairs as he did the math. "Brian isn't from Hank, but he thinks he is. I'll explain it to him when he's old enough to work it out. We have two other Wolves staying at the moment, convalescent leave," she added, putting the smile back on. "I'm sure you'll be eager to meet them."

"I would, Mrs. Walbrook."

"First rule of this house is to call me Donna."

She went through the other rules. They were brief and clear, militarily precise, and covered visitors, mealtimes, the gun locker, and the necessity for stoking the boiler if there was to be enough hot water. After negotiation involving Valentine reducing some of her cordwood to kindling, they settled on twelve dollars Southern Command script a day for his room and two meals. If he did his own bedding and laundry. Lunch he could scrounge, buy, or have for free if he cared to walk all the way to the Guard canteen.

"Any questions? I've been here fifteen years. There's nothing about the town I don't know."

Valentine wondered how to phrase his request. She wasn't officially part of Southern Command, but—

"Out with it, young man. I've heard it all." She covered her ample décolletage with a hand. "You got a case of something you don't want down in your Q file? I won't scream and faint." Her eyes sparkled with interest.

"There's supposed to be a Command Intelligence Division office about somewhere. I've seen bulletins issued from them, and the Western Border ones are marked 'Fort Smith.' But I didn't see it on the guide at the Fort, or the town map." He held out his map. "You wouldn't know where it is?"

She looked disappointed. "It's hardly a secret. They just don't have enough people to staff an information desk for every Tom, Dick, and Jane off the riverboat who saw a strange footprint."

"I need to file a report, in person." He'd tried through channels once, and nothing came of it. "It's more than a footprint."

"They're in the old museum building. Three stories, red brick, curved windows at the top. There's still a nice little one-man museum on the first floor. Schoolkids and recruits spend some time there for lectures. CID has the rest. You go in through the museum."

"Thank you."

"And there's a wonderful laundry just catty-corner. Tucks, it's called, and they will make those buckskins look like they've just been sewn. They can get the bloodstains out. Along with the . . . ahem . . . natural masculine odors."

The museum filled out about one quarter of the first floor of the building Donna had described. Valentine had bummed a pair of jeans and a clean shirt off one of the con-valescing Wolves—Gupti had a head wound and Salvador a knee brace; Salvador's advice was to borrow from Gupti because there was every chance of him not remembering he'd ever lent out his clothes. Valentine borrowed clothes from Salvador and reported to the fort to let them know where he was staying; then went into town.

The museum was on his map.

He spent a few minutes chatting with the curator, a one-legged veteran with a solid build and a pistol in a quick-release holster—a former Bear. A single key dangled from a breakaway chain around his neck; Valentine suspected it was for a case of captured assault rifles.

He took a polite look at the exhibits, tracing everything from the last newsmagazines, stained and dog-eared, covering the earthquakes, tidal waves, and volcanoes of 2022 before Big R hit. The next cabinet covered the Ravies plague—photographs of wild mobs caught in action, cities aflame, stacked corpses riddled with bite marks and bullet holes. Then the hopeful headlines from the few remaining newspapers about the Kurians, visitors from another world who had come to restore order to a shattered civilization. Alongside these were pamphlets, amateurish and smeared and filled with horrific sketches about how the Kurians were the cause of it all. There were drawings of the robed Crisis Governors with captions asserting that the "Reapers" were nothing but death-collectors, vampirelike creatures who fed on humans for their masters.

Then came a few fuzzy shots on bad stock of the Lost War. Drawings of the Grogs, a polyglot of beings brought by the Kurians from other worlds. Blasted tanks. Crashed planes. Mushroom clouds. Ruins. Flags being hauled down as bases went up in smoke to save them from capture.

A room, shielded from the rest of the museum by a black curtain, was devoted to the Kurian Order as practiced across the planet save for a few remote Freeholds. Valentine decided not to look in there. He'd seen enough of the KZ with his own eyes.

Valentine stated his business. The custodian picked up a phone and dialed, and he told Valentine one of the "upstairs men" would be with him in a minute.

*   *   *

Bone Lombard was about Valentine's age and had thick glasses. He introduced himself as a CID "filter."

"What's that?" Valentine asked.

"I'll show you."

He took Valentine back to the loading dock. Like a big garage, the dock had a series of metal doors on rails, a wide-open interior devoid of anything but structural supports. Painted lines crisscrossed the floor. The lines organized a sea of wire crates and metal trays filled with documents, binders, folders, and books.

"We get a lot of captured paperwork," Lombard said. "*We* meaning a big we—Southern Command. Anything that isn't obviously useful, like the details of a column, where and when it'll be, ends up being carted here. We get everything from Quisling cookbooks to personal letters, complete with perfume and snips of hair. I don't want to bore you with all the procedures, but the filters read through it." He waved at another young man and a woman. The other filters sat on wheeled chairs with a built-in desk, pencils handy under a droplight hanging from a hook attached to the back of the chair, going through loose paper. "It can sometimes give us a picture of what's really going on outside our borders. Where there are shortages, weak spots."

"You divine trends from paperwork?"

"Once, based on requisitions that the logistics commandos found in a hospital, we saw that huge amounts of bandages and surgical supplies were going to Shawnee Oklahoma. Turned out that the Fassler Revolt was in full swing."

Valentine remembered hearing something about it while he was studying for his lieutenant's bars at Pine Bluff. "It ended badly."

"Fassler and all his men got hanged, yes."

"I heard crucified," Valentine said.

"Maybe. Couldn't get them enough guns in time. The Oklahomans really locked down the counties in revolt. But again, if it weren't for some paperwork, we might not even know the name Fassler."

"I've got a name for you. What do you know about the Twisted Cross?"

Lombard shrugged. "I don't know. Let's index it."

One of Lombard's associates kicked out sideways and sent his chair-desk rolling down an alley between the boxes. A white cat jumped out of the way.

The "index" turned out to be an old library card catalog in a separate room, thickly insulated behind a safelike door. There were several of the huge wooden cabinets filled with index-card-size drawers. Valentine opened a drawer; under typed headings there were handwritten notations in a mix of letters and numbers.

Gannet, Pony A. (Capt. "Chanute Leadership Corps")
MIL-KAN ACT206928 11NOV61
Append CAP -6 INT -15(m, v) EX 61-415

"Don't even try," Lombard said. He took the card. "Seems this Pony—strange first name—Gannet was a captain from a Quisling body called the 'Chanute Leadership Corps.' Action Report 206-928 describes the fight. You see the date. Looks like he was taken, and there was something interesting about the capture—it appears as a separate appendix. His interrogation is also appended, and copies went to Division V, which deals with atrocities, and M, which deals with people missing in action. They must have caught him more-or-less red-handed at something. He was executed in '61 sometime between eleventh November and the end of the year. That's pretty fast nowadays. If you go to a card for the 'Chanute Leadership Corps,' you'll see—"

"I'm impressed. But the Twisted Cross?"

"Quisling unit, I bet," Lombard said.

"Yes."

Lombard went to a file drawer. "They have any other names?"

"I don't know. I wrote out my report. You want to read it?"

"Sure, in a sec. Okay . . . Twisted Cross. They're designated a Quisling unit. Looks like they get around by train. That's odd. They're cross-referenced to Eastern Division."

"Why's it odd?"

"They provide railroad security, maybe?"

"Why is it odd?" Valentine asked again.

"Usually Quisling units stay in one area, under a lord or a group of lords. You wouldn't find the late Captain Gannet's Chanute Leadership Corps operating in, say, Illinois. Unless that particular Kurian family was invading Illinois, I suppose."

Valentine gave him the copy of his supplemental report that he'd attached to his description of the battle at Little Timber. Lombard looked through the three pages at the rate of ten seconds a page.

"Aren't you going to read it?"

"I did. Shall I quote the key passage? *Ha-hem . . .* 'The destruction of Lieutenant Caltagirone's platoon and Smoke's report of heavily armed Reapers employed in groups as a cohesive fighting force demand investigation. Any information on the General—' "

"Sorry. I wrote a report on these guys once before. I might as well have tossed it in a swamp."

"Fear not. I'm sure it lives forever in an index just like this one, so it can be located in a climate-controlled warehouse. Wish we filters got the same treatment—you should smell this place in August. Let's go talk to Doug; he's our Quisling expert for everything west of the Mississippi."

As he followed Lombard to the stairway, Valentine congratulated himself for passing through the filter.

Lombard took him to an office this time. Doug Metzel had a nameplate on his door, which opened only partway thanks to the volume of binders in his office. They lined shelves, filled corners, and cut off the light from the room's big, arch-topped window. A cat napped in the sun atop one labeled BRIDGE SECURITY. But the man himself wasn't in.

"Two weeks' leave. His mother—cancer, I guess," his assistant reported. She was a slight woman, perhaps in her late thirties, and wore a Guards uniform. Her nameplate read SGT. LAKE.

"Shows you how often I make it to the third floor," Lombard said.

"What is it, Bone?"

"I've got a Wolf just in from . . . ah . . ."

"Lake of the Cherokees," Valentine supplied.

"Memory's great short-term." Lombard shrugged. "Five minutes later, it's mush. Comes from doing sort after sort after sort."

Lombard made further introductions. Metzel's Southern Command associate shook hands with Valentine. "I'm honored," she said gravely. Valentine hadn't heard that expression very often from either a civilian or a Southern Command Guard. He wasn't quite sure how to respond.

"It's a pleasure," he said.

"I'm Doug's liaison, and I'm filling in while he's gone. What do you have, Lieutenant? Sit down and give me the highlights."

Valentine sat across from her and began with his first encounter with the Twisted Cross swastika logo when he'd seen it on a canoe belonging to some Reapers hunting a Cat named Eveready in the Yazoo Delta. The Illinois Quislings who feared an organization with that insignia called the Twisted Cross. The Twisted Cross man he'd met in Chicago who spoke of a comrade who "fed" and suffered a bad leg wound. The man's own feeding, somehow inspired by the others. Then more recently, Smoke's description of Reapers with guns.

She listened attentively and brought down a binder. Inside it were pages of snipped insignia from uniforms. She consulted the legend in the front and then opened it before Valentine. "Like this?"

The card within had a black piece of fabric attached. On the fabric was a white piece of metalwork, a reversed swastika.

"That's their insignia. I saw one just like it in the Zoo in Wisconsin. The owner . . . he fed like a Reaper." Valentine's voice cracked, embarrassing him.

The liaison and Lombard grimaced. "Maybe just a sicko? Monkey see, monkey do?"

"I only saw him for a few minutes. He was definitely Twisted Cross."

She made a note on a pad of paper. "We don't know much about them. We think it's railroad security. They've been spotted in a couple different places." She looked in another folder. "Looks like the current theory is they run what we call 'Q-trains.' Trains filled up with soldiers that look just like normal cargo trains. You Wolves or whatever hit the train, thinking you're going to score some tires and penicillin, and out jumps a regiment of men. But there are no action reports having to do with the Twisted Cross attacking Southern Command, so we can only theorize about methods or numbers."

"It's got to be more than that," Valentine said. "There were border trash in Illinois that were scared—"

She turned the book around and looked at it again. "I don't doubt it. Lots of Quislings use Nazi insignia. Trying to be tough or scary." She waved at the binders. "I can name half a dozen groups that use that crap. There's a gigantic biker gang in California's Silicone Alley that has SS death's-heads and the twin lightning bolts plastered everywhere. Up in Idaho, there are brownshirts with those goofy cavalry pants and boots. The Quislings open a history book, find something that looks intimidating, and copy it. Hell, even our own guys—Colonel Sark's Flying Circus in the Cascades uses the Iron Cross as a decoration for valor. I'm sure there are others in the East; the West is my field."

"Will you read my report?" Valentine asked.

"It's informative," Lombard added.

"Of course."

Valentine passed it to her. "While I'm here."

She smiled at him. "You always been a Wolf, Valentine? Seems like you don't trust our department."

"Always been a Wolf, unless you count my year in the Labor."

"The millstones of Southern Command grind slow but exceedingly fine," she said. She rotated a pencil in her mouth as she read, looked up, and extracted it. "Sorry. Old habit."

Lake finished it, put a star in the upper righthand corner. "That means 'interesting,'" she explained. "I'm kicking it higher in the food chain."

"What would two stars mean?"

"Immediate threat," Lombard said.

"I don't see anything like that here. Southern Command has other fires nearer its foot to piss on. But thank you for bringing it to our attention. I'll see if I can find that Cat's report; I'll send them on together. Thanks for bringing him up, Bone."

Valentine had done all he could. Perhaps he'd given his story enough inertia to keep the Twisted Cross moving through Lake's millstones. He thanked her for her time, and Lombard escorted him to the door. A calico cat rubbed itself against his boot as Lombard fumbled with his key.

"What's with the cats, Bone?"

"Mice. They love to eat paper. We've got a lot of it here."

"Do you think what I came in with is important?"

Lombard took off his glasses and cleaned them with his shirttail. He didn't bother tucking it back in. "Yeah. Anything that can surround and kill a platoon of Wolves is dangerous. But your Cat's story—it's hearsay, kinda. Operating out in the KZ for months on your own, it's enough to queer anyone's judgment. I've read a few Cat reports. . . . Some sound like the products of a disordered mind."

"Will you make sure the paper trail stays in view?"

"I'm just a filter, like I said. I'll do what I can."

They shook on it at the museum door.

The weather turned sunny, almost hot. Valentine sweated on his walk back to the boarding house.

"You missed a courier, Valentine," Donna Walbrook said when he returned to the Den.

She handed him a sealed envelope. "Bad news when it comes special delivery."

He read the sender's imprint. It was from the colonel's

office, Second Wolf Regiment. Maybe they'd cut his survivor's leave short so he could take command of a reborn
Foxtrot Company. Foxtrot deserved to live after the fight
they'd put up at Little Timber. He broke the seal.

Mrs. Walbrook watched him, saw his face, patted him as
he read. "Sorry, son. Someone you know die?"

"I've got orders to report to Montgomery next week."
The rest of the words were hard to say; he had to force
them out of a thick throat. "Under escort. There's a court of
inquiry being formed to investigate my actions. I'm subject
to court-martial."

Four

Southern Missouri, April: Even the rebuilt islands of humanity surrounded by the bloody sea of the Kurian Order no longer resemble the quiet past. The settlements and towns are in the tradition of medieval villages, with stout buildings huddled together like a threatened elephant herd, presenting horns and hide to the world as the mothers and young shelter within. People take care to be indoors by nightfall, and trust only the faces known to them. A few radios and even fewer printing presses distribute the news. A telephone call is a rarity. Trusted elders and community assist the smallholders with everything from education to sanitation.

On the north "wall" of the little town of Montgomery, folded into the foothills of the picturesque Ozarks of southern Missouri, Jackson Elementary School stands stolidly as one of the hamlet's oldest buildings. Architecturally uninspiring but thickly bricked, it protects the north side of one of the newer towns of the Ozark Free Territory. A series of classrooms, with windows bricked up except for a few rifle loopholes with sandbags ready on nearby shelves, look out on a playground cleared of swings and trees. The roof of the school is covered with a slanted shield of fireproofed railroad ties, which, along with a thirty-foot watchtower are the only additions to the school in the last half-century of its existence.

Inside the building, in the old half-underground library on the lowest level of the school, three long scarred wooden tables have been rearranged into a U. At the center of the table, a sober-faced woman in a heavy uniform coat sits

*with three small piles of paper in front of her, sorting
through the handwritten and typed pages with the aid of a
younger officer. To her left, another gray-haired officer
waits in self-important isolation, his fingers laced primly in
front of him, tired-looking eyes gazing across the empty
space in the hollow of the U at another figure.*

*The object of his gaze is David Valentine, wearing the
closest thing to a uniform the Wolf officer posesses: creased
blue trousers, boots, and a pressed white shirt. He has
bound his shining black hair close to his scalp out of respect for the occasion. Valentine has none of Foxtrot's complement in Montgomery, but were any of them to look at
him, they would know he was angry. His chin is down, jaw
set, and he wears the fixed expression of a wounded bull
about to try a final charge at the matador. A brother Guard
officer leans toward him, speaking calmly and softly into
his ear.*

Col. Elizabeth Chalmers, who rumor said had written the
book on Southern Command's military jurisprudence,
cleared her throat. After the days' proceedings, Valentine
learned that the sound was her version of a judge bringing
the court to order with his gavel.

"This investigation is drawing to a close. Captain
Wilton," she said, addressing the older man who sat facing
Valentine, "you've had the unhappy duty of attempting to
substantiate the charges brought by Captain Beck against
Lieutenant Valentine. Namely that on the date in question
Lieutenant Valentine willfully and without cause disobeyed
orders and withdrew from Little Timber Hill, turning Fox-
trot Company's hard-won victory into a defeat."

Two weeks ago, when Valentine first heard that Beck,
from his hospital bed, had ordered charges brought against
him, he had been shocked. During the course of investigation to determine if a court-martial should be convened,
Valentine came to the slow realization that Beck was using
the investigation of his subordinate as a smoke screen to
obscure the debacle at Little Timber Hill. Foxtrot Company,
so laboriously built up and trained over the last year, was

again well below half-strength and rendered useless to Southern Command for the rest of the year at least. Judicial proceedings against a disobedient subordinate would befuddle the issue.

Who knows, Valentine thought, a touch of gallows humor appearing, *Beck might even get another promotion out of it.*

Captain McKendrick of the Advocate General's office, the tiny legal team that handled most of the military and civilian justice in the Free Territory, had been assigned to Valentine as his official "friend and spokesman." His counsel consisted of, "Keep your mouth shut," and "Colonel Chalmers prefers to be addressed as *sir*, not *ma'am.*"

He did not inspire much confidence in Valentine. Especially after he heard that if brought to court-martial and convicted, he could be shot by firing squad.

The colonel's voice broke him out of his dark musings. "Captain Wilton, your summation, please."

The prosecuting officer stood up, a slightly bent figure with the slow voice of grandfatherly wisdom. "Yes, sir. I think we should concentrate on two essential facts. The first being that on March sixteenth, the day in question, Foxtrot Company was victorious on Little Timber Hill. In no small part due to the courage of Lieutenant Valentine here, the Grogs were thrown back each time they tried to take the hill. Their attacks grew less and less frequent as the day progressed, until finally they were reduced to sniping and the occasional mortar shell. Lieutenant Valentine's own report, read out at this hearing, states that plainly. They were beat, and they knew it."

"Colonel, please," Valentine's adviser interrupted. "There's no evidence to support that last statement."

"Don't let rhetoric carry you away, gentlemen," Colonel Chalmers said. "Let's stick to facts, please. The statement about the Grogs being beaten will be removed from the record."

"My apologies, Colonel. But that would have been my judgment, having served in the field most of my career. Within minutes of Captain Beck being wounded, Lieutenant Valentine assembled what subordinates he could and began planning a withdrawal. Despite the fact that Captain Beck, before relinquishing command temporarily owing to wounds, ordered that hill be held."

"Colonel, sir . . . ," McKendrick said, holding up his hand.

"You'll have your chance to speak, Captain McKendrick," Chalmers shot back. "Please continue, Captain."

"Lieutenant Valentine's reasoning for disobeying his Captain's orders is given in his report. This Cat out of Oklahoma somewhere believed that some kind of 'paramilitary Reaper unit,' " Wilton read, referring to a copy of Valentine's report, "would be there by midnight, having already destroyed Lieutenant Caltagirone's short platoon of Foxtrot Company. Unfortunately, this Cat disappeared as quickly and mysteriously as she came."

Captain Wilton let that hang in the air for a moment.

"We know she is no figment of the imagination, but wild stories about Reapers behaving contrary to everything we know about them might seem more frightening on the battlefield with Grogs prowling the woods than here. Lieutenant Valentine acted on this intelligence, for whatever reason"—Valentine gritted his teeth and dug his fingers into his thighs to keep from speaking—"and left a strong defensive position with a long column on night march through territory of unknown enemy strength and disposition. I think we should count ourselves fortunate that any of them returned at all.

"Of course, I must leave it to the colonel to decide whether the withdrawal from Little Timber Hill constitutes a court-martial offense."

Colonel Chalmers turned to Valentine's side of the table. "Captain, are you ready to give your final statement, or shall we break so you can reread the record before your response?"

McKendrick stood. "Colonel, I believe there is no basis for a court-martial; in fact this hearing should never have been called. Charging Lieutenant Valentine with disobeying orders makes no sense, for as soon as he assumed command when Captain Beck was wounded, no one of superior rank was present. The only orders he could disobey were his own.

"Lieutenant Valentine holds a commission in the Wolves, an honor that says we trust him to make decisions about the lives of those under him. As a commander, he made a decision to abandon the position under the same authority that Captain Beck had to order its defense. Wolves in the field usually operate outside the formal command structure; he had no one to refer to, so he used his own judgment. He made the right decision, in my opinion, but even that is a moot point for the purposes of this investigation. Even a handful of Wolves are worth more to us than the entire Grog force assaulting the hill is to the Kurians. A Grog force that was being reinforced as the day progressed as evidenced by the artillery fire that started that afternoon.

"As to the issue that Captain Beck's final orders should have been obeyed, I agree that it is traditional to follow the orders of a wounded commander being carried from the field. But we are talking about a court-martial here, and a sentence that could include this officer facing a firing squad. So we must be very careful about how we apply the law, as opposed to applying tradition.

"As soon as Lieutenant Valentine assumed command, any action he took that did not violate the Stated Rules and Regulations or Emergency Articles was by definition legal. We have had Guard colonels withdraw their forces despite orders to the contrary from immediate command authority, and at each instance, we have deferred to the judgment of the officer in the field. This proceeding should go no further. The fact that it has gone this far speaks more eloquently of the nature of the officer who brought these charges than I—"

"Colonel Chalmers! This—," Wilton protested, but Chalmers cut him off.

"Captain, Lieutenant Valentine is being discussed here, not Captain Beck. I believe this is the second time I've had to warn you about this. I want those remarks removed from the record," she said to the young officer typing on the recorder. "Another statement like that, and I'll put my own censure of you on record, Captain McKendrick. Please continue."

Valentine would infinitely rather have been back at the breastworks on Little Timber Hill than be subject to this cross-court sniping. He shifted in his seat, a bitter taste at the back of his tongue.

"Thank you, Colonel," his defender continued. "I just want to ask the colonel to keep the good of the service in mind. If we hamstring our officers by court-martialing them for decisions made under fire, we are going to get a very timid group of Wolves. Lieutenant Valentine was at Little Timber Hill; we were not. What's more, he was in command. For us to punish him for exercising that command would be the height of folly."

McKendrick sat in his wooden chair and pulled it forward with an authoritative scrape.

Colonel Chalmers looked at the piles of paper before her. "Lieutenant Valentine, do you have anything to say before I make my decision?"

McKendrick elbowed him and gave the tiniest shake of his head.

Valentine stood up to address the colonel. "No, thank you, sir."

"Then would you please step into the waiting room while I discuss this with the captains."

"Sir," Valentine said, and left the room.

A very welcome face met him in the tiny room. Baker, the Wolf who had aided him in the attack on the Rigyard, was stretched out full on the sofa, reading a yellowed book.

"Hi-yo, Lieutenant. What's the story?"

The sight of a familiar face was like a cool breeze in hell. "Baker!" Valentine said, trying not to drop his mask of assumed stoicism too far. "What are you doing here? Foxtrot is supposed to be at mustering camp getting replacements."

"I'm outta Foxtrot Company, sir. I applied for a post in the Logistics Commandos."

"You, a scrounger?"

"Yeah. 'The backbone of the army is the noncommissioned man' and all that, but we need beef and shoes that aren't made out of old radial tires."

"Good luck, wherever you end up. The Wolves'll miss you."

Baker shrugged, his big shoulders making the gesture evocative of a turtle withdrawing to its shell. "I liked serving under you, but by God if it weren't for you and that Cat, we'd all be dead. And what happens to you over it? A court-martial."

"Not a court-martial. An 'inquiry.' There's a difference." The words came easy. Valentine had told himself the exact same thing hundreds of times a day for the past week:

An inquiry can't shoot me.

Baker began rummaging in his rucksack. "Now, where is that—? Here Mr. Valentine, I brought you some liquid morale." He said, extracting a sizable corked jug. "This ain't no busthead, either. It's genuine Kentucky whiskey. Berber or some such. Every man in the platoon chipped in and bought it off a cart trader. Bill Miranda from second squad grew up in Kentucky. He tasted it and vouched for the authenticity. Tasted a couple times, as a matter of fact, but we'd bought a big jug, and no one thought you'd miss a sip or two. Taste?"

"I'd love to. But I've got to go back into the courtroom, or whatever they call it. Not the best time to show up drunk."

They chatted over the small doings of the platoon and the company, from the smooth-faced kids who were supposed to be turned into Wolves to the lack of adequate blankets to replace those lost.

"This last batch," Baker was complaining, "turned to mush when they got wet. How the hell do you make a blanket outta sawdust, that's what I want to know. They'd unravel, if only there was material in 'em to unravel in the first place. Does all the wool go to the Guards' fancy dress uniforms?"

The young officer who transcribed the inquiry poked his head into the room. "They're ready for you, Lieutenant."

"Good luck, sir," Baker said, suddenly serious.

As he walked back to the table-filled room, the stenographer walking next to him at a wedding-march pace, Valentine fought the urge to ask what the verdict was. He would find out soon enough, and the last thing he needed was this kid looking down his nose at a weak sister of a Wolf.

He stood in the center of the U of tables, the faces of the three officers conducting the inquiry impassive.

"Lieutenant Valentine," Colonel Chalmers began, "by all accounts, you are a fine young officer. I have tried, behind the scenes so to speak, to see if we can just drop this with some kind of simple reprimand. The basic facts of this case are in your own report, which you have sworn to and stood by, that Captain Beck ordered you to defend Little Timber as the new commander of Foxtrot Company. In that you heard and acknowledged that order, I have decided it would take a court-martial to decide whether you disobeyed said order."

Valentine's heart fell at her words. Innocent or guilty, the very fact of being court-martialed would ruin his career. No commander would want a junior under him whose ability to obey orders was the subject of a military trial.

"However, I do have certain powers. I am going to give you a choice. Face the court-martial, and take your chances. If it means anything to you, your friend at this inquiry, Captain McKendrick, has offered to defend you before the court. And, interestingly enough, Captain Wilton also very passionately offered his services in your defense. You can come away from this assured that the officer investigating on behalf of the complaint against you is sympathetic to your situation.

"I am also giving you the option to resign your commission rather than face court-martial. You can serve as a Wolf, or go into one of the other branches of service discreetly, or return home to Minnesota if you wish. I advise you to consider this option. In my experience courts-martial are tricky affairs—no one on either side ever comes out smelling like a rose, so to speak. What say you, Lieutenant?"

Valentine felt the room reel around him for a moment,

and then he straightened. "May I think about it for a day, sir?"

"Of course. I am holding a hearing in the matter of a theft of civilian property tomorrow, and I believe there are two more cases before I move on in the circuit, so you can answer me at your leisure. Good luck to you, Lieutenant Valentine."

She rose, as did Wilton and McKendrick. She left the room by a back door, walking a little oddly with her artificial left leg, and carried away the formality of the proceeding with her.

"Damn shame, Valentine," Wilton said as soon as the door closed behind her. "The colonel of the Second Regiment should have shut Beck up, but good. Does he have friends in Mountain Home?"

"I don't know, sir."

McKendrick approached him, and Valentine offered his hand. "Seriously, do you have enemies in high places, Valentine? I can't see why this is being pushed through. She should have rolled that complaint up and tossed it in the fireplace. Bullshit like that usually walks with the colonel."

"Captain, you want a drink? There's enough bourbon for you, as well, Captain Wilton," Valentine offered.

"No thanks, son," the old man said. "Gives me a sour belly."

"Good," said McKendrick. "More for us, then."

The informal party, which Valentine dubbed "the Wake in Honor of David Valentine's Lieutenancy, May It Rest in Peace" broke up about 2 a.m. Baker had left around midnight in the company of a very companionable "widow lady" who joined them in the shanty bar just outside Montgomery's walls. But not before he turned over his pocket watch and most of his cash to Valentine. McKendrick proved to be a loud, roaring drunk who recited obscene jokes at each round but exhausted himself at the stroke of one. "The stronger the wind, the quicker it blows itself out," Valentine quoted to the other drinkers, not sure if he was quoting

himself or someone else. Valentine shared the rest of his jug
with the barflies and ne'er-do-wells of Montgomery, assur-
ing himself of their undying friendship while the liquor
lasted.

Nobody seemed to own this oversize shack; the pack
trader who had been selling drinks went to bed at midnight.
Valentine decided that returning to his room at the old
school was too much effort. The dirty linoleum floor
seemed much more cool and soothing than any bed. Clean
sheets were not worth the walk, anyway. He was a Wolf, by
damn, at least for now, and used to sleeping rough.

"This how you always take bad news, Lieutenant?" a sarcastic and vaguely familiar female voice sounded from the
whirling world above.

"I'm the king of bad news, lady. Ask my parents. Ask
Gabby Cho. I'm King Midas and the Angel of Death all
rolled into one. Whatever I touch . . . dies."

"Ahh, the jovial kind of drunk. My favorite. C'mon,
Ghost, let's get you up." She lifted him to his feet. Her
compact body had a good deal of wiry strength, Valentine
noticed through the drunken haze. She also smelled good, a
faint, soapy aroma.

"Errhuh?" Valentine said, not sure that he wanted to be
pulled to his feet by the Cat he knew as Smoke—even if his
nostrils were attracted to her. "They used to call me that in
the Wolves. Which I'm not anymore, and neither are you."

"You're coming with me, Lieutenant Valentine. Can't
have you doing yourself any harm, not on my watch, anyway."

Valentine cleared some of the bourbon fog with an effort
and a few lungfuls of the cold spring air of the Ozark
Plateau. It really was Smoke, the Cat from Little Timber.
"Okay, okay, I'm fine. Hey, how did you get here? I could
have used a deposition from you today, you know. My ass-
hole captain intends to salvage his next promotion by
putting me in front of a firing squad."

She escorted him to a caved-in house on a hill overlooking Montgomery. Tree branches through a window held up
the one remaining wall.

"It's got a good basement," she said, leading him to a still-standing door within the ruins. She shoved open the door and helped him down the steps. The embers of a dying fire glowed within an old backyard grill in the center of the room, the wisps of smoke drawn up through the remnants of furnace vents.

"All the comforts of home. There's even a washtub. Until I got here three days ago, I hadn't had a hot soak for a month. I had to kill some rats to claim the room. I'm worried that they're reorganizing for a counterattack, though." She reawakened the fire and stared into its orange-yellow dance for a long moment.

Valentine sagged onto a pile of musty discarded clothes piled in a corner. "Three days ago?"

"Yes, I've been listening in to the trial."

"Funny, I didn't notice you in the room. Were you disguised as the colonel?"

"Valentine, you're talking to a Cat. The militia cretin in the watchtower wouldn't see a hundred gargoyles flying in a V-formation on a sunny day, never mind me sneaking into the building before dawn. I found a spot in the basement where the echoes were favorable and listened. We Cats have about as good hearing as you Wolves, you know. You didn't say much in your defense."

"I didn't want to spoil anyone's fun. They were having a fine time dissecting me."

"The words you use. You're a regular dictionary, Valentine. I can read pretty good, and I've been doing a lot of it lately. I've been checking some of your reports they have copied at the Miskatonic. I'm starting to think we were fated to meet."

She avoided his eyes, laying out blankets and matting.

"How's that?"

"I'll explain when I'm rested and you're sober. Too tired now."

"Give me a taste."

"No. Shape you're in, you wouldn't remember anyway." She crawled into her bedroll. "*Brrr*—I've been waiting for you to come out of that dive for hours. What are you going to tell them tomorrow? I notice you didn't ask anyone's advice."

Valentine rubbed his 2 a.m. shadow thoughtfully, making the bristles rasp. "They got me pegged as a retreater. I was thinking of fighting it out. Beck would have to take the stand, and there are a few questions I'd like to ask him."

She kicked her shoes out from under the blankets. "Do yourself a favor, Valentine. Just resign. Go quietly. There's more important things at stake than your ego."

"Just a second, lady. Where do you get off talking to me like that? I've got four years in the Wolves. I don't see what my choice has to do with anything you're interested in."

"Valentine, go to sleep. We'll talk tomorrow. Now be quiet before I start asking myself those exact questions."

"Speaking of questions, you've never even told me your name."

"Duvalier. Alessa Duvalier."

"Appreciate the assist, Duvalier. Never thanked you properly." He reached out and gave her shoulder a gentle squeeze.

"Don't press your luck."

Gold-plated bitch.

"I meant for back in Oklahoma. You saved—"

"Cats need their sleep. Good night, Valentine."

With a diamond setting.

Frustrated, Valentine wrapped himself in a blanket and let the booze win. He turned his back to the fire, feeling as though he were in the bottom of a canoe in white water. The pair vented their mutual hostility in deep, regular breaths. As Valentine drifted away to calmer waters, he noticed that they were also breathing in unison.

Valentine hadn't smelled real coffee more than twice in the last year. So the aroma of Duvalier brewing it in an aluminum percolator over the rebuilt fire startled him into wakefulness.

She saw his head rise. "I figured you could use some coffee. I'm glad you're not the puking kind of drunk."

Valentine's tongue felt and tasted like the defensive end

of a skunk. "The morning is still young. That can't be coffee."

"You'd be surprised at what I get out of the KZ. Here,
have a cup." She poured a generous amount into a
scratched plastic bowl. Valentine wondered if he was supposed to lap it up, but eventually got some down without
burning his lips.

The sharp, stimulating taste made the morning appear
rosier.

"Ever read detective novels?" he asked.

She shook her head. "Where I usually circulate, I'm
lucky to have old dishwasher warranties to read."

"They're stories about really smart people who solve
murders. They always spot a tiny little clue everyone else
missed, and explain themselves to the rest of us poor idiots
at the end. Once you start reading them, they're kind of ad-
dictive."

"And?"

"My point is I feel like one of the idiots, waiting for the
puzzle to be put together under my nose."

She smeared something in a skillet and reached for her
jacket. "Your file said you were well read. Wish I could
help. My puzzle is missing a few pieces, too. Maybe together we can fill in the blanks."

He met her gaze, but she didn't elaborate.

Depressed, half-sick, headachy, Valentine wished he
could just spend half the day in bed, as he had during the
long Minnesota winters when there wasn't much else to do
but read away the short days and long nights.

She cracked a pair of eggs in a pan, and they immediately began sputtering in the hot grease. Her elfin features
were the picture of concentration as she poked at the eggs
with a handleless spatula. "Don't get used to this. I don't
know if it's because I feel sorry for you, or because I know
what it's like to have a hangover. The bread might have a
little mold on it, but the eggs were freshly swiped this
morning from one of the good citizens of Montgomery. The
only trade good I have right now is the coffee, and I don't
want to part with it. Besides, I'm keeping my presence here

quiet. I've got only one plate, so I'm just going to eat out of the pan if you don't mind."

She passed him the cooked over-easy egg and a hunk of green-dusted bread. Valentine mopped up the egg with the bread and ate the sticky combination. "This is great, thanks."

"You like it that way, too, huh?" she said with a smile, eating her own egg-yolk-smeared bread. "Okay, how do you want the story, from now working backwards, or from the beginning?"

"I don't think I can think backwards, so you'd better do it from the beginning."

"Easy enough. I came across some interesting stuff reading your reports. Four years ago you had a run-in right after you were invoked as a Wolf. You stumbled onto some Reapers hunting a Cat in the Yazoo Delta."

"Yes. That's the first time I saw that Twisted Cross insignia."

"At first we just brushed it off as another faction of the Kur. Sometimes they use little symbols to note their houses, or clans, or whatever you want to call the groups of Kurians." She consulted a thin notebook in a leather case, like a waiter's order pad he'd once seen in Chicago. "The summer you ended up hiding in Wisconsin, one of the Freeholds we communicate with went silent. It was a small one, really just a valley or two in the Smoky Mountains. Scouts from the New England Freehold found buried Quislings. And some mass graves. But back to the Quislings, they had Twisted Cross insignia on their uniforms. A swastika is another name for it, I'm told. So the Cats kept their eyes open, and now and then these Quislings were seen in other parts of the country. So the insignia did not mean just one geographical group of Kurians.

"The people at Miskatonic have an idea that the Kurians have taken some of their Quislings and created Reaper-human half-breeds, kind of a specialized striking force." She looked at him expectantly.

"Is it under someone called the General?"

She looked puzzled. "Where did you hear that?"

"From an old railroad man we brought out of Oklahoma. A little addled. Not much of what he said made sense, so I abbreviated it in my report. He stumbled across some Quislings under this Twisted Cross banner in a yard. They took him before this General, who then decided to kill him as a precaution."

Duvalier digested this information along with her moldy bread and egg. "This General is someone we've heard of now and then. I think he's a very highly placed Quisling. So they have a special train?"

"Yes, he said it was a sizable one."

"That doesn't fit with the rest. As far as Miskatonic knows, they go in small groups, without heavy weapons or a big escort. Do they just want to look like another supply train?"

"Guessing is interesting, but facts are better." Valentine returned to a subject much on his mind lately. "What happened at Little Timber Hill after you went back?"

"I was getting to that, because I think it's important. I built up the campfires and shot down at the Grogs from various points in the line. They didn't come at night. Some Harpies flew overhead, but they didn't risk dropping down for a close look, so they never saw that the breastworks in the trees weren't manned.

"Well before dawn, could have been three a.m., eight Reapers came up the hill. I just hid and watched. They were loaded for bear, assault rifles and everything. Mean-looking Kalashnikovs with banana clips.

"But here's the kicker. They make the top of the hill, and they get . . . confused. I've never seen a Reaper that looked like it didn't know what to do. So they group together and talk. Who ever heard of Hoods talking to each other? Usually when you see a group of them, they're all puppeted by the same Kurian, so they don't have to talk. Same hissy voices. If these were some kind of Reaper-human cross, they sure left the human parts in their other pants. They looked and sounded like Reapers to me. Just didn't act that way."

Valentine put down his plate. "How did you get away?"

"They picked up your trail, sent out the Grogs. I just slipped away back to the south in the dark. I wanted to have another talk with the Miskatonic people about this, so I caught a barge from Fort Smith to Pine Bluff. That's where I heard about all this. I was told to come up here and talk to you."

"Told? Told by whom?"

"Don't worry about that right now. An old friend of mine, who knows some old friends of yours. I was hoping you'd do some work with me in the KZ for a while."

Valentine narrowed his eyes, wondering what she was getting at. "I thought you Cats worked alone."

"We do. Unless we're training another Cat."

Dear Sir,
    It has been my privilege to serve in the Wolves for four years. I wish to spare myself, my company, and my regiment the pain and disruption of a court-martial that would be the inevitable result of my fighting the charges brought against me. Please accept my resignation from duty in the Second Regiment of Wolves, Southern Command, immediately.

            I have the honor to remain, etc.,
            David Stuart Valentine

Duvalier looked up from the handwritten, slightly smeared note. "Brief and to the point, Valentine. I expected more flowery 'the clock has struck the hour of fate' type stuff out of you. I like you better already."

"After I turn this in, where are we headed—north or west?"

She shook her head as she shouldered her pack. "Back into the Free Territory, actually. You have to meet with someone. We also need to outfit you with a little better blade than that sawed-off machete before our little welcoming ceremony with the Lifeweavers."

Valentine remembered his. The cave, Amu the

Lifeweaver and his retinue of hairy, sleeping wolves. Amu had called it an "operation," though he'd never opened Valentine with anything but a tasteless drink and his mind.

"Another invocation? Like when I became a Wolf? I felt like I was wearing a different body the first few days. Nothing worked right. I couldn't pick up a mug without knocking it across the table."

"Same here. Maybe it'll be different for you. I've only been a Cat. But don't let it worry you."

Valentine buttoned up his buckskin tunic, thoughtfully running his finger up the familiar fringe. The Wolves of Southern Command decorated their jackets with leather strips of varying length on the arms or chest or some combination of both, a token to friends and enemies alike of their clan. Supposedly they helped shed rainwater, but Valentine had been soaked to the marrow enough times to smile at that bit of frontier myth.

They took the short hike into town in silence and parted at the main gate. His first duty was to hunt up Baker and return the ex-Wolf's money and pocket watch. Then Valentine made for the old school to see Colonel Chalmers. Duvalier went into the Montgomery market with Valentine's remaining money to acquire some provisions for the trip.

Valentine found Colonel Chalmers in the court's temporary offices, going over the organization of her schedule with her ubiquitous shadow, the young clerk. Valentine smelled sawdust in the air and heard distant sounds of construction. More rooms in the school were being renovated.

"Ahh, Lieutenant," she said. "I take it you slept on your decision. I haven't seen your counselor yet this morning; they tell me he's a little indisposed. Kenneth, would you excuse us, please?"

The clerk exited, shutting the door behind him.

Valentine tried to stand as straight as possible. The letter in his hand trembled a little, and he fought to still it. "I've thought over your offer, sir, and I gratefully accept. Would you forward this with the report of the inquiry to Headquarters, Second Regiment?" He handed her his spidery-scripted letter.

She glanced down at it, and back up into his eyes. "I'll handle it for you, Valentine. The colonel will be relieved. Everyone ends up looking bad in a court-martial. Although I'll bet my next quarter's pay that he's sorry to lose you as an officer."

"Thank you, sir. In any case, I'm lucky not to be in the ground next to Sergeant Stafford."

Valentine got the feeling he was being judged for the second time in twenty-four hours.

"He died for something, David. Most people just end up dead."

"I'll let you get back to your work, sir."

She held up a hand. "Valentine, I did what I could for you. Off the record, I sympathize with your situation. I can't say very much about the inner workings of Southern Command, but we make more mistakes than we admit. This may not turn out to be a mistake after all.

"You know, I met your father once. At a ball. I was a lieutenant in the Guards, perhaps your age. The dance was in this fine old convention center right across from the hospital. Electric chandeliers, if you can believe it. Good food on gold-rimmed plates, an orchestra. But I didn't feel like dancing. I had just lost my leg from the knee down at Arkansas River; a sniper got me when I was spotting for artillery. Your father had been in the hospital, too. A piece of shrapnel had taken a chunk out of his arm. I just sat in a corner by myself, feeling like it was all over. I didn't do my physical therapy. I didn't want to get used to walking with a prosthetic. Just wanted to sit. I suppose I would have been in tears if I were the crying type.

"Your father came over and made me dance with him. I would have said no to a man around my age, but your dad was maybe fifteen years older—it made him seem like an uncle or something. We had to have been the worst-looking couple on the floor: I was sort of hopping on my good leg, and his arm was in a sling. We lurched our way through a waltz, and I could tell everyone pitied us—or rather me, I suppose. So he goes to the band and makes them play a polka. Now a polka you can sort of hop to, and before I knew it, we were flying around the floor. I had a tight hold on his shoulders and he just sort of bounced around, taking me with him. The band started playing faster, and he kept spinning us in a wider and wider circle. People got out of our way rather than get run over. When the song stopped, we were in this big circle of people, and they applauded.

"I got a look at myself in a mirror. I had this huge smile on my face. I was laughing and crying and gasping for air all at the same time, and very, very happy. Your father looked down at me and said, 'Sometimes all it takes is a change of tune.' "

She stared at the wall, plastered with poorly printed handbills, but Valentine could tell the wall wasn't there, just a big room filled with a band, food, and dancers in some broken-down corner of Southern Command. Colonel Chalmers returned to the present after a moment's silence.

"I read you were orphaned. How old were you?"

"Eleven."

"I didn't really know him, apart from that dance and talking to him a bit afterwards. He was kind of remote, in the nicest possible way, and I think the wound hit him hard. He left the Free Territory shortly afterwards, moved up to Minnesota and married your mother, right?"

Valentine could deal with his own memories of his family. Other people's left him feeling wistful, wishing he could talk to his parents again.

"I never even knew he was a soldier until I was older. The man who raised me afterwards didn't exactly keep it secret, but I think he wanted me to make up my own mind about things."

"You're probably wondering where I was going with that story. I ended up in the Advocate General and never found anything else I could do half as well. I just wanted to tell you that perhaps you just need a change of tune, so to speak.

"Good luck to you, Valentine."

"Thank you, sir." He saluted and left, closing the door behind him.

"They don't waste any time," she said quietly after he shut the door. But not quietly enough. Valentine still had his Wolf's ears, if not his commission; she might as well have shouted it.

They don't waste any time. He passed the loitering clerk with a nod, already analyzing her words. Did somebody want him out of the Wolves for a reason? Duvalier seemed to be a veteran Cat for one so young, but could she have the pull to get him dismissed from the Wolves just to help her run down the Twisted Cross? He doubted it.

He walked out of the school. The hardworking residents of the town were in the fields surrounding the village. A flock of sheep passed through the main gate under the stewardship of a boy and two dogs. Valentine looked at their heavy coats—they were due for their spring shearing.

Duvalier rounded a corner, pack already over her shoulder and Valentine's hammock roll in her left hand. She waved a knotty walking stick with a leather wrist strap in her right hand.

"That was fast, Valentine."

"It takes a long time to build a career. You can wreck it in a couple minutes."

She handed him his pack. "Crackers and cheese to get us where we're going. I lost my taste for dried beef a long time ago, so I got us each a three-pound wurst. Some new cabbage, turnips, and a few beets. I make a pretty good pot of borscht. No rice and not much flour to be had, at least not for strangers."

"Where are we going?"

They passed out of the gate, waving to a half-awake deputy at the gate. "First stop is not far at all, just over the border in Arkansas. Why couldn't you have been one of those officers with half a dozen horses, Valentine?"

"Try covering thirty or forty miles, mostly at a run, with full equipment sometime. I'll never mind just having to walk somewhere again."

Duvalier looked up into the wooded hills of the Ozarks.

"I can never get over it when I'm in the Free Territory. No checkpoints, no ID cards, no workbooks. You were in the KZ once, right?"

"Yes, in Wisconsin and Chicago."

"Never been to either; my ground is between here and the Rockies. I was in the desert in the Southwest once, too. Lost all illusions about how tough I was when I ran with the Desert Rangers there for a winter. Sometimes out there you get . . ." She let out an exasperated breath.

"You feel impotent against it all. You'll die, your friends will die. . . . ," Valentine said.

"Yeah. But then you get back here, where the kids don't have that quiet, haunted look. Then you pick up and do it again, because . . . you know."

"I know."

As the day progressed, they moved deeper into the old growth of the Mark Twain Forest. At the crossroads, there were new maps, burned into planks and painted and anchored, sometimes covered with glass, showing which road led where. People clung to the old names, as if as long as the names existed, the past existed, and a future that might be like the past.

Valentine's nose picked up life everywhere in the rich, rain-soaked spring soil. The trees and undergrowth flourished in green tangles all around the walkers. An empty tanker truck returning to one of the Free Territory's minuscule "backyard" refineries in eastern Oklahoma gave them a ride up old Route 37, the driver and his shotgun letting them ride atop the tanker, giving them a bumpy entrance into Arkansas. By evening, they were south of Beaver Lake in Spring Valley, when the truck turned southwest for refilling.

A pig farmer by the name of Sutton hailed them off the road and offered them lodging that night. He was an older man, in need of a couple of strong young backs for a few hours, and glad for the company. The men who helped him run his place stayed with their families in the evenings, and visitors to the rather pungent farm were limited to days with a stiff easterly breeze. Valentine was happy to cut fire-wood in exchange for the hot meal and lodging.

Reducing tree trunks to cordwood and kindling was Valentine's way of sitting cross-legged and chanting. He often lost himself in the steady, muscle-draining effort. He had chopped wood as a kid in Minnesota, bartering his labor to the neighbors for a few eggs, a sack of corn flour, or a ham. Even as an officer, he cut wood on mornings when he could get away from his other duties, causing his sergeants to shake their heads and find other forms of uninteresting labor for the men who fell into their bad books. The satisfying, rhythmic *chop* of ax blade or wedge into wood cleared his mental buffers, a psychological reset that left his torso rubbery with fatigue.

He finished up with the wood by moonlight and returned to the house in time to say good night to the obliging Sutton. "You and the missus got the whole upstairs to yourselves. I don't like trips up and down them stairs any more than I have to; I got a nice bed now in the office. I showed her where the linens and such are—sorry if they're a little mothbally."

Valentine padded up the creaking staircase in the faintly piggy-smelling house. A steaming bucket of water, soap, a basin, and a towel waited for him.

"Whoever last used this had a lot more hair than me," Duvalier commented, looking at one of the long hairs caught in the brush she held. She had a towel on and was playing with the three-plated mirror in the small bedroom vanity.

"He's a widower. He told me when we stacked wood. Her name was Ellen. They had two kids, Paul and Wynonna, and she died giving birth to Wynonna. The kids are both dead in the Cause's service."

Duvalier set the extracted hair carefully on the marble tabletop.

Valentine stepped into the old bathroom across the hall. The fixtures were operational, though they gave only cold water, and the electrical lighting in the house was a pleasant surprise. Sutton must be fairly well-to-do, or the area between Fayetteville and Beaver Dam better maintained than most parts of the Free Territory.

He washed up with the pail of hot water and returned to the bedroom. "So you're 'the missus,' huh?"

She peeped out at him from under a thick quilt. "My conversation with him wasn't quite as serious as yours. He assumed, and I didn't correct him. I'm not looking for sex, but you are a warm body. It's a cold night."

"Your hot water bottle is turning in. Ready for light's out?"

"Mmmmph," she agreed, turning facedown in a feather pillow.

Her rich, female smell both lulled and excited him as he lifted the covers to climb into bed next to her. His nostrils explored her even if his hands remained tucked under his pillow. He toyed with the scents in the room, locating them with his eyes shut: the wet hair of the woman next to him, the out-of-mothballs sheets, the dusty quilt, the warm, soapy water remaining in the bucket and sink, wood smoke, and the faint, omnipresent smell of pigs. He counted scents like some people count sheep, and was asleep when his companion Cat pressed her back against his.

The next morning, after sharing two steaming cups of coffee from Duvalier's shrinking supply of beans, they packed up again. Sutton drank the coffee with lip-smacking pleasure and presented them with a slab of cured bacon wrapped in brown paper.

After exchanges of gratitude and good-byes, the pair turned east. The ground grew more rugged, and the roads began to break down into trails. Worn-down mountains loomed ahead. They walked in companionable silence, pausing at little streams for water and brief respites.

"I've never been to this part of the Territory," Valentine said. "Where are we headed?"

"Cobb Smithy. One of the best weapons men and all-around blacksmiths in the Free Territory."

"I think I've heard of him. I recall some of Major Gowen's Bears talking about him."

"Actually, it's a bunch of them. There's old Cobb, his son, his daughter, a couple of journeymen, and apprentices. It's quite an operation. They probably made that chopper of yours."

"My parang? How can you tell?"

"What, you never looked at the blade closely?"

"To oil it, sharpen it . . . Wait, the *CFS* on the blade, in little letters right by the hilt?"

"Cobb Family Smithy, Valentine."

He drew his old, notched parang with its hardwood handle. He held the blade so the light fell on it, and looked again at the faint letters scrolled in tiny, precise calligraphy up against the hilt. "Funny, I never thought to ask what it meant."

They reached the smithy and outbuildings early in the afternoon. Faint hammering sounds from two different workshops sounded in the little hummock of land between Arkansas ridges. A stream ran down from the high hills to a half-pond, half-swamp on the other side of the road.

A pair of sizable but indefinable dogs trotted up to greet them, warily hopeful. Valentine took a step forward to greet the canines, and the pair began barking to raise the dead. A boy on the short side of ten ran down the drive to meet them.

"Who are you, and what's your business?" he squeaked. Then to the dogs, with more authority, "Still, you two! We know company's come."

"Smoke, Cat of Southern Command. Her Aspirant, Ghost. He needs a weapon or two."

"You're welcome here, then," the boy said, swelling with self-importance. "Follow me."

The house was a single-story conglomeration, a long rambling rancho growing like a rattlesnake's tail: an extra part every year. Whatever their skill at steelwork, the Cobb family knew little about architecture esthetics.

A middle-aged woman came out onto the nearly endless porch and squinted down at the visitors. She broke into a grin and clapped floured hands together. "Why it's Smoke, our little Kansas State Flower. How's that straightsword working out for you?"

"Needs a professional edge put back on. The hilt could use some rewrapping, too—the cording is a little frayed."

Valentine looked at the Cat, puzzled. "Did you bring it? It must be awfully small."

Duvalier exchanged glances with the woman and shrugged. "He's new, Bethany." She twisted her walking stick at the knob on the head and exposed a black handle. In a flash, she had the sword out from concealment within the stick. Valentine guessed the blade to be about twenty-two inches, single edged, with an angular point. The metal was dark, burnished so as not to reflect light.

Bethany examined the hilt with an expert eye. "I'll get a man on this. Can't have our precious Smoke losing her grip in a fight. What does your Aspirant need?"

"Apart from about two years' training in the next two months—which is my problem, not yours—he's going to need a set of claws. I'd like to see about getting him a decent blade, too. He's a Wolf, but by the look of it, he's been digging holes with that cotton chopper of his. He needs something to bite a Reaper."

"You want the old man to work with him, or my brother?"

"The Ghost here has had a hard enough week. Nathan will do."

"I'll be happy to oblige," Bethany said, moving to the screen door and holding it open. "C'mon in, and I'll make some tea."

"I've got better than that. Coffee," Duvalier said, handing over the rest of the bag.

Bethany Cobb smelled the beans. "I declare! You are just too good, rosebud."

They went into the kitchen, a vast cavern with two stoves and a large brick oven. After ringing a bell on the end of a carved wooden handle, Bethany reached high on a shelf for a coffeepot and grinder, and began to work on the beans while the water heated. "My brother will be with you shortly."

Nathan Cobb was a lumbering man with bulging arms and a substantial potbelly. He clapped Duvalier on the back, a blow she absorbed with some grace, and came close to crushing Valentine's hand in a vigorous shake. "Always, always happy to see a new Cat out there. Raise some Hell for me, would you, ummm, Ghost?" he said before getting down to business.

"I take it you need a set of claws?" he asked Duvalier.

"Yes, please, and time is a little bit of an issue."

"He seems to have average-size hands. You want talons like yours, or blades?"

"Talons, and make the fingers stiff—concealment won't be an issue on this job. I want him to be able to climb with them as well as fight."

"That'll save some time. Let's measure you up, son." Cobb extracted a stained tape measure from his work apron, and wrapped it around Valentine's palm. He then measured each finger from the little well in the center of his hand to its extremity, making notes in neat block numbers in a little pocket pad. "How about a weapon or two, Smoke? Are you going to train him?"

"I'll have to."

"Then you'll want a sword for him, I suppose. We may have something already made up."

An old man appeared at the kitchen at a door from one of the adjoining rooms in the endless house. "Is that coffee I smell?"

Bethany began pouring. "Sure is, Dad. We have visitors, and they brought it. Smoke Duvalier and her apprentice, Ghost."

The elderly man paused in his appreciation of the java. "Ghost? What's your real name, son? Don't worry, my memory's going so fast, I wouldn't be able to tell anyone if I wanted to."

Valentine looked at Duvalier.

"He's named Valentine," she said.

"Then your father was—"

Valentine rose. "His name was Lee Valentine, Mr. Cobb."

The senior Cobb's eyes narrowed suspiciously. "You sure don't look like him, except a little round the eyes. You sure you're mother wasn't just making a brag?"

Valentine ignored the insult. "My mother was Sioux, sir. North side of the Great Lakes."

"You're a fair size, but not as tall as your father. Nat, he needs a weapon?"

"Something for a Cat, not a Bear," the son answered.

"C'mon, boy, follow me," he said, blowing on the scalding mug of coffee and shuffling off down the hall. He opened a door to a stairwell and slowly started down into the basement.

Valentine looked around at the others, who simply smiled. He followed the senior Cobb.

The basement had a collection of everything from swords to antique farm implements. Daggers hung next to sickles on one wall, and opposite, pitchforks shared a rack with long pikes. A cavalry saber occupied a place of honor over a fireplace. Valentine stepped up to it and looked at the rather ordinary hilt and scabbard.

"That belonged to Nathan Bedford Forrest, son, but I don't expect you know who that is."

"Confederate cavalry commander in the Civil War. He wasn't a West Pointer, but he sure outwitted a bunch of them."

"Glad to be wrong once in a while. Bound to happen every year or two. See anything you like?"

Valentine picked up a heavy blade with a basket hilt sharing a rack with a similarly sized claymore. He swung it experimentally.

"Valentine, what are you thinking?" Duvalier chided him from the bottom stair. He hadn't heard her on the stairs. "You don't want to be lugging that halfway across the country. Mr. Cobb, let's look at something he can draw fast and swing quick."

"Hummph," Cobb grunted, not exactly disagreeing, but not wanting look like he was taking her advice, either. "I have a beautiful blade and scabbard. Last carried by a Guard with a different taste in sword. They usually like sabers and épées. Let's see what you think of this."

He opened a footlocker and began sorting through long, slightly curved shapes wrapped in blankets and twine.

"Which sumbitch is it? Here we go," he said, extracting a shape. He handed it to Valentine.

Intrigued, the would-be Cat unwrapped it. As soon as he saw the hilt, he recognized it as a samurai sword of some kind. His brain searched for the term.

"Called a katana, Valentine. That's a helluva piece of fighting steel. Looks old, but it's actually from this century. We'll have to fit you with a new hilt, but that won't take too long. Only twenty-four inches of blade."

Valentine drew it experimentally. The blade carried a few cryptic ideograms etched in the metal.

"Can you cap the scabbard like mine?" Duvalier asked.

"Easy enough, missy. You should use it two-handed, boy, lets you put your whole back into it. But you can use it one-handed, from horseback, say, or if you want to parry with those damn fighting claws."

"I like it," Valentine said. "What's the cost?" he asked, wondering where he would come up with the money.

"That's Southern Command's problem, not yours, Valentine. You and little missy here will just have to sign a chit for what you take."

Duvalier wrinkled her freckled nose. Valentine could tell that the *missy* was getting under her skin.

The claws, he learned the next day, were a pair of metal hands held to his palms by thick leather straps. They arced out like a second skeletal system from there, ending in sharp talons that capped his fingers.

"You can climb a tree with 'em, and they do gruesome in a fight if you use 'em right," Duvalier explained. She put on her slightly smaller pair and looked around for a tree. "It takes a little practice," she said, stepping to the bole of a mature oak. She jumped up the side of it, reaching around either side until her palms were opposite, and began climbing. She was among the branches in no time.

Valentine imitated her and learned to his chagrin that if he failed to grip the trunk with his legs, a single set of the claws weren't enough to hold him up. He arrested the slide before falling off, then managed to hump his way up the trunk neither as quickly nor as gracefully as Duvalier. But he succeeded.

He also learned about putting a new hilt on his sword. A craftsman named Eggert showed him how to encase the naked tang in a wooden handle shaped more or less to fit Valentine's hands. Then he wrapped it in wet pigskin, applying a series of small bumps to the blade side in fastening the leather. "They used to use skin from stingrays and sharks, but those aren't too common hereabouts," Eggert explained. Finally a fine cording was wound round and round the hilt. Duvalier insisted on tying the last knot herself.

"For luck," she said, planting a tiny kiss on the newly reconstructed hilt. They worked on the scabbard together, fitting an old rifle sling to the mahogany wooden tube. Valentine decided he felt most comfortable carrying it over his shoulder.

"We can add a spring to the bottom—it'll help you draw faster," she observed, after watching him pull the sword a few times.

They moved on as soon as Valentine's sword was finished. They shouldered their packs one more time, newly laden with food supplied by the generous and Southern Command–compensated Cobbs.

"Now for home," Duvalier said, turning on the road east once more.

Five

The Ozark Mountains, May: The Free Territory had its genesis here, among the river-cut limestone, caves, sinks, and thick forests of America's oldest mountains. Like the armadillos and scorpions found in these timbered, rocky hills, the residents here are scattered, alert, tough, and dangerous. They know the stands of oak and hickory, trout-filled lakes and streams, and each other. But one area they avoid out of respect for its inhabitants, more wary and hermitlike than the most remote woodsmen. That is the ground around the headwaters of the Buffalo River, home to a cluster of Lifeweavers.

The locals call them wizards. Some fear them as a branch of the Kurians and their otherworldly evils. When the residents come upon a Lifeweaver, perhaps among the beeches running along the river as he fills a cask with water, they gather their children and avert their eyes. The Lifeweavers draw trouble like corpses draw flies. The Reapers, when they break through the border cordon to stalk and slay amongst the Freeholders, gravitate to this area in the hopes of killing Kur's most ancient and bitter foe: their estranged brethren.

Perched halfway up Mount Judea, a stoutly built A-frame lodge stands in a thick grove of mountain pine. The foundation of the building was cut from the old seabed a few miles away, thick slabs of varicolored stone that support the massive, red-timbered roof. Two monolithic lodgepoles of granite, etched with obscure designs that suggest Mayan hieroglyphs, gradually narrow toward the peaked roof. The building dwarfs any other house in the area; you would have to travel to the old resorts of the Mountain Home region to find a larger construct.

The Cats of Southern Command call it Ryu's Hall or just the Hall. They also call it home.

Valentine liked the look of the building from when he first set eyes on it, in the afternoon of the day after leaving Cobb Smithy.

"I was expecting another cave," Valentine said as they walked up the hill-cutting switchback leading to the Hall. "This part of the Ozarks is full of them."

"The Wolves like to lurk in their holes. We Cats like shared solitude and comfort," Duvalier said, leading the way with her swordstick used as a staff.

"Shared solitude? Sounds like 'fresh out of the can' to me. Or 'military intelligence.'"

"Watch it, Valentine. What 'military intelligence' Southern Command has feeds you now."

He didn't need his Wolf's nose to scent pine trees and wood smoke. They were cheery and welcoming odors after their days on the road.

The pair walked across a pebbled path to a metal-reinforced door. A cylinder of wrought iron with a thin steel bar hanging down the epicenter hung next to the door, and Duvalier rang it until the hills echoed.

A face appeared at a high, horizontal window. Female, amber skinned, with sharply slanting eyebrows. "Duvalier! You made good time with your new boy. Let me get the door."

Valentine heard a heavy bolt being drawn back and noticed there was no knob or handle of any kind on the outside of the door. It moved, and he got a good view of the six-inch-thick timbers that constituted the main door.

"David Valentine, meet Dix Welles," Duvalier said by way of introductions. "Dix was the toughest Cat between here and the Appalachians once upon a time."

He noticed that the darkly attractive woman held herself very stiffly and used a cane. "That was a long time ago, before my back got busted up," Welles explained. She was wearing ordinary blue overalls and had a bag of tools hanging from her hip.

"Pleased to meet you, ma'am—," Valentine began.

"Dix does just fine, David. For the last—I guess it's nine years now—I've been the Old Man's assistant, or major-domo, or whatever it is I do here. Have you ever met Ryu, Valentine?"

"No."

"He's met his brother Rho, though," Duvalier said. Intrigued, Valentine looked at the two women. It never occurred to him that the Lifeweavers had families.

"We can talk later," Welles interjected. "Come in, come in. I'll find you some space. We're almost empty right now. The Cats that wintered here left for the summer. About all that's here are some Aspirants like you, Valentine. What are we going to call you, anyway?"

"Ghost," Duvalier answered. "Some of his old friends gave him that name in the Wolves."

The conversation barely registered to Valentine. His eyes had adjusted, and he stood and gazed at the cavernous interior of the lodge.

Ryu's Hall was one big room built around a central fireplace. The fire pit was a good thirty square feet, with a wide metal chimney that disappeared up into the dark rafters. Valentine's eyes followed the metal tube up to the peak of the ceiling, which he estimated to be at least sixty feet high. A series of beams crisscrossed above his head halfway to the roof, holding up two chandeliers. They glowed with formed drops of liquid illumination, bathing the entire lodge in a golden light and deep shadow.

Welles saw the direction of Valentine's gaze. "Those little fancies are something the Lifeweavers brought across the worlds. Leave them out in the sun for an afternoon, and they'll glow like that for weeks. But don't ask me more—I only work here."

The main room of the Hall was subdivided around the edges of the room into a series of six-foot-by-six-foot platforms projecting out of the walls like shelves, all at various heights and connected by little staircases, climbing poles, and even rope ladders. A handful of figures lounged on the platforms, eating, reading, or simply sitting and looking at the new arrivals. Tapestries and sheets and rugs hung from the rafters or from the platform above provided some measure of privacy. Plates and mugs and casks were stacked at the centers of two long tables at opposite sides of the fireplace.

"You like it small and cozy or open and airy, Valentine?" Welles asked as they walked into the hall. She moved with a back-and-forth motion of her upper body that reminded Valentine of a metronome.

"Open and airy, I suppose. That's what I'm more used to."

"I'll take my usual spot," Duvalier said. "Just put him up above."

"Easy enough. These tables are the common eating area." Welles led them into the depths of the lodge. "You are free to make your own food, of course, but we usually have a morning meal and a night meal made up by the Aspirants. That's you now, Ghost-man. We have genuine toilets in the back, along with two showers and a tub, but you have to attend to the boiler. When there are a few more bodies here, we take turns with that duty so there's always enough hot water for all. There's a sauna that works whenever we got the boil up. This place is built practically on top of a mountain spring, so there's the best drinking water you've ever had whenever you want it. We don't even have to work a pump handle. Sweet, no?"

Valentine felt the warmth of a few dying charcoal bricks as they passed the massive fire pit.

"The fireplace is more for heat than cooking, but we've had a pig roast here on occasion. The main kitchen is in back. You wouldn't be any good at making bread, would you Valentine?"

"In an emergency."

"Great, you're our new baker. These kids go bluescreen whenever they try to bake anything but flatbread. Ryu has the rooms above the kitchen, and he doesn't take to visitors, so stay away from the back staircase. Questions so far?"

"Just as long as you don't have him in the kitchen at all hours," Duvalier grumbled. "We've got a lot of work to do if he's going to be ready to come out with me in a couple months. When can we see Ryu?"

"You know that's not up to me. Okay, here we are. Your usual spot, Smoke, and the Ghost will be in the attic."

Duvalier had a small space beneath Valentine's platform and its stairs. Valentine noticed she already had curtains up, blinds made from some kind of wicker. She dropped her pack under the stairs and sat on a footlocker to unlace her boots. He looked up at his own platform directly above, bare and featureless.

"I can find you a futon if you want, Valentine," Welles offered.

He didn't relish spending too many nights in his ever-ready hammock. "Thank you, I'd appreciate that."

"I'll let Ryu know you've arrived," she said, and rocked her way back to the doors at the rear of the Hall.

As he placed his possessions on the platform, connected by a stairway to the main floor and by a little walkway to still another platform, it occurred to him that his whole life amounted to two little heaps of gear: his carbine and the new sword, a pack containing a few tools and utensils, pans, and spare clothes, and one moldy-smelling nylon hammock. He had a locker back at Regiment with some heavy clothing, books, and odds and ends that he would have to write to somebody about.

"Hey, Duvalier," he called.

"Yes?" she answered from below, like a fellow camper in the bottom bunk.

"Where am I?"

"Southern Command calls it Buffalo River Lodge, Newton County. We call it Ryu's Hall. You confused about something?"

"What are we going to be doing here?"

"Didn't you listen? You're going to bake bread. That and learn how to kill Kurians."

*   *   *

Ryu himself woke Valentine the next morning. The nearly windowless hall slumbered in darkness, lit only by the red glow in the fire pit.

The Lifeweaver chose to appear as an ordinary man, with a hooked nose and a regal bearing that made Valentine instantly think of Pharaoh from illustrations in the Padre's storybook Bible. He wore a simple black loincloth and sandals.

"I am glad of this opportunity to meet you, David," he said as Valentine sat up, a little startled. "Would you share the sunrise with me?"

"Yes, just give me a moment," he said, rubbing the sleep from his eyes. The futon didn't look like much, but it was bone-deep comfortable. He slept heavy in the hours before dawn, but duty seemed to require him to awaken then more often than not.

Ryu turned and slowly walked down the stairs. Not sure whether that was a yes or a no, Valentine hurriedly pulled on his pants and followed. The Lifeweaver led him, with slow, graceful steps, almost floating back through the kitchens and spring-cave. They stooped into a rocky passage cut into the side of the mountain. They walked, and at times climbed, in silence through the shoulder-wide tunnel. They arrived at a wooden ladder, and Valentine smelled outside air.

"This is my private entrance. The ladder ends at a little fissure in the mountain."

Sure enough, the predawn quasi-light came faintly down the tunnel. The Lifeweaver began to climb the ladder, and Valentine followed. They emerged in the trees on the north side of the rounded-off mountain with birdsong all around them.

"It will be a fine morning. My spot for dawn-keeping is up the hill."

Valentine followed him up the slope, eventually coming out at a pile of boulders. Ryu sat down on the cold stone without even wincing, and Valentine joined him on the broad slab of rock. To the east, the green-carpeted mountains of the Ozarks bent away to the southeast. The high, scattered stratus clouds were turning from pink to orange as the unseen sun began to touch them.

Ryu said, "It will be a morning of rare color."

"What should I call you, sir?" Valentine asked. Amu, the Lifeweaver who'd been in charge of the Wolves, had acted like an old man who enjoyed teasing his grandchildren with riddles, and spoke as though he knew Valentine his whole life. Rho, the Lifeweaver who'd trained his father, he'd known only a few hours before he died. Ryu seemed cold and detached compared with the other two.

Valentine shivered in the chill morning air. The rock they sat on leached his body heat, but that was not the reason for the shudder. Ryu looked solid enough—he brushed aside small branches and flattened grass with his feet—but the Lifeweaver had no *presence*. Valentine thought it like having a conversation with an unusually lifelike portrait.

"Just Ryu. In our Old World, we had long and complex names describing our family, profession, planet of origin, and planet of residence. My brother and I were young then, born when the old Interworld Tree was still intact, and the rift with the researchers of Kur just beginning. We are old now, but not what we consider ancient. I mention my brother because my first duty to you is to thank you for getting him free. The torments and humiliation he suffered at the hands of the fiends . . . I had no idea until you brought him out of there. His death was free of grief. He went in peace, among friends."

Valentine couldn't find the proper words, so he resorted to a quiet yes.

They sat side by side, staring off into the warm palette of the coming sun.

"You have questions for us. You have an inquisitive mind."

"Sometimes I sense the Reapers. They say there are others like me, but I've never met one. Is that something Amu did? When I was invoked as a Wolf, one of the men said that I'd been 'turned all the way up.' "

"Some bodies are more ready for the change than others; the genes are there to do more. Your family had an aptitude, I understand. But as to this *sense*—I cannot say."

" 'I cannot say' isn't the same as 'I do not know.' "

"In the earlier war, before you wrote your histories, we tried a great many modifications to humans. Some we shouldn't have. Vestiges of those live on. It could be that."

Ryu let that sink in a moment before he continued. "Another possibility is that you could be a genetic wild card, a leap in natural selection brought on by the new stresses on your species. If I knew for certain, I would tell you."

Valentine felt like a bug under a light. The Lifeweavers were strange sort of leaders. They didn't inspire the Hunters to die for them, for all that they helped in their own secretive way. They just happened to be on the same side of a war—a very old one, in the case of the Lifeweavers. "You use us," Valentine said, and then thought that the fact had sounded like an accusation.

"Yes, we do. Do you know why? When we fell under the first onslaught of the Kur, we were in panic. We had no aptitude for fighting. We needed a weapon, something flexible and powerful, a species we could both use to attack with and hide amongst. A sword and a shield all in one. Your race fit the bill, as you say. In a span of nine planets, you were the material that best answered our need: cunning, savage, aggressive, and organized. You are a unique race. The deadliest hunter in the world is a tiger, but put five of them together and they still hunt no better than a single tiger. A beehive is a miracle of organization, but three beehives cannot cooperate. Army ants make warfare, plan campaigns, and make slaves of their captives, but do all this on group instinct and could never work together with an ant from a different queen. In microcosm, that is what we found on the worlds we explored: individual greatness or collective ability, but never both. You humans, you are tigers alone and army ants together, able to switch from one to the other with ease. You're the greatest warrior species we have ever encountered."

"Considering all that, the Kurians beat us pretty handily."

"They had surprise on their side. Had we known they were coming, we might have been able to warn you in time. Unlike Kur, we had no friends in your various govern-

ments; we did not wish to reveal ourselves to you. Perhaps
it was a mistake, but we felt your society needed a chance
to develop on its own. We had no idea Kur could organize
such an effort, had bred such a variety of what you call
Grogs, or that so many of your so-called leaders were willing to sell their species for some iteration of thirty pieces of
silver. Ah, here is the dawn. Let us enjoy it."

The sun tinted the clouds above and trees below, renew-
ing the world in its warmth. Its welcome touch restored
him; Valentine felt ready for whatever challenge Ryu might
put in his path.

They sat together in silence. When the shining orb separated from the horizon, Ryu turned and sat facing Valentine.

Valentine tried to pierce the psychic disguise, to see the
real shape of the Lifeweaver beneath—a grotesque mixture
of octopus and bat—through sheer force of will, but Ryu
did not change.

"David, you've proved yourself as a Wolf. It may not
seem that way to you right now, but we think well of you.
Amu's Wolves succeed through hearing and smell, speed
and endurance. My Cats are different. They depend on
stealth and surprise, and a certain amount of pure daring
that we cannot give but only encourage. To become a Cat,
your body will undergo some difficult changes, and there is
a risk. Perhaps you remember a Wolf or two who could not
adapt."

"Yes," Valentine said, remembering a cabin mate who
had thrown himself off a cliff in the confusion brought
about by the Wolf invocation. After Val's own invocation,
the tiniest noise and movement made him jump, before he
learned to soften his new senses. It was too much for some.

"It is a hard, lonely life, often without even the comrade-
ship of your fellow soldiers. You lived once in the Kurian
Zone. Are you willing to go back? Perhaps to disappear,
nameless and unavenged? Every year there are Cats who do
not return."

"Ryu, I've heard enough stories about the Cats to know
all this. The only time I ever knew I'd made a difference
was when I got Molly and her family out. If there's any

way I can help the people in the lost lands . . . I'll take the risk."

"Good words. But are they enough? Is there another reason? A personal one? Forget about your father, your fellow men and women, the Carlson family, or the graceful Alessa. Forget all that's happened with your old captain. You don't have to prove anything to us. Are you going to do this because you want to?"

Valentine sat back a little, perplexed. "Ryu, if that's the case, you should count me out. My desires are at the bottom of my list of why I'd like to do this. Of course, I agree with her about what we need to hunt."

"Forget about the Twisted Cross for now. I want to know what's in you."

So do I. "It's because of my parents, and for my people, that I want to do this. You talk about what an amazing species we are, like we're some kind of work in progress. We're a species that's either headed for extinction or permanent branding as livestock. Whatever potential you saw in us is going to waste as long as the Kurians are here.

"Sir, given my druthers, I'd like a house with a lot of books in the woods on a lake where I could fish in peace. I volunteered for this life, and I've sought responsibility because somebody has to, or there's not going to be a future for any of us. So if you're looking for a samurai mentality, dedicated to its own perfection in deadly self-annihilation, it's not me."

"Nothing more? David, do you like to kill?"

Valentine's heart stopped for a moment, then restarted with a thud that bounced off his ribs. How far into his mind could Ryu see?

"The old Cat took your tongue?"

"I can't—," Valentine said.

"David, how did you feel when you knifed that sentry on the bridge, when you killed that policeman in Wisconsin, the one who disparaged you as an 'Injun.' What did you feel when you strangled that man in the Zoo?"

"How—?"

"Hows take too long. What was in your soul?"

"Guilt, but—"

Ryu waited.

"I felt guilty."

"Guilty because you chose one path over another, leading to their deaths? Or guilty because you reveled in it?"

Valentine shrank away. Ryu suddenly frightened him; he wasn't sure he wanted this conversation to continue. But he had to answer, and no answer would do but the truth.

"I don't know. I don't know myself well enough."

Ryu nodded. "Then leave it at that. I like to know what is in my Cats' hearts. Once you've learned what's in you, I hope you'll share it with me someday. Very well, you'll have this opportunity to aid your people in their crisis. And perhaps one day learn why David Valentine feels guilty."

"Then I'm in?"

"You are in."

The ceremony could hardly have been simpler. Valentine was brought to a warm little room in the back of the Hall, escorted by Duvalier. He wore only a towel wrapped around his waist. "It's a waste to wear clothes for the Change," she said as butterflies began to beat their wings on the inside of his stomach.

It resembled a wedding in a way. Ryu entered, wearing a heavy robe with more cryptic designs woven into the lapels and cuffs of the garments. He had Valentine stand next to Duvalier.

"Alessa, are you ready to take on the responsibility of training this one?"

She nodded. "I am."

Ryu turned to Valentine. "David, are you ready to take on the responsibility of joining our ranks?"

Valentine nodded. "I am."

"May the bond between you meet with success."

The Lifeweaver emptied a small vial into a plain ceramic bowl of water and swirled it in his palm like brandy in a snifter.

"Drink this, and become a Cat," Ryu intoned.

Valentine drank it, as tasteless as water.

Ryu handed Duvalier a small knife. "Now share your blood."

With a quick slash, she opened a small cut across her right palm, then took Valentine's left hand and did the same. They then clasped hands tightly. Valentine felt the sticky warmth pressed between their palms.

Ryu looked at Duvalier. "Explain to your bloodshare what is coming."

"David, the next few days are going to be a little difficult. Within a few hours, you're going to feel jumpy. I had trouble breathing, and it made me very panicky. Most people get very dizzy; people who've been on boats say it's like seasickness. Your heart will beat very fast. There's no real physical pain, but a whole new part of your body that you didn't know was there is going to be waking up. We'll keep you in this room for a couple days, safe and warm. Relax and ride it out. Try not to tear your hair out or gouge yourself."

Valentine stiffened. He'd been awkward and twitchy after his first invocation, but hadn't felt the desire for self-mutilation.

She continued: "If you have to bite something, we've got a leather-wrapped plastic tube in there for you; gnawing at the wood's no good, you'll just wreck your teeth. After the second day, I just did jumping jacks till I collapsed; then it was done. Maybe that will work for you, too."

Ryu shook his head. "David, she's making it sound worse than it is. If it helps to have a goal, keep this in mind. The first test of a Cat is how silently one goes through the Change. And you're lucky; the Wolves who've come into our caste adapt quickly. There will be someone outside the door at all times. We'll be keeping an eye on you."

The Lifeweaver clasped Valentine's blood-smeared hand between his palms in a gesture that was half-handshake and half-bow. Duvalier gave Valentine a tight hug, then showed him the old white scar across her left palm.

"You'll be fine. See you in three days."

They shut and locked the door to the little room. It reminded him of a sauna, right down to the little glass window in the rough cedar door. A single slatted bench was the

extent of the furnishings, and a drain hole in the center of
the wood-paneled room evidently served as the sanitary fa-
cility. There was a water spigot fixed into the wall, and
Valentine gave it an experimental turn. Cold springwater
cascaded onto the floor.

They left him the hunk of leather and plastic, like a dog's
chew toy. He did not feel uncomfortable, at least not yet.
He spread the towel on the unyielding boards of the bench
and stretched out. The light shining into the little room illuminated one edge of the bench, and Valentine recognized
human teeth marks.

The human psyche has a wonderful capacity to remember pleasant things: the taste of a superlative meal, the feel
of a lover's lips, a refrain of inspiring music. It hurries to
dispose of the unpleasant. Valentine was always grateful for
that ability later: the three days in that little room were
among the worst in his life.

The first tremors hit within an hour, and by the afternoon, his muscles screamed for action. He wanted to run
until he dropped. Sweat poured off his body, his ears
pounded, the tiny amount of light coming in through the
window hurt his eyes. He felt disoriented. The room
seemed to be a tiny cork bobbing on a sea of five-story
waves. He did not vomit—he would have loved to do so,
but it was one long stretch of nausea absent the relief of
vomiting. His stomach alternately cramped and spasmed,
leaving him twitching and listening to his own overloud
heartbeat. To keep his heart from exploding out of his
chest, he curled into a fetal position and locked his arms
around his body, at war with his own desire to climb the
walls, pound down the door, then run and run until the
maddening electricity coursing through his body left him.

He bit the leather loop to keep from screaming.

The second day was better. His wooden cell seemed
oddly shaded, the red browns of the room became muted
and faint, the shadows more sharply defined. The room no
longer swooped and plunged around him; it rocked like a
cradle moved to and fro by a cooing mother.

But he wanted *out*.

He did push-ups until he collapsed in exhaustion, drank a little water, and passed out into electric nightmares.

The third day was a hangover to end all hangovers. His empty stomach hurt, his head ached, his hands would not stop trembling. When Duvalier's face appeared in the little window, he threw himself at the glass, clawing at the door and leaving a smear of saliva where he'd tried to bite.

Then he slept.

When she came again, he was too drained to react.

She entered cautiously, a tray holding a shallow bowl with some kind of soup in her hand. "How do you feel, cousin?"

Valentine eased himself onto the bench, feeling light-headed. "Weak as . . . as a kitten?"

It turned out that the soup meant the general consensus was that his ordeal was over. While he ate, Duvalier went to get him some clothes, leaving the door open to air out the stuffy room. Forty-eight hours ago, he would have run howling into the hills, but now he was content to just sip at the soup and wait for her to return with something presentable. The blood-and-filth-smeared towel deserved a decent burial; all four corners were gnawed to shreds.

He finished the meal and got dressed, still trembling a little. When he followed Duvalier into the brighter light of the little honeycomb of rooms that composed the toilet and washing facilities at the rear of the Hall, he put a hand on her shoulder. She, and everything around her, didn't look quite right. There was little color in her skin, and the wooden walls were ashen, like bleached-out driftwood.

"Just a second," he said. "Why do you look different? The light is all odd."

"I know what you mean. It's not the light—it's your eyes. A Cat with some medical training explained it to me once. It has to do with the cells in your eyes. I guess there are two kinds; he called them rods and cones. The rods are good at picking up low light levels. You've got a whole lot more rods now. Your color vision will return once your eyes get used to it; right now your brain is just not processing it right. That was his theory. You'll adapt. In any kind of light short of pitch black, you're going to have no trouble seeing from here on out."

"Did the doctor explain the drunken feeling?"

"That was even more confusing, and it's got to do with your ears. We have these little bags of liquid in our ears that help us keep our balance. Some animals, cats in particular, have a whole different set of nerve fibers attached to them. You know how a cat always lands on its feet, or at least nearly always? It's from these nerves. Their balance corrects as involuntarily as your leg moving when your knee gets tapped. Right now you're oversensitized again."

She walked into the kitchen and picked up a sack of flour.

"Stand on one leg. Raise the other one like a dog marking a tree. Higher. Okay, keep it there," she ordered.

Valentine obliged, noticing that as he raised his leg he barely moved. Normally he would wobble a bit.

"Now catch," she said, tossing the ten-pound sack of flour with a shoving motion.

He caught it a few inches from his chest, causing little puffs of flour to shoot in the air. What's more, his leg was still raised.

"Interesting," he said, returning his leg to the floor. He shifted the bag of flour in his hands, and quick as a flash hurled it back at her.

Her reflexes were no less than his. She snatched the bag out of the air, but while she was strong enough to halt the ten pounds of flour aimed like a missile at her head, the bag wasn't quite up to the task. Its weakened fibers opened, and a white bomb detonated full in her face.

"Mother—!" she screamed, emerging from the cloud in kabuki makeup and fury.

Valentine let out the first squawk of a laugh and then read her expression. Their eyes locked for a second, like a gazelle and cheetah staring at each other on the veldt. He ran for his life.

"Dead meat, Valentine!" she shrieked, after him in a

flash. Valentine went to the stairs up to his little flat, and jumped. To his astonishment, he made it up to the top of the flight in a single bound. With only one foot down, he changed direction and leapt onto the next platform over, a jump he normally would have needed a sprint to cover.

He slipped on the landing and sprawled. Duvalier was on his back in a moment—she must have equaled or exceeded the speed and power of his bounds. He tried to wriggle out, but as he turned over, she pinned him with legs that felt like a steel trap. She nailed his arms down in a full pin. He found the situation arousing: Duvalier in the classical position astride him, the flour liberally coating her from the waist up adding its own strange zest to the moment. But her eyes were lit only in triumph.

"Okay, gotcha," she said. "Let's have it."

"Sorry," he panted. "Didn't mean to make you the monkey's uncle."

"What's that?

"A monkey's uncle!"

"Can't hear you, Valentine, speak up."

"Uncle!"

"That's better," she said, rolling off him.

He took a deep breath, still goosey with the half-drunken, half-hungover sensation.

"Ghost, how do they do it?"

"Do what?"

"Change us like that."

He shrugged. "I've wondered about that myself. Some of the Wolves used to say they were just awakening something already inside us. I was talking to a cabin mate named Pankow one time, and I remember he took a gas lamp that was barely on, just a flicker, and turned it all the way up. It hissed and roared and lit up the whole room. He said that's what the wizards do, they just 'turn up the heat.' "

Valentine wondered if he could share his fears with her, as well. He looked at the healing wound on his hand. "But the bigger the flame, the sooner the gas runs out. You swap heat and light for longevity. It worries me. I haven't met many elderly Hunters."

She shook her head, flour cascading off her face. "Gimme a break, Val. You know how long the average Cat lasts in the KZ? Two or three years. Ask Welles—she'll confirm it. Me, I'm already well past my 'lifespan.' I'd like to switch subjects.

"Now that you've been tuned up, it's time to start training. We'll be cutting a lot of corners. I'll try to fill in the holes on the road."

"Okay, Sarge, what's next on the agenda?"

She began to dust herself off. "Sarge? David, as a courtesy, Cats are treated as captains by the other ranks in Southern Command. So you got promoted after all. But rank doesn't mean much to us. As far as the *agenda* goes, you're going to get some food and sleep in you. Then we're going to run your ass ragged. When I drop, Welles will take over. So you take it easy while you can."

Over the next weeks, Valentine decide that Duvalier held an epic grudge against him for the flour bomb and wanted to see him lose life or limb if at all possible. When she was unavailable to personally torment him, Dix Welles made sure he sweated.

He had to carry the sword everywhere, to ridiculous extremes like the shower and the toilet. If Duvalier caught him exiting the head with a dog-eared copy of *Reader's Digest* instead of his sword, he got to spend the rest of the day running up and down the mountain. He learned a few basic stances, cuts, and thrusts from Duvalier the first day, then practiced them endlessly, first with a wooden replica until he got the motion right, and then with the naked blade. One day Welles took him outside and had him climb up the sharply slanted lodge roof, and draw, swing, and move with the sword back and forth across the narrow peak, carefully straddling the top as he fought wind and momentum.

He took bundles of twigs, wrapped them in old rags, soaked them, and then attached them to poles. The target was then placed on a gimbal-mounted teeter-totter. He tried to hit it while Duvalier, at the other end of the ten-foot plank, made it dodge his blows. She succeeded in knocking him over with it more than once. When she wasn't bashing him with straw men, she was doing it herself, in fencing duels with wooden swords. She struck like lightning, and more than once laid him out with stars in his eyes.

Even when he was off his feet, he had to read. Poisons, explosives, powders both natural and chemical that blinded or sickened. Acids and bases. A grizzled old Cat, toothless and bent, lectured him on how to sabotage everything from tank engines to hydraulic brakes to a backyard water pump.

He learned to climb and fight with his claws. Duvalier taught him to always keep them in the pockets of an old overcoat, so that all he had to do was slip his hands in to become armed. He clawed, climbed, and parried with them until they felt like old friends, but that wasn't good enough. Duvalier had him practice with them until they felt like a natural extension of his body. A couple of the other Cats-in-training shook their heads and privately made fun of Duvalier's fixation with them.

"Waste of time," one of them said at dinner. "You end up using them one fight out of a hundred, I've been told."

Welles overheard and stiffly turned on the other Aspirant. "That one time in a hundred he'll be alive. And you won't."

Ryu appeared now and then and took Valentine in order to work his mind. First Valentine had to reduce his aura at rest, and as the days progressed, he had to do the same while running or climbing, or even practicing with his sword. He'd learned the basics of hiding lifesign from an old Cat named Eveready the summer after he'd been invoked as a Wolf. Now he was learning from the Lifeweaver who had taught Eveready.

Valentine could satisfy Ryu at rest, but in action, the Lifeweaver upbraided him again and again. One afternoon, as he crossed a rock-strewn creek under the Lifeweaver's eye, Ryu lifted his arms, the signal to stop. "You're still in your own mind, David."

The obvious joke about "the perfect Cat is always out of his mind" had to be bitten back—again.

"You're not a Kurian. You don't need it to survive. How can you sense it?"

"Aura is a lot of things, David. Thought, emotion, sensitivities, fear. I am able to perceive these to an extent. So can you, by the way. There's more to intuition than guesswork. Sometimes I can read you as easily as you read printed words."

"Sorry. I saw a fish dart away."

"Forget about your empty stomach for a while."

Valentine stood in the shin-deep water and tried to reduce himself again, become a part of the stream and the rocks rather than a traveler over them.

"The energy they feed from, what we call lifesign, is as individual as a fingerprint," Ryu continued, "and you're putting out far too much into the world. You're the wind on the rocks, the water flowing on its natural course, a swarm of gnats over the dead log there."

Valentine imagined himself part of the stream. The fish he'd alarmed resumed its vigil, waiting for a meal to drop onto the surface of the slow-flowing pool. *Just water and rock, trout . . .*

"Quit thinking, David. Just float across."

Valentine followed the water, ignoring the fish and the gnats until he stood beside Ryu.

"Better. Look back at the stones. Try to trace your path."

He squatted and looked for marks of his field boots on the stones. He'd come up and out of the stream without overturning a stone or leaving a telltale track of mud.

He didn't say anything, just felt the breeze.

"Now be that wind and let's talk again at the top of that hill," Ryu said, pointing to a limestone-scarred slope.

He worked inside the lodge, as well, leaping from rafter to rafter with his arms tied behind his back.

"Everything is balance, Valentine," Duvalier shouted up at him from the floor, a long hard fall below him, as he teetered for a split-second after a jump. "It keeps you from being hit in a fight, lets you hold your rifle steady, and makes you silent when you walk."

A Cat named Cymbeline—a tattooed woman with a milky eye and hairless even to her eyebrows—taught him unarmed combat. Her philosophy for unarmed combat was to arm yourself as quickly as possible with anything handy, even a piece of chain or a good solid stick. From her, Valentine learned to use everything from his instep to his skull—Cymbeline called it a readily available, ten-pound brick—to disable an opponent.

His spare locker from the Second Regiment depot found him after five weeks at the Lodge, along with another pad-locked case of back-straining weight. A note and a small key came in an envelope forwarded with his other mail. He looked at the unfamiliar handwriting and opened the letter. Written in heavy block printing was

Dear David,
This better make it intact, or I'll have something to say to the Territorial Post. I've become good friends with Molly and her family. They told me what happened and what you did for them in Wisconsin. We're glad to have people like the Carlsons in Weening.
I don't have any family worth speaking about. I never served with your father but I know he'd want me to help you along if I could. I'm enclosing a very dear friend of mine, one of my favorite guns from my days in Jorgensen's Bears. It's over a hundred years old now, and been rebuilt a time or two, but it's a damned murderous weapon and I want it in your hands. It's an old Soviet PPD-40. Reliable in any weather and dirt. I've enclosed a thousand rounds I loaded myself, plus tools and casts to make reloads. I've also sent a little manual on it I wrote myself. I suppose it was captured by the Germans when they invaded Russia. The German Army loved this gun and grabbed every one they could. It got captured again by our troops and brought back here. I got it from a collector in Missouri who was handing out his

guns left and right in the Bad Old Days of '22. Later taught me to take care of it.

Hope it takes care of you as well as it did me. Watch the full auto—you'll empty that big drum in less than eight seconds if you hold the trigger down. You can get shells for it at Red's in Ft. Smith, or the Armory in Pine Bluff, or go see Sharky at Gunworks in Mountain Home. Just tell them you need 7.62 X 25 or .30 Mauser. Better yet, learn to do your own reloads. More reliable that way. READ THE DAMN INSTRUCTIONS, kid.

Always liked you when you spent that season in Weening. I respected the way you went after them Harpies and took that Hood that got the Helm boy and your Labor Regiment pals. Stop by anytime, there's always a bed and a beer waiting for you at my place.

Your friend,
Bob Bourne

Valentine remembered the man named Tank from four years ago and the firelit night when Gabriella Cho, the closest thing Val had had to a childhood sweetheart, died.

He put the memories away.

So the gun was the mystery mentioned in Molly's last letter. He took the key from the letter and opened the case. The gun was smaller than a carbine, but solidly built, with a thick wooden stock. The barrel was encased in a larger, vented handle. Amongst the little reloading tools and instructions were three heavy ammunition boxes. He picked up the gun, ruggedly manufactured from heavy steel. Cyrillic characters were printed above the trigger.

"Thanks, Tank."

Tank had enclosed three drums and a banana magazine. The fully loaded drums held seventy-one rounds. Valentine hastily referred to the manual, a mixture of weapons jargon and how-to hints, like instructions for replacing a worn spring in the drum and using a piece of leather to cushioning a part in the gun's simple action. He stripped the weapon experimentally, an operation that involved simply opening the hinged receiver to expose the bolt and spring, and found that it broke down as easily as it went back together. Valentine, who had some experience with various guns used by both the Free Territory and their enemies, was all in favor of simplicity, but he had his doubts about using exotic ammunition. The stock was clearly new; perhaps that was what Molly was referring to when she said Tank was working on something for him that winter. Gleaming with rich stain and polish, the stock had been fashioned out of a beautifully grained piece of ash.

Duvalier joined him on his little platform. "Heard a Logistics wagon was by with some stuff for you. Did your locker arrive?"

Valentine replaced the gun in the case.

"Yes. Even better, an old Bear came through."

The next night they ate dinner alone. Dix had led the rest of the Cats to the nearest Southern Command trading post for supplies. Valentine was grateful for the quiet—he'd spent the day running pursuits on Duvalier. If he was unlucky enough not to catch her after an hour, they'd turn around and she'd chase him. He hoped he'd get time for a long shower and then a sweat in the steam room.

Ryu emerged from his refuge, a beautiful woman accompanying him. In fact, she was so striking, Valentine assumed she had to be another Lifeweaver. Such beauty had to be illusion, the stock-in-trade of all Lifeweaver interactions with humanity.

The Cats greeted the stranger with short bows.

"My courageous ones, please greet my sister from the East, Ura," Ryu said, standing aside so she could come forward. Radiant in a simple teal gown with a roped belt of gold, she walked without bending blades of grass beneath delicate feet. Valentine thought she looked like a princess out of a storybook.

"A little rough around the edges, like everything here,

but you seem capable," she said, smiling. She shook each of their hands with a cool, firm grip.

"Ura, Alessa Duvalier and David Valentine are also concerned with the Twisted Cross. Could it be that the evil has been reawakened, like so many others?"

"I fear so. Certainly they have unfurled the old standard. Perhaps they march again."

"What's this, Ryu?" Duvalier said. "When you tasked me with this, you didn't tell me you knew anything."

"I thought it might be coincidence. Many things appear to be different now. Certainly they never used Reapers before."

"Maybe you should start from the beginning." Valentine mined his memory, trying to bring back every detail, every word of the brief encounter he had with a member of the Twisted Cross in Chicago. All he could remember was the unknown man's kill in the grotty Zoo basement, the sight of the gaunt figure's blood-smeared face, the ripped-out throat of that poor condemned girl.

"Come and sit then," Ryu said, leading them to one of the long tables. "Ura, would you care for food or drink? No? David, to start from the beginning would take years. As you should well know, you've learned more of these matters in your youth than many of your elders, even ones who should know better.

"The Twisted Cross go back to the first onslaught, when the Kurians came across the Interworld Tree as the great schism turned to war. On Earth and six other planets, they attacked us without warning. Their first human allies were a group known as the Aryans, originally from the middle of Asia.

"Because of their favored status with the Kur, the Aryans considered themselves superior to other men. The baubles the Kurians gave them made them able to convince others of this, and soon the Aryans led armies that would do the bidding of Kur."

Ura held up her hand. "It is worth remembering that the Kurians failed in their first invasion, and the Aryans' power was broken."

"So what does the Twisted Cross mean?" Valentine asked.

"I do not know," Ryu said. "Some have interpreted that glyph to mean 'life.' As an extreme example, there is no physiological reason that a human couldn't live off vital aura and gain what amounts to immortality. It requires not much more of a Change than the one that you recently experienced, David. Your body already generates and uses vital aura; it is the loss of this in the declining years that causes you to age. It is just a matter of being able to acquire and utilize another's aura."

Valentine took a moment to consider this. Perhaps that was the carrot dangled before humans who betrayed their own species. If offered eternal life, what would his answer be? How different was it, truly, from eating a steak or a slice of ham?

"Alessa, David, do what you can to learn about this new threat. In the mountains of the Eastern seaboard, my sister tells me, we suffered a mysterious loss two summers ago. One day there was a thriving freehold in a guarded valley. Ten thousand of your people. And the next, a wasteland. Last summer we lost all contact with some allies on the Gulf Coast at the Florida peninsula. We fear the Ozarks may be next. I've sent out other teams with the same orders I'm giving you: Find out all you can about this General and those who follow his banner."

"Of course we'll learn what we can," Duvalier responded. "I've got an idea of where to start. But the trail's already cold. We may be back soon."

"You're not ready yet, but then neither am I," Duvalier told Valentine a few days later. "Doesn't matter, though. We're leaving."

The lodge echoed emptily. Aside from Valentine, the lone remaining Cat was Duvalier, and even the other Aspirants had left to join their tutors for the summer. Of course the ubiquitous Welles still lingered, but she was a permanent resident. They busied themselves with last-minute preparations: putting together an assortment of photographs—Welles had a pair of cameras and a darkroom—that could be used on identification papers, collecting blank forms they might need in the Gulag, going over the latest news summaries so they understood conditions in their operational area.

Valentine had grown into his new senses and skills. He handled his sword with the same confidence he once felt in his rifle and parang. He practiced with the gun Bourne sent him—it wasn't any use at all over two hundred yards, but in the rough and tumble of close-quarters action, it would be a deadly asset.

His night vision rivaled that of daytime except at the most extreme distances, and he could play follow-my-leader with Duvalier over a single-strand rope footbridge without thinking twice. As he did it, he concentrated on "quieting his mind," obliterating his higher consciousness as Ryu instructed. He needed no training in moving quietly; his skill at that had earned him the nickname "Ghost" long ago from his Wolf teammates.

Even Duvalier found his ability to move silently a little eerie. He overheard her discussing it with Welles one evening when they assumed he was asleep. Duvalier explained that she was resting against a tree one afternoon and knew he was next to her only when he touched her shoulder.

"Hmmph, maybe it's the Indian blood. He got the hair, anyway."

"His mother was Sioux. Listen, there's more. I read this in his Q-file: he can sense Reapers. It happened on a couple of occasions, and there are witnesses. But only if they're active. He picks up on them when they're moving around, but if they're asleep . . . nothing. He can almost locate them with it. It's like their reading of our lifesign, only reversed."

Welles paused, perhaps thinking it through in her mind. "Weird shit. Maybe he's sensitive to the connection they have with their Masters, do you think?"

"Could be. I've heard of people being able to ping off them; never met one, though. I'll feel a lot more comfortable sleeping at night knowing he's right there."

"I bet he could make you a lot more comfortable at night," Welles said with a very uncharacteristic giggle.

"Get off, Dix. My interest in him is purely professional."

"Mmmmm-hmmmm. Good thing I just fell off a turnip truck, otherwise I might not believe you. I will miss the fresh bread and biscuits, though. He worked that cute ass of his off in the kitchen. Never mind the firewood to last until next spring."

The Hall echoed with the sounds of their packing. Valentine looked up at the glow bulbs, tempted to take one. It would be a useful souvenir.

"Feel free to store your gear here," Duvalier said. "We all do. This is the closest thing to a home you're going to have for a while."

Welles appeared, a bundle tucked under her arm.

"Made this for you, young Ghost. In return for a lot of tasty bread and some great fireside stories. Who ever thought I'd like hearing about Roman emperors and moldy old English plays? Here you go," she said, handing it over. "I can't move around so good anymore, but I still sew like the wind."

"I don't know if I'd call *Richard the Third* a moldy English play, but you're welcome," he said, taking the folded green cloth. He untied the twine around it and unfolded a long riding overcoat.

"Sorry some of the buttons don't match, but you know how it is. I used wooden pegs at the stress points—they hold up a little better."

Valentine held it up and then tried it on. It was a faded, slate-colored green, reversible to black like Duvalier's natty relic. It hung to just above his ankles, and was split up the back for saddle use, including loops for his legs to go through. There were pockets galore, and a built-in muffler that could strap around his throat and closing heavy collar. A hood hung neatly down the back, cut so skillfully it looked like decoration. "So you weren't taking my measurements for 'statistical reasons' a month ago, huh?"

"Guilty. Keep out of sight, would you, Valentine? It'll

keep out the wind, but not bullets. The damn Bears grab all the Reaper cloaks, you know."

"You going to cry or thank her, Val?" Duvalier asked.

"Thanks, Dix. I really appreciate this."

"You'll appreciate it even more the first rainstorm you walk through. Wear it in good health, Ghost."

They opened the heavy front door and stepped out into the morning light. A pair of roan horses browsed amongst the grass and weeds of the front lawn. As Ryu followed the Cats out the door, the horses raised their heads and nickered.

"A farewell gift," Ryu explained. "This pair is out of a very wily herd of wild horses that runs the mountains. I called and they came."

"They won't do us much good, then," Valentine said. He had spent some time training wild horses to pull timber in Minnesota. "It'll take days to break them properly."

Ryu patted Valentine on the shoulder. "That will not be necessary, David. I imprinted the two of you on them, if that is the proper expression. They should take to you quite readily. Try it."

The horses, as if listening to Ryu's words, walked up to the pair.

"I'll go grab some oats out of the kitchen," Dix said. "That'll last you until you reach a border fort for supplies."

Valentine looked at the mare a trifle dubiously, but she looked calmly back at Valentine from her white-freckled face as if she had known him her whole life. She gave the collar of his new overcoat an experimental nibble. He grabbed a handful of mane and slipped onto the horse's bare back. He pressed against the horse's side with his calf, and it sidestepped to face Ryu and his ethereal companion.

"We have some saddles and blankets in the outside shed, do we not?" Ryu asked.

Duvalier looked over at the little outbuilding next to the smokehouse. "Yes, I think we can rig something up. Thank you, sir—this means a lot to us."

Ryu turned his piercing eyes to Valentine. "Seventy-one

days ago, you accused us of using you. At times I think my people take you humans for granted. We share the same war, but you do most of the dying. Some hold that if we do too much for you, you will become dependent on us and cease growing. I sympathize with that belief, but arguments over not interfering with a civilization become moot when the Kurians have already reordered your world to suit their purposes. So if I can help my children with a simple trick, I do it.

"Speaking of simple tricks, I have one for you, David. A small gift," he said, holding out his hand. In it a tiny, triangular glow bulb glimmered faintly in the daylight. " 'May it be a light to guide you in dark places, when all others lights go out,' " he said. Or did he? The quotation seemed to drop into Valentine's brain, a windfall from the abundant orchard of his reading, without benefit of the Lifeweaver's lips moving.

"You know how to charge it, I believe," he said, again speaking with his voice.

"Leave it in the light," Valentine said, taking the little pyramid-shaped object.

"In the Old Days, we had ones that generated heat, as well, which would be far more useful. But that Art, like so many others, is lost to us in the here and now."

Ryu and Ura exchanged a long look, making Valentine wonder if in that time they shared the mental equivalent of an evening's discussion.

"Alessa, follow your spirit when your mind falters. David, if you keep an open mind, you will find friends unlooked for," Ryu said. He drifted up off the ground, touching their foreheads, first Duvalier's and then his, with his fingertips and spreading his arms before them as if in benediction.

"Go, the two of you," Ura added, imitating the gesture. "Turn away this old evil, and in doing so, change evil fate into good fortune for our Cause."

While you are at it, find King Solomon's mines and a splinter of the True Cross, the contrarian part of Valentine's mind added. He looked over at Duvalier, standing next to her newly appointed horse with a rapt expression on her face. She looked hypnotized. Did she know more than he, or was she just more gullible? Evidence of the Lifeweavers' special abilities stood quietly between his legs at that moment, or were the magically appearing horses some kind of elaborate put-on?

He could not argue with his enhanced senses, from vision to balance. He could spend most of the day running, but not be exhausted. There was no question that they had awakened something inside him, but did they create it, or just ring the alarm clock?

Duvalier and Valentine bowed in thanks and left their horses to see if they could find bridle and saddle in the jumble of odds and ends housed in the outbuilding.

Valentine looked at the Hall one more time. He remembered something his mother used to tell him: *There are two kinds of people in the world—those who look back and those who look forward.* She also said that most people in their youth look forward, and a sign of advancing age was looking back. *Always look forward, David,* she'd told him.

Being atop fresh horses and under the summer sun felt fine. The Kurian Zone was far away; if it were not for the July humidity, the day would have been ideal. After an easy stretch to warm them to travel again, the well-shaded old highways of the Ozarks guided them back up to the Missouri borderlands in a second hard day's ride. Duvalier showed her usual flair for finding discreet shelter in a pre-Overthrow ruin.

Valentine always bedded down in the old homes and businesses with a certain amount of trepidation. He would sometimes find an old weather-stained family picture and stare at the carefully combed and braided hair on the children and wonder what the fate of this or that family member was. The Ravies plague that swept the world in 2022 took the majority; war and upheaval claimed the rest. He had seen enough death at close hand to wonder how any of the old-timers had come through it with sanity intact. The population in the first years of the Kurian rule was thought to be somewhere around 10 to 15 percent of its pre-2022 height, with the urban areas suffering the worst losses. Valentine once passed through the nuclear blast site in Little Rock on a trip up the Arkansas River, where nature had returned but not man. Trees now grew amongst the naked girders and piles of rubble, but people shunned the site as if it lay under a curse.

"What's on the agenda for tomorrow?" Valentine asked after they had seen to the horses.

"We're a team now, Valentine," she said, lugging her saddle indoors. "We both share the decisions. You're sensible enough."

"That sounded an awful lot like a compliment."

"You cut me off before I could say 'most of the time.' I was thinking we should stop tomorrow at Fort Springfield. That's the last stop before we hit no-man's-land. That old man from the Oklahoma City rail yard, he said the 'Nazis' traveled by train, right?"

"Yes. He also mentioned that new lines were going in west of here."

She set down the saddle and dug out a tin of some kind of tallow from her pack. She worked the tallow into a rag and then used the rag to clean the summer dust off the saddle. Valentine began to put some dinner together using the fresh food they brought with them from Ryu's Hall. The best of the summer vegetables had come in, and he began to peel and pare into a pot of chicken stock.

"There's three sides to a job, Valentine," she said, drawing a triangle in the dirt. She put three letters at the corners. "Fast, safe, and right. You get to pick any two when you're out in the KZ. You can do something fast and right, but you sacrifice safe. Or safe and right, but you won't get it done fast."

"Then there's fast and safe."

"That's how most Cats operate. In and out quick. Me, I like to live around my objective for a while. Then when it comes time to act, I know what I'm doing. Your lead from the old nutcase is the only trail we have, at least in this part of the country. I'd just as soon not go stumbling around in the Smoky Mountains, where I don't know anybody."

"Then you know people in the plains?"

"How does that old song go? *'I got friends in low places . . .'* Sure, Valentine, not everyone in the Gulag is a Quisling."

Valentine covered the little pot hanging over the fire burning in an old stainless-steel sink they had propped up on two cinder blocks.

Duvalier unfolded a map of the Old United States. "We know the General moves by train, right? They didn't raid into the Free Territory, which I kind of suspected they might do. Could be he doesn't have the muscle for that job yet. They were heading north out of Oklahoma City. The Kur don't have a reliable east-west rail line south of Iowa and Nebraska—your old buddies the Wolves raise too much hell between Kansas City and St. Louis—they don't even try to keep that line repaired anymore. In Kansas or Nebraska, they could have turned west, to hit Denver or one of the Freeholds in the Rockies. I can't believe they turned back east. Why come west in the first place?"

Valentine looked at the map. "North out of Oklahoma, they might have turned west at Wichita, Junction City, or maybe even Lincoln. Lincoln seems like a long shot, but if I were trying to recruit, Iowa might be the place to do it. It sounded like a long time ago, there was a pretty big army under that Twisted Cross banner. Maybe they're trying to do the same thing again. A lot of loyal Quislings have land in Iowa granted to them in exchange for services rendered. We used to draw a two-hundred-mile circle around Des Moines and call it Brass Ringland. I imagine these Quislings are raising families. Could be they want some sons and daughters to join up."

Duvalier looked at the map for a moment and thought. "Funny, I'm just not picturing these guys as leaders of a huge army. They seem secretive, more like a tight elite unit. In a way, if they had a huge army, it would be better for us. We could track—hell, even infiltrate. I feel like they're more the Kur's answer to our Bears: small teams of very serious badasses who crack nuts the Kur don't want to risk their own Reapers on."

"Reaper mercenaries? Okay, you've seen Reapers, I've seen men. Maybe it's their version of a tag team. The men guard the Reapers when they sleep away the day, and the Reapers do the killing at night."

"That system's in place already, Valentine."

"Perhaps they're just perfecting it."

"I still heard Reapers talking on the hill where we met. That means they weren't being operated by the same Master."

A Kurian Lord animated his Reapers through a psychic bond, the same bond that fed him the vital aura of humans killed by the Reaper.

Nothing made sense to Valentine. "How about if a group of Kurian Lords decided to spread the risk in destroying common enemies. They each contribute one Reaper, a flying strike force to . . . No . . . damn, that makes no sense. A Kurian's hold gets weaker the farther the Reaper is from him."

Duvalier nodded. "That would mean the Kurians had to travel around the country. To much risk. Nothing, but nothing, gets them out of their little fortresses once they are established. They're the biggest cowards in creation."

"Yes, you're right. Doesn't make sense." His stomach rumbled at the smell of cooking food. "But I can understand my insides. Let's eat."

They turned to their bread and soup and concentrated on the hot food. For dessert they shared a bag of summer plums, seeing who could spit the pit most accurately. Valentine won on distance, but Duvalier expelled hers with bull's-eye control. They laughed at the wine-colored stains left on their faces and turned in, giggling like kids.

"How'd you get to be a Cat? Were you always a troublemaker, or is it just the training?"

"Both, in a way. I grew up under the Kur in Emporia, Kansas. It's a town about halfway between what's left of Topeka and Wichita. My daddy had been shipped off to some work camp God-knows-where. My mom made clothes, mostly for the labor. We call that part of the country the Great Plains Gulag. Gulag: I thought it was some kind of hot dish until someone told me it means concentration camps. My mom was a little too young and pretty, though. Some of the Society used to visit her. Society is what we called the Quislings. She got extra food and stuff out of it, but I hated Society calls."

"You don't have to elaborate."

"I have the high ground on you, Valentine. I've read your Q-file. But you don't know much about me, other than that I saved your ass, then recruited you.

"I started causing trouble, sneaking around, spying on the Society guys. They lorded it over the rest of the Labor, driving around in their cars. God, I hated them. I started lighting fires. A real dynomaniac."

"Pyromaniac," Valentine corrected and instantly regretted it. The habits of growing up in the Padre's schoolroom, where he helped teach the grade-schoolers, died hard.

Duvalier didn't seem to mind. "Pyro-maniac. It started with the uniform of one of the Society. I swiped it while he was with Mother and torched it in a culvert. I used to watch them burn off fields when I was little, and after a fire everything was clean and new for the spring, and the bean sprouts coming up were always so bright green against the black. The uniform just started me. Ever afterwards I liked to see things go up in flames, especially if they belonged to Society. One time I burned up a police van that had a bunch of equipment in it. They hauled twelve people off to the Reaper, one every twelve hours, waiting for a confession. I knew old Mrs. Finey saw me do it, too, but she didn't turn me in. I've always wondered why not. I felt so bad about it, I told my mom. . . . I mean, people were being taken off to be killed because of something I did. My mom about died on the spot. She sat down and put her head between her knees and started crying. She had been sick a lot that year—I think now she had syphilis. She grabbed my baby brother and went to the phone—the phones worked in that part of Kansas. I figured she was going to call one of the Society guys and turn me in. I ran out of the house with just the clothes on my back.

"I lived for nearly a year on my own. I got picked up by the law once, pretty early on. An old guy and a young guy in a car." Her voice got low and monotone. "The young one convinced the older one to pull off the road so he could haul me into the woods and rape me. The old one just opened a bottle of beer and said, 'You have ten minutes.'

"He took me into the woods, I can't imagine why—I was dirty and thin, didn't look much different from a boy at that time. My boobs had shrunk from not eating to practically nothing. I had handcuffs on. He bent me over and got my pants off, then threw me down on my back. He was getting set on entering me, fumbling around with his prick, I think. I got my teeth around his Adam's apple and bit for all I was worth. Then blood was everywhere, and he was making this weird wheezy sound. He tried to get up and was drawing his gun when he tripped over his own pants. I stood up and started just kicking into him, right in the face, with my heel. He was stunned and about half bled to death, and I jumped in the air and landed with both feet right on the side of his head. His jaw broke, but he might have been dead already, I couldn't tell.

"I knew what a handcuff key looked like, but it took me forever to find it and then get it into the cuffs. I was doing everything by touch behind my back, and I was shaking so bad, I kept dropping the key. It seemed like it took hours and I kept thinking his partner was going to show up and kill me.

"I got the cuffs off finally and picked up the gun. It was a revolver with this really nice white handle and scrollwork on the barrel plating. He had probably stolen it somewhere. It had bullets in it. I sat there for five minutes, hiding in the bushes with the hammer of the gun pulled back, waiting for the partner to show up. Finally I hear him honking his horn on the car.

"I got up and left my pants off, and wiped the blood off my face mostly. I pretended I still had my handcuffs on and came running out of the woods up onto the road with my hands behind my back holding the pistol. I was screaming and crying, which wasn't too hard to do given what had just happened.

The old guy was looking at my crotch when I ran up to the car, and he said something like 'Where the hell's—' or 'What the hell's—' and I never heard the deputy's name because I shot him right in the face from three feet away. I shot him twice more just in case through the window of the car, even though his brains were all over the place.

"I got a nice leather jacket, some food, blankets, a compass, camping stuff—all kinds of things I needed from the car and the dead Society men. Guns—pistols, a shotgun and a rifle, too, but I threw the rifle away after the first day because it was so heavy to carry all the shooters and my other stuff, too. I burnt the car with them in it, which was a dumb idea because it attracted a lot of attention and I only just got away by crawling through a swamp. I knew from when I was little that there was a place in the mountains to the southeast where they didn't have to live like us, and I decided to go. I made it just as winter was setting in. A nice family named the Duvaliers took me in. They didn't know what to make of me: I talked almost nonstop. You'd think I would have been quiet, but no. The poor bastard who had to take my statement had a lot of writing to do. I had a good eye, noticed a lot of things: where there was militia, what kind of vehicles they had.

"So the next spring they had this raid planned into Leavenworth. There are all these prisons there that the Reapers use. They needed scouts and guides, and my name came up. I was young, but they put me out ahead of the column. I got pretty chummy with the other scouts; one was a Cat named Rourke. He liked what I did, and before I knew it, I was his disciple. I've been back to the Free Territory only four times in the eight years since then. Five now, if I count this time with you."

Valentine woke early with a plan. While Duvalier slept, he turned it over in his mind.

"We ride the rails," he said as they split what was left of the fresh bread for breakfast.

"Hmmm?" Duvalier said. Valentine had learned that she was something of a bedbug; it took her a while to wake up.

"Have you ever bummed a ride on a train? Not a military train, just one hauling corn or potatoes?"

"Not too often. Being on a train means pulling into train yards. They're well guarded."

"I did it in Wisconsin. It wasn't without risk, but it's doable. In fact, it seems to be a pretty common way for the people in the KZ to get from A to B. I think it's kind of winked at. But you have to be somebody."

"You mean a Quisling?"

Valentine nodded. "In this Gulag, what do the Quisling militia wear?"

She thought for a moment. "Generally they're called the Society in most of Kansas. They wear kind of a khaki police uniform with epaulet. From Nebraska on north, they're a little more anything-goes. They're generally called Marshals for basic law enforcement, but since it is a borderland, there's a military unit called the Troop. Individually, they're 'Troopers.' The Marshals wear this black uniform, usually with a tie and everything. The Troopers wear any old thing, but they almost always have old police bulletproof vests with insignia patches on them and their name stenciled across the back."

His mind gaining momentum; he put down his tin. "Okay, we go up into Nebraska and get our hands on a uniform and some papers."

"I've got a few forgeries for us. I worked on them while Welles was giving you a hard time. Or I can make them as we go. It's a talent you should learn, Valentine."

"We just pose as a couple of travelers. Better if one of us could be a Somebody, or at least military. Everyone in the KZ lives in fear of offending a big shot and winding up in the hands of a Reaper."

"Pretty nervy. I like keeping away from towns and stuff. Too easy for something to go wrong."

He turned the thought over in his mind, looking for holes. "We could pull it off, I've met a few Quislings. Having you along would add a little realism."

"How's that?" she asked.

"Anyone who is anyone in the KZ travels with a woman.

You're attractive, just the kind of pretty young thing a Quisling officer might have hanging on his arm."

"Dream on, Valentine!"

"Just a suggestion. Even if you're in uniform, too, we're just a pair, traveling to see relatives in Kansas, or an old friend in Omaha."

"Omaha ain't ours no more, Valentine. It's a ruin on the Missouri River. Hip deep in Grogs. Harpies, Tunnel-Snakes, Bigmouths—"

"Sorry, I forgot. Anyway, we can crisscross the Gulag and try to pick up the scent. Maybe your sister ran off with a Twisted Cross guy and I'm helping you look for her. Are there a lot of checkpoints—say at the Kansas–Nebraska border or something?"

"No, the Gulag runs from northern Oklahoma to the Dakotas, from the Rockies to the Missouri River. Just little princedoms, you might say, with Satan's own on the thrones. Something for bribe and barter would be handy. I've found tobacco pretty useful."

"We can pick up all the tobacco we need in Fort Springfield. They might have some whiskey that's hard to acquire in the KZ, too. Thank God we're still in Southern Command. Cash crop."

She smiled at him. "Okay, Valentine, you sold me. A-riding-the-rails we shall go. But I've got a few visits to make, so let me do the navigating once we get into the KZ."

They requisitioned feed for the horses at the Fort Springfield depot, the last post on borders of the Ozark Free Territory. Duvalier and Valentine turned in their Southern Command ID to the officer commanding; he'd hold it until they returned or a year passed, when the next-of-kin protocols would be put into effect.

Valentine found a healthy pack mule and did not even have to throw their weight as Cats to acquire the beast. The stable master handed over the pack and leads with a chuckle. "He's a damn thing. Fifty bucks says you'll be eating mule steak two days from now."

They also signed a chit for enough script to load up on

cheap cigars, cigarette makings, and rolling paper, and a few bottles of labeled liquor. Some feed for the mule and provisions for themselves went onto the mule's pack.

At Duvalier's insistence, they went out of town and traveled a half day east back into the Ozarks.

"We aren't the only spies in Missouri. Kur has eyes in every border fort we have, without a doubt," Duvalier explained.

Valentine made sure they weren't being followed, dropping off the horse behind high points in the rolling ground and letting Duvalier lead his horse while he scouted. The pair turned north after a column of patrolling Guards jumbled their tracks.

"Nice work. You're shaping up, Valentine."

"How about you just shorten it to *Val*?" he asked. "It's what most of my friends use."

"Funny you should say that. Duvalier gets shortened to *Val* a lot, too. Can't say that I want to be the Val twins, though. You can use Alice or Ali if you want."

"Okay, Ali. I'll answer to David, then."

"We'll see. Every time I say *David*, I hear Ryu in my head using that fatherly tone of his. I like *Val*. But if you want to wake me up in a hurry, use *Duvalier*. That's what old Rourke used to bark in my ear when he wanted me on my feet."

They decided that for now they would stick to Missouri, keeping to the west side of the state in the hilly region east of Kansas City. Then they would cross the Missouri River somewhere north of St. Joseph, angle into Nebraska, and start hitching rides on westbound trains around Lincoln.

They switched over to night travel while still within the nebulous borderlands of Southern Command. If they were to encounter enemies, daytime was more dangerous than night, for the Grogs that lived along the Missouri Valley preferred to fight in daylight. After a long afternoon's rest, they turned up an old road at nightfall. The mule had its own ideas about nighttime travel, and took a good deal of convincing to get it in motion. It then showed a tendency to stop at every opportunity, leaving them with the task of getting it in motion all over again.

"No wonder that stable master parted with him so fast," Valentine said.

"Maybe we can tempt him with something," Duvalier suggested, pushing on the back end while Valentine hauled away at the front. "Do we have any plums left?"

"That would work, until we ran out of plums. Then he'd never move without one."

The quest seemed to be off to a mule-stalled start when Valentine finally solved the issue with what Duvalier laughingly called the "wugga-bugga dance." The mule bit Valentine, nearly clipping off his ear, as he tried to pull it by the throatlatch. With blood running down the side of his face, he ran into the woods, returning with the better part of a poplar sapling. He yelled gibberish at the mule, thrashing pack, ground, air, and mule with the noisy branches. The leaf-shaking spectacle sent the mule trotting down the road of its own accord. Any time thereafter that the mule balked, Valentine just brandished his leafy shillelagh, imprecating against it in the glottal nonsense that worked on the recalcitrant beast. The mule put itself into high gear to get away from nasty voice and noisy leaf.

"We'd better start taking turns scouting soon," Duvalier said later, after a break for a cold meal.

"Why's that?"

She pulled down a young sugar maple bough. "Stripped clean," she said. Something had torn off the leaves and bark, leaving the thin limb as naked as a rat's tail.

"Grogs?"

"Yeah. They don't digest much of it, if you've ever looked at the droppings close."

Valentine swept the woods with ears and nose and picked up only a distant owl. "Duty in the Wolves denied me the pleasure. I've never patrolled Missouri, just passed through it a few times. More east of here, though."

"Don't know if it aids their digestion, or they just put something in their stomach to fool themselves out of being hungry. Anyway, if you see stripped branches, you can tell they pass through. The evidence hangs there a lot longer than footprints. Or droppings."

"First point goes to—"

She tweaked his nose, held up to better catch the soft nighttime breeze. "Me. God knows I can't keep that mule moving."

Mule problems aside, Valentine found he enjoyed nighttime travel. With his cat's-eye vision, the color-muted landscape looked clearer than he remembered the brightest of moonlit nights. His ears worked to their best advantage, as well; the sounds of nighttime insects carried farther, though they made a good deal less noise than their daylight counterparts. The Cats bedded down after dawn with a hot meal and dozed away the heat of the day. Even the mule grew accustomed to the routine.

They cut a few trails of Wolf patrols, but these grew more and more rare as they approached the old Kansas City–St. Louis corridor. If there was a danger point on the first leg of their journey, this was it. They took turns leading the mule, with one of the pair on point a hundred yards ahead, looking and listening, and the other guiding the mule. As Valentine peered down onto the area around the old interstate that the Grogs frequented, the mule decided to bellow into the night. He swore he'd dine on a mule steak for breakfast. Either nothing heard the animal, or whatever did hear it did not want to bother to investigate the source. In any case, they crossed the corridor without seeing anything but tire tracks and footprints.

Valentine was on point when he scented them. Three Grogs, sleeping upright back to back like Buddhist statues, rested on a thickly forested knoll.

He drew his sword and waved Duvalier forward.

"Pistols or blades?" he whispered.

"Neither."

"They're snoring."

"Of course we could kill them. But ten would come looking for them. You're good; we would probably kill those, too. But then a hundred would close in from either side."

"In the Wolves—"

"Don't ever want to hear that again. You're a Cat now, and it's all about the mission. Killing a Grog patrol has nothing to do with that."

By dawn they were miles off the corridor and pushing northwest. The land began to flatten out with the beginning of the Great Plains. They supplemented their dwindling supplies with, and fed the animals on, the wild corn and beans common to the area. They set small game snares on likely ground, two or three every morning, and it was a rare day when they could not come away with at least one animal for the stew pot. Even if it was only a wild rat.

Valentine and Duvalier began to know each other's minds. They approached abandoned buildings communicating through hand gestures and learned to rely on each other more and more as the days passed. When Duvalier spent a day in the cramped agony of dysentery—she would devour meats the new Cat wouldn't even touch—Valentine gathered a shirt full of elm bark and poured boiling water over the strips, then picked out the floating parts once it had cooled. He made her drink the infusion three times over the course of a day, and the symptoms subsided.

They released the mule and horses at the Missouri River. Valentine gave the mule its freedom with a kind of sadness; he would miss their combative companion. Like parents with a rebellious child, dealing with the bloody-minded beast together cemented the relationship between the two Cats. They left the beasts grazing in a grassy field thick with white clover-heads, shouldered their newly heavy packs, and crossed into the Gulag.

Six

Southeastern Nebraska, July: The Great Plains Gulag produces the wheat and corn of the Kurian Order. Collective farming settlements, managed under discipline that would make Stalin envious, dot the flat expanses of the Plains. Good farmland is divided into roughly fifty-mile-diameter regions from the main railheads with their towering grain elevators. At the center of the circle, like the spider in the middle of its web, is the well-guarded fortress of the local Kurian Lord. His eyes and ears and appetites are in his Reapers. The Reapers pass the Master's orders to the Marshals and Managers below them, making sure they attend to duty with the devotion expected of ones absolved from any chance of providing auric fodder for the Kurian Overlord.

The trade in this part of the country is a tragic exchange. Boxcars full of grain and corn leave the Gulag to feed the urban population elsewhere and return with a few dozen assorted captives, criminals, and disposables as payment. The Marshals then unload the unfortunates from the boxcars and route the prisoners to their doom with the knowledge that each unknown fed to the hungry Kurian Lord means one less friend or neighbor selected and sacrificed in the dead of night. Rumor has it that in Dallas, Chicago, Atlanta, and Seattle there are trading pits, run with the same frantic energy of the Old World, and devoted to buying and selling wheat, corn, soy, barley, and legumes with human lives. The trades are administered and run by the accountants and dealers for their Kurian Lords, seeking the best deal in living bodies per ton in what might be called a futures market for those who have no future.

Lincoln, formerly the capital of Nebraska, is a good example of the Kurian Order in the Gulag. The Dark Lord lives, appropriately enough, in the fourteen-story stone tower that looms over the reduced city skyline. Its solid construction, commanding view, and numerous carvings and statues appeal to the megalomaniac temperament within. Though one valuable statue from the pre-Kur days is missing: the Daniel Chester French study of a pensive, standing Lincoln. Some say that the Kur destroyed it as they did the larger, more famous seated one at the memorial in Washington, D.C., but others maintain it was spirited out of the city and now resides in one of the Western Freeholds, a hidden icon of liberty.

The people within his realm call the Kurian Lord "Number One," and nothing gets the local Quislings' attention like someone walking in a room and announcing, "Orders from Number One." Just across from the dreaded tower is the old City-County Building, now just referred to as the Hold. The local Marshals are quartered here, and the ample prison space is the last stop for those on the way to the Reapers. The city is now home to artisans and technicians in the employ of the Kurian Order, as well as being a main depot of the Troop. Their armored cars and trucks are maintained in a huge garage, once the Pershing Auditorium. The Regional Director, a Quisling in charge of the thick belts of farmland within the Kurian's realm, lives (at the pleasure of Number One) in the Colonial-Georgian governor's mansion. The house has a sad history: assassination and suicide, as well as the occasional Reaper-led housecleaning, have plagued the series of Regional Directors and their families. The suicides especially drive the Kurian to distraction—he sees it as a tragic waste of aura.

The Lincoln Lord has six Reapers. One or two are usually at the Capitol Tower serving as bodyguards and mouthpieces. Another is circulating in the city, checking up on the doings in Lincoln, and another will almost always be on tour in the farmland with a dreaded retinue of Marshals, *spreading fear wherever he goes. Finally two more hunt in the unclaimed buffer zone between the Kurian principalities, looking for threats to the realm and feeding their lord with drifters, runaways, and the occasional sleeping-on-duty Trooper.*

"Why'd it do that?" Valentine asked, peering through the empty window of the parked patrol car.

It was a ridiculous-looking vehicle, an old police cruiser on a jacked-up suspension, sitting on fat on-and-off-road performance tires and missing its trunk hood. Camouflage greens and browns replaced the old state-trooper markings.

"Haven't you ever seen a Reaper hole?" Duvalier said, looking at the grisly scene within. Bronze-colored flies clustered around a ragged wound. "They poke their tongues in right above the collarbone. Pretty good chance at hitting the heart or a big blood vessel."

"This just happened." Valentine's hair was standing on end from something other than cold river water hitting his nethers. The Reaper must have been just over the hill when they crossed.

"Lucky for us he was here." Duvalier grabbed a key ring off the body's belt. "Crap—no codes."

"But what I meant was, why would a Reaper take out one of his own militia?"

Duvalier touched the corpse. "Not quite cold. Either it was a Reaper from down Kansas way poaching—which is pretty unlikely, they might grab some farm boy but not a soldier—or the Hood caught him sleeping on the job."

"Kurian justice is efficient, I'll give them that."

"Solves one problem. You were talking about scrounging a uniform. Here's your chance."

Valentine ignored her buttocks as best as he could as she rooted in the car through the window.

"The vest you mean? We'll have to clean it. We'd also better take the whole body."

"Why, you want to give him a Christian burial?" She summoned a tongue full of spittle and let it drop on the Trooper's forehead.

"No, they're going to be a little suspicious if they find a body missing a vest and identity papers."

"Your idea. You carry him, then. Better get him over the shoulder. Rigor will be setting in," she said, putting on her claws.

"Why the metal? Think the Reaper is coming back for seconds?"

"Nope. Omaha is Grog country. We're near enough to make it look like they made off with the body."

"Would they touch a man in uniform?"

"They're kind of freebooters. I've heard that they don't take orders from the Quislings to the east or the Kurians to the west. As long as they don't interfere with the rails or roads, they do as they please. Maybe a few Harpies smelled the blood and came down for the body."

She scratched the paintwork on the roof and hood with the claws, a sound painful to Valentine's sensitive ears. She looked inside. "I'd put marks in the upholstery, but I don't think anyone would notice. Three generations of corn-fed Troopers have done their worst."

Valentine searched the car, but was disappointed at the results. A little bit of food, some tools, a pump-action shotgun, and a box of shells were the extent of the booty. He also carried a fist-sized key ring, which had a number of varicolored disks threaded on it like beads on a string. Duvalier explained that the disks served as money, useful enough in Lincoln itself but no good in another Kurian's territory. He pocketed it nevertheless. Grogs would definitely take the shotgun, for trade if nothing else, so he took it and the shells. "Not even a radio. Kind of primitive up here, huh?" he said, shouldering the body.

Duvalier erased their footprints as they moved off the road and to the west.

They weighted the body with rocks and sank it in some swampy water along the shallow river they'd been following when they came upon the car. In the distance they saw a few lights, the first they had seen since Missouri.

"We're on the outskirts of Number One's land around Lincoln. If we keep heading north, we should hit the rail line between Lincoln and Omaha. Then it's just a matter of catching the first westbound."

Dawn brought a blush to the sky, and they found some tall growth at the banks of the river to sleep away the day's heat. Duvalier believed in hiding in plain sight, so to speak, when this close to enemy territory, rather than looking for concealment under old bridges and in barns. She examined the vest and papers of the dead Trooper.

PRICE W was stenciled across the back of the body armor, and the identification card had "Price, Wesley" typed in the blank for name.

"Hmmmm. Okay, Val, how does 'West Rice' sound?"

"Like a Texas side dish. Can you do it?"

She took out a small scalpel and a bottle of ink. "O ye of little faith. Think I'll get some rest first, so I can concentrate. Wake me with some lunch at midday, Rice."

"Sure thing, Beans."

She was good to her word and spent the afternoon removing the *P* from the back of the vest, then dabbing black ink in to cover the worst parts. Valentine tried it on; the Trooper had gone to some trouble to make it more wearable by adding leather panels to the inside with a layer of cotton mesh sewn over them. It was still hot and heavy even with the side panels open all the way. Duvalier did a masterly job with the ID, right down to placing a new photo over the old complete with imprinted seal. This last she managed with the tip of a small screwdriver. After the ink dried, she folded it and had Valentine place it under his armpit for an hour. "Nothing like a good sweat stain to add some realism," she said.

"You'd think they could make these up for us before we left," Valentine said, unfolding the damp ID papers and looking at the details again to refresh his memory.

"Sensible if we were just going one place, but there are many, many different Kurian Camps just in the Gulag. A lot use different kinds of ID. We'd have to carry a whole satchel just with forged papers. We're safe enough around Lincoln, as long as we don't run into one of Price's close personal friends. If we go in the town, it should just be Marshals."

"The sword won't be suspicious?"

"You got it off a dead Grog. It was valuable, so you took it. I once saw an Oklahoma Territorial walking around with a battle-ax, God knows why. The thing must have been heavier than hell."

"You're the boss."

"I'm more worried about the gun. That big round magazine, it makes it look pretty memorable. Anything no one's ever seen before is suspicious. It makes sense to stand out a little, but not too much."

"I've got a regular clip for it. Or better yet, I could leave it unloaded."

"That would work," she said. "It's such an ugly thing, except for the stock. Looks like you put it together yourself."

They angled around the village that night, moving through fields of tall corn. Most of the houses showing lights were clustered in little groups, but an isolated farm here and there appeared to be occupied. "Not many big harvesters and combines left," she commented as they passed a tall John Deere that looked well maintained. "Most everything is done with horses again. The Kurians like having a lot of labor under them."

"Where do you figure on jumping on the train?" he asked.

"I thought you were the expert on train travel. Maybe we should stick to the Platte River—it's between Omaha and Lincoln. Follow it north until we hit a bridge, and jump a train there. They always slow down crossing a bridge—you never know when one of those resourceful long-range Wolf patrols are going to take out something like that."

When they settled down for the evening, Valentine had the first watch. He stood above the camp, wishing they could run across some Wolves. It would be good to see the beards, the hats, the sweaty buckskins again. Hear the rude jokes. Life was simpler in the Regiment: you followed orders, camped, moved, slept with the assurance of your comrades all around. He felt naked moving in the Kurian Zone without the companionship of his pack.

On the other hand, being a Cat brought independence and its concomitant responsibility. Best of all, freedom to use his judgment.

All things considered, he'd take it. Even at a price of loneliness. Of course, he'd been paying that bill since he was eleven years old.

Duvalier opened sleepy eyes. "Val, relax. I can hear you grinding your teeth all the way over here."

"Sorry."

He watched seed-laden grass bend in the soft summer breeze and tried to quit thinking, to be that breeze. The tension left his neck and shoulders.

"That's better." She rolled over onto her side.

By dawn they struck the Platte where it threw a wide loop south around Omaha before joining the Missouri. They camped in a thick patch of timber, about halfway up the slope to the crest of the river valley. Their spirits rose for a moment at the distant clatter of a train, but they realized it was eastbound when they found a vantage point allowing them to see the line of cars.

As Valentine ground some stolen ears of corn into flour in the predawn clamor of rising birds—it was Duvalier's turn to set the traps or try for a game bird with the wrist rocket they carried for small game—he suddenly felt his luck was in. They would catch a train that day, or at worst the day after. He felt confident enough to walk into the Tower in Lincoln and see what Number One was up to, for that matter. Or maybe he just looked forward to the excitement of train travel after weary weeks of walking.

Duvalier returned, bearing a pheasant. "I think it was asleep. It never knew what hit it. I probably could have just reached up and grabbed it," she said, sitting down on a rock and opening her small clasp knife. She cut the bird's throat, nearly severing its head, and bled it into her canteen cup.

"Pretty feathers, these things have," she said, beginning

to pluck it. She picked up the cup. "Blood, Val? Nice and warm. Chock-full of vitamins."

Valentine chewed dandelion leaves and young fern buds, among other things, for his vitamins. "Thanks, no. I only like it with lemon and sugar."

"Great for the eyes, my friend. But it's your choice. I can use the iron anyway." She drank it down, smacking her lips in appreciation, and continued plucking the bird. Valentine enjoyed the taste of fresh blood only in cold weather for some reason, perhaps because it reminded him of winter hunting trips with his father.

The pheasant turned out to be an old and stringy specimen, so they made soup, plucking the painfully hot joints out of the broth with their fingers and gnawing the bones clean.

"Is this breakfast or dinner, Ali?" Valentine asked, watching the sun come up.

"That's a philosophical question; I'm too tired to care, Valentine. Put the fire out and let's get some sleep."

Valentine relaxed, and she stretched on the rattan mat she rolled out to keep herself off the cold ground. He listened for trains and watched her nod off. Her angular face softened in sleep; and he decided she was altogether desirable. *You've been without a woman for a good year now,* the responsible part of him said. *Keep your hands to yourself. She's a comrade, not a lover.*

It was a three-day wait for a westbound train. Valentine hoped his lucky feeling regarding the train timing was an aberration, and the rest his premonition of good fortune would come through.

They spent the time reconnoitering the bridge region, making a few cryptic notes in Valentine's journal. You never knew what knowledge might come in handy to Southern Command. A small sentry shack stood at each end of the bridge. Only the western side post was manned during the daytime, but both had a pair of soldiers at night. The sentries were supplied by a little guardhouse at a settlement called Gretna, which marked the start of the unoccupied area leading to the

Omaha ruins. Trooper vehicles patrolled north from there on the east bank of the Platte and rolled out due west, probably as far as the Missouri River south of Omaha.

They heard the train before it appeared atop the lip of the shallow river valley.

The western side bridge post was a good spot to hop on. It would give them the added authenticity; a pair of deserters or runaways would hardly shelter somewhere run by the local Authority.

With the train still well in the distance, they approached the guard post. A single middle-aged sentry, with a functioning radio and a bicycle for his commute, stepped out of the slant-roofed little blockhouse with his shotgun in his hands. He had the hairy, crusty look of someone who spent a great deal of time in the elements.

"Howdy," Valentine said, breathing heavily as he climbed up the hill. He paused, put his hands over his knees, and faked exhaustion. "We didn't think we'd make it. I sure want to hop this train."

"Then you have a lot more running to do," the guard said, gun pointed at Valentine as he watched the pair suspiciously. "Train doesn't stop here."

"Oh, great, the difficult type," Valentine said to Duvalier, loudly enough for the sentry to hear. He looked back up at the guard. "Listen, I'm in a jam here. I just want to ride it, not blow it up. My name's Westin Rice, and this is my bride-to-be, Ali. We're getting married in two more weeks out by Grand Island, where I'm stationed, and we were here visiting my folks out by Fremont. They never met her, you see? I've been away from my unit—it should've been just the weekend, but old friends and relatives showed up, you know how it is."

"Can't say that I do," the man said, but at least he didn't move for the radio. Valentine noticed a brown stain at the side of his mouth.

"My sarge is covering for me, of course. If we can catch this freight, everything's Toyota."

"Not on my watch, kid. Don't know how you do things out there, where about all you got to guard against is prairie dogs, but here where we're staring down the wildthings in Omaha, rules mean something."

Valentine was about to reach into his pocket for some cigars when Duvalier unexpectedly burst into tears. "Th-th-there goes your promotion, or w-w-worse," she sobbed. Valentine looked almost as startled as the sentry. She sank to her knees, pouring tears into palms clasped against her face. "Your mom b-b-being so n-n-nice an' all, and giving me her mother's wedding ring. Wh-wh-what're we gonna do?" she blubbered, staring up at him with tear-strained eyes.

Valentine picked her up. "Don't worry, hon, I'll figure something out. Don't I always?"

"Look, er—you two," the man said, rubbing the back of his neck. "Hop the damn freight. But if anything happens, I was taking a break in the bushes, you follow me? You never even got a good look at me, I was too far away."

Valentine pulled out a cigar. "Thank you, sir. My pa gave me these. He has a connection over in Cedar Rapids with those rich big shots across the river. They're for the groomsmen, but I want you to have one."

"Save it for the groomsmen, then. No, I won't take it, and that's final. Just take my advice, and don't do stuff like this. The way I got to be this age, pulling easy duty, is by not bending the rules. Get me, you two?"

The train started down the opposite bank of the Platte and rolled onto the bridge.

"We get you—thank you, sir!" Duvalier said, kissing him on the cheek as they hurried past him. "Sometimes the rougher they are on the outside, the more tender on the inside," she added sotto voce as they took positions alongside the tracks. "It's the ones who just seem not to give a damn one way or the other who make me worried."

Valentine took a good look at the train. It burned oil, judging from the blue fumes emerging from the engine. Behind the engine came the main guard car: a mountain of sandbags and a tripod-mounted machine gun. Behind the guards was a pair of passenger cars followed by the freight and tanker cars. A caboose, looking like it was modified from an old observatory car, brought up the rear. Most of its windows were missing.

Valentine and Duvalier ran for the little balcony welded onto the rear of the armored caboose. A bored-looking guard started to wave, then stared at them as they dashed to catch the train. They both leapt up onto the platform and grabbed railing.

"Help her over, dammit!" Valentine said to the paralyzed soldier, who complied.

Valentine swung his legs over the rail. "Good arrangement here," he said casually as a sergeant appeared with an infuriated look on his face. "If there's one thing I hate, it's riding on top of a boxcar. Can't even roll a cigarette, you know?" he said, carefully taking out a paper and a pouch of makings.

"Look, Trooper, I dunno what you two think you're . . . Hey now, is that the real thing?" the sergeant asked, looking at the aromatic brown shreds going into the cigarette.

"Real Tennessee Valley Tobacco, or so they tell me."

"You wouldn't be able to spare a puff? Haven't had a real cig in a week, just chew that's half sawdust. Bastard Chicago clip-joints."

"The Zoo, eh?" Valentine said with a knowing wink. "Only thing I ever came home with from there I needed gunpowder to cure, you know? I'll do better than a puff or two—you can have the whole thing, how's that? Can never have too many friends in the New Federal Railways, you know?"

"This train is Consolidated Overland. Federal has the gray uniforms with the black epaulet. We've got patches."

Valentine looked over at Duvalier, who appeared to be making herself agreeable to the sentry who helped her over the rail.

"Stopping in Lincoln, right?"

"Of course, and then on west. End of the line is Mc-Cook."

"Passing near Grand Island?"

"Err, Grand Island . . . I don't know the Plains that well, beyond our route. Let's see the map." They went inside the caboose. Only one more soldier was on duty there, looking forward from the observation platform. The sergeant checked at a map pinned to the wall. "Okay, yes. We stop in Hastings, that's just south of Grand Island. What's in Grand Island?"

"Our wedding. I'm bringing her back from meeting my folks. My unit and her family are up there."

"You two are carrying a lot of iron for just visiting relatives," the sergeant observed.

"I have to have my piece, Sergeant. Regulations. But even if that weren't the case, you can't be too careful near Omaha, sir," Valentine said. "Ali got us a pheasant the other day, too. She shoots well for a civilian."

"You could get in a lot of trouble back east letting a civilian carry a gun, even if it is yours, West. But hell, this calls for a drink, celebrate you two taking the bonds," the sergeant said, but the guard chatting with Duvalier looked disappointed.

Valentine grinned. "Yes, it does, and I'm buying. If you'll bend regs for a shot."

"If we took duty that seriously, you wouldn't be here, Trooper."

Valentine took out a bottle of whiskey, and three glasses appeared as if conjured out of wind and dust. He poured everyone two fingers' worth and faked a swallow from the bottle himself.

"Be sure to save enough for the wedding toast, baby," Duvalier said. "Your dad went through some trouble to get that."

"Have pity, miss," one of the guards said. "Awfully hard for a man to walk around with quality likker like this without having a sip now and then."

The rest of the journey passed in a much more convivial atmosphere. They discussed various kinds of duties, comparing being in the Troopers in Nebraska with guarding trains. In the process, Valentine and Duvalier learned a good deal about railroad routine. A second round of drinks, with formal toasts for the would-be newlyweds, cemented the temporary friendship. Unfortunately for Valentine's sense of satisfaction with the day's events, they learned what two of the boxcars held.

"Food for *them*. You know what I mean," the sergeant confided. "Twenty in each car this run, but we've crammed in as many as sixty. Half getting off in Lincoln. Glad it ain't our job to clean the cars out afterwards. We're just making sure they don't break out. They're chained up in there like dogs in kennels, but you never can tell."

"How long is the stop in Lincoln?" Valentine asked, desperate to change the subject.

"Four hours. We'll get some sleep. But don't worry, West. Some nosy-new comes checking in here, you two can hide in the john. We'll get you back to your sergeant and your wedding on time."

"Four hours?" Duvalier said, unusually enthusiastic. "I can do me some shopping in Lincoln. You know they have a real shoe store in town, Sergeant?"

"Knock me over with a feather, miss," the sergeant said. He winked with the eye on the side of his face turned toward Valentine. "I was really hoping to pass the time with a deck of cards and your fiancé here, though."

"Oh, he doesn't have to come with. Shopping bores him to death. Honey, can I please have some of the money Uncle Max gave you?"

"Money?"

Duvalier glared at him. "You aren't playing tricks on me now, are you, Westin? Uncle Max, I saw him give it to you through the window of his patrol car. The one you said looked dumb, all jacked up."

Valentine reached into his pack. "I guess I can't fool you. Here, but don't spend all of it, okay? It's supposed to be saved for starting us off." He passed her the ring of money.

The three Overland guards exchanged half sneers. One made a tiny motion with his wrist that might imply a whip being cracked.

The train pulled into Lincoln Yard for unloading, and Valentine dived into the card game to avoid looking at the doomed souls being unloaded. As long as he didn't see the faces, he would be fine. He started a game of gin with the soldier who had to stay on duty in the caboose, while the sergeant and the other guard left to lend a hand at the off-loading.

Duvalier gave him a peck on the cheek and disappeared into town, leaving her pack in Valentine's care and twirling the ring of coins as she went.

"Hooo . . . welcome to married life," said the sergeant, returning to the caboose as Duvalier left.

"You married, Sarge?" Valentine asked, trying his best to let the other sentry win a cigarette off him at gin.

"Is he married? You might just say that!" Valentine's partner said. "What are you up to now, Sarge, four?"

"Seattle, St. Paul, Chicago, and Atlanta," the sergeant said, leering at Valentine. "Each one waiting for the next run that will allow me to return to hearth and home. Travel has its advantages, Trooper."

"You don't say," Valentine said, picking up and laying down a card. "How do I get into this outfit?"

"I could put in a good word. You could write Capt. Caleb Mulroon, care of Overland Consolidated in Chicago. That is, if you think you could get out of your present post with no hard feelings."

"Gin!" said the sentry, laying down his cards and picking up the cigarette ante.

"I think I can make the Troopers happy to be rid of me," Valentine said, passing his cards across to be shuffled.

Four pairs of eyes widened when Duvalier returned later. Her appearance wrecked a perfectly good game of poker.

The transformation was nothing short of incredible. She had changed from slightly grubby scarecrow to head-, neck-, and shoulder-turner in the space of the afternoon. Her short red hair was now in carefully arranged, slightly curly disarray. She wore a midriff-revealing, sleeveless jeans jacket unbuttoned to a hint of lacy red bra and more than a hint of cleavage. Short shorts hugged assorted curves where they didn't reveal long, athletic legs ending in white canvas rubber-soled shoes. Her lips matched the fire in her hair, and her eyelashes seemed longer and thicker. Valentine was not used to makeup, especially not on Duvalier.

"Better, sweetie? Hardly spent any money at all."

"You are a lucky son of a bitch, West," one of the Overland guards said.

Valentine got up and took her hands in his. "Much better. That's the Ali I dream about at night." He gave her a hug and experimentally patted her on her backside as he planted a kiss on her ear.

"Now, now, Westin, can't have these men thinking you're a *pig*," she said, locking her eyes on his. "Don't let's get carried away now—we still have a lot of traveling to do before we're home safe."

The miles rattled off pleasantly until Duvalier killed the Overland guards.

She had been napping in one of the little bunks set atop the caboose's wooden storage cabinets. It had tiny rails to keep her from rolling out.

As evening fell, the card game had died off, and Valentine put some clothing in to soak in a soapy basin, getting in a badly needed laundry between stops. One Overland guard kept watch from what the sergeant called the "catbird seat," a cupola high at the train-side end of the caboose, and the sergeant retired to the bunk opposite Duvalier.

The other guard, suspenders dangling and in a sweat-yellowed tank top, kept up a pretext of conversation with the man on top as he eyed the sleeping Cat from an angle that allowed the best view down her décolletage. Valentine heard her stir as he wrung out a pair of socks, and she looked up in alarm at the presence looming over her.

"Ever think about trading up?" the guard asked, touching her hair before sending his fingers walking down her shoulder and across the exposed top half of her freckled breast.

Duvalier locked on the guard's eyes and wrist at the same time. Valentine felt a horrid trill of danger from some inner alarm as she pulled the exploratory hand down under the sheet and between her thighs. "I thought so . . . ," the guard said, giving Valentine a wink across the rocking caboose interior.

She clamped his hand there.

The knife came up fast—so fast, the guard never saw it. He let out a surprised cough, gaping at the handle sprouting from his armpit. Duvalier rolled out of the bunk, walking stick ready.

Valentine smelled blood. His pack and weapons were in a locker at the other side of the room. He grabbed the washbowl. He needed something—anything—in his hand.

Duvalier thrust with her stick just as her would-be lover opened his mouth. She caught him solidly below the breastbone; the yell for help died into a gasp of a contracting diaphragm. He grabbed at the weapon, and Duvalier left him holding the empty scabbard as she drew twenty inches of naked blade.

She became a blur. To Valentine, it was like trying to watch a hummingbird.

"Hol-huh?" the waking sergeant asked just before she stabbed him up and under the chin. The guard in the catbird seat brought down his rifle. Not knowing what else to do, Valentine threw his bucketful of water and laundry in his direction.

The splash of water brought the man with the blade in his armpit out of his shock. He dropped Duvalier's scabbard and pulled the bloody-handled blade out of his armpit. Duvalier danced out of the way of the arterial spray and spun to slash up at the legs of the seated guard. At one time or another, Valentine had heard the expression "cut off at the knees." Now he saw it in practice.

Blood pouring from under his arm, the guard made one half-swipe at Duvalier with her knife before he sank to the floor, face calm and beatific as though relaxing into sleep.

Tchick-BANG went the guard's rifle and splinters flew and Duvalier stabbed up and up through the seat and the blood came down as though from a broken pipe and the rifle fell on the man bleeding to death on the floor. *BANG*—Valentine ducked as the rifle fired again as it landed and Duvalier pulled the mutilated guard out of his seat and threw him to the floor and jumped on his back and pounded his face again and again into the bloody floorboards until broken teeth lay like dropped candy and clear fluid ran out and the screams ended.

Valentine pulled her off the guard.

"Damn them all," she said, leaving a bloody smear as she wiped her nose with a trembling hand.

"What was that?" Valentine asked.

"A helluva killing." She moved some of the spilled laundry out of the way of the blood. The thirsty wood could absorb only so much. She smiled and planted a bloody kiss on his lips. "Good work with the water."

"Are you insane?"

"Maybe. We have to beat the heat. Let's jump off."

"Just a minute." Valentine couldn't leave it at that. If they set the caboose on fire and fled, there'd be a pursuit as soon as the engineers radioed for help. They had to make the deaths look plausible, sow a few doubts for when the train pulled in at the next stop to drop off people and take on corn and cattle.

As Duvalier gathered their gear, plus wet laundry, and rooted for supplies, Valentine put the sergeant and the half-dressed guard among spilled cards and whiskey on the floor, bloody utility knives in their hands. The guard who had been on duty they set out on the open rear galley for the moment, until they were ready to jump off. As the train slowed at the top of a gentle slope, they threw dead man, their packs, and themselves off. After the train disappeared into the night, Valentine concentrated on making it look like the wounded guard had somehow got caught under the train and succumbed to blood loss at the side of the tracks.

Duvalier removed traces of their presence from around the body. He watched her, greenish gray to his night-widened eyes.

Only after they were well off the rail line and moving south in Nebraska incognita did he vent. They cut across ancient fields, now returned to the prairie plants and insects.

"I thought we were 'all about the mission'?"

She let out an exasperated breath. "I don't like being pawed."

"You could have said something."

"You ever been attacked? You know . . . for sex?"

"You led him on."

"I woke up, and there's a soldier with a hand on my boob. Maybe they had a gun on you. I didn't think, I reacted. Panic."

"So you just lost it?"

"Something like that."

"And when a posse comes?"

"Posse? Val, we killed some Overland rail guards. It's Overland's problem. You think the local Kurian is going to round up a bunch of men to search deserted silos? Hell no—he's got better things to do. At most, Overland will bitch to whoever's running the show here, and something will get negotiated. Meanwhile that sergeant's wives are going to be in for a surprise when they try to claim pension."

"This negotiation—it'll probably involve some aura changing hands, you think? It's the only thing Kur values."

She reached up and slapped a fly out of the air. "Not necessarily. Could be just corn."

"Hope it was worth it."

They took another twenty paces in silence.

He thought he heard a sniffle. "You want to talk abou—?"

"No!"

They caught a road at dawn, and Valentine stopped and unrolled a map. As they tried to guess their whereabouts, she was as calm as though they'd spent the last few hours berry-picking. Valentine couldn't help thinking that she'd killed the three Overland men for touching an old wound. A woman like Duvalier might attract male attention anywhere they went. A reaction like that in the wrong place—

His mind went back to when he had first met her. The shapeless old coat, the dirt, the half-starved flesh. Was she at war with her own looks, as well as Kur? He wondered if he was chasing the Twisted Cross under the guidance of a woman who was, to use Bone Lombard's phrase, of "disordered mind."

He couldn't think that. He'd lose hope. She'd just reacted. She wasn't disordered. Disordered wouldn't find the General and then get them home again safe.

Duvalier found them a little town the next day, and they walked in with a tale of stolen horses. They didn't get so much as a suspicious glance when they said they had business south. There was a truck loading for a southbound trip to Manhattan, Kansas; the driver was making notes as townspeople listed their needs. The Cats needed a quick ride, so they entered Kansas in the back of a diesel truck baby-sitting a load of eggs.

The driver was glad to have them. If there was anything besides eggs in the back—for instance, black market clothing or jewelry, the driver hinted—it might be a good idea to have a uniformed Trooper visible riding shotgun.

Duvalier had a contact near the truck's destination.

"Who?" Valentine asked as Duvalier did everything but lick her lips in anticipation.

"A friend."

She described her contact as they rattled south in the back of the carbon-spewing truck, which due to some idiosyncrasy in its suspension shimmied side to side like a duck shaking its tail feathers.

"Roland Victor is an odd sort of black marketeer. Lots of contacts in the Militia; Roland's so well connected, he might as well be part of their logistics support."

Valentine didn't hear her refer to other men by their first names.

"He deals in items appealing to Kansas Society's women, but ninety percent of his clientele is men. He's also something of a loan shark. I think every Militia officer above the rank of lieutenant owes him money or a favor. He gets clothes, jewelry, wines, chocolates, teas, and almost any kind of luxury you can think of, little favors that powerful men like to give to their whores after giving the wife a new apron for her birthday. He's not the sort of man you invite to your daughter's wedding, but when you and your brother officers are planning a binge, he's the one to see for a case of Canadian whiskey. You wouldn't think wealth meant anything anymore, but it does to Roland."

"Know him well, do you?"

"He has very good manners, and he has a lot of—what's the word, style?—no, call it class. He plays he's a baron and looks the part. You're going to have to see him to believe it."

"I suppose he knows better than to paw at you."

Her eyes pleaded with him as much as her voice. "Drop it, Val. Please? I'm sorry about back there in the train, okay. Cross my heart."

"We got away. I'm ready to forget it."

"Start trusting me again. You've been all stiff and watchful lately."

"I don't mean to be. Sorry."

"Buddies, you know? Like before?" She held out her hand, turning her palm up so he could see the scar she'd made at his Cat invocation.

He shook it, their common wounds touching. But it was still hard to meet her eyes. He'd found a soft spot in a woman he'd come to respect as he respected only a handful of other teachers in his life: the Padre, Eveready, Captain LeHavre. He relied on her, and up until the incident on the train, would have gladly followed her into any danger.

He sneered at himself: Who was he to judge? Had he always made the perfect decisions?

The Kurians would have relished the moment. Sworn allies suspicious of each other despite the danger all around. They would have gladly sacrificed the Overland guards to set a pair of Cats against each other. He had to quit letting his sensibilities do the enemy's work for them.

By the time they reached Manhattan, Valentine knew as much about Roland Victor's operation as Duvalier did. She explained that his couriers always showed a *V* somehow when in public. For example, the driver of the truck they had swayed southward on had a pocketknife open in a

V shape resting on his dashboard. Victor had his own network, which extended to Canada, the Mississippi, and down into Mexico—a web of friends of friends of friends who specialized in the underground trade the Kurians didn't bother to suppress, as long as it was furs instead of firearms.

The driver had his own legitimate market to visit at a Militia camp, so they had to travel on foot the last few miles. They walked through the empty husk of learning that once was Kansas State University. They saw crates being taken out of a from a three-story hall, with new bars on the tall windows, but most were burned-out shells.

"Just warehouses now," Duvalier explained as Valentine instinctively counted trucks and guards.

She turned them up a road, the asphalt as black and smooth as molasses.

Valentine marveled at Victor's well-tended grounds on the shores of Lake Milford. The smuggler made no attempt to hide the fruits of his luxury-goods labor. Clipped lawns, statues, neatly trimmed trees, decorative gardens, flower beds, and shrubs arranged to form secluded grottoes were a new experience to Valentine. He found himself estimating how many potatoes could be grown on the front lawn before him.

The sturdy pinkish-gray brick house seemed built to flaunt its ostentatiously oversize door. Val wondered if guests dismounted outside or rode their horses into the entryway.

"We'll go around the back. He uses the front door for Society. He has a smaller door to his office for business."

Roland Victor greeted them after a discreet tap from Duvalier on the plain wooden door. He already had company in the form of a sawed-off-looking man in a leather cap. Or perhaps Victor's companion just looked small in comparison with the big, bluff smuggler. Victor had the hearty, meaty features of a beer-and-beef diet, concealed to advantage by a well-fitted suit. Valentine had seen only a half-dozen suits in his entire life, and never one with a starched shirt underneath.

Victor's square face, framed by thick black sideburns and an equally bristly mane, broke out in a welcoming smile. "Ahh, out-of-town guests. From Nebraska, judging from the uniform, Trooper. Please, come in and don't worry about the boots. Can this be my dear Dee? It's been too long." He turned to his current guest. "I'm sorry, Mr. H, but we'll have to cut our pleasant afternoon short. Can I look forward to the pleasure of your company when you get back from your commission?"

"Gladly, Mr. Victor," the man said, aping Victor's pleasantries if not his educated accent. "I'll be sure to stop by directly."

Victor escorted his courier to the door. Mr. H was slightly hunchbacked, and seeing the two of them move toward the door together made Valentine think of an entertainer with a trained monkey he had glimpsed during his time in Chicago.

The smuggler returned to his new guests. Duvalier introduced Valentine as simply *David,* and Victor shook his hand and gripped him by the upper arm as he did so. From another man his size, the gesture might be intimidating, if not overpowering, but from Victor it conveyed only bonhomie. "Coffee? Something to drink?" he asked, moving to a mirrored liquor cabinet.

Valentine and Duvalier accepted Victor's coffee with appropriate *oohs* and *ahhs* at its aroma, and sat. At the first taste, Valentine's eyes widened in pleasure; the coffee had a rich, smoked chocolate taste and a stimulating kick. He watched Victor pour something from a crystal decanter into his own coffee and looked around the room. Victor had a fondness for statues, mostly blackened bronze interpretations of cowboys, riding like fury with horse, lariat, and gun. Valentine looked at the label. He'd never known the old Remington gun company made art, as well.

"Now what can I do for you children?" Victor asked, taking a sip of his Irish coffee, hardly enough to wet his lips.

"Information," Duvalier said. "We're hunting something. Or someone."

Victor leaned forward in his leather chair, which silently

bore the shift in his respectable weight. He braced his massive head on a bipod created by his forearms, chin resting on the back of his right hand. "Yes? I shouldn't wonder the hunt isn't going well, if you don't know whether you're hunting a *who* or a *what*."

Duvalier took a breath. "That's because it's a little bit of both. The *what* is some kind of new military organization the Kurians set up. Their banner is sort of like the old swastika one from the twentieth century. Only backwards. The who is a man. We don't know his name; he goes by the rank of General. 'The General,' his people seem to call him."

"How do they get around, truck or train?"

"We know they use trains," she answered, "disguised to look like ordinary freight cars. The last solid information we have is that they were in Oklahoma in March. Headed north, we believe. No information on trucks."

"Hmmm, I've not heard anything about a 'General' from the Kansas Society. You never learned where they were going?"

"No," Valentine chipped in, wishing to contribute to the conversation.

"How large? Do they have enough men and equipment to make a try to conquer, say, Denver?"

Duvalier shrugged. "We just don't know. It can't be too large an army. Anything bigger than a couple of regiments, and some of the other Cats would have picked it up and brought it to Southern Command's attention."

Victor's jaw worked as he stared at the ceiling in thought. "I know there's a new line being driven west into Colorado. First new construction in that direction I've heard about in ages; our venerable Masters don't go in for civic improvement. You do know that they're also putting in new lines on your western border, right?"

"We've had some word. Southern Command isn't taking it seriously," Valentine said. "They think it's just another rail corridor to make defending the border easier."

Victor brushed out his sideburns with the backs of his hands. "I wouldn't be seen around where they are building.

They'll either shoot on sight or impress you. Best case is you'll be cutting embankments and driving spikes for a daily issue of corn bread for what's left of your future. But you could ask my man out there. I've got an agent that does an occasional run into the Denver Zone. He sometimes comes back with word of what's going on in the mountains."

Duvalier brightened. "How do we get there?"

"I'll put in a word with the East-West Line Chief, and that'll get you as far as the high plains. I'd recommend horses once you're out there. I'll give you a letter of introduction to Cortez. He'll get you supplies and mounts if you want to head west from there. He might even agree to guide you."

A gentle knock at the back door announced the arrival of another visitor.

"It never rains; it just pours," Victor quoted. "Last week I sat and twiddled my thumbs, but today you're my fourth caller. You will stay the night, of course."

Victor told his visitor that he would be just a few minutes, and introduced the Cats to a combed, pressed, and manicured servant named Iban. He charged Iban with preparing meals and bedrooms for the pair, and returned to the door to greet his latest arrival, a dust-covered man with a hat so wide it was just short of a sombrero.

The well-tended rooms, rugs, and furnishings made Valentine long for a bath more than for a meal. Iban somehow telepathically picked up on his desire and suggested, "If you want to wash up before you eat, there is fresh soap and towels in the first-floor bathroom."

"Dibs," Duvalier said quickly. "Victor's bathrooms are incredible. Hot running water at the twist of a knob, and a razor so sharp, you can shave with its shadow."

"Prove it. What are you going to shave, anyway? I'd like to watch."

"Oh fu— Dream on, Valentine."

Valentine plunged into the prewarmed tub after a quick washup in the sink, fearing he'd leave a ring like a moon crater if he dipped immediately into the steaming water. The servant had poured some sort of scented oil in the tub; it smelled vaguely of cedar. Valentine lathered and shaved with a small hand mirror placed in a tub caddy, lingering over the rasping strokes and enjoying himself immensely.

Iban discreetly knocked and entered, taking Valentine's dirt-encrusted clothing and replacing it with a heavy cotton garment, a thin robe the servant called a *kimono*. Valentine lingered in the tub, then finally rose and put on the wheat-colored wrap. His hiking boots had disappeared, as well, and as the efficient Iban had not replaced them with anything, even socks, he left the bathroom barefoot to find Duvalier wolfing a fruit salad in an airy corner room. French windows let in the warm afternoon air.

"Quite a place," Valentine commented, feeling the rich texture of the draperies as he parted them to take in the lawn and sky.

"Quite a person," Duvalier countered.

"I didn't know they still made fabric like this."

"Probably just well preserved," she said. "Every time I'm here, it makes me think of stories I heard of the Old World. It's like a museum or something."

"Some of the higher-ups in the Kurians' favor live like this, I'm told," Valentine said. "You sure he's not one of them? How does he get away with it?"

She paused to finish a forkful. "He doesn't fight the system. He provides things the Society wants, and that the Kurians can't be troubled to deal with. The nearest Kurian is seventy miles away. The Quisling who runs Manhattan has a brass ring, but all he knows is a lot of shiftless types come around this house. I've heard of Reapers visiting the area, and I know the Milita searched his house and buildings. No guns, no problem. The Kurians don't seem to realize that wealth and influence can be a weapon, maybe a better weapon than a battery of howitzers. He uses that wealth now and then to help us. Or Denver, I suppose."

"What does he ask in return?"

"That's the funny part. Nothing."

* * *

They rested for two glorious nights on clean sheets, groaning from stuffing themselves at Victor's table. Rack of lamb, roast beef, and delicate baked rolls that fell into buttery quarters left them torpid, barely able to make conversation. Their host asked no questions beyond pleasant inquiries about after-dinner drinks.

After a hearty breakfast of pork chops and fried potatoes, Victor saw them off with the dawn. Wearing cleaned clothes and bearing Victor's letters of introduction, they shouldered their refilled packs bulging with canned food and hearty biscuits, and thanked their host.

"I hope it puts you back on track," Victor said. "The length of Kansas is a long way to go on a wild-goose chase."

Valentine said, "We'll be riding most of the way. You've made it a quick trip."

"I'm a little worried about those guns. Nebraska Trooper's uniform or not, somebody might decide you shouldn't be carrying weapons. They'll be taken for 'safekeeping,' and you'll never see them again. The Line Chief will give you passports, but his stamp won't help much in that case."

Iban produced a small, two-wheeled basket cart.

"On the road you can pull it," Victor said, "and if you can't use the wheels, you can carry it between you. Negotiables. The usual assortment: tobacco, alcohol, watches, pens, and good paper. I've put in some real gold coins and some fake pearls that are very good. Optics are popular with the soldiers: you have two binoculars, a spotting scope, and two spyglasses. Once you get rid of those, it'll be a lot lighter. Always better to bribe your way out than fight your way out."

"Amen," Duvalier agreed.

"If you have to, use my name as an IOU with anyone in my network, but please use discretion. If you're caught burning down a police station, Dee, my name won't help you and will only hurt me."

"Thank you. We're worth your trust, sir," Valentine said.

"Then go out and prove it. I hope you'll have another

Kurian notch in your scabbard the next time I see you, Dee."

"Seems to me you're doing pretty well for yourself under them," Valentine said. He just as quickly regretted it.

"Val!" Duvalier said.

"It's okay, Dee." Victor looked at his nails, bitten to the quick. "Am I well? You try living your life smiling and dancing at parties and picnics and weddings of people you despise, boy. Cheering at Militia games where the teams are made up of murderers who keep their one sorry life in exchange for hundreds of their fellows. I've got a chronic ulcer, and my doctor says my liver is going to throw in the towel."

He seemed to sag, ruddy skin now almost purulent. "It's not as easy a life as you think. I only hope my liver gives me enough warning so I can go to the Governer's New Year's Ball wearing an explosive belt."

Valentine felt his face go hot. "I'm sorry. I should be grateful. Not my place to criticize unless I'm in your shoes."

"Live and learn. Emphasis on *live*."

Seven

The High Plains of Eastern Colorado, August: A better name for this upland might be the Dry Plains, as running water is scarce much of the year. The pumps and sprinklers that fed circular patches of crops, which had dotted the flats like some giant variety of lily pad, are now nothing but rusting empty skeletons and dry as marrowless bone. A little more rainfall, and the high plains would be a lush paradise: the sun shines three hundred days a year, and the winters are comparatively mild.

Perhaps it is the sun that keeps the Kur away, or just the lack of sustainable population for their feeding. The inhabitants of Denver and the Eastern Slope might also have something to do with it. Their outpost garrisons scattered in this empty land imitate the forts of the Old West, with wooden walls high enough to prevent a Reaper's leaping over them.

The few souls living in this expanse hide their paths and habits from both the vigorous Denver Freehold in the West and the Kurians to the East. The Denverites have been known to "relocate to safety" anyone found on their borders, confiscating property too large to move at the point of a gun. As for the Kurians, it is the old story. Any group larger than a family is too hard to feed, and too big a risk of becoming a lifesign lure for a roaming Reaper.

So only the occasional house is inhabited, though the isolation can be as hard to live under as the Kurian avatars.

*   *   *

Valentine did not know whether to call it a sod house or a cave. The House of Cortez had none of the scope and glitter its conquering namesake inspired. The front of the structure protruded from the side of a grassy hill, as if it had been fired from a gigantic cannon and embedded there. An overhang sheltered the wide porch, with rough wooden trunks holding up the dirt-and-grass-covered roof. Flowers in hanging baskets and planters added a splash of color to the weather-beaten wood and straw-colored grasses covering the hillside and the crown of the house.

They drew near the house to a crescendo of barking. Valentine guessed three dogs, and he and Duvalier approached empty-handed.

"At least we know we have the right house. We haven't seen another one for five miles," Duvalier said.

"I've got a gun," a female but not very feminine voice called from the shadows of the house. "You're welcome to water from the pump, but there's no food or roof here for strangers."

"We're here to speak to Tommy Cortez," Valentine called over the barking.

"No one here by that name. You're lost, sounds like."

"We have some messages from Mr. Victor. We got the directions from him."

The unseen figure contemplated the news for a moment, and even the dogs went silent. "My husband's not home. Your business is with him. If you want to wait, just tell me where you'll be, and I'll tell him when he returns."

"Ma'am," Duvalier said, "we've come clear across Kansas, and we're heading farther west. We've lugged this case all the way from the railhead, hoping for some help when we got here. Food and horses, in other words."

"Horses? You see a barn here?"

Valentine put a restraining hand on Duvalier's shoulder.

"Mrs. Cortez, we're here to help if we can. Is your husband missing?"

Valentine felt the hard casing of the unseen woman's manner break inside the shadowy interior. "Three weeks and two days," a much smaller voice said from the shadows. The door opened, and a short raisin of a woman in a denim smock stepped out onto the porch, gripping a rabbit gun. Years of dusty Colorado summers were written on her face in vertical lines. "Never been gone this long. I'm about out of my head with worry. It wasn't even much of a trip, just up to Fort Rowling."

They ate a meal of corn bread and drippings and drank prairie tea under the low ceiling of the Cortez home. Like a rabbit warren built for humans, the house behind the half-buried facade was a series of rooms and passages, mostly filled with cobwebbed relics as a sort of indoor junkyard. A generator chattered away; judging from the piping, it burned local natural gas to light and ventilate the house. The musty smell was offset, to Valentine's mind, by the welcoming, earth-insulated coolness of the interior after the hot August sun.

"My husband brought me out of Garden City, Kansas, almost thirty years ago, now," Mrs. Cortez explained while moving about the tiny kitchen. She had grown garrulous after letting them in. "He always was a traveler. Tall and handsome, he was. Still is, even with the mileage. Just his size made most of the varmints in Kansas avoid him. He made money getting messages into Denver, New Mexico, wherever. The New Order had just got itself worked out by then, everything all organized to suit them. After years of fighting and starvation, lots of folks were happy to stay put where they were told and do what was ordered. But I saw there was no future in it, and when Tommy asked me to go, I went. He had found this place in the middle of a whole lotta nowhere and had been slowly fixing it up. We were happier than we had a right to be, considering what was going on beyond the horizon." She removed a pistol from her apron and sat down to her own meal.

"It's always been just the two of you?" Duvalier asked.

"Yes, we couldn't have children. Something wrong with one of us, I expect, but no way of knowing these days. Not that we failed on account of trying," she said, a shy smile creeping across her face. "There was Karl, an orphan boy

Tommy picked up on one of his trips. He stayed with us about three years, but moved on to Denver when he was seventeen. Nobody around here—he was lonely, poor boy. Or I should say nobody around here worth knowing. These lands get all sorts of trash passing through, and I'm not as brave as I once was. I get scared if I'm left alone. That's why we've got the dogs."

The curs in question snored in a companionable heap on an old sofa. They sported the curled tails and short-haired, irregular coloring of mongrels, and as soon as their mistress had dropped her suspicions, they turned into a tail-wagging, tongue-lolling trio of family pets.

Valentine cleared the table and worked the pump in the sink. As he washed the dishes, he noticed a half-folded note on the counter. Making sure that his body blocked him from the table, he dried a finger and turned it open.

> *To Who Finds This Note:*
>   *The house and all in it are yours. Tom's been gone these days and I must find him. I can't stay alone in this house no more or I'll be a suicide God forgive me the nights are too much and I don't sleep with him away. I will find him or . . .*

Valentine folded it closed again. "I'm sorry he's overdue. Bad for us—we were hoping he could serve as a guide to this part of Colorado. But of course that's not important compared to you."

Mrs. Cortez brightened. "I used to know the land between here and Denver real well. In the years since, I've changed but the hills haven't. With you two along, I'd feel safer following the trail to Fort Rowling. And yes, we do have horses. The stable's just hid; it's in an old foundation you'd think was just a collapsed house unless you got within spitting distance. There'll be news of him there. Whether he's there or not, you can pick up a guide. Good place to hear news, too, if that's what you're after."

"Sounds like the best plan for all of us," Valentine said.

*   *   *

Valentine enjoyed riding the dry, lonely country. The horses, tough mustangs with muscles of steel and adamantine determination to accomplish whatever the rider asked, whether bearing packs or saddles, were in better condition than most horses he had known. The three dogs added an air of a picnic to the trip, for they explored the countryside with such canine joie de vive that the accompanying humans could not help sharing in their high spirits. They were out of the KZ, no checkpoints to dodge, watchful eyes of the residents no longer on them. Finding water was the only problem, but between their guide's memory and Valentine's nose, they went from waterhole to waterhole without too much searching.

The nights passed a little more nervously. There might be slim pickings for any Reapers wandering away from Kansas, but human lifesign in such an empty land would show up all the brighter on a Hood's psychic radar. Mrs. Cortez must have thought the Cats a quiet couple. Valentine and Duvalier sat at the tiny, shielded campfires, in a lifesign-lowering trance that had many of the benefits of sleep. Her small talk continued despite her unresponsive companions until she drifted off to sleep.

Then came glorious dawns. The horizon always seemed a little higher than the observer. To Valentine, it felt as if he were in a vast shallow arena, with only high, wispy stratus clouds watching their performance.

They were a matter of "a few more hours'" ride from Fort Rowling when the dogs alerted. All three narrow snouts pointed northwest at the same moment, ears cocked to attention. Valentine's ears picked up the sound of vehicles.

"Motors. Maybe two," Valentine said, and Duvalier nodded agreement.

"It's most likely Denver soldiery, but we might want to get under cover anyway," Mrs. Cortez said, sliding off her saddle. "Guess my ears aren't what they used to be."

They took cover in the lee of a horseshoe-shaped hill among a spread of scraggly oneseed junipers. Mrs. Cortez held the horses, which took the opportunity to nose among the branches for the dark blue berries, and ordered the dogs down next to her. Valentine and Duvalier chose a spot on the crest to observe.

Two wide-framed cars, minuscule in the distance, bumped along the remains of a former road, moving south. As long as they stuck to the road, they were little threat.

"Just brownish off-road cars," Valentine called back down.

"You sure they aren't green? Denver folks have their rigs painted green, sometimes they got a white star on 'em, too."

"Maybe they're just dirty," Duvalier suggested, but even she did not sound convinced.

They traveled more carefully after that. They found the road the jeeps had used, but the tire tracks told no clear tales, except that the jeeps weren't the only vehicles that had used the road recently. A mile past the road, Valentine picked up the smell of humanity on the light afternoon breeze as they walked their horses.

"People up ahead," he said to Duvalier. "Don't look startled—it's probably a stillwatch. Let's worry about it behind some cover."

They wound around a bend in a hill, cutting off the scent, and stopped. After that it was a matter of outwatching the watchers. Sooner or later curiosity would force them to reveal themselves. Duvalier volunteered to go after them while Valentine and Mrs. Cortez made a pretense of tending to the horses.

Valentine was wondering how to phrase it when Duvalier let out an exasperated breath. "Don't look like that, Val. I'll be gentle."

Within an hour she descended from the grassy hills carrying an unfamiliar rifle behind a matched pair of uniformed soldiers. A second gun bobbed on her back.

"Look, she found one," Valentine said.

Mrs. Cortez narrowed her eyes. "Good-size boy. That's a Denver regular, not one of the Rangers they use here on the Frontier. Something must be going on. I hope she was polite; the Denver troops get riled easily."

Duvalier walked her prisoner into camp, chatting with him as they approached the horses. The soldier spoke first.

"Look, friend, you're in Colorado now. Ambushing and hitting a soldier brings a heap of trouble your way, especially now. Better tell your girl to give me my rifle back. In about five minutes, you'll have twenty guns pointed at you from these hills."

Valentine shrugged. " 'My girl' is actually in charge here, more or less. I wouldn't get too heavy-handed with the threats, Private. Your sergeant might ask us some questions, and if he finds out this 'girl' about half your size surprised you and got your gun without even having one of her own, well, I wouldn't care to be you."

The soldier, who had PARKSTON stenciled on his breast, glanced around at the crests of the low surrounding hills, as if the unnamed sergeant were in danger of overhearing that someone had taken his gun.

"But we don't want that to happen," Valentine continued. "As far as we're concerned, you hailed us from good cover, having sense enough to ask questions first and shoot later, and from our conversation you decided to bring us in to see your officer. If we give you your gun back, can we trust you not to do anything foolish?"

"Yes, sir," Parkston agreed. His comrade nodded, dispelling the suspicious air hanging between them.

Duvalier returned his rifle, a restored version of the old M-16 battle rifles of the U.S. Armed Forces. "What are you doing so far from home? I've never seen a Denver regular this far out on the frontier before," she observed.

"I probably shouldn't say," Parkston said. "Maybe the sarge can tell you more—he's leading this patrol."

The patrol in question chose this moment to reveal themselves. A line of men came over the top of the hill from the same direction Duvalier had appeared with the boy. Valentine heard others moving at the crest of this hill, staying hidden from sight but not being quiet enough to fool either him or the dogs, who at this moment were startled out of making themselves agreeable to Parker by the new arrivals.

The sergeant and a small team approached, rifles ready but pointed down.

"Howdy, folks," said the thirty-something man with the stripes. He exuded calm confidence, which was just as well since none of his team looked over twenty, and nervous boys with guns in a potentially hostile situation needed a lot of reassurance. "What are you doing this far into the DPZ?"

Mrs. Cortez ended up doing the introductions, her nasal western twang being similar to the sergeant's own. "My name is Cortez, and I'm looking for my husband, a pack trader last on his way to Fort Rowling. These two are with me—you might say they're helping a nervous old woman."

One of his men opened his mouth to say something, but the sergeant cut in. "Seen anything unusual west of here?"

"Two vehicles a couple hours back, moving south," Valentine spoke up.

"They were too far away to tell who they belonged to, you or someone else," Duvalier spoke up. "Sergeant, I'm no stranger to the Protective Zone. I've been to the South Platte Trading Post before on a cattle drive. None of us are friends of the New Order."

The sergeant lit a cigarette, and Valentine recognized the noxious smell of clove tobacco. "The jeeps were ours. But whether you're friends of Kur or no, it won't hurt you to know that Fort Rowling's gone. Burned right to the foundation. Done from the inside too, not artillery or any kind of heavy weapon as far as we know."

"What?" Mrs. Cortez and Duvalier said, nearly simultaneously.

Valentine rooted in his pocket and came up with a pack of cigarettes. He passed out two or three each to the sergeant and his men. The youths hooted, and the sergeant lit his and threw away the homemade smoke.

"Only bodies left to tell the tale," the sergeant continued. Valentine saw that the sergeant still held his gun in a way that wasn't threatening, but the barrel had to rise just thirty degrees to put a bullet through his chest. "Never saw anything like it before. They must have been surprised; there's a secret bunker in the gulch well back of the fort where the dependents are supposed to go if trouble's coming. Not a soul in there, or any sign of a fight, for that matter, at least at the refugee bunker. Fort Rowling put up a struggle, judging from the shell casings. They were at the walls for a bit. The gate was blown to bits. Some officers say a rocket, but I think demolition charge. The blast was just too big for anything else that you wouldn't need railcars to haul. Whoever planted the charge must not have minded machine-gun bullets."

"What was the garrison?" Valentine asked.

"Full complement is around eight hundred, but about half that is almost always on patrol or doing escort duty. Arming the camp casuals would mean six hundred men available for the defense. Fort Rowling wasn't just some little hole in the wall either. It was our strongest Frontier post. Mortar pits, two howitzers, I don't know how many support weapons. There's even a rail line that goes out to within ten miles of the fort, a project that don't look like it's going to be completed now."

"Tell them about the dependents," one of the sergeant's men said.

"Mrs. Cortez doesn't want to hear that."

"No, go ahead—I need to know. Please, Sergeant," she implored.

The sergeant tossed away his butt. "I've seen plenty of death, but not like this. Heads stuck on the ends of sticks, babies flung against walls and left on the ground like some sparrow that hit a window, houses burned with the people handcuffed inside them . . . I'm gonna be thinking about what I saw till the day I die now, and I thought I was a hardcase." He paused to take a gulp of air and to swallow. "Mrs. Cortez, I'm sure your husband died on the walls if he was in there—if he could have carried a gun, they would have armed him."

Mrs. Cortez let out a deep breath, blinking back tears. "Maybe he ran for Denver. Oh, I do hope so."

"We'll get you there and you can find out, ma'am," the sergeant said. Valentine met his eyes and gave the NCO a tiny bow of his head in gratitude.

"Don't make sense," Parkston said. "I mean, whenever the Reapers hit somewhere, they take prisoners. It's the whole point. If people go dying on them in the fight, they're no use for . . . for food."

"I'll tell you what really doesn't make sense," the sergeant said, recovering from his memories somewhat. "The tracker's report. He said that his best guess was three two-and-a-half-ton trucks carrying about fifty men. Fifty men. Fifty Reapers couldn't have taken that fort, I don't think, not that I've ever heard of that many Reapers all together anywhere but a big city. What fifty men could wipe out six hundred in a defensive position?"

"I think you'd better take us to whoever is in command now at Fort Rowling," Duvalier said.

Valentine saw what was left of the fort up close. It had been in a good defensive location, with water for man and livestock and stands of timber nearby. The wooden parts of the walls were burned, the blockhouses and bunkers demolished. The first order of business of the troops on the scene had been to decently tend to the bodies; long rows of fresh graves stood a little distance from the fort, looking out over a gully through which a sluggish stream still flowed in this, the hottest month of the year.

After surveying the burnt ruin, Duvalier asked for a chance to speak privately with Colonel Wilson and his adjutant, Major Zwiecki, of the Denver Free Colorado Corps. They left Mrs. Cortez hunting through the personal effects of the dead, looking for evidence of her husband. The colonel obligingly gave them his time. He was as desperate for an answer as any of the Denver soldiers or what was left of the Fort Rowling garrison, now returning from the patrols and convoys that had preserved their lives.

Rather than reoccupying the fort, he had pitched his men's tents on some high ground a half-mile from the fort, so the men didn't have to spend the night among the bloodstains and burned timber. Night had fallen, and the tent was lit by electric light provided by a mobile generator.

"Gasoline we got," the major said when Valentine asked

about the logistics that allowed mobile electricity. "There's a lot of shale oil in Colorado. We make it in blasting furnaces; you get the shale hot enough, and it bleeds oil. I've got a brother-in-law there. He says the refinery is really something. Up in the mountains. They call it Hell's Penthouse. The name comes from the huge slag heaps everywhere, and the furnaces that run over nine hundred degrees."

Duvalier cut in. "We're here to find out what happened—let's stick to the subject at hand."

"If you've got an answer, or even a good guess, I'd like to hear it," Colonel Wilson said as the major turned to pour coffee.

"Colonel, have you ever heard of Reapers using guns?" Duvalier asked.

"No, but I'm ready to listen to anything. Because other than an attack by a few thousand flying Harpies who carried off their dead and never landed so's to make tracks, you have to get to really weird theories to explain this."

The major added, "The more I see of the Kurians, the more my definition of 'really weird' gets pushed further and further out."

"We work for Southern Command," Valentine broke in after a look and a nod between him and Duvalier. "We're looking into some new unit the Kurians have, a group called the Twisted Cross under somebody known as 'the General.'"

The major and the colonel exchanged looks. "That's substanial," Wilson said, "and I'll tell you why. We've kept this from the troops, but there was one survivor of the Fort, a very old woman who lived there with her daughter and her daughter's family."

"Pretty tough old bird," the major added.

"She didn't see anything of the fight—they were in a basement. She heard a lot of gunfire. Some men busted into the basement, dressed in body armor with heavy black helmets. They dragged the others off, but they pulled her up into the compound and made her watch what was going on. She said when they were done, one of the men in body armor 'hissed' at her *'Tell them the General did this.'* Also something about coming back. That's why we kept it from the troops."

"Hissed?" Valentine asked. "Those were her words?"

"Yes, 'hissed,' " the colonel said. "I've never been close enough to hear a Reaper, but I guess they have kind of a breathy voice."

"That big tongue doesn't leave much room for vocal cords," Valentine said. "They hiss, all right. I'd like to speak to her."

"Then you'll have to chase her to Denver," the colonel said. "She's been sent there for debriefing. I didn't want the men worried about what happens if this General comes back. I'm doing enough of that for the whole regiment.

"I don't know what could stop them. If they can do this to Fort Rowling, I don't know that any of our posts outside Denver could."

They said good-bye to Mrs. Cortez inside the Denver Corps camp. She had found a bloodstained hat belonging to her husband; a bullet had come in through the side of the wide-brimmed ranch fedora.

"At least I know it was quick," she said fatalistically.

Duvalier hugged her and whispered something in her ear that Valentine did not even try to hear. Sometimes using his "hard ears" just depressed him, giving him glimpses into others' private lives he wished he had not heard.

"You two take the horses, and mine besides. I'm going west to Denver with the dogs. Make myself useful in a hospital or stable. Been out there so long, it'll be nice to be among people, even if you're living under a set of rules long enough to choke a horse." The tears were in her voice, but not in her eyes.

They held a final meeting with the colonel and his adjutant. The colonel had requested a briefing about the Twisted Cross for all his officers, but Duvalier demurred, wishing to keep a low profile in camp. They told all they knew of the General, speaking on the record as Cats "A" and "Z" of Southern Command as Major Zwiecki took notes. As far as everyone else in the Denver Free Colorado Corps was concerned, they wanted to be known as just a pair of concerned relatives looking for one of their dead at Fort Rowling. That they also were remembered as some drifters who inexplicably had their horses shoed, were given a pack saddle, canteens, food, fuel, and a pass allowing them on Denver Protective Zone Territory at DFCC expense, Valentine never learned.

They followed the Republican River east out of Colorado, traveling slowly and carefully. Avoiding contact with farm, camp, or town, they worked their way back up into Nebraska. Valentine changed back into his Private Rice attire when Duvalier judged it safe enough, and they worked out yet another cover story to explain their presence. But this corner of Nebraska, so close to the Colorado border, was empty enough to allow them to move without being noticed. And so they came to the river Platte and its adjoining roads and tracks. After looking for their faces on wanted posters at station offices and finding none, they traded the horses for travel warrants from a corrupt rail-yard chief. Soon they rode again on the railroad, this time working for their passage—riding in and cleaning out eastbound cattle cars.

They were inside an empty cattle car on a siding outside their original pseudo-destination of Grand Island, sharing a bag of corn bread, when a train approached from the west. It moved with a mile-eating speed as the powerful engines pulled it. When the train roared by, Valentine counted an extra guard-car, thirty nondescript freights, and another heavily armored guard-car before the steel-colored caboose passed by. Whipped by speed and wind, two flags fluttered next to each other on the caboose: black with a spiderish design centered on the standard.

It was the white swastika of the Twisted Cross.

Eight

The Sand Dunes, September: Stretching north from the Platte River is the rolling, empty expanse of Nebraska's dunes. Sitting above one of the great aquifers of the world, the coarse, dark brown soil is not suited for crops, but supports some of the world's best ranching country. It is the Sahara transformed into a grassy garden. The Dunes, a beautiful green ocean in the spring before being burnt into straw by the summer's heat, cover an area larger than the state of Connecticut. They start to the west, and like the ocean, the great rollers are found the farthest out, thousand-foot-high, wind-rounded ridges a mile across and ten miles long, almost all running east-west according to the prevailing winds. East from the great ridges are smaller hills of varying squiggled shapes but still mostly long and thin. These gradually fade off into tiny steep hillocks, as the great rollers of the Atlantic turn into the chop of the English Channel. So like little waves are these hills that the residents use a nautical term for them: choppers.

While much of the soil is too dry to easily grow crops, the area is anything but a desert. It is ideal ranching country and supports more than horses and cattle. The little valleys between the hills are thickly wooded: lakes and ponds, marshes and soggy meadow can be found among the teeming cottonwoods and box elms. Trout streams and lakes filled with pike are dotted with beaver homes and dams, and a newcomer is sometimes startled to see a pelican fishing after descending from one of the high, dry ridges as seagulls ride the breeze overhead. Game is plentiful, mule deer bound through the long grass like giant jackrabbits,

*and antelope herds graze while the younger males at the
edges keep watch for coyotes. Bird hunters come home with
everything from waterfowl to wild turkey, pheasant to
sharp-tailed grouse. But the residents of the Dunes ride
with rifles for reasons other than shooting game.*

They hunt the minions of Kur.

Valentine and Duvalier caught up to the Twisted Cross
train at the fork where the North Platte and South Platte
converged their sandy banks. The town of North Platte no
longer existed on the spit between the rivers, having been
burned in the chaos almost fifty years ago. A hand-lettered
sign announced that they were pulling into Harvard Station.

Their train did not stop, even though they had been assured by the engineer—this being a cattle car, unguarded
except for a few rifles in the hands of the railroad men—
that it would pause at Harvard Station before moving on to
Ogallala and Scottsbluff. As they passed through the station, they saw squads of Troopers milling all over the yard,
crates being unloaded and organized, and sentries posted on
either side of their track for the express purpose of making
sure no one got off. A small, single-engine plane came in
for a landing on the old airstrip southeast of town, adding to
the panoply of war. He and Duvalier openly stared; in fact,
had they not watched the plane, it would have been even
more suspicious, flying machines being a rarity even in the
Kurian Zone. Valentine looked at it through his binoculars:
it was tiny bush hopper, white with red markings. He half
expected to see a swastika on the tail, like in pictures in
World War II books, but could identify no markings.

"I've been here before," Duvalier told him, "but I've
only seen it from the other side."

Another Twisted Cross train was on a siding by a dock
with some chutes and pens for livestock. They could see
figures lounging in the sunlight, wearing what looked like
black jumpsuits, but unlike the men at the other train, they
seemed to be in no hurry to unload the contents of closed
boxcars. Around the caboose, a team of the most formidable-
looking Grogs Valentine had ever seen stood guard, taller

than the slab-skinned gray ones he had fought at Little Timber and partially covered with fawn-colored fur.

A concrete blockhouse, surrounded by razor wire and gated, looked out over the ruins of the town and the river below. Men in a sandbagged platform smoked as they stood watch with machine guns. The black-and-white banner fluttered from the blockhouse's flagpole.

"They're setting up shop," Valentine said as their train pulled away westward. "Supplies, men, weapons, a plane. But what's the target? We haven't heard any news of a uprising in the local Gulag."

Duvalier gazed off northward into the rolling, grassy hills. She looked terribly, terribly sad. "If there were, it would be news they'd keep quiet. This isn't even a Kurian center—this is an outpost of the one down in McCook, right on the border."

"Border? Border with what?"

"The Dunes. They must be after the Dunes." She sighed, as she had done one day in Kansas, when they saw a police truck lumbering down the road with human fodder for the Reapers chained in back.

Valentine followed her gaze, not exactly doubting her, but waiting to hear more. "Who or what are the Dunes?" he finally asked. Duvalier liked to make him ask questions for some reason, perhaps as revenge for his occasional corrections to her English.

"It's more of a where, Val. The Dunes are that," she said, pointing. "It runs from here up to the Dakotas. Kurians never really controlled any of it, and every time they've tried, they got their ears pinned back. It's a huge area, maybe half the size of the Ozark Free Territory. I don't even think the Reapers dare hunt there."

"Why is that?"

"The Trekkers. Wanderers. The only way to describe it is big moving ranches that go with their cattle and horses. Everything in their life is packed onto their wagons, they move from winter to summer pasturage and back again, but not always the same spot. Their whole world is their cattle; the herds feed them and buy what they can't make."

"Buy from whom?"

"There are a few outfits that trade with the Quislings, no doubt about it. Oh, they call Quislings 'Jacks' out here. I've asked six different people and got six different stories. Some say its short for 'jackals,' but I'm not even sure what those are."

"They're a sort of scavenger dog—in Africa, I think," Valentine explained.

She ignored the zoology. "Others say it's because they used to be led by a man named Jack. Some more say it's because they run like jackrabbits if someone starts shooting at them. I forget the others. Doesn't matter. They're Jacks to folks out here."

"You know the people in the Dunes?"

"I do. Good people, damn good people. I got friendly with one of the larger clans, a group of families under the Eagle brand. They identify themselves with the marks they put on their cattle, you see. The brand looks kind of like an old set of air force wings, or an American Indian thunderbird. I guess it got its start from some Strategy Air Controller people who helped them fight off the Kurians in the worst years."

Valentine wondered if she meant "Strategic Air Command."

"They don't care for strangers too much, but I got to know them when they were running stock to Denver. I ended up riding scout for two cattle drives. Good days. Learned a lot about the land between here and the Rockies. The area between the two Platte branches is real anything-goes country. A couple Kur ranching settlements, bands of Jacks riding for the Kur, Crow Indians trying to live on the Pawnee, and a few little villages just trying to keep out of everything."

"So you've been to Denver?"

"No, the Denver Outriders would meet us outside the city. I always wanted to go, though. See a city. Of course, they tell me it's pretty empty, just like everywhere else. A fair amount of damage, but it's still free soil, and that always feels good."

Valentine watched Harvard Station disappear into the distance behind them.

"So you think they're going to clear out these Trekkers?" She nodded. "It kind of fits the pattern. That other Lifeweaver, Ura, she mentioned that a couple of small Freeholds got torched by these guys. Maybe they're training before taking on bigger game, like us or Denver."

"If Denver depends on these people for food," Valentine theorized, "could be this is a step in a campaign against them. That might go a long way to explaining the attack on Fort Rowling. It was a probe."

"This will be a chance to see how they operate," Duvalier said. "We can see how they organize, scout, prepare for a battle. Find out about these Reapers with guns. Do they have artillery? It looks like the Twisted Cross has an air force, even if it's just one plane. Southern Command will need to know what's coming."

Valentine felt another, more important battle coming on. His duty and his humanity, his conscience and his code silently warred within. It wasn't much of a fight this time. Too many lives at stake.

The wind at the top of a rise pulled at his hair. He pulled it back into place, and as he did so came to a decision. As if a yoke had been lifted from his shoulders, he straightened.

"Ali, that's exactly what we should do. But first we've got to warn those people."

They jumped from the train as it slowed to climb a hill east of Ogallala. Rather than leaping immediately into the bushes, they waved at the railroad men watching from the caboose. The railroaders waved back, smiling.

"That's always fun," Valentine said, pulling a teasel weed's prickly head out of his hair and picking up his pack. "You okay?"

"Did it knock some sense into you?" she said as she changed back into her stained traveling clothes. At least she was speaking to him again. They had argued briefly, until she quit talking to him after he asked her if she could just watch her friends from the Denver cattle drives die.

"Not yet. Ali, I didn't say that you had to come. I didn't even suggest it. One pair of eyes can see as much as two. You can keep an eye on the Twisted Cross, and I'll try and get the word out to the people in the Dunes."

"You did suggest it. You said, 'We've got to warn those people.' *We* is plural, Mr. Professor."

"Okay, I hoped you'd want to come with me. After all, you're already known to them."

"Irresponsible. What we're doing—recon—is *really* important. As far as Southern Command is concerned, the Twisted Cross is just another gang of Quislings. I wanted to take you on because after reading your reports, it seemed like you were just as worried about them as I was. But you want us to go up into the Dunes, where all that's going to happen is we'll be on the receiving end of their attack, instead of evaluating it and learning about their numbers and methods."

Tears trickled down her face. "I liked those people, Val. They're good people, as good as I've met anywhere. There are families in those wagons, Valentine. They're going to be dead in a little while, and there's not a thing we can do about it—and it's killing me. Now you just want to throw our lives away, too."

"Our duty is to Southern Command. What about warning them? Didn't you take an oath when you became an officer, or a Wolf or whatever they put you through when you joined up?"

"Maybe if I can warn them they can hide the kids. We, or I—whatever—I just have to let them know about what's coming." He tightened his pack. "I'm going in there. Unless you want to try to stop me."

The stare-down was brief.

It ended when Duvalier looked at the dirt beneath her hiking boots, poked the loose soil with her walking stick. Then she gripped it firmly by the middle, and for a second Valentine thought she was planning to knock him out with it. But the tears disappeared.

She even looked a little relieved.

"Okay, David. We warn them. But that's all."

*   *   *

The Cats decided to risk crossing the North Platte River during daylight, starting as early as possible in their race against time and death.

It wasn't hard; at this time of year, the brown-streaked river was at its lowest point. They crossed into the Sands at the wreckage of the Kingsley Dam, passing a sign that read UNSECURED TERRITORY. TRESPASSERS SUBJECT TO SUMMARY JUSTICE. Although the road had been destroyed, a drift of sorts existed, allowing them to make the treacherous crossing without wetting anything below their knees. A few anglers, perhaps out of Ogallala, plied their rods from the banks. If hidden border sentries also watched the pair, Valentine's Trooper vest perhaps confused the guards enough to keep them from shooting.

Rather than disappear into the Dunes right away, which would look more suspicious to a stillwatch, Valentine decided instead to walk up the banks of the Platte among the birches and poplars of the floodplain.

After a rest, they found enough wooded cover to cut up into the Dunes, running parallel to the old State Route 61 north into Dune Country.

Valentine pushed the pace. He carried Duvalier's pack across his chest, so Duvalier, who hadn't spent years running from point to point in the Wolves, was light enough to keep up with his trot.

They jogged carefully along the hills, making sure they did not skyline themselves. At sunset they stopped to rest and watch the daylight go out in a blaze of glory. Valentine had been in some wide-open spaces before, but something about this rolling sea of straw and grainy soil felt endless.

"It's funny," Duvalier said. "What we're trying to do is just . . . nuts. Hopeless. I feel liberated, though. Like I'm about to go shoot some rapids in a barrel and it's too late to worry."

Valentine looked at her as he massaged his aching legs. The fading sun tinted her skin the color of beaten copper. "No, it's not that. You're doing the right thing. When I was a kid, the man who raised me after my family died, he was a teacher. He used to have the older students read about the Holocaust. The Holocaust was when—"

"I know what the Holocaust was," she said, but without her usual vexation. "Kind of a dress rehearsal for all this."

"He made us study it for a couple reasons. One was to learn that there were people who went through times as bad as these and survived, although it wasn't that bad in the Boundary Waters of Minnesota. I think the other reason we read about it was to learn that evil, even if it seems all-powerful for a while, always collapses eventually. He used to say evil was like a rabid animal: it was very dangerous and should be destroyed as soon as possible, but even if it couldn't be attacked from the outside, the sickness within would put an end to it.

"But back to this one book I read about the Holocaust. It started with this diary kept by a little Jewish girl in hiding. She was killed, but her diary survived, and the rest of it went on about people who helped the Jews and others hide from or escape the Nazis. People would ask them afterwards how they found the courage to do it, when the Nazis killed people who helped the Jews. They said it took no courage at all; it was the easier choice to make. By doing the right thing, they kept their humanity. I think being able to keep their self-respect gave them strength. There's a power in doing right."

Valentine opened an old tobacco pouch and took out his little pyramid-shaped stone so it could absorb the remaining sunlight and charge.

Duvalier looked at the tiny crystal pyramid. "Do you ever think the Lifeweavers are angels?"

"What? Err . . . no, I heard you. What do you mean, I should say."

"When I first got to the Free Territory, and that Cat Rourke began to sort of be a father to me, he took me to see Ryu. It was a sunny day, and he was wearing that white loincloth he goes around in, only he had another white thing he was sort of wrapped up in, too. I remember I was looking at him, and something about the sun must have warmed him—he turned to it and spread out his arms. Suddenly I saw this man with a halo, and these big white wings billowing out from his back. Of course, it was the white shawl or whatever he was wearing and the sun in his hair."

"Be a funny kind of angel, making killers. The Lifeweaver who turned me into a Wolf, he said the only kind of people who were going to be able to beat the Kur were ones filled with hate and fury, not so much soldiers as berserks. At least that's how I remember it. The whole thing is a little hazy."

"I never heard anything like that out of Ryu. He always seems"—she sought for a word—"lonely. Lonely and sad."

Val shrugged. "You want to get a little rest before we push on?"

"I think maybe you should get some. You always carry most of the load, plus that god-awful gun and ammo."

Back in the Regiment we should have been called mules rather than Wolves. They selected us for a sterile life of endurance. He stretched out on the grass with his coat as a pillow. "I can handle it."

"You still carry too much," she said, and suddenly leaned over and kissed him on the forehead.

He opened an eye. "It's a good thing you didn't do that while you were still wearing that bra-and-shorts combination. Otherwise I would have performed a very convincing newlywed act on you."

"Dream on, Valentine," she said, sending a peanut shell his way. They had picked up a bagful somewhere during a trade.

"I wish I could have seen you buying that red bra. That would have been a memory to treasure. No one at the hall would have believed me. I suppose you burned the evidence."

"No, I didn't buy that in Lincoln. Actually I found it, still hanging on a little plastic hanger in a ruined store in Amarillo a year ago. Still wrapped up in tissue paper and plastic. It fit so well, I decided to keep it for days when I just can't deal with my boobs."

He laughed. "You carried a red bra around with you for a year?"

"It's a hidden little piece of me, okay? You're a man, you don't know how important a good bra is."

"Your little pieces weren't so hidden under that jean

jacket. What does it feel like to have a tan inside your belly button, anyway?"

"Cretin."

"Bitch."

"Quit being an ass. Get some rest—we're up again in an hour."

A day later, they cut a broad trail moving east. Cattle, wagon ruts, and horse hooves all churned a wide swath through the grassy dunes.

"You don't have to be Red Cloud to follow this," Valentine said, pushing the dirt in one of the deep wagon ruts aside to see how far down it had dried.

"Red what?"

"Red Cloud. He was a Lakota Sioux chief. My mother used to say that when I tracked mud across the kitchen."

She tipped her head, a faint smile on her face. "Do you have a picture of her?"

"Only in my mind."

"I bet you have her hair."

Valentine shrugged, and they began to follow the trail. A distant, buzzing *errrrrrrrrm* made them take cover as the little plane they spotted at the Twisted Cross depot came up from the south.

"Now wouldn't that be a timesaver," Duvalier said, looking up at the scout plane. That little thing can do in an hour what it takes us days to cover."

Once it had moved off to the north, Valentine and Duvalier continued on their course, trailing the marks of the mass of men and cattle into the Dunes. They walked hard for an hour, and then rested for fifteen minutes, then got up again to jog for a while. After six hours, even Valentine began to get dry-mouthed and rubber-limbed. Duvalier groaned whenever they rose from a rest break, but otherwise endured the hard miles in silence.

It was afternoon when they spotted a pair of riders, the rearmost part of a rear guard, cutting across the path ahead. The pair rode smart, avoiding the skylines, and frequently paused their horses just to look and listen.

"Those are Trekkers," Duvalier pronounced, passing the binoculars back to Valentine. They began to jog in the open, trying to catch up with the outriders.

The riders spotted them soon after they started running, and moved with their horses to intercept. Valentine had his gun slung where he could get at it, but he had no weapon in his hand, and Duvalier just had her walking stick.

The men sat their horses, rifles on their hips, and awaited events.

"That's close enough, Trooper," one of them called from beneath a wide-brimmed Western hat. "What are you, a deserter?"

"Parley, riders," Duvalier called. "He's no Trooper. We took that off a dead 'un for disguise. What brand do you ride behind?"

"Barred Seven. Glad you're not a stranger here, little lady. What brand do you ride behind?"

"The last time I visited here, I rode with the Eagle's Wings. We have to speak to your Wagonmaster."

"Always happy to talk to a brother brand, 'specially when the visitor's such a pretty one. Does your boy here talk, or did somebody fork his tongue?"

"I can talk, friend. I just like to see which way the wind blows."

"Out here, it's usually west-east," the other man said, his lips hidden by a long drape of a mustache. The wide-brimmed man guffawed.

"You still got a good two miles to go before you hit the wagons, I'm afraid," he said. "But we'll get you to the edge of the herd." They turned their horses neatly and began to follow the trail.

"Bar Seven," Duvalier said quietly. "Not one of the larger groups, but tough as nails. They keep to the border country. Rumor has it that they trade with the Jacks, but let ye who are without sin cast the first stone. A lot of the Trekkers do, one way or another."

"What about your Eagle's Wings?" Valentine asked.

"No, they have a serious feud with Kur. Lots of memories from grandfathers in the military. And too many losses while running cattle to Denver. But in a way, this is good—Bar Seven might not want to offend the Eagles by being difficult, since the Eagles are the biggest of the Trekker groups. Once in a while there are disputes over winter pasture, and Bar Seven can't afford to make enemies."

They caught up to the herd, mostly Herefords that looked like they had been toughened up by the addition of a longhorn bull or two. Beyond the herd they could see a little spread of twenty or so wagons. A cowboy with a yellow bandanna tied at his hatband had a few words with the scouts and then rode up to the Cats.

"You want to see the Wagonmaster, huh? You got anything that's worth Mr. Lawson's time?"

"I think Mr. Lawson would like to be able to make that decision, friend," Valentine said.

"Ain't your friend, half-breed. Would like to be your friend though, miss."

Duvalier reached up to shake his hand. "Mister, we've come a long way. Could we please see the Wagonmaster?"

"I'll ride in and ask. Best I can do."

"How about you bring us with you. Saves a little time."

The man pursed his sun-dried lips. Either he had trouble thinking on his own or he had a very strict set of orders to follow.

"The Wagonmaster is a busy man. Where do you come out of?"

"The KZ, to the south," Duvalier said. "But I've ridden with the Eagle's Wings."

That seemed to make the decision easier for the rider. "Be back soon," he said, putting his horse into a trot toward the wagons.

Night blanketed the grassy hills. The Bar Seven cooks rang the supper bell as Valentine and Duvalier finally caught up to the loose ring of wagons. After a boring wait among the cows, the yellow-marked foreman rode back out with news that Wagonmaster Lawson would see them.

Lawson was a broad-shouldered individual with a heavy

scar over his forehead, giving him a scraggly eyebrow that looked permanently raised in surprise. He used the back gate of a large wagon as a combination desk and supper table, and was tearing into a blackened piece of beef when they were introduced to him.

"Boy, you might want to take off that vest in here. One of my men might take a shot at you, just out of habit."

Valentine removed the vest, feeling strangely naked without its weight.

"I hear you two rode with the Eagles?"

"Just me," Duvalier said. "Actually, I'd like to get back to them in a hurry. We think the Kur are planning a major raid into you out of North Platte. A real clean sweep."

"Uh-huh," Lawson said. "What makes you say that?"

"A sizable force offloaded from a train in North Platte. Everything from Reapers to Grogs, armed for bear. Even the Reapers will be carrying guns."

"Haw, that's a good one. Skulls with guns! Since when?"

"We both saw it. They're fighting with new tactics. They're scouting the area, and they're going to strike soon. Haven't you seen that little scout plane?"

Lawson looked suddenly uncomfortable. "Ee-yup. As a matter of fact, it circled here a couple times. You think they might be aiming to hit us? Bar Seven, I mean?"

"That we don't know," Valentine said. "We're just trying to warn you."

Lawson scratched his growth of beard. Judging from the whiskers, he shaved only once a week, and according to Valentine's sensitive nose, bathed even less often.

"We really need to get to the Eagle's Wings," Duvalier said, almost pleading. "It's a lot to ask, but if you could loan us a couple of horses . . . We don't have much to barter with. A few cigars, a little tea."

The Wagonmaster stared at them through narrowed eyes and sucked in his cheeks. "Nice-looking lady like you always has something to barter."

Valentine watched cords pop out on Duvalier's neck. She glared at the Wagonmaster.

He lost the staring contest and shrugged. "But charity's

always been my middle name. Okay, looks like I might be out two horses. How's this: if what you say is true, as far as I'm concerned the information is worth two good horses. If you're wrong, I'll be relieved but expecting either their return or payment. Tell Mr. Hendricks that a couple calfs out of one of those big reds he breeds would be adequate. Sound like a deal?"

Valentine looked at Duvalier. "Deal," they said in unison.

"I'll even throw in saddle blankets. Sorry I can't do any better, good tack is hard to come by. We ain't short of leather by a long shot, but good saddle makers are rare."

"Do you have any idea where we can find the Eagles?" Valentine asked.

"You aren't leaving now? It's getting dark in an hour or so."

"Afraid so, sir," Valentine said.

"Hope you know what you're doing. Hard riding in the dark is a good way to lose a horse. The Eagles are about forty miles northwest of here. It's calving time, so they're in a good anchorage, with water and wood under one of the big ridges."

"And where's that?" Valentine asked.

"Go dead northwest until you come to a big ridge, runs the whole skyline, a good ten or fifteen miles long it is. If you hit a little stream, turn left; if not, turn right. They're at the head of that little stream. You should see the cattle a long way off—Eagle's got thousands."

"Thank you, sir," Duvalier said.

"Good luck to you, Mr. Lawson," Valentine added.

Lawson began barking out orders, and his men hurried to comply.

"Nice diplomacy, Smoke," Valentine said as they left the wagon with one of Lawson's riders. "Never would have guessed you had it in you."

She squeezed his hand. "You'd be surprised at what I've done with my mouth, if it gets me where I need to go."

They rode out at nightfall, heading northwest. Valentine's stomach sometimes got ahead of his brain, and his insides were doing flip-flops from fatigue. And he had a new worry. When they dismounted from the improvised, blanket-and-rope saddles to walk the horses for a while, Valentine's concerns finally made it to his voice box. "I don't get it, Ali. How does he know so exactly where the Eagle's Wing camp is? They camp in different spots every year, don't they? You said Bar Seven and the Eagles aren't even friendly."

She stopped for a second, then shook her head.

"Valentine, their horsemen range pretty far. Hunting, rounding up strays. Sometimes looking for other Trekkers' strays, if I know the Bar Seven. He gave us the horses, didn't he? If he were in cahoots with the Twisted Cross, which is what you're suggesting, why not just hand us over to them, dead or alive? They had a good twenty guns hanging around those wagons, and their men know how to use them. We wouldn't have had a chance. Stop being paranoid. The Bar Seven are on the shady side of the line, sure, but I've never heard of one group of Trekkers betraying another. Every other Trekker brand would come down on them from every direction but up, and they'd try that if their horses could jump high enough. It'd mean the death of—"

"Enough. You win. You get hold of a man's ear so he has to chew it off to end the arguments."

The hard miles crossing the Dunes left Valentine's brain swimming. He finally convinced himself that the disquieting feeling he had from the Bar Seven came from lack of sleep.

They cold-camped for a couple of hours, deciding rest was more important than hot food. Duvalier kept his spirits up by promising him a sizzling steak on their finding the Eagle camp. While the horses cropped grass, they shared a soda-cracker-and-cheese meal that brought them back to their first journey together.

At noon the next day, they caught sight of their destination. Lawson was not kidding about the ridge. The grassy monster loomed like a tidal wave over little lines and clusters of trees at its base, following the eastward-flowing stream he described. Herds of cattle were scattered on the floor of the valley and the steep slopes of the dune.

Valentine traced the base of the hillside with his binoculars. At last he spotted it, an irregular triangle of wagons parked on a hummock at the base of the hill. The base of the triangle spread out as a concave arc, and the peak trailing up the hillside. On top of the ridge, like the mast of a ship, an observation post stood on a single trunk of timber. He whistled in appreciation.

"You don't know the half of it, Val," Duvalier said. "They've got other herds we can't even see. Counting all the families, there're over sixteen hundred people in this traveling circus. There's about a five cows to every person."

"What about that steak," Valentine said, training his binoculars across the red and red-white herds.

"Coming right up, sir," she said, touching her heels to the horse's sides lightly. Their horses broke into a trot, catching the smell of their kind coming from the three-sided enclosure.

On closer inspection, the wagon laager was even more impressive. Hundreds of wagons made a wall centered on the little spring in the hummock.

"They have three kinds of wagons," Duvalier explained as they cut through the herds. A bull or two stared at them, but most of the cows took no notice. Valentine noticed a lot of calves—a few still knock-kneed newborns—dutifully trailing behind their mothers. "Most of them live in little house-wagons, which they told me are based on Gypsy wagons, whatever Gypsies are. No, I don't want any history lessons, Val. Those are drawn by horses. Then there are the supply-wagons; those are the ones with the big rear wheels and the small front ones. They take oxen because of the heavy load, sometimes as many as sixteen. Most of what you see on the walls are those or the long battle-wagons. The battle-wagons are drawn by draft horse teams, and when they stop anywhere for longer than a day or so, they fortify. The battle-wagons have sheets of metal that they put on the outer face, joined kind of like double-paned windows, with rifle loopholes. They fill the space between the aluminum sheets with sand. The kids even help with this. They have little shovels and buckets they carry. In the space of an afternoon, they can build a pretty substantial wall by hooking the wagons together, and within a couple of days, they have trenches dug and the walls filled in."

As they grew closer, Valentine saw the battle-wagon scheme in practice. The triangular fort even had little mini-forts at the corners, clusters of four wagons projecting out like towers at a castle's corner, covering the main gate.

"Keeping the fires going, that's the teenagers' job," she continued. "Whenever I tell this story to people with kids, they laugh. The Trekkers don't cut down trees for firewood unless it's an emergency—they use deadfalls and trim branches, sure, but when the wagons first used to roam, they'd cut down too many trees and screw up the whole area for everybody. So they conserve wood. They use the cowshit. They mix it with grasses and twigs and leaves and press it into dried bricks. It makes a good fire, practically smokeless. Gathering the droppings and turning them into fuel is how you spend your youth from twelve years old to sixteen, or whenever they allow that you're ready to get your own horse and gun.

"Wherever they stop in a camp, they plant, potatoes, tomatoes, and peas mostly. They mark the crops with stakes before they move on if they can't harvest themselves. It's called 'leaving something for the future.'

"The Eagles have some allied brands, groups of families that have split off to form their own brands. It happens every generation or so. These wagon trains can only get so big before they become impossible to feed and water without permanent digs."

Valentine noticed that no outriders came up to ask them their business; the men watching over the cows just looked at them from under the brims of their felt hats. Presumably some sentry in the observation tower signaled strangers coming in long ago.

The wide gap in the wagon wall that served as the gate was also the outflow of the spring that watered the camp. It splashed down a rocky watercourse to meander into the trees to the east. They dismounted and led their horses up the final slope to the camp. Valentine expected it to reek of burning dung after Duvalier's travelogue, but he smelled only people, cooking food, and cattle. He eyed the layout of the camp, the trench and fortifications, with admiration.

A lanky man with a thin beard and a dusty top hat waved and came out to greet them. He recognized Duvalier with a smile.

"Glory be!" he said, stamping his foot and tossing his head like a horse. "If it isn't Little Red outta Kansas. It's been nigh on three years, sister."

"Hi, Deacon. I see you're still in the baptizing business. I've brought in another stranger from the south. This is David Stuart, out of Minnesota originally. We've traveled hard and ask your hospitality."

"The Eagle's Wings grant it to both you and the brother. With pleasure, Little Red, with pleasure."

"We're also going to need to speak to you, the Wagonmaster, and anyone else concerned with the Common Defense."

"This has anything to do with that plane that's been passing overhead?"

"Yes, Deacon."

"I knew that machine was a bad omen, soon as I saw it. We'll talk later, woman. Why you're thin as a rake! Let's get you into camp and get some food into you. Boy, come here!" he hollered at a scrawny kid gaping at the new arrivals. He spoke a few urgent words to the youth and sent him running into the camp.

They passed through the wagon barricade. An inner ring of wagons, a mix of the house-wagons and larger supply-wagons, formed a second wall within the first. A corral held a reserve of horses with saddles draped on the trek-tow fence. Valentine guessed the camp could mount a hundred men in a matter of minutes. Another wide loop of wagon wall sheltered a mass of oxen downwind, and more could be seen just outside the walls, grazing. "Animal husbandry must be second nature to you," Valentine remarked.

"We live and die by the stock," the deacon agreed.

They made their way past women washing clothing in the stream, lines of laundry drying on ropes stretched between the house-wagons cracked in the fresh breeze. At the center of the second circle of wagons, another pole-mounted crow's nest held a sentry, and above him a flag with the symbol that looked like a thunderbird—or perhaps a set of United States Air Force wings.

A train of dogs and curious children followed the deacon and the Cats as they walked their horses into the center of camp. The children were dressed in the final tatters of hand-me-downs, but they looked healthy and energetic.

"The widow knows you're coming in," Deacon said. "Since a fever took Mr. Hendricks, rest his soul, last April she's been running things. They had a son and a daughter, if you remember, Red, and Josh and Jocelyn have both grown into fine people. Good woman. Those were some big shoes to fill, but no one's missed the old Wagonmaster except in their hearts."

Mrs. Hendricks did not look like a Wagonmaster to Valentine; she looked like your favorite aunt who always bakes a thick cherry pie with a perfect lattice crust. She wore a simple dress with an apron containing everything from pen and notepad to scissors. Her sun-streaked hair was tied back into a bun, and she had meaty, work-reddened arms, well-padded hips, and cherubic cheeks. The only thing hard about her was her eyes.

Seeing the deacon and the visitors, she waved over some young women with platters from the cooking pits. A long table with a blue-and-white checkerboard tablecloth was filled with still-sputtering food, joining tall pitchers of water and prairie-herb tea.

"You poor tired things. We're in the middle of calving festival, so I want you to try this rib roast and tell me what you think. Doris, what's keeping those peas?" She turned back to her guests. "Now, clean up in the bucket over there, don't spare the soap, and tell me what brings you in. Red Alice, I remember you from a few years back, but this young man is new, isn't he? Have you taken a husband?"

"Some days it seems like it," Duvalier said, freckled skin going a trifle redder. "Other days it's like I've had a son. Questions all the time."

After washing his hands, Valentine swung a leg over the bench when the woman motioned them to sit. He reached for his knife and fork, mouth overflowing with saliva, when Duvalier grabbed his hands and thrust them in his lap. The deacon had just bowed his head at the end of the table.

"Heavenly Father, for what we are about to receive may we be made truly grateful." He raised his head. "Lord, that looks good. Let's eat."

Valentine could not have agreed with him more.

With supper cleared away, the dinner table became a council of war. The hot meal had left Valentine sated and sleepy. Through some internal resource, Duvalier was as bright as ever. Valentine struggled to imitate her.

"Red Alice" summed up the threat in a few concise sentences, giving her experiences with the Twisted Cross in Oklahoma, and their supposition that the Dunes were on the list to be cleared out.

The Hendricks woman listened impassively, shaking her head in sadness when Duvalier described the dead Caltagirone and his Wolves and the massacre in Colorado. Her son, Josh, and her daughter, Jocelyn, joined them at the table, mostly listening. Waldron, the Camp Engineer, who looked as though he had a bit of longhorn in him, asked sensible questions. The leader of the outriders, an almost baby-faced young man named Danvers, who proudly claimed he was eight years old on the ground and eighteen years old in the saddle, wanted to know details about the Twisted Cross weaponry.

Around the tables, many other members of the Eagle's Wings Brand stood, squatted, and sat, all listening. The Wagonmaster was not one to hide her doings and decisions behind closed doors. The others kept a respectful silence, allowing the words to carry, and the few who asked ques-

:ions held up their hands and waited to be called on like
disciplined schoolchildren.

"I wish we had a better idea about what you're facing,"
Valentine said in answer to a question from Danvers.

"We only ever worried about artillery," Waldron said.
'So far, every time those Troopers have brought it into the
Dunes, they've lost it. We even have a couple of their
pieces in camp, but the mortars are the only ones that still
have something to shoot out of them. Air power or armor
would whip us, but if any of that's still being made, it's not
finding its way to Nebraska."

Valentine nodded. Duvalier had briefed him on how the
cavalry harassed invading columns, assembling and striking at them like sparrows pecking at a hawk, and dispersing
again to leave the Troopers capturing nothing but hoof-
prints and air.

"Fact is, those creatures can't cooperate for shit, or
they'd of took us long ago," Josh Hendricks said. The boy's
clothes didn't fit; his adolescent body was lunging out in all
directions.

"Language, Josh," his mother warned. "I should say
English, too. I didn't teach you to talk like that."

"Sorry. But one time that bast—that bad'un in Scottsbluff came at us with everything he had, trying to take the
whole land up to the Niobrara. He was doing pretty well
until his cousin in Cheyenne hit him from behind. I hear he
lost half his territory. Been all he can do to hold on to the
rest ever since. I can't see a bunch of them ganging up on
us. Not like 'em."

As darkness fell, a bonfire and music started, almost at
the same time, from the south end of camp by the gate-
stream.

"It's still calving festival," Mrs. Hendricks said. "I hope
you young folk will join in the fun after your hard ride."

"Just some sleep would do nicely, ma'am," Valentine
said.

"We won't keep you, then. We're going to talk over what
you told us and decide what to do. Don't let the music fool
you. We're taking this very seriously. We'll have extra rid-

ers out tonight and people on the walls. Please feel free to stay here as long as you want—we'll handle the Paul Revere job from here on out. Jocelyn, show our guests to the visitors' cabin."

A saddle-muscled young woman stood up. Jocelyn Hendricks wore a man's moleskin hand-me-downs brightened by a red neckerchief wrapped around her thick brown hair. She stepped around behind the Cats.

"Thank you for the dinner, Mrs. Hendricks," Valentine said, swallowing the last of his milk.

"Yes, it was wonderful. Thanks for the bed, too. It's going to be very welcome," Duvalier added.

They zigzagged through the maze of wagons, tentage, washing lines, and campfires.

Jocelyn paused at the little ladder and door of one of the house-wagons, set apart from the rest. "People are going to be asking me what our chances are. What should I tell them? They'll be worried about their children."

Valentine looked at Duvalier, who shrugged.

"I can't tell you what to say, Miss Hendricks," Valentine said. "If there's somewhere safe they can put their kids, I'd recommend that they do that right away. Reapers move fast at night when they want to. They could be here tonight."

"We'll be here with you, at least tonight," Duvalier added. "I believe that if anyone in the Dunes can beat them, it's your brand."

Jocelyn showed them the cozy little cabin, with its bunk beds, tiny cabinets, and built-in basin. "There's water in the pitcher," she explained. "Clean bedding on the mattresses, real horsehair stuffed, and a thunderbucket in the corner in case you don't feel like a trip to the pits. I'll check on your horses and tack before I turn in; they're in the north corral.

"There will be dancing until midnight or so. You sure you aren't up to it? A lot of the folks would be interested in meeting people from elsewhere."

"We just spent two days traveling hard," Valentine said. "I'm sure you understand."

Duvalier added, "Another time."

"Maybe tomorrow night, then," Jocelyn said, smiling as she closed the door.

Duvalier placed her sword where she could reach it easily. "If there is a tomorrow night, Val."

No call to arms, no attack from the darkness disturbed their dreamless slumber. It seemed only a matter of minutes before Valentine heard a gentle tap on the door and opened his eyes to light pouring through the window.

The door opened, and Mrs. Hendricks entered, bearing a tray. "Good morning!" she half sang, half whispered. "Anyone up? I've brought you a little something to get your eyes open."

Valentine realized he had collapsed in his clothes, and guiltily looked at the mess he'd made of the sheets. Duvalier had stripped down to her shirt, and she swung her legs from the bottom bunk with a groan.

"I thought I might kill two birds with one stone. So I brought some sausages and wheat bread and a cup of tea for each of you. Nothing happened over the night. The meeting went until late, and we decided to scatter some of the herds and families. We sent out riders to warn the other brands and asked them to send what men and guns they could this way. We're going to have to unite to stand any chance at all, from what you've told us."

"How soon will they be arriving?" Valentine asked.

"Days. The Dunes are big, and in the summer the smaller brands get to the most remote places they can. If the Troopers raid into us, it's usually between May and September."

Valentine removed the fly-cloth from his breakfast and began eating. Duvalier nursed her tea, content to listen and look out the window.

"How can we help?"

"You've done enough, by my reckoning. But if you want to, go around, speak to the men, maybe tell them a little more about those Reapers. We don't have much experience against them, and what we do know has us all frightened."

Duvalier nodded. "We'll do what we can." After the

Wagonmaster left, she looked at Valentine. "I'm frightened, too."

"Never thought I'd hear that from you."

She went to the basin and wrung out a washcloth, wiped it across her face. "Hear me admit it, you mean."

Valentine shrugged.

"We've warned them, Val. Let's head out."

"I'm staying. You've got more experience at this. You'll be better without me."

"Staying? Staying like in desertion?"

"Staying like in helping them fight. We've been over this before."

She lowered her voice in case anyone was outside the wagon, listening. "I figured once you saw them, you'd either figure there were enough guns for the fight so that you being here wouldn't make a difference, one way or the other. Or you'd see it was a lost cause."

Valentine stood for a moment. He feared the coming fight but wanted it, as well. *Do I have a death wish?*

"I'll quit trying. You're a lost cause, Valentine. No wonder your captain had you court-martialed."

She must have seen the hurt in his eyes, because her tone softened: "Sorry. You—well, you deserved that, but I shouldn't have said it. I'm going to scrounge up some supplies. Think about it before I ride out."

Valentine spent the day with Waldron, the Camp Engineer, trying to forget about Duvalier by inspecting the defenses.

The Eagles had a trench around the camp, hurriedly being made as wide and deep as the sandy soil would allow. Shovelfuls of thrown dirt rained dust and pebbles that made skittering noises as they bounced off the metal panels of the walls. Some of the corrugated sheets that served as armor on the outside of the battle-wagons still had sections of vaguely familiar logos from the Old World.

"We took a lot of these facings from old rigs. Big engines called semis used to haul these trailer affairs. The metal is light and strong."

Valentine ran his hand along the dirty old surface, printed in huge letters. ADWAY. Farther down, the red Coca-Cola label protected one of flanking corners. Strange that one of the most persistent holdovers of the Old World was its product marketing; like the advertisements for gladiatorial contests that he'd read could still be seen on a wall or two in Rome.

"Been a long time since we've had to shoot from the walls of the camp. Last time it was because we got surprised," Waldron said as they walked the perimeter. "A few years back, the Troopers reinforced a bunch of their trucks and loaded them with men. Came barreling at us across the plain; I think the idea was to ram through the walls. Sure, tin and sand stop bullets, but not a truck moving at forty miles an hour or more. They either didn't know much about physics or they forgot about the trench; they hit it and killed most everyone in the trucks. We hardly had to fire a shot."

He lifted up his shoe, and Valentine smiled at the serrated pattern of a truck radial. "Got a darn long-lasting pair of shoes out of it, and a good laugh."

"You said you had some artillery?"

"Ha! A pair of mortars and less than thirty shells. Eighty-one millimeter. Let me show you what we have come up with, though."

They cut through a hidden angle in the battle-wagons, and climbed up into the bed. A shiny cylinder that Valentine recognized as an old artillery shell casing, probably a 155-millimeter, sat in a metal trough secured by a heavy steel cover. A fuse, curled like a pig's tail, dangled behind. The whole affair stood on a tripod welded to an old metal wheel.

"This is kind of based on a swivel gun. You can point it using the mount, but your aim doesn't have to be very precise with this cracker. It's an artillery shell casing sitting in the half-cut pipe there. We loaded it up with powder and put a bag of taconite pellets on top of the wad. No range to it whatsoever. But it'll sweep twenty yards in front of the gun like you were using a broom, and more beyond if you get lucky. We've got a version that goes on the ground too, in a wooden holder. Strictly one-shot, takes us a good while to clean and reload it if the casing doesn't crack." Valentine thought it looked like as much of a threat to the men behind the weapon as the enemy in front, but he kept silent.

"We also have some grenades we took off the Troopers, but not enough, and coal-oil bombs—which are really just sawdust and the oil mixed in an old vodka bottle. And that's our artillery."

After lunch he met with Duvalier. She had spent the morning after her scrounge riding with Danvers, going from point to point looking for signs of the Twisted Cross.

Eagle Brand families took a portion of the cattle and dispersed to hiding places among the dunes. "They're great trackers and the best horse-riding guerrilla fighters since the Apache—plenty of rifles but not enough support and artillery," she said.

Valentine was happy to find her equitable—or just resigned to him staying. "Same thing in camp. The Reapers will tear this place apart from a couple hundred yards, and there won't be much they can do about it. All the guts in the world aren't much of a help against Kalashnikovs in the hands of something that isn't disturbed by catching a bullet."

The little red-and-white plane appeared just then high in the sky, hardly audible even to Valentine's ears. He felt a chill as it threw a wide circle around the camp before moving off eastward. It was like the ravens of the Middle Ages, who would gather along with the armies in anticipation of the coming carnage.

"Rider coming in," the sentry mounted in the crow's nest at the central cluster of wagons called. Valentine saw Josh Hendricks go toward the gate with the deacon. Valentine and Duvalier looked at each other, shrugged, and joined the cluster of people, wondering what new calamity the rider portended.

It was a boy on a lathered horse. Valentine guessed him to be somewhere between fourteen and sixteen. He was dressed like a Comanche, in a leather loincloth and vest, and had a blanket-saddle on his black horse. His mount dribbled, foamed, and glistened with sweat.

"Boy's out of the Q or Twin Triangles Brands, is my guess," an older man by Valentine predicted. "Don't look like good news either."

The kid rolled off his horse, half-fall and half-dismount. Josh Hendricks poured him some water out of a canteen.

"Triangles' camp's been burned," the boy said flatly, once he had caught his breath. "Last night. We were camped between the Middle Loup and the Middle Branch. I was outrider to the north, and I heard shooting. All a-sudden the wagons was going up in flames. Then up came the Grierson family. Mr. Grierson was shot and looked real pale; his sons were carrying him. Mrs. Grierson told me to ride and warn you. She said they weren't no Troopers, they came with guns and explosives, and the bullets didn't seem to touch 'em. I asked about my pa and ma, and she didn't know, she said she was sorry," he said, his voice cracking before he realized he'd voiced his thoughts.

"Damn," the older man next to Valentine said. "That isn't far at all. Just east of here maybe four hours' ride—and not a hard ride, neither."

"Big difference here, though," Valentine said. "We know they're coming."

The elder man spat. "We know the sun's going to set in about five hours, son, but there ain't a thing we can do about it."

The deacon handed the boy the reins to his horse. "See to your horse, son."

Then he turned on the gloomy man next to Valentine. "Have a little faith, Brother Tom," the deacon said. "The Lord's seen fit to bless us with warning and some help. He'll be with us tonight."

Tom's words troubled Valentine as the sun lowered toward the horizon, as slow and deadly and inevitable as Poe's pendulum. He learned more about the Twin Triangles: though not numerous, they were as good a group of riders and shooters as existed in the Dunes.

The Eagles had more fighters, but would that just mean more bodies to be buried? With the teens and older men armed, the Eagles could horse a force of five hundred men. But nearly a hundred of these were with some of the women and children and livestock who had scattered into hiding after the decision by the Common Defense Committee last night. Dozens more were riding across the Dunes now, as messengers to the other brands. The foundation of the brand, their wealth and their sustenance, was the cattle, and the animals had to be moved and protected. This deducted another hundred and fifty riders. That left a force of a little over two hundred women and men able to stand in the wagons, backed up by teens old enough to shoot for the camp.

One of the scouts sent back word during supper that a convoy of vehicles had been spotted west on the old Highway 2. The Trooper-marked column wasn't making good time—weather and actions of the Trekkers had reduced the road to little more than a bad path—but they were clearly heading for the Eagle camp. The Twisted Cross were intent on smashing the largest brand in the Dunes, probably sometime after nightfall.

A few voices suggested that they pull up stakes and move at dusk, leaving nothing but empty space for them to attack, but Hendricks vetoed the idea with the weight of the Common Defense behind her. Valentine explained that with the Reaper's ability to read lifesign, the mass of moving wagons would shine like a lighthouse across a calm sea, and they would be able to cover whatever miles the wagons put between them and the camp that same night. They were better off fighting it out from behind trench and wall.

As the sun set, a mist began to steal across the valley beneath the great rolling hill.

"That's strange for this time of year, especially in the evening," Mrs. Hendricks said, watching the veil thicken around the camp.

"It's the Kurians. They can shape the clouds when they have a mind," Duvalier said. She'd lingered through the day, saying she wanted to rest her legs and her horse. "Val, I'll ride now. You still staying?"

Her tone was nonchalant, but he read concern in her eyes. "Yes."

There wasn't a fight this time.

The pair went to their packs in the guest wagon. Duvalier stripped down to a utility vest, perhaps some old angler's jacket or photographer's rig at some time, now dyed. She now loaded it with everything from her claws to screw-topped pipes filled with chemicals designed to burn or blow up. She began to apply black greasepaint across her face and arms as Valentine sharpened her sword. The straight, angle-pointed blade had a dull coating everywhere save the very edge, where it glinted with cold reflections.

"I'm going to be outside the camp before the sun goes down," she said. "I plan to stick to them like a tick. You live through this, you can catch up to me south of Omaha, where I got that pheasant. Remember? Just head east till you hit the Missouri."

"I'm not leaving these people until things are decided one way or the other," Valentine said.

"Neither am I. This column means there's a headquarters for it. I'm going to find those Troopers and see what I can see. Could you help me with this greasepaint?"

Valentine coated her shoulders and the back of her arms with the ebony grease, leaving the occasional strip of sun-darkened flesh exposed to break up the human pattern. She looked like a black-and-tan tiger. Her torso finished, Duvalier slipped into baggy black pants with enormous cargo pockets on the thighs and her trusty old hiking boots. She tucked her red hair under a dark, insignia-less kepi. It was the standard-issue hat of Southern Command dyed black.

"Technically I'm in uniform, not that it makes a difference if they catch me. If I learn anything useful, I'll try to leave you a message somewhere outside the Twisted Cross camp. Look for a pile of four of anything sticking up, rocks, sticks, whatever. I'll leave a note under it."

"Be careful."

"You, too. Don't get your head blown off, Ghost."

"Don't get caught lighting any fires, Smoke."

She took a step toward him, and evidently thought better of it—instead she opened the door. She touched the side of her hand to her eyebrow and then dragged her index finger down her grease-painted nose, and left.

Fog and night closed in on the camp; the lantern lights glowed like amber gems, each surrounded by a tiny halo. Valentine stepped out of the guest house-wagon. He wore his old Wolf buckskins instead of his traveling coat, now like Duvalier's night gear darkened to a chocolate color. The heavy vest weighted his shoulders. His parang and revolver still hung from the sweat-darkened leather-and-canvas equipment belt he could not bring himself to let go. But now it had additional gear added: the old curved sword hung across his back, and the two spare drums for the submachine gun were clipped above each buttock where once canteens had ridden. His fighting claws, worn more for luck than because he expected to use them, hung around his neck from a breakaway leather shoelace like Eveready's old necklace of Reaper teeth.

Even with the seventy-one-round drum in it, the submachine gun had a nice balance. He sat down on the tiny steps to the wagon, broke down the gun, cleaned and oiled it, and put it back together again. He flicked the little switch in front of the trigger from full automatic to semi-auto, and back again, listening to the inner workings of the gun. He put the drum back on and chambered the first round.

He looked at the stock, and looked again, before he recognized what he saw. Someone had marred Tank Bourne's carefully stained and lacquered finish and carved a little heart in the stock, no bigger than the nail on his pinkie. A valentine? It must have been Ali, in one of her sentimental fits. He wondered if she kissed it after she had etched the icon. Of course he knew many soldiers with strange little rituals they practice to bring fortune. One of his Wolves used to chew a terrible gum made of pine sap before action, as though as long as his jaws worked, he knew he was still alive.

Valentine tried to relax, but his body refused to cooperate. He rose, deciding to walk the perimeter as darkness fell.

The inner ring of wagons had been drawn into a tighter circle, trek tows lashed under the wagon in front of it, with the little house-wagons parked in the gaps. The remaining women and children were huddled in a quiet mass around the main campfire. Jocelyn Hendricks read by firelight from some children's books, reciting the well-known tales of Pooh and Piglet. Piglet was voicing his worry over meeting something called a Heffalump when she looked up and met Valentine's eyes.

"Rin, read the rest of this, would you?" she asked a boy, handing him the book before getting an answer. She stepped lightly between the children in her pointed-toe boots and joined Valentine.

"These are the kids whose parents won't let them go. They figure if anything's going to happen, they want it to happen to everyone. Is it as bad as that?"

Somewhere on the walls a sentry started up a tune with a Native American flute. He or she was skilled; it sounded like two instruments accompanying each other. The woven notes soothed.

"Are the kids okay?"

She shrugged. "The little ones just know something is wrong. The older ones are so busy pretending to be brave, they don't ask questions, but I can tell they're listening. Not to my story or the music—they're trying to listen for the sounds outside the camp."

"And you're pretending to be brave reading, and I'm pretending to be brave walking around with a gun."

"It's not pretending. At least not with you."

Valentine looked down at the young woman, scarecrow-lean in her hand-me-downs. Duvalier was the bravest person he'd ever met, and she voiced her fears. Why couldn't he admit to them, as well?

"I'm scared all the time. Scared of dying, scared of doing something stupid that causes others to die. Scared that no matter what I do—" Valentine stopped, not wanting sink into nervous garrulity. Especially not in front of this young woman he had just met.

"No matter what you do? What's that mean?"

"Not making a difference."

A quick, embarrassed flush came over her, and she rose to the points of her boots and brushed her lips against his cheek. "I feel safer with you here. With our wagons. So that's a difference, isn't it?" Then she fled the kiss's rebuff, or return, to the circle of children.

Outside the central ring, he met Waldron, setting up the last of his one-shot cannons to cover the outlet for the spring. More battle-wagons, ready to roll, had been placed to block the gate. "The lookout up on top of the ridge says the fog isn't thick at all, doesn't even come up to the hilltop. Says he thought he saw movement on Stake Ridge. Where's your lady?"

"Out there," Valentine said, gesturing with the ugly muzzle on the gun.

Waldron whistled in appreciation. "No kidding? You wouldn't get me out there on a night like tonight, not with them Reapers on the prowl. They can see through fog, right?"

"Fog, night, rain—it's all the same to them. They can read off of something else."

"Body heat, like old infrared equipment?"

Valentine shook his head. "No, but it's generated by our bodies. Some kind of energy. It's what they, or rather their Masters, feed off of. Your cattle create it, too. . . ."

"Rider coming in," someone called from the wall. The observation tower was useless in the fog.

Mrs. Hendricks hopped down from the wall, where she had been talking to some of the men on guard, showing fair athleticism for a woman her age. The deacon stepped forward, putting on his tall formal hat, but she moved in front of him.

Valentine half expected one of Tolkien's nazgul-shapes to appear out of the misty darkness drifting thick around the camp, but it was only a tired-looking rider.

"Don't shoot, now," the man said, riding forward with his reins in one hand and his other in the air. "I'm Deak Thomas, with the Bar Seven, speaking for Wagonmaster Lawson. Where's Wagonmaster Hendricks?"

"Dead, son. I'm his wife, I'm filling in. Say your piece."

"He heard you were gathering outriders, and he's come himself with ninety-five, horsed and equipped. We came as fast as we could, so we need provisions."

"Glory be!" the deacon muttered, raising his eyes to the fog-shrouded heavens.

"Tell him he's welcome. Tell him he'll get his payment for helping those messengers along, and a lot more besides. Tell him I'm grateful for his help, and I'm glad to see that the bad blood between him and my man is forgotten. Now's the time to put aside our differences if we're going to get through this."

Thomas nodded out his understanding. "He's a half hour away at most. We've had to ride carefully, before this fog set in we spotted some Troopers. They must have forgotten what happened the last time."

"With your Wagonmaster's help, we'll teach 'em another one, Mr. Thomas," Josh Hendricks said, coming up in support of his mother. Thomas walked his horse back into the fog, and they heard it break into a trot.

"That's news we can use. Close to hundred!" Josh said. "He must have emptied his camp."

Valentine felt his stomach tighten in turmoil.

All wrong. Something's all wrong about this.

"Funny . . . ," said Mrs. Hendricks out loud.

"Ma'am," Valentine said, wondering how to say this. "I don't like the sound of this. When we spoke yesterday, Mr. Lawson just didn't seem right to me. He looked nervous when I asked him about that scout plane. He was sure of your camp's location—like it'd been on his mind."

Josh Hendricks interrupted.

"Nothing unusual in that," Josh said. "Are you trying to

start something, stranger? Didn't the man help you on your way? He could have just killed you or turned you over to *them* when you were in his camp."

"Quiet, now, Josh," his mother said. "Let the man speak. I've got a worry or two, and I want to see if his are the same."

Valentine lowered his voice, not wanting to have rumors spread in case he was wrong. "First, it sounds like there's some history between your brands. I don't know what it is, but bad blood can make people do crazy things. Especially if the hurt is recent. Second, is he the type of Wagonmaster to strip his wagons, leave his herd almost unguarded with enemies in the area, to come to the aid of someone else? Unless he was sure they wouldn't be touched, that is."

"That's true enough," the deacon said.

"Third, he knew a lot about your camp, where it was, the calving, but none of his men must have talked to yours or he'd know you were the new Wagonmaster. Finally, his brand was also on the line of march from the Platte, but the Triangles got wiped out and his wasn't. You'd think his whole brand would've spent the last day running for their lives."

Josh Hendricks shook his head. "Pa used to say I could think better than most, Mom. I'm thinking this is plain stupid."

"Hush now, Josh."

The boy ignored her with fifteen-year-old certainty. "No Trekker has ever rolled over for them, and I don't think even Lawson would be that low. His men would string him up. They can't all be bad apples. I'd bet my life on it."

Mrs. Hendricks looked out into the fog. "I've got to think about more lives than just my own. But we'll see. You may have to bet just that, with the help of our new friend here."

Twenty minutes later, Lawson and his outriders came into the camp through a gap in the gate battle-wagons. Two tables laden with food and drink stood near the gate on one side, opposite the little shallow with the stream running out of camp. A fire burned cheerfully in the center. The deacon stood in the light enjoying a bottle of beer and one of Valentine's cigars.

Valentine watched events from beneath a house-wagon in the second line in the center of camp. Rocks, cases, kegs, and dirt were piled up under the wagons, hiding him and two dozen men good at rapid rifle fire. A few feet in front of him Josh Hendricks stood, Valentine's revolver tucked in the back of his belt.

"Look at those guns," a man sighting down his lever action muttered to Valentine. "There ain't a man there who isn't ready to shoot. Think they suspect us?"

"No, I think they're supposed to do this in a hurry," Valentine breathed. His heart sounded loud in his chest. A fight was coming; he felt it in every raised hair.

At the sight of all the ready guns and the antsy-looking men, Josh Hendricks seemed to shrink back into his clothes as he stepped forward. Lawson stood up in his stirrups and looked around the walls, where a few of the Eagles were on guard. He scratched his heavy growth of beard with the front sight on his pistol.

"W-w-we sure are glad to see you, Wagonmaster Lawson," Josh stammered. The deacon edged closer to the boy. "We're short men on the north wall. After you eat, you think you could get your outriders to screen us from the ridge side?"

"Those your orders, boy?" Lawson said, squinting at Hendricks.

"No, my mother's. She's Wagonmaster of this camp."

"Not anymore," Lawson said, pointing his pistol like a striking rattlesnake. He shot Hendricks in the chest twice, and the youth toppled backwards, falling almost in front of Valentine.

Valentine's riflemen brought their guns up as the Bar Sevens wheeled their horses toward the walls. The men and women to either side of him fired in a long, ragged volley, followed by a second as the Eagles worked the bolts and levers on their guns. The food and drink tables upended, men appearing from underneath like shotgun-armed jack-in-the-boxes, blazing away at the surrounding horses. From the walls, men fired down into the mass of emptying saddles and screaming horses. Three Bar Seven outriders managed to get outside the gate before the battle-wagons were pushed together behind them, but explosion-flashes from the swivel guns swept them into a bloody, dying heap in the trench.

The deacon crawled through the flying lead and dancing hooves, pulling Josh. He dragged him beneath the wagons and stayed put.

It was over in less than a minute. With the gate shut, a few of the Bar Seven men flung their rifles down and dived off their horses. Some tried to crawl out out under the wagons, only to be rounded up by the men from behind the tables who advanced into the slaughter-yard to pistol the crippled horses and pick up the wounded men.

Valentine raised his gun over his head and waved it. He and the snipers emerged from beneath the wagon to join the deacon and Josh. "How is he?"

"Gasping for air, scared, and a Godly man for the rest of his days, I'll bet," the deacon said, pulling apart Josh's shirt to reveal Valentine's bulletproof vest on the coughing youth. The deacon extracted out the flattened remnants of a slug and tossed it from hand to hand like a hot chestnut. Josh Hendricks got to his feet and removed the vest, handing it to Valentine.

"I guess I owe you an apology, sir," he said, rubbing his breastbone.

Valentine looked at the deacon. "No harm letting them think the sneak attack worked—"

The deacon's eyebrows came together; then a grin split his face. "Good Lord, yes." He turned to the walls. "Fire off a shot now and then . . . like they're mopping up." A few shots cracked off into the night.

"Ghost! Ghost!" Valentine heard a female voice call from out of the mist.

Duvalier.

He ran to the front gate. His fellow Cat stood, barely visible in the mist in the light thrown by a reflector lantern.

"Can't stop for more than a moment—can you hear me?"

"I'm here," Valentine said.

She spoke quietly, but Valentine's ears picked up her words. "A Trooper and another of these Bar Seven turn-coats were waiting about a couple hundred yards out."

"What did she say? Why's she so quiet?" one of the men on the wall asked.

"Anything we have to be worried about?" Valentine asked.

"No, I took care of them. One's just behind me, and the other's in the stream, if you want to get their weapons. I listened in at their camp; they're waiting for a signal. Watch your north wall, too."

"For what?"

"No idea."

"Get out of here."

"It's a good night for hunting, Ghost. You were right about the Bar Seven after all. I'm impressed. Good luck." She disappeared into the fog-weighted night.

Waldron was replacing the expended charge in the trough of the swivel gun with a new shell.

"Signal, huh?"

"Yes. I think I need to ask a few questions."

The deacon was finishing his cigar as a woman in a white calving smock tied a tourniquet around the leg of Wagonmaster Lawson. Lawson looked around at his shattered outriders, tears of pain or anguish streaming down his cheeks.

"Shot up bad," the deacon muttered.

"They made all kinds of promises," he confessed to the deacon as Valentine approached. "I thought I'd become the biggest cattle king in the history of Nebraska, able to run the Dunes as long as I didn't cause them trouble. But as soon as they got into camp, they started showing who was boss. That damn General guy, ordering us around, treating my men like dirt. But what could I do? All the women and kids are in their hands now."

Valentine approached the pair. The medic looked up at

him and gave a tiny negative shake of her head. The ground beneath Lawson was black with blood.

"Damn, that tobacco smells good, Deac," Lawson said weakly. "I haven't had a real smoke in months."

"Give him one, Deacon," Valentine said.

"Thanks," Lawson said, through a grimace of pain. He took a deep puff on the cigar and closed his eyes. For a moment Valentine thought he would die; then they opened again. "Hey, you're the one with the horses, trying to warn people. They asked me some questions about you two. I gave them a wagonload of bullshit."

Valentine whispered something into the deacon's ear. He nodded.

"Lawson, here, hold my Bible. The Good Book's about the only comfort I got for you. You don't have much more time in this here world, so maybe you want to think about the next. You can help us, tell us what you were supposed to do once you took the camp."

Lawson's breathing became labored. "Sure. In my pocket. Flare pistol. Fire when we . . . got the camp."

Valentine found the wide-mouthed pistol, listening to the occasional shot or two still ringing out.

"My men . . . have pity . . . wounded . . . ain't . . ." He faded away.

The deacon checked his pulse. "Not dead yet, but soon," he decided. "God have mercy on you, Wagonmaster," he said, taking his Bible back from the relaxing fingers and mumbling a prayer.

Lawson gave a faint gurgle, and Valentine waited for the deacon to finish. When the deacon's hat was back on, Valentine picked up Lawson's pistol and handed it to Josh. "Souvenir for you, Josh." Valentine turned back to the preacher.

"Deacon, get me Waldron."

Mrs. Hendricks looked out over the slaughtered men and horses, shaking her head and patting down her hair, as the bodies began to be dragged away and lined up. Valentine didn't need his Wolf's nose to tell she smelled like gunsmoke.

"Wagonmaster," Valentine said. "This may work to our advantage. They were supposed to send up a flare when they seized the camp. If we send it up, the General's men might come in. I expect they'll be careful about it, but they'll still get close enough to have a look. I think if we can hit them then with some of Waldron's one-shot wonders, we can shorten the odds."

Waldron joined Valentine and the deacon. The four hashed out a plan, and then gave it to the leaders to pass among the Eagles. They would fire the flare, and the gates would be opened. When the Twisted Cross, or the Troopers, or whatever walked or rode in, they would fire every one of Waldron's cannons on command. Valentine described the main targets: "Tall humans, probably in body armor or at least heavy robes. They'll also have some serious hardware, battle rifles with curved magazines. Don't waste your cannon on the Troopers if they come in—just try to get the Reapers."

Mrs. Hendricks fired the flare herself, which arced up into the mist and bathed the camp in its red light, glowing as it descended from the heavens like the Star Wormwood.

"Remember, cheer as they approach the gate," Valentine said to the men, some standing and some hiding in the battle-wagons flanking the gate. Every cannon Waldron could load was clustered around the gate, and the wooden mine versions were hidden behind dead horses and in front of the wagon wall. They would explode in a hail of splinters and scrap metal. Valentine crouched in the cold waters of the spring, waiting.

He heard an engine approach, filling the night with the rattling, wheezy sound of a big diesel.

"What the hell?" one of the men on the wall said, peering into the mist.

"Cheer, yell your heads off!" Valentine called up at them.

"Would you look at that Goliath," the deacon said, crouching behind a dead horse. His cigar tip glowed above the cannon fuse.

"Let it in, let it in," Valentine called over the increasing noise of the engine. "The troops are coming in behind it." He half closed his eyes.

Quiet.

Centered.

Valentine pictured his consciousness as a large blue ball filling the horizon, and breathing deeply, he shrank it and shrank it, all the while inhaling and exhaling from a point at the bottom of his rib cage. He felt his heart slow, felt the whole world slow. The people around started to look like mannequins, dummies like he'd seen turning round and round in shop windows in Chicago. With his mind faint and open, he felt the presence of Reapers. A lot of them, terribly near. And coming closer, cold will-o'-wisps of death drifting toward him out of the fog.

Valentine's first view of the Twisted Cross, coming straight at him out of the midnight fog, froze him in place. A tracked vehicle, like a bulldozer with armored plate on its arms and front instead of a blade, towed a tanker-trailer that someone had torch-cut and welded into a mobile fortress. Crew-served machine guns pointed out of each side of the trailer and the windows and doors of the tractor were covered with slitted armored plating.

Behind them, in two columns, came the Reapers of the Twisted Cross. More like insects than men, they wore carapaces of heavy body armor, topped by visor-covered helmets that hung down at the sides and back like old samurai versions. The battle-Reapers held assault weapons at the ready and bulb-headed tubes in a harness on their backs.

The Eagle men cheered, some of them almost hysterically, others tentatively. A few inched away, ready to run for cover at the first shot.

Valentine crawled and flattened himself into the depression cut by the stream of water as the battle-rig rolled overhead, its bulk straddling the little spring with ease.

C'mon, Waldron. Now!

A whistle trilled in the night, to immediate effect. The swivel guns began to go off in such quick succession that it sounded like one continuous roar; an avalanche of sound and air pressure washed over Valentine. From beneath the still-moving trailer, he saw armored figures knocked down, some never to rise again. Others seemed not to even feel the blasts, and they turned to fill the night with muzzle flashes like yellow flowers blossoming.

Valentine, deafened by swivel-gun blasts and the gunfire, crawled out from beneath the trailer.

A Reaper ran toward the back of the truck, trying to take cover from the cross fire streaming down from the battle-wagons.

He rose to his feet with his gun at his shoulder. It pulled up and stared, perhaps surprised by his sudden appearance. It brought up its gun but caught a chattering blast from Valentine's PPD through its visor and into its face.

He heard the machine guns in the armored trailer firing, stitching the side of the battle-wagons to either side. Men toppled and dived for cover.

Valentine turned. He took two steps toward the rear of the sawed-off tanker and leapt, vaulting into the air as if lifted by an invisible pole over the ten-foot moving wall. The Cat landed on a walkway that ran along the spine of the converted tanker. The top hatch was round like a man-hole, locked tight. He found a fan mounting on one of the sloping sides, the exterior closed by wire designed to keep grenades out.

Quisling mechanics take no pride in their work. Quick and cheap does it every time.

He squatted next to it, ignoring bullets whistling all around. Balancing on the balls of his feet, he coiled his body, grabbed, strained, and tore the thin grating free. Then he kicked the plastic blades out of the way.

He tucked the gun and dropped inside.

Only one had time to even look in astonishment at the in-truder who had appeared in the their midst as if conjured out of the fog before Valentine swept the forward half of the gun bay with a burst from the submachine gun. The PPD roared in the confined space of the platform, sending men sprawling.

Valentine sensed movement behind—ducked as a pistol

shot ricocheted off the armored wall where his head had been. He put a burst up into the soldier, lifting the man clear from the deck. He squeezed a second blast into the other rear gunner as the Twisted Cross man struggled to put a new magazine in his rifle.

Eight dead or dying men lay inside the back of the truck. Valentine moved forward to the crew-served weapons, shooting one crawling soldier in the side of the head as he did so. The semi was turning, bringing its deadly sides to bear on the main gate, the drivers in the cab still unaware of the destruction wreaked in the rear.

He pulled the machine gun facing the wall of wagons out of its mount and looked in the box magazine at its side, half-empty of shells. He decided it was enough and climbed up to the firing position at the front of the old tanker, using a step that gave him a clear view out over the top of the tracked dozer. The driver and his companion traded shots with the Eagles on the wall from within their reinforced cockpit. Nothing but canvas and wire mesh stood between him and the two men in the cab. He shoved the gun tight into his shoulder and pressed the trigger, snarling down at the unsuspecting Troopers. The muzzle flash blinded him. When he lifted his finger and could see again, both men lay dead in the bullet-riddled cab.

He went to the other machine-gun slit in the tanker wall. It was a well-designed weapons bay: a slit cut in the armored side of the trailer, with the gun mounted on a tripod behind a second bulletproof shield. Through the slit, he could see a triangle of Reapers. They had made it past the gate, firing all around as bullets hit their body armor. They seemed invulnerable. A grenade exploded amidst the three, causing one to drop to its knees. It righted itself and continued firing.

Valentine sighted the weapon and loosed a long burst, the tripod easing his aim. The weapon hardly shook as the bullets poured out of it, cartridge casings sounding in the gun's deafening chatter like faint bells as they tumbled to fall through the holes in the wire grid deck, where they wouldn't be tripped on before they could be collected from the belly of the tanker.

The first Reaper went down, broken in half by the machine gun. Another's head vanished when it turned to look at the first, and the grenade-wounded third tried to crawl away after he knocked it over with a blast. Valentine must have put a hundred rounds into it—in short bursts that alternated with mindless obscenities—before it finally lay still.

Get a hold of yourself. Use your brain as well as this gun.

Fighting the madness still heating his blood, Valentine dropped two more Twisted Cross off the wall. Another team vaulted into one of the battle-wagons. One removed the head of the defender in the wagon with a single hand-thrust up and under the Eagle's chin; its companion fired a weapon that looked like a plunger with a football glued to the end of it. The warhead took off in a whoosh of rocket-sparks and exploded under a battle-wagon, tossing men and debris into the air.

Valentine emptied the weapon into that pair, knocking one—its midsection torn to a pulp of black goo—into the bullet-riddled wall and blowing the other off the parapet. It fled, swinging over the wagons and into the trench minus an arm and a leg.

Working as though possessed, he lifted a new ammunition belt from the locker at the base of the weapon and opened the feeder at the top. As he placed the first round in the gun, a Twisted Cross rushed out of the darkness. In two seconds, it covered the distance to the truck.

When Valentine saw it leap, he drew his sword, and by the time it ripped through the top hatch, he had the blade held ready.

It came through headfirst.

His first slash removed the thing's arm at the elbow; it just dodged his backswing designed to take off its head. Had it immediately dropped in clawing fury on Valentine, it might have ended the fight there, but whoever was animating the Reaper decided to use its gun.

It dropped and spun to land on its feet; as it fell, it

brought up the Kalashnikov, giving Valentine the instant he needed to roll forward under the burst of bullets. He opened its stomach just beneath its vest, where the groin-guard joined the armor above, then used the return thrust and skewered it under the armpit.

It turned, plucking the sword out of Valentine's hand like a wounded bull taking off with a banderilla. It staggered a step away as Valentine reached for his parang, drawing the machete-like knife and striking the back of its neck with one fluid motion. The body took one more step with its spinal cord severed before crashing to the deck, smearing a tarry black substance on the wire flooring as it rolled and flopped.

The men at the walls and figures outside the gate were still exchanging shots. Valentine heard a great deal of fire on the hillside at the north end of camp, not the chatter of the Kalashnikovs but the *pop-pop-pop* of aimed rifle fire. An occasional heavier *whump* sounded as one of the swivel guns discharged, joined by sharper explosions Valentine knew now to be rocket-propelled grenades.

Feeling thick-limbed and dull-eared, he retrieved his PPD and replaced the drum. Shaking himself back to coherence, back sore from adrenaline-burn, he readied the mounted machine gun and trained it on the gap at the gate, but even the muzzle flashes of the Twisted Cross guns had ceased. The gunfire around the camp faded into a moaning chorus of the wounded calling for help or screaming out their pain.

There was nothing left to kill.

Valentine sagged against the butt of the gun, aware of nothing but the smells of cordite and hot metal; he waited for someone else to make the decisions.

As the Twisted Cross Reapers withdrew, the barrage started, a fall of mortar shells blasting man, animal, and wagon into pieces. Valentine had never experienced anything like it. Though they fell all around the wagons, each explosion seemed aimed at him.

Thirty minutes later, it stopped. Then the cleanup began.

"If this is victory, I'd hate to see a defeat." The outrider leader, Danvers, looked across the smoldering ruin of the campsite as dawn burned away the fog. Valentine had joined him in the survey, asking that he might also employ the outriders in looking for a "pile of four" message from Duvalier.

The Eagle's Wings Brand dead lay in a long row, blanket-covered bodies with feet, at least in the cases where the deceased had both legs, protruding from beneath the earth-toned shrouds. Among them was the Camp Engineer Waldron, killed by a Reaper while reloading a swivel gun.

As they waited for the dawn and organized what was left of the defense, Danvers told Valentine about his outriders' fortunes on the hill above the north wall. During the Twisted Cross retreat, they discovered insectoid Grogs they called "Sandbugs" scattered on the hill above the camp.

"Sandbugs we can handle. They're out of the Dakotas—they live mostly in the unoccupied prairie and Badlands area," Danvers explained. "They look kind of like big sow bugs—they grab you in their front choppers and stick a needle with some kind of venom into you. If you're lucky, it kills you; if you're not, you get paralyzed. Either way, they throw you in a hole with a bunch of their eggs."

"Weaknesses?" Valentine asked mechanically, watching a widely spaced line of men on horses checking the grounds around the camp.

"They're the dumbest damn things, they don't organize at all, just scuttle in to the attack whenever they spot motion. Of course, if they had made it to the walls, there would have been trouble, they can dig like hell and they would have just hit the trench and gone right into the sand, come up in camp. That wouldn't have been pretty. What's left of my men are trying to hunt them down. They'll be hiding from the sun now that it's coming up. All we need are Sandbug nests on top of everything else."

Valentine's business was with the Twisted Cross, not new Grog physiognomy. He hadn't seen Duvalier, or discovered any message from her.

He found the deacon overseeing the care of the wounded and preparations for interment of the dead.

"I can't find Mrs. Hendricks, Deacon, so I thought I'd say good-bye to you, and ask you to tell her I'm on my way."

"Hold on now, son. You need a break as much as everyone else. Mrs. Hendricks is riding with the outriders. Let them see what those people have found out. No point in you wandering off half-cocked. Besides, we still haven't found sign of your friend. Don't you at least want to see her given a decent burial?"

"I think she's alive, Deacon."

"Now look, here comes the Wagonmaster now. Talk it over with her."

Mrs. Hendricks rode in, bearing her exhaustion and loss with the same mild manner she used to order her camp. A man ran up to help her off her horse.

"Thanks, Brent," she said. Valentine and a few others approached her, anxious for news.

"Yes, they're gone—their camp is empty," she announced. "And no, we haven't found any of the missing people yet, except for Peter and Judith Reilly. They're down amongst the trees, shot. That should take care of most of your questions."

The crowd mostly turned away, but Mrs. Hendricks chose to speak to Valentine first. "No sign of Alice, young man. But no body, either."

"Wagonmaster, I don't think you have to worry about the Twisted Cross for the immediate future. They'll need time to regroup after this. I'd like to move on. Maybe I can follow them back to their hole. Seems like they're retreating."

"We've survived before; we will again. You'll always be welcome among our teams, David. I saw you with that mobile bunker," she said, looking at the battered tanker. It had been emptied of weapons; the automatic guns were now in the capable hands of the Eagles. "I didn't grow up in this area—I was born into the Freehold out in the Wind River in western Wyoming. I was a dispatch runner at one time, before I met my husband while he was scouting for the Eagle

Brand cattle drive. I know the Hunter's Arts when I see them. Back in those days, I used to use my ears and nose just as much as my eyes. I'm sure you know what I mean."

She turned to her son. "Josh, we'll need a good saddle horse and rig for our friend here. He has to be riding on. Put a couple of bags of feed for the horse and something to keep him going on the saddle, would you?"

"Yes, ma'am," Josh said briskly, despite the pain and fatigue in his eyes. The boy had changed from opinionated adolescent to dutiful outrider in a single night.

Danvers added, "It might take a while. The horses that had bolted during the mortar barrage are still being rounded up."

She smiled at her son's back. "I think they pulled out south." Her rosy features turned fierce. "We really gave them something to choke on. Oh, there was a pair of burned trucks, and one heavy tow-rig that looked like it plain blew up. Could be your Alice got in their camp when they were busy with us. Hope she didn't go up with their powder."

"She said she'd leave word if she could," Valentine said. "Did you see any markers, any piles of stones or wood?"

"No, but then the camp was a mess. She sure can cause a lot of trouble when she sets her mind."

"You could say that," Valentine agreed. "And now I need to find her."

"You've been up all night, son. Crossing the Dunes with Lord-knows-what still out there bleeding and angry isn't a job for someone who's half-asleep. You need two hot meals and some sleep in between before I let you walk out my gate."

He opened his mouth, but shut it again when Mrs. Hendricks planted hands on her hips. She jerked her chin down in a nod, putting the same authority in the gesture as a Chalmers tapping her gavel.

Valentine returned to the house-wagon, grateful to give in to the wisdom of her words. Jocelyn Hendricks sat on the wooden steps, a cup of something steaming in her hands that smelled faintly of whiskey.

"I put breakfast in there for you," she said. There were

circles under her eyes. "There's so many dead. It felt . . . strange to make coffee and food with bodies laying in rows. I feel like everything should stop for a while, but the cows still needed to be milked."

She got up and opened the door for Valentine. He dragged himself inside and sat at the tiny table. Rolls and a slice of pie stood on the table next to a pitcher full of milk.

"I couldn't touch meat, let alone cook it. Sorry," the young woman said, opening a window.

"I'm not that hungry," Valentine said. He poured himself some of the still-warm buttermilk and drank. The rich taste triggered something in him, and he raised the glass, gulping it down. What did not go into his stomach went down his chin. He put the glass down with a shaking hand.

She stared at him, biting her lower lip. Valentine, in a fog matching last night's, couldn't bring himself to make conversation.

"Was this a bad battle?" she finally asked.

"No. You won."

She shifted her weight closer and brought up a rag to wipe off his chin.

"There's . . . blood or something all over your clothes. From when you were in that truck, so I hear. Though it's already turning into a tall tale: they've got you jumping like a deer, practically flying. . . . Let me wash them for you; they can dry while you sleep."

He stood, still chewing, his mind taking in her movements, the taste of the food, and the little cabin, but not processing the information. He began to undress. She blushed and stepped outside, and he handed her the bundle through the window.

"Thanks, Miss Hendricks," he said.

"Jocelyn."

When he woke, Jocelyn was sitting on the cabin's tiny stool, oiling his boots. He either felt safe in the Eagle camp, or she had sneaked in during his deepest cycle of sleep: he did not remember her reentering the house-wagon.

"You're leaving?" she asking, getting up to show him his
newly washed traveling clothes.

"Soon." He sat up, still wrapped in the blanket, and tried
to blink the gum out of his eyes.

"To find your wife?"

"Wife? She's more of a guide. I suppose I rely on her
better than some men do their own wives."

"I know it's none of my business, but do you and she—?"
She trailed off, darting an embarrassed look at him from her
lowered head.

"No—we joke about it. Maybe under different circum-
stances I'd think differently."

"I had a boyfriend. He went on a drive to Denver, never
came back. That was over a year ago now. I guess he
wanted to see the city. I was hoping for a letter, a message,
but he never explained himself."

"I'm sorry."

"He used to make me feel . . . all warm and safe. Last
night, when you talked to me, I felt warm and safe again. I
wanted to kiss you."

Valentine felt lust and compassion war within him. She
was an alluring young woman, but he was leaving almost
within minutes. "Jocelyn, I'll bet every young man in this
brand would walk through fire to kiss you. We're
strangers."

"The guys here are good men. I've known them all my
life. All the older ones act more interested in the fact that
I'm the Wagonmaster's daughter. The young ones are
just . . . kids in men's boots, if you know what I mean.
You're . . . serious."

Valentine thought it a strange word. Perhaps it was apt.

She placed the boots on the floor and sat at the edge of
the bunk. "Since that meal after you rode in, I've been
thinking about you. You probably think I'm just some silly
hick girl. I'm not looking for a man permanent. If anything,
you going away makes it better for me—I can just lose myself in it without worrying about the future. Know what I
mean?" She took off her bandanna and shook out her thick
chestnut hair. She planted her palm between his pectorals;

his heart thumped hard against his ribs, as if it were trying to touch her.

Valentine rose from the bed toward her, and they fell into each other's arms, need making the embrace smooth and unembarrassed. Even better for Valentine, it was unself-conscious. Instincts sublimated during months without touching a woman surged inside him, spilling out like rising floodwaters over an earthen dike—in an instant the barriers dissolved. He took her rich, sage-sweetened hair in his hands as he kissed her.

"David, who *are* you? I . . . feel like I'm in heat," she gasped as he explored her neck with his mouth, the rest of her with his hand. He helped her wriggle out of her clothes. His blanket had already fallen away, leaving him nude and aroused and pressed hard against her.

He laid her down to the sheets, and she parted for him. Her hands gripped, pulled at his back as he entered. She melted around him, greedily taking what he gave her, but what she gave him was even sweeter. Forgetfulness. For those minutes there was no battle, no hunt, no responsibilities or fears, only a trembling woman in his arms. Their lovemaking was just kisses and softness and warmth and wetness and lust and motion, thrusting motion in which there wasn't a last night or tomorrow just a climax like a lightning flash in the dark of the angry void that was his life, a paroxysm that left him even more hungry for her and the oblivion of her body.

He trotted out of the Eagle's Wings camp on a bay quarter-horse gelding. It was like riding on a mobile tower: the horse measured over seventeen hands and had a rear end like a rowboat. The Eagles lined up to see him out of the gate. Valentine felt honored by the gesture, though he flushed at the little half-wave Jocelyn gave. He saw her hands clasping and unclasping as he rode out, and felt guilty.

Valentine's only souvenir of the fight was a metal helmet, a piece of Kevlar with coal-scuttle flanges protecting the neck. With his battered vest, it would add to his disguise should he have to resort to posing as a Trooper again. Whoever had worn it invested in a cork-and-webbing liner and khaki cotton sun sheath, which did an admirable job of keeping him cool.

He searched the Twisted Cross camp. It stood in the lee of the little ridge south of the larger, horizon-filling one that sheltered the Eagles' camp.

A pair of outriders scavenged the wreckage, throwing everything from useless-looking scrap metal to expended shell casings into a wagon. Valentine rode up to them.

"The man with the tommy gun," one of them said, waving back. "Hey, mister, we got word you were looking for piles of four of anything. I think we found what you're looking for—that or these boys sure have a funny way of taking care of their dead. Look at Sam beside the trail yonder." He pointed down the rutted cross-country trail.

Valentine joined the waving outrider and found a little collection of four Reaper heads, arranged in a neat pile like cannonballs in an old fort. Bluebottle flies were already thick on the dead flesh; in places, masses of maggots had already exposed black bone.

He closed his nose and mouth and knocked over the pile with his toe. Beneath the gruesome marker was a folded piece paper. He picked it up and recognized Duvalier's hand.

Ghost,

I'm moving south to the Platte. I listened to the camp, and there's another contingent over in Broken Bow. Just go south to the highway and follow it east, or read your map. If they've pulled out of there, let's meet south of Omaha where we talked about. I listened in on their General, and their Headquarters is there. They call it the "Cave," whatever that is.

Don't be impressed with the pile. This is wounded I finished off while they were trying to get back to their camp.

—Smoke

Valentine folded the note and put it in his map case. He returned to his horse, which already had its nose down in the dry grass, cropping some green weeds beneath the longer growth.

"Broken Bow it is."

He camped that night near an old highway intersection, in a former Nebraska national forest.

The indefatigable horse covered nearly sixty miles that day. Valentine was astonished at the distance. In his first year as a laborer in the Free Territory, the horsemen in the Ozarks had passed on their preference for mustangs, saddlebreds, palominos, and tough ponies, claiming quarter horses lacked stamina. The bay's energetic, mile-eating walk proved the Ozark horsemen wrong.

Valentine had seen some wisps of smoke to the northeast in the afternoon, but decided that whatever happened was probably over with before dawn. He had no desire to investigate another gruesome battlefield and risk being seen by a straggler. He saw fresh tire tracks on and beside the old highway, but even the little plane that had appeared every day previously was grounded. His only companionship was the occasional wary coyote and a few far-away hawks.

The campsite felt lonely. He missed Duvalier's jabs and sarcasm, and the smell of the woman's sweat over the campfire. He made a cold camp, and not knowing what might be out there, decided that his old Wolf habit of switching campsites around midnight was called for. He waited for the moon to go behind a cloud, and then he picked up his blanket, pack, and saddlebags.

As he placed the western-style saddle on the bay, preparing to walk to a new campsite, the horse grew restive. Valentine tried to stroke the horse's forehead, making soothing sounds, but the animal wouldn't be quieted. It danced backwards. Alarmed, Valentine turned to see what the bay was backing away from. A hummock of grassy ground bulged beside him, and he caught a wet moldy smell, like decayed wood swollen after a rain.

Valentine agreed with the horse. He vaulted into the saddle. The animal turned, but the saddle did not turn with it: Valentine had just placed it on the bay's back in preparation to walk the animal and never fixed the girth. He tried to grip the horse's barrel chest with his calves, but saddle and rider slid sideways off the fear-crazed animal.

He rolled to his feet and drew his sword. He felt the ground shift under his feet and sprang away. Something attacked the saddle and bags in a spray of dirt. He ran a few steps to the old highway, wanting broken pavement beneath his feet instead of soil that might conceal an enemy.

Something crashed through the woods and brush on the far side of the embankment. He saw a boulder shape bouncing downhill. It altered its course slightly—and intelligently. It headed for him, even as he sidestepped to get out of its way.

He dived, and the thing bounced over him. His peripheral vision picked up movement from another direction, and he put up his sword. A carpet of living muscle threw itself on his legs. Something poured liquid fire into his calf. He shifted the grip on his sword and plunged it into the thing, working the blade like an awl right and left in search of something vital. Valentine gasped for breath, and his sword and the pinned Sandbug suddenly looked distant to him, like the optical illusion a glassless telescope creates.

He had no inner sense of peace as consciousness died, his life did not flash before him . . . just a confused *What the hell?* And then darkness.

His little sister's puppy liked to nibble feet. It would lie down and cross its paws over his shin in the yard, and chew at his toes with sharp young teeth. David would lie in the yard and shriek out in ticklish agony while his sister sat on his chest and her mutt worked at this foot. Then his sister started in on the knee on his other leg. He felt her tearing at the soft flesh at the back of his leg. "Ouch, Pat—cut it out!" Then someone put a pillow over his face, and he had to struggle to breathe.

Valentine felt dirt in his mouth, but he couldn't spit it out. His tongue felt dry and withered, like a desiccated toad. He was in darkness, every muscle frozen. He tried to shake his head, move his arm, but his body wouldn't answer. Something was thumping at his chest. It was easier to fade back into sleep. *You sleep, you die,* a little voice told him, and he fought to stay awake, to break out of the enclosure binding him, but it was too hard, and he faded again.

Pat was at his face, strong beyond her years and trying to force a tube into his mouth. Using his last iota of willpower, he kept his jaws clenched.

"David! David!" his mother called from the back door.

"Mom?" he called back. "Pat's being—"

A hard probe entered his mouth, and some kind of fiery liquid hit the back of his throat. He couldn't breathe through his nose; he swallowed.

"David!" Jocelyn implored. "David, I'm here, it's okay. We killed the Sandbug grubs, you're going to be all right."

Valentine felt neither one way nor the other about the matter. He was too tired.

"Give him another jolt of whiskey. Best thing for the damn Sandbug venom," a gruff voice said, but his foggy brain took its time with the words.

More liquid forced in, his mouth held closed, and his nostrils shut. He had no choice but to swallow.

He woke feeling like a broken victim of a cattle stampede. But he could see now through blurred eyes. Jocelyn, the deacon, and Danvers sat around a campfire, staring into the flames and sipping something out of tin cups.

"Water," he croaked.

Jocelyn grabbed a canteen and knelt beside him. Danvers got behind him and lifted him so he could drink properly. The cool water infused him with enough strength for him to look up at Jocelyn.

"What?"

"Your horse wandered back yesterday. We knew something must have happened," she said, her hair tickling at his face as she stroked his brow.

"The Sandbugs are loose everywhere," Danvers explained. "We're losing cattle right and left. But the Wagonmaster, when she saw your horse come in, had us drop everything and track you down, just in case. We've pulled guys out of Sandbug holes before, and if they ever come out of the coma—well, they're like stroke victims a lot of the time. You being a tenderfoot and all, I figured about all we would be able to do is kill the grubs and bury what's left."

"It hurts. . . . Anything help the pain?" he said.

"I've got a soda poultice on it now," Jocelyn said.

Danvers patted Valentine's scratched and dirt-covered hand. "You'd clawed your way to the surface. We saw your head and arm sticking out of the burrow. You must not have got much of a dose."

"Don't let him scare you," the deacon said from the campfire. "You'll be fine. They only nibbled on you a bit, and all your fingers and toes still twitch. You were buried at least a day. Have another swallow of whiskey. That old saw about it being good for snakebite is bullfeathers, but some alcohol in the bloodstream sure helps with whatever it is they sting you with."

Danvers uncorked the bottle, poured another mouthful into Valentine, and gave him a chaser for good measure when he swallowed the first.

"That good, eh?" Danvers said. He took a swig.

"Chuck, you stop that, don't forget we're far from home," the deacon admonished.

"Sorry. First drop since calving festival, Preacher. Lot's happened since."

"It's your last till we're among the wagons again. When dawn comes, I'll ride back and let them know to call off the trackers."

Dawn came, and Danvers roused the deacon from his watch. The old Bible-thumper went to his horse and eased himself in the saddle.

"Time was, life got easier when you got old," he grumbled, and walked his horse over to Valentine. "Young man, you're welcome at our wagons anytime you like."

The deacon pulled his hat down firmly on his head.

"Thank you," Valentine said. He still felt drained, but his mind was back in the alcohol-numbed world of the living.

His left leg throbbed at the ankle, but it was the healthy pain of a body healing. "Now I know what Sandbugs smell like, sir. I'll be fine."

"Jocelyn, he doesn't saddle his horse for two more days. Lots of water and rest will flush the stuff out," the deacon ordered. "Danvers, I'll send out some of your men to take your place so you can get back to work."

"Thanks, but no, Deacon. I'll keep an eye on Jocelyn."

"As you like. Good-bye again, Mr. Stuart. God be with you."

The poultice cooled the wound. Valentine bowed his head and shut his eyes. "He was when I met the Eagles."

Valentine napped in the shade whenever he wasn't drinking. His Eagle companions fed him on bread soaked in broth. Jocelyn put vinegar-soaked compresses on his wound, and the cool antiseptic bite of the vinegar brought some relief. Valentine watched the two work: Danvers's eyes never left the girl when he was in camp. But there was restlessness to the man; he continually went out to fetch water or survey the road, or set snares for small game, and hallooed from a quarter-mile off when he returned.

"He likes to be on the move, doesn't he," Valentine said, as Danvers rode off to exercise Valentine's bay on another sweep of the ground to the south.

"He was born and raised in the saddle, more or less. His mom climbed off her horse and had him two minutes later. His pa says she climbed back on five minutes after that, but no one takes him seriously. He's leaving us alone out of politeness."

"I like your company, but there's no need."

"He . . . I made kind of a scene at camp when your horse came back. I told my mother I was going to find you and go with you."

Valentine read the anxiety in her eyes.

"I think your people need you," he said after a moment. "More than I."

"They'll be fine."

"I'm not going to tell you you couldn't keep up, or that I

wouldn't want you next to me, Jocelyn. So I'll rephrase. You need your people."

She looked at him, eyes wet. Perhaps she had expected a different argument.

"They're your family. You're at exactly the age where that doesn't mean much to you, but as the years go by, you might regret your choice."

"I might not, too."

"I wish I had the chance to regret my family. I had parents, a brother and a sister, a home. It all was taken away when I was eleven. If you've got any respect for me, set aside whatever it is between us, and listen to this: Stand by your mom and Josh. We're two people who needed each other for a little while. Your family will always need you."

"You're just saying this to keep me from . . . tagging along. Tell me you don't want me to go with you, and I won't."

"I don't want you to go with me for the reasons I just explained."

Her face hardened. "That's not what I meant. You, David, the man."

"Man? Am I?"

"Well, you're not a mule, except you're stubborn as one."

"You need a man with possibilities. I'm—"

"Used up?"

"What makes you say that?"

She sat still for a moment. "It's what my father used to say. About the older generation, the one's who'd seen too much death and change. He said they were still walking and talking, but something in them died—'used up' in the wars. Their families, if they had any, had a hard time."

"I was going to say you need someone to grow old with. I've had . . . bad luck with friends."

"It can't be better to be alone."

He shook his head. "Of course not. But it's easier."

Jocelyn was chipper as a robin in spring sunshine for the rest of his recovery. Valentine couldn't tell whether it was a

mask or not. The three of them talked long across the firelight as the stars circled overhead, until the embers dimmed
and they were only shadows and voices in the darkness.

The next day Jocelyn and Danvers rode southeast with
him for a few hours, before saying their good-byes. Danvers shook his hand, and Jocelyn hugged him when they
rested their horses at the farewell. Jocelyn broke off the embrace and resaddled her horse; perhaps she was not as eager
to leave her brand as she seemed.

"Thank you," Danvers said, taking his reins. His gaze
darted to Jocelyn and back again. "For everything."

"Remember . . . us," Jocelyn said.

"I will. Your people helped more than you know. The
General's been given a bloody nose. Maybe he'll run home
to his hole for a while. Then I can catch up to him."

With the good-byes said and an annoying mist in his
eyes, Valentine turned his horse's head to the road, and
tried not to listen with his hard ears to the slow hoofbeats of
friends leaving.

This land was thick with stands of cedar, with small, irregular hills sheltering wetter country and woods. Wildflowers and bees ruled this part of the Dunes. He saw no
sign of cattle or the trails of the Trekkers. He was into the
borderlands.

He tried to remember what Kurian controlled this area,
and thought it to be the one in Kearney. He doubted he
would see any Kearney Marshals out this far yet, but there
was a chance of a Reaper at night or Trooper patrols in the
day. He walked his horse and rode with more caution, keeping to low ground farther from the road.

He approached Broken Bow by throwing a wide loop
around to the south. He had known some Quislings to be
suspicious as hell of someone riding in from the no-man's-
land, but let that same man just circle and come from the
other direction, and they were nothing but smiles and "have
a cup of java."

Night was falling by the time he approached the little

cluster of pre-Overthrow gas stations and markets, houses and roadside stops.

He came across an old railroad track and dismounted to inspect it. There was no question that it was both little used and had recently had a train pass over it. The rails and ties were in poor shape—even for Quisling-maintained lines—yet the overgrowth had been damaged by a passing train.

He paralleled the tracks and the road, coming into town as the shadows disappeared and evening claimed the town. Only one building, a whitewashed cinder-block corner shop of some substance, had any light burning from windows covered by makeshift shutters. Only the wind moved through the streets.

If there had been a train in town, it had passed on.

Valentine saw the glow of a cigarette in the shadows of an alley, and a Trooper appeared, gun held ready in sentry duty. He pointed the barrel down the road at Valentine.

"Hold it right there. Who are you?"

Valentine halted his horse. "It looks like I'm too late. Did the General's men pull out? I was supposed to deliver a message."

"I don't know you."

"I wouldn't expect you to. I'm from Columbus, not Kearney. I'm going to turn right around, friend. He's obviously gone, and I just had a hard day's ride for nothing."

"Why didn't they just radio it in?"

"Not that it's any of your business, but the General likes to see certain things on paper, or so I'm told. Could be they didn't want everyone with a scanner picking up the transmission."

"Well, go on inside if you want. You could at least have a bite before turning around. Leave the horse and gun out here, though. Better leave that oversize shiv, too. Where did you get a thing like that?"

"A Grog in Omaha, two summers ago. It better still be here when I come back outside. I have a revolver, too—can I put that on the bench over here?"

The gun didn't waver from Valentine, but he could see the soldier relax a little. "Sure. You're well armed."

"You'd be well armed, too, if you were this far out, riding alone."

The sentry went to the door. Its glass was badly scratched but intact. "Dispatch rider coming in. I got his horse and guns."

Valentine strode into the little corner building. Four soldiers, two of whom were sleeping on cots, filled the post with sweat and smoke. Sandbags filled the windows, and a line of rifles hung on the wall. There were new sheets of paper lying here and there on the freshly swept floor; perhaps the building had recently been a headquarters.

"Evening," one of the men said gruffly. He looked like a sergeant, even if he wasn't dressed like one.

"Good evening," Valentine answered. "I'm a day late and a dollar short, story of my life. I was supposed to deliver a packet to the General or his most immediate subordinate. Looks like he pulled out."

"Yep, you're about eight hours late of a done deal. Don't know about a General, but that Twisted Cross bunch were here. I understand they burned out three whole brands in just two nights. There was some orders came through, and they left."

"Hell. To where?"

"How should we know? Those guys are damn close-mouthed. They gave me the shakes, I can tell you that."

"I know the feeling," Valentine said, honestly enough.

"They said they'd be back. Not that I'd recommend you waiting. Some snafu out west with the goat-ropers. Bank on this, though, when they do come back, it's going to be with enough guns to plant every last cowboy out there. Not that it's any blood outta my veins."

"Mind if I help myself to some coffee? I have to be moving on back, then."

"No, go ahead. It's old, but it's hot."

Valentine poured himself some of the acorn-and-hazelnut swill. He missed Duvalier's stolen coffee.

"Hey, son, if you want to take a real break, in the back

room we have a nice little piece of runaway. If she's over seventeen, I'll eat my hat. They found her family by the river two days ago, and I sort of inherited her from a buddy of mine who drives a squad. Spooks got her parents. You're free to take a turn."

Valentine took a step over to the doorway and peered in. The other soldier stepped over to his NCO and whispered, "Don't like the look of him, Bud." Not that a whisper mattered to Valentine's ears.

Valentine tossed down the rest of the coffee. "No, but thanks for the offer. I'd just get all sleepy, and I have some riding to do." He walked up to the sergeant, putting his hands in his pockets. "Let's see, I've got a tin of Indian tobacco in here somewheres, and if you'd be willing to swap a—"

He lashed out in an upward swipe, fighting claws on his fingertips reducing the sergeant's eyes to red jelly. With his left hand, Valentine raked the other Trooper across the face, opening four furrows to the bone from his ear to his nose. As the sergeant staggered backwards, palms to his bloody face, Valentine kicked over the cot holding one sleeping Trooper.

The other rose in time to have Valentine almost sever his head from his shoulders.

Valentine slipped off the claws and grabbed a rifle from the wall, aiming it at the soldier rising from the overturned bunk. The hammer came with an impotent click. Misfire or unloaded—he reversed his grip and laid the man out with a swing the Jack was too slow to duck. He struck the other Trooper solidly over the head, breaking the stock at the grip. The Trooper fell to the floor, dead or senseless.

Valentine finished the grisly work, killing the wounded with his parang. He took a pump-action shotgun from the rack, made sure it was loaded, and crossed to the sandbagged window. There was no sign of the sentry; he had either run or was crouched somewhere, covering the door.

Keeping below the windows, Valentine set the shotgun carefully next to the door, picked up one of the dead Troopers, and launched him through the window. Glass shattered, and he heard a shot. Valentine burst through the door, shotgun at the hip, and saw the sentry standing over the body, pointing his gun at the prone figure. Valentine's first shot caught him in the shoulder, and the second load of buckshot tore off part of the man's head.

The quarter horse was dancing in fear, pulling at the bench he had tied it to. Valentine calmed the animal, retrieved his gun and sword, and went inside.

The girl, the object of all this death, was in the bare little back room. She huddled in a corner, wearing only her fear and a ratty blanket. Two large brown eyes stared out at him from under a tangle of almost-black hair. She screamed when she saw Valentine take a step into the room, but he lowered his gun and spread his hands, palms out.

"My name is David. I'm not going to hurt you." He took another step toward her.

"No!" she shrieked, closing her eyes and turning her chin to the wall.

He stopped. "Sorry, this isn't much of a rescue. You're going to have to do all the work. Do you like horses? Do you know how to ride?"

"Ride?" It was only a whisper, but it had hope in it.

"Yes, ride. Ride away from here, on a horse that can run all night."

"Away from here?" she said, a little more loudly.

"Now you're getting the idea. Do you want something to eat, some water?"

"No . . . I'd like to be away from here. Like now."

"Get dressed. Take some blankets."

Valentine returned to the room and looked out on the intersection, if two unused roads sprouting sunflowers from the cracks could still be called an intersection.

The girl had seen enough. He threw bedding and jackets over the dead eyes of the Troopers and returned to the back room.

"Are they dead?" she asked.

"Are who dead?"

"The Authorities. They came in the night and took them. Took them for-forever."

"Who, your parents?"

She nodded, tears reawakening in her eyes.

"Yes, little sister, the Authorities are dead."

She walked out of the room, the blanket draped over her skinny frame like a poncho, in a torn pair of pants and some thick military-issue socks. "Wow," she said with a sniffle, looking at the corpses.

Valentine took her out to the horse. "I want you to ride on this road, straight as an arrow. I don't think you'll see any trucks, but if you do, hide. Find some people who have lots of cows and wagons—you got that?"

"Cows and wagons, sure."

"You know how to take care of horses, right? I've never seen a teenage girl who couldn't do it better than any man alive. Now that I think of it, I never did name this guy. I guess you'll have to do it."

She patted the big horse on the neck, making friends. "Yes, sir. He sure is a big one. I think I'll call him Two Tall. He has two stockings, you see?"

"When you reach the cows and wagons, find someone called a Wagonmaster. Tell the Wagonmaster that you need to get to the Eagles, and they'll help you. Are you okay with that?"

"Wagonmaster. Eagles. Sure."

"There's a woman with the Eagles who just lost a lot of people to the Authorities. She'll look after you. Now what road are you going to follow?" He asked, taking his pack down from the horse but leaving the food and water.

"This one," she said.

"Any questions, little sister?"

She climbed onto the saddle with the agility of a monkey, a skinny young girl in the saddle of a very big horse. She pulled back on the bit and turned Two Tall. The excited horse sidestepped; she knew how to neck-rein.

The girl's eyes followed the road into the night, confidence rather than fear on her face, and then turned down to Valentine. Her eyebrows furrowed. "Who are you?"

Valentine wondered himself sometimes. He adjusted her stirrups as she looked at the dead Trooper lying in the street.

"I'm the one who comes in the night for the Authorities."

*   *   *

The rail terminus turned out to be a treasure trove of equipment abandoned by the hastily departed Twisted Cross. Valentine found the Troopers' pickup truck, a heavy-framed conglomeration of dirty windows under wire grids, wooden cargo dividers in the bed of rusting bodywork over a double axle. But the mechanical heartbeat within the diesel cylinders was still strong. He examined the engine, added motor oil, and loaded the bed with food and fuel, all the while keeping his ears open for approaching patrols.

The Jacks had either stolen from or been equipped by the Twisted Cross. There were stenciled crates everywhere. He read the labels using the light from Ryu's stone. It fit easily in his palm, allowing him to shine it this way and that. He found a case of grenades and another of thermite bombs. The aluminum–ferric oxide mix, when ignited, burned hot enough to weld metal, and was a favorite incendiary device of the more destructive-minded Quislings. He loaded up with maps, guns, and ammunition from the dead "garrison" and got behind the wheel—looking through a newly cleaned windscreen and the armored wire grid over it.

As he drove—not very well at first, he was inexperienced with such contraptions—he tried to get to know the ancient truck as he would a horse.

Valentine would never know it, but his slow drive through Northeast Nebraska became the stuff of local legend. He wanted to avoid any chance of encountering either patrols or hunting Reapers, so he stayed well clear of the Number One's territory north of Lincoln. He crawled along on the backest of back roads through an area claimed by Kurian, Grog, and Man. He stopped at the occasional lonely homestead, trading guns and boxes of ammunition for a meal and a night's rest.

The residents at each stop asked no questions of him, but were eager to tell him about their problems. He cleared out a nest of Harpies that were plaguing a little bottomland settlement from the old college at Wayne by burning their roost, and ambushed some armed ex-Trooper thugs who prowled in a two-vehicle convoy as they camped at night.

He killed one of the deserters as he went to relieve himself in a gully and returned in his hat and shot the others before they could rise.

He finally gave away the truck from Broken Bow to a co-op of families in the picturesque country north of Blair. On his legs again, he proceeded afoot into the ruins of Omaha.

Omaha was a burnt-out husk. The outskirts of the city were falling apart, the inner regions a charred and collapsed wreck, and everything south of the city between Council Bluffs and Papillion flattened by the nuclear air and ground bursts designed to knock out the old Strategic Air Command base at Bellevue. He planned to move around the edge of the ruins, perhaps along the old I-680 line, when Fate decided to lay down one of the face cards that She sometimes used to change his life.

Nine

Omaha, September: The Old World transportation hub set in the wide, wooded valley of the Missouri is a sad shadow if its former self. The skeleton of the Woodman building looks out over smashed walls and collapsed roofs, where people and commerce once thrived. Like its sister St. Louis, farther down the wide Missouri, Omaha proper is now the breeding ground for assorted Grogs and human scoundrels. The city and its surrounding lands were deeded to the Grog tribes in exchange for their help during the Overthrow, and the Grogs have shaped it to their taste. Control over the vital communications lines passed to the Quislings in Council Bluffs, who oversee the railroad bridges and the river traffic. On the western shores, the nineteenth-century brick buildings of the Old Market are now home to an assortment of human smugglers, traders, and plug-uglies plying perhaps the second-oldest profession—that of getting goods into the hands of those with the ability to pay. But even that nest of vipers just south of what's left of Heartland Park now thinks about relocating to a new city; there have been stories of fighting throughout the city between the Grogs and tall, well-armed men. The city is being cleared of its Grogs.

Which would be fine with the smugglers. But the recent destruction of a barge full of contraband and the death of its entire crew have the Old Market gangs worried. The Quislings always winked at the trade that supplies them with a few luxuries from other parts of the country, the Grogs in the ruins depend on them for weapons, and since the Freeholders are too far away to go to such lengths just to burn a few barrels of rum and brandy, they are forced to wonder if they have also been selected for destruction.

Someone with a plan is making a power play for the city, and playing for keeps.

He was on the northwest side of the city, near one of those multilevel, indoor shopping centers of the Old World. Now the cement structure was black and green and hollow as a diseased tooth. It reeked of Harpies from a half mile off, so he avoided it.

Valentine wanted to make time, so he walked well out in the open, intimidating-looking gun over his shoulder, sweating freely under the heat of the September sun. He pushed through the green chaos of what had been either a golf course or a park and moved out onto a series of parking lots in the midst of being reclaimed by forest, with the overgrowth-dripped roof of the mall in the western distance.

He came upon an east-west road, no more or no less clear than any of the others he had crossed, littered with the rusting ruins of weather-beaten cars, many with small terrariums growing in the sheltered detritus within, like a series of rust-colored planters. But he picked up a battlefield odor—flesh rotting in the sun.

He followed the smell and saw stains, recent but faded to brown, splashed on a car, and his nose located the fresh, overripe smell of bodies in the afternoon heat. A little farther down, Harpies, the snaggletoothed, ugly, bowlegged, and bat-armed Grogs that Valentine despised from his earliest days in the Free Territory, lay dead on the road and tossed atop cars.

Among their broken forms he found a huge fallen backpack—far too large to be carried by a Harpy, even on its feet, in the road. It was fashioned out of wood and skins, grafted on a core of what looked like a tube-steel frame of a kitchen chair, clearly homemade but showing a great deal of delicate craftsmanship in the numerous leather laces and braces. Obviously some Harpies had survived the encounter with the backpack-wearer, for it was empty.

Curious for some reason, Valentine tried to read the story of the battle from the placement of the bodies. The Harpies first attacked their victim in the middle of the road, judging from the two that lay dead to the east with bullet holes. His restless mind welcomed the challenge; he got on his hands and knees to find discarded shell casings. Their victim tried to make it to the trees Valentine had just emerged from, killing one on the way by tearing a leathery wing, breaking its neck, and throwing it into a car. He was strong, whoever he was. And tall—the Harpy had been thrown through the sedan's sunroof. Around the fallen pack, there was more dried blood, an increasingly heavy trail that became a torrent as it reached the broken windows of an old McDonald's. Valentine saw a final dead flier, but nothing else, in the stripped-out lobby of the restaurant.

McDonald's built its restaurants to last; this one's roof was still more or less sound after nearly fifty years of Nebraska's seasons. Stepping softly, Valentine followed the blood trail into the back of the building, through the debris and growth springing up wherever swirls of dirt accumulated. The trail ended in the dark, cavelike metal walk-in that had once been a refrigerator, or perhaps a freezer.

Valentine smelled more blood and heard slow, labored, breathing. He opened the door to the freezer a little farther, and looked inside.

A Grog lay curled up on the floor. An enormous one. It looked to be a type he had glimpsed among the Twisted Cross trains, taller and not quite so broadly built as the fierce gray apes he was familiar with. This one's exposed skin, rather than resembling the thick slabs of armor plating like that of a rhino that the Grogs on Little Timber bore, was rougher and deeply wrinkled, pebbled like an elephant's. It was also wearing fitted clothing. He had never seen Grogs in anything more than simple loincloths or vests. It was dusted with soft, fawn-colored fur, in patches on its chest and somewhat heavier on its back and shoulders. Blood matted the sparse fur. An ugly brown streak ran from the Grog to a drain in the center of the floor.

It was unconscious, obviously dying. Valentine almost

shut the door, to leave it to expire in peace, when he heard the slightest whimpering sound from the Grog, lost in some pain-diffusing dream. Whatever else, it had killed six Harpies, four with its bare hands. It deserved some thanks as far as Valentine was concerned. He began to rummage around for something that could be used as bandages.

The store was empty, but while exploring the basement, he found a few rags and old towels. The uniform closets and employee lockers had been stripped long ago, but he found a large red flag, well trodden on and obviously once used as a carpet on the cold floor by some unknown resident, long gone. He found an old box with packets of mix labeled SANITIZER, read the label, opened one up and experimentally added it to some water poured from his canteen into one of the buckets scattered around the basement.

Absently he stuck the empty packet in a pocket. Going over the Spanish instructions and comparing them to the English half would give his mind something to do later on.

Working with speed now, he went back outside and found rainwater in a crumbled sewer. He filled two buckets with water, and then rinsed out the rags and the dirty flag as best he could in the standing water. After that he filled two buckets and poured some packets of sanitizer into one, starting the material in on a cleansing soak. Returning with the water, he gathered deadfall branches under his arm and came back to the restaurant. Using a match for expediency instead of his usual small magnifying glass, he built a fire in one of the old fry-vats with the branches and set a metal bucket of water on a rusty grill over the fire to boil.

Valentine wondered how long the material should soak in the sanitizer. He made more trips for water, until he had every portable vessel he could find full up, then began to turn the cloth into bandages. He stripped and tied the cloth with almost hysterical speed, and forced himself to calm down. After a few deep breaths, he brought the boiled water and the strips of chlorine-scented cloth into the metal-walled room and began to wash and dress the limp creature's wounds. It was wearing a sleeveless, short robe that tied behind it in the small of its back, now badly torn and bloodstained. Valentine removed it and tossed it in the sanitizer bucket, where it joined the bloodstained rags that he used to dress the wounds.

Its cuts and gouges and bites bled again, but slightly. Whatever else might be said about Grogs, they died hard. With more time now, Valentine took the bloody rags to the fire and threw them in another bucket of bubbling water to boil clean.

He had a little brown sugar and a jar of honey, a gift from one of the farms in Northeastern Nebraska. The bee enthusiast had also given him pieces of dried honeycomb along with the syrup. In Valentine's next boil, he dissolved some sugar, honey, and honeycomb, and brought it in to the Grog. Using a washcloth-size piece of material, he poured the warm sugar-water into the cloth and then placed it in the creature's mouth, cradling its bearlike head in his lap. It began to instinctively suckle at the liquid.

Twenty-four hours later, having given it six more feedings and another change of bandages, Valentine prepared to leave the Grog. He arranged the honeycomb, a large supply of water, and some dried beef within reach, along with a bag of all the edible fungi he could scour from the nearby woods.

He hurried to pack up, for the Grog showed signs of returning to consciousness. Its breathing was slow and regular, and it no longer alternately groaned and whimpered. The Grog's remarkable body, perhaps more than Valentine's fit of tenderness, had pulled it through its numerous injuries.

Valentine took a last look at his patient. He had made a bed for it out of some of the scraps downstairs and padded it with moldy-smelling paper, but at least it was a cushion of sorts. Oddly enough, he felt the time spent treating the Grog was not wasted. He'd needed a day or two's rest anyway, and the empty restaurant was as good a place as any. He wished to be off well before nightfall, however, since the Harpies evidently hunted the region.

Valentine turned to leave and began to walk out of the

kitchen area, when his sharp ears picked up a hoarse croak. "Wait . . . man."

Valentine had never heard English out of a Grog before. Intrigued, he returned to the freezer.

"Was . . . this . . . you?" it asked, pointing to the dressings around its head and chest. It had a voice like a rock slide, a low, clattering rumble.

Valentine nodded. "Yes."

"Food . . . drink . . . also?" It tried to sit up, failed, but managed to raise its ursine head. Its pointed ears extended, sticking up on either side of its head like a bat's when unfolded. The ear tips tilted toward Valentine. "Why?"

He shrugged, before it occurred to him that the Grog might not know the meaning of the gesture. "You fought outside very . . . bravely. Call it a tribute. Do you understand?"

It closed its eyes for one long second. "No."

"It means I think you're strong, a warrior. Give help then."

The Grog chuckled, a low sound like subterranean grinding. "No . . . man. Your . . . words . . . I . . . understood. You . . . purpose . . . I . . . not . . . understood."

"That makes two of us. I will leave you now. I think you'll be all right."

"Thank . . . you . . . but . . . gratitude . . . is . . . owed."

"No."

The creature rolled onto its stomach. It lifted its chest off the floor with two muscle-wrapped arms. First one leg, then the other was drawn up under pectorals the size of manhole covers. Somehow it got to its feet, leaning as raised itself with an arm like a child's slide. It stumbled toward the door, and Valentine moved forward to catch it, forgetting that the Grog's full weight would probably knock him flat at the very least. But the Grog extended one of its five-foot arms, bracing itself against the wall.

"No!" it said between gasps. "A . . . gratitude . . . is . . . owed. Please . . . wait . . . one . . . day."

Curiouser and curiouser, Valentine thought. "Very well. One day."

"As . . . Men . . . do . . . I . . . am . . . Ahnkha . . . Krolph . . . Mergrumneornemn," Valentine thought it said. He got the first part, partially understood the second, but the final word in what sounded like its name was a set of trailing consonants as unintelligible as his old pickup's transmission.

"My name is David Valentine, errr . . . Ahn-Kha." He pronounced it best he could, as if saying, "Ah-ha!"

"Valentine is your clan name?" the Grog asked, catching its breath.

"You could say that. But it is a small clan. As far as I know, I'm it."

"David is your close name?"

"We say first name."

"My David, I am grateful to you," Ahn-Kha announced, crossing its left arm across its chest, palm outward, and bowing with ears folded flat.

"Ahn-Kha, I am pleased to meet you," Valentine responded. His knowledge of Grog habits was limited to what part of the human anatomy they liked to eat first. He extended his hand. The Grog either recognized the gesture or had some knowledge of human customs; he solemnly engulfed Valentine's hand with his own leathery palm and shook. "We didn't just get married or anything, did we?"

The Grog's features split into a wide smile. It threw back its head and opened its satchel-mouth, like a baby bird looking for a feeding, and laughed. The sound reminded Valentine of a certain braying mule of recent acquaintance.

"I hope that was a no."

Valentine gave Ahn-Kha one more day than he asked for.

Ahn-Kha's strength returned exponentially. Valentine admired the powerful construction of the Grog. Although he stood like a man and had longer legs than his "Gray One" relatives, when Ahn-Kha wished to move quickly, he made use of three or four limbs. Valentine eventually learned he could outrun him on the flat, but if it came to moving up or down a slope, especially one cluttered with trees or rocks, the Grog could vault and pull himself up using his enormous arms with an agility Valentine could match only with Cat jumps.

Fully erect, Ahn-Kha stood seven feet tall. His arms formed an inverted U, with an arc of muscle at the shoulders that bulged and writhed like separate creatures riding his back. He had three fingers and a thumb, the index and middle finger a good deal longer than the digit on the end, which was nearly as opposable as the true thumb opposite. His feet mirrored his hands, but he kept the former covered with something like a thick mitten shod with leather that allowed him to better use his toes climbing.

The two males of their respective species agreed that each was the ugliest thing they had ever met in Creation. Ahn-Kha thought Valentine looked like a flat-faced birth defect, and found the contrast between hair and skin revolting in contrast to the Grog's own all-over tan-blond body hair. For his part, Valentine kept thinking of the Grog as some kind of weird miscegenation between a shorthaired bear and an ape. He had something of the calm wisdom of a bear in his expression, with deep-set black-flecked eyes of the richest brown. The fanged mouth below marred the effect, making him look like a predatory beast of ravenous hunger. Ahn-Kha's snout was wider than a bear's. He bore a set of long white catfish whiskers that hung out and down from the sides of his mouth, though they looked more decorative than functional.

Ahn-Kha ate constantly, giving Valentine endless opportunities to examine the Grog's mouth. He watched Ahn-Kha eat with the same fascination that he once had when he studied a rattlesnake as it ate a rat. Hinged far back, Ahn-Kha could drop open his mouth like a steam shovel, wide enough to take a grapefruit down his gullet as easily as Valentine could swallow an aspirin. His front teeth, including the overlarge incisors that projected up and down, just visible behind his rubbery lips, projected forward like a horse's, but his back teeth resembled Valentine's own, proving him omnivorous. The Grog sucked rather than lapped water. For the size of his mouth, he had a small tongue, preferring to use his lips to move food around in his mouth. When Valentine, while discussing eating habits over dinner, extended his tongue out of his mouth to touch the bottom of his own nose, the Grog choked back vomit and turned his back on Valentine for the remainder of the meal.

Valentine learned to watch his companion's ears. The pointed shells telegraphed his mood. When interested in something, they projected slightly up and forward and narrowed into points at the top, giving him a devilish appearance. When asking for a favor, even something as simple as passing a knife during a meal, the Grog flattened his ears against the sides of his head. When he was tired, they drooped; when something pained him, they went almost horizontal. When he and Valentine were moving over unknown ground, as they did when the Grog first got up and about and started to exercise, they twisted this way and that like radar dishes, fanlike flaps of skin spread wide.

One mannerism that took a good deal of getting used to was Ahn-Kha's habit of closing his eyes to mean no. Until Valentine got used to it, he kept asking questions twice, a practice that annoyed both of them no end.

They relocated a mile south as soon as Ahn-Kha felt well enough to travel. Neither said a word about accompanying the other as they set out, but the Grog's presence felt natural to Valentine. They explored and finally settled in to a ranch-style house by the wooded shores of a lake. The others in the neighborhood were burnt ruins, but this one had solid brick walls and a slate roof. The fresh air and movement had seemed to do the Grog good at first, but he fatigued quickly. The lake turned out to be rich in walleye, and Valentine decided they could feed themselves without going out of hearing distance from the house for the remainder of Ahn-Kha's recovery.

"How did you know about the mushrooms, my David?" Ahn-Kha asked the day they found the ranch, sharing a bowl of fungi-based soup with Valentine. "You say you have never lived among us, traded among us, yet you know our tastes?"

Valentine could take or leave mushrooms. They provided

easily gathered protein, and in some cases fats, but given his choice, he would prefer to set rabbit snares or trap snakes rather than eat the chewy, tasteless growths.

"I've tracked a lot of your kind and watched them from a distance. What did you call them again, the gray ones with the thick hides?"

Ahn-Kha made a noise that sounded like he was getting ready to spit.

"That's not a word, that's a bodily function," Valentine demurred. "The Hur-rack? Is that close enough?"

The Grog nodded—a born diplomat, he adapted to David's gestures more easily than the other way around, as Valentine's ears were as fixed as his teeth—and concentrated on his meal. Cooking for Ahn-Kha was like trying to feed a lodge of lumberjacks.

"We've had some dealings with them down south. I knew a captive one once, he lived with some researchers. Loved root beer."

"Root beer? I know beer. I know root."

"It's a sweet drink—you wouldn't believe how good it tastes after a hot day's running."

"The mushrooms?"

"I've seen the Hur-rack stop and break off mushrooms from fallen trees and eat them on the march, even fight over them. I figured you found them tasty."

"Yours are adequate, no more. You have never tasted a heartroot, my David, which surpasses even your bread."

"How did you learn to speak so well?"

"We have a tradition, my David. When one asks a question needing a story to answer, the asker must then be prepared to tell a story in turn. Fair?"

Valentine nodded. "Fair."

"I was born here, my David, one of the first of my clan to be brought into this world once our people had settled. I am forty-one years old, and call this land home. The 'Gray Ones' you fight come from my parent's world, too; they are jungle dwellers—they do not write or shape metal and stone. We are the Golden Ones of hill and valley, builders of dams and bridges and makers of roads. Kur lured many of our clans and the Gray Ones' tribes to this world with promises of land and space, ours for the taking from a filthy and weak race. They gave us guns and trinkets, training and promises; we did the dying and helped win their victory. My parents despised your parents, many of whom sold their species for power and small wealth. In their opinion, you got what you deserved.

"We Golden Ones are happier as builders and planters than destroyers, and we claimed our land from Kur as soon as we could. Our clan settled around a fine stone building, once a library in this place you call Oma-Ha. My father was an overseer of our human laborers, and I heard your tongue. In my youth, I learned the English-speech and the English-script. I read many, many of your books, played your music on the electric toys, and grew in knowledge of your kind. I began to disagree with my parents, in simple rebellion at their narrow view at first, and later through conviction. A clan seer said my destiny would be with men, and so I chose as a profession trading. I was often in the house of the Big Man in Omaha, drinking his tea. I met smugglers who drove gasoline-powered off-roads. After being cheated more than once, I learned a valuable lesson: Know the man before sitting down to bargain; examine the product before making the trade. I learned that some men I could trust with my life—others were lower than dogs.

"By my thirtieth year, I sat at our Principal Elder's side during any meetings with your race, to help translate and advise. Men sometimes give themselves away when they lie. By my thirty-fifth year, I was an Elder, ten years before custom usually grants such an honor, and I looked forward to one day surpassing the achievements of my father.

"Our people had fine gardens of heartroot in the old brother buildings. Heartroot thrives on moisture and waste and little else. It is our staple. We learned to care for your animals, finding chickens tasty and easy to keep. We had a good land and busied ourselves tearing down the old and planting or putting up the new in our deep, rich soil.

"Then came the Twisted Cross, the emblem of our doom. I was optimistic when they first came; they showed us every respect. Their human 'ambassador' called for warriors to serve the new lord called the General south of the city, promising in exchange the General's protection for our lands.

"The ambassador, who had spoke fair words at first, turned foul when he learned we would not immediately give him all he demanded.

" 'We always protected our own before this day,' said the Elder. 'I suspect what you really offer is protection from the General himself. Look for your tribute of clan-flesh elsewhere.' "

Valentine tried to picture the scene, on the steps of the Grog-restored library, the Golden Ones talking amongst themselves, facing a uniformed contingent under the black-and-white swastika flag. Ahn-Kha, as he warmed to his tale, switched to the cadence of his native tongue, speaking slowly, his tone rising and falling like a ship in a heavy swell.

"After many words, sometimes hard, sometimes soft, the Principal Elder decreed that any free spirits who wished could go along.

"The General's man promised rich rewards of land after 'actions to destroy certain bands of rebels and terrorists' were completed. We Golden Ones had heard such before in the times of our parents and grandparents, and after much death and suffering were granted ruined lands near poisoned ground. Nevertheless, a number still returned south with the ambassador.

"He came again in the fall, again asking for a quota of able bodies. With fewer words and more anger, the Principal Elder turned him away, and only one or two malcontents went with him this time, rather than the dozens he had swayed before.

"Then came the third and final visit in the spring, now over three years ago. One of the malcontents who went with the ambassador on the second trip returned with him. The news they bore caused such shock that were it not for the many guns in the hands of the ambassador's men, there may have been bloodshed. Kur had named this malcontent,

Khay-Hefle (may he forever wander from hell to hell), to be our new ruler. Not Principal Elder, but *ruler*. Of course, this Khay-Hefle did not voice himself with brazen demand, knowing the gods would not allow his treasonous tongue to speak such words. All were shocked into silence at the ambassador's announcement, even the Principal Elder.

"A great anger came upon me, and I stepped forward and said: 'Go, all of you, or you will be killed where you stand.'

"The ambassador ignored me and spoke to the Principal Elder. The Elder quoted the agreement that deeded us this land, ruined and poisoned as it was, to us to be used and governed as we saw fit.

" 'Ah,' said the ambassador. 'It does say that, but as a Golden One would still govern, the agreement is still valid and Kur is still keeping its promise.' And many more words of deception like it.

"The Principal Elder grew angry, and his hair bristled. 'This is the second time in my life I have heard plain words twisted to mean the opposite of what they say, and both times your Masters are involved. Go back to your kennels, dogs, and never come again. Khay-Hefle and all who follow him no longer belong to our clan unless they return in seven days.' At this there was sorrow from the families of those who left in the two times before.

" 'You may try to enforce your demands and place this usurper over us, but do not think this task will be an easy matter,' said the Elder. 'You will go back with none of our warriors and less of your own.'

"I supported his brave words, and all the Elders stood silent and grim until the ambassador and his dog Khay-Hefle left. Then there was much argument, some saying that it would be better to preserve what we had built than suffer in a war that we would lose. Others said we must leave: go north at once beyond the reach of this General or Kur.

"In the end, the Elders sent away One of Ten, to travel north and then west to a range of mountains we knew of in the place you called Canada, beyond the reach of the Kur who care not for such cold. I was selected to lead the flight because of my skill in speaking to humans, but refused. I still felt the heat of my words before the Clan Hall and wished for nothing more than to see Khay-Hefle come with his new masters and try to enforce their wicked will."

Ahn-Kha paused for a moment and stared into the glowing coals of the fire kindled in the stone fireplace of the house. After their morning meal, it was still far too hot during the day to keep the fire going, so they let it die.

"For the rest, I shall be brief. We turned our gardens into trenches, or homes into forts, our halls into castles. Everyone carried a weapon at all times, and we gathered the children in the basements. I thought we stood a good chance, or at least would make such a struggle that in our destruction they would be destroyed, too, and our children would grow free of them.

"They came, and we had never encountered such soldiers. Our bullets knocked them down, but did not kill them. Even arm against arm, their strength matched ours by some demonic power, and we killed only one for each ten of us who died. They were as the Hooded Ones but they fought with the weapons and skill of men. They came with explosives, guns gushing streams of fire, and cannon mounted on tracked vehicles. The fire-guns were the worst. My people fear fire the way some of yours fear snakes or spiders, or great heights. Our end was bitter. Some comrades, and my father, as well as myself were holding a building in the garden before the Hall. They came with boxes of explosives, and when I saw this, I called for all to follow me out the secret tunnel going back to the old library. When the explosion came, it buried all behind me in the blast and rubble. I went to the Hall. A bomb or shell had gone off in the basement with the children, killing all there. I took another tunnel to the post where the Principal Elder commanded, but found nothing but bloodstains on the floor.

"I determined to avenge the Clan on Khay-Hefle, and lurked outside the ruins of our lands, waiting for a chance to kill him. But he set about ordering the lives of the survivors, surrounded by humans and a bodyguard of the Gray

Ones. Imagine that illiterate rabble chewing on gum-root and watching Golden Ones toil as they scratch themselves.

"Strangely, I was shunned by the few other survivors who lurked in the city. Perhaps they had their minds poisoned by Khay-Hefle, who told them that I brought this on our Clan with my proud words, and the death and destruction of our Clan came about because a few mad ones controlled the mind of our Principal Elder.

"My people live now as many of yours, my David, little more than slaves who live under the lies of a Golden One who speaks the words he is told to speak. I have had to move to the outskirts of the city and live alone. I still hope for my chance, but sometimes I think of going north and seeing if the One in Ten ever made it to the mountains of Canada."

Valentine reached into his map case. "I have some maps here, if you think they would help."

"I recovered with some from the old human library. But I will not go north before I pay off my gratitude to you."

Valentine shook his head. "Do we have to talk about this again? You owe me nothing. I had to see what could have killed those Harpies barehanded, and then I felt sympathy for you. It was a tribute, not a favor."

"We shall see, my David. You agreed to tell a story in return for mine. To know yours would make me happy. I have not really talked to anyone in a very long time. We are brothers under the skin, I feel, for you also carry many sorrows that trouble you."

"I could use a drink," Valentine said.

"You mean wine, or liquor?" Ahn-Kha asked. "My people made a wonderful wine from a fruit we call *ethrodzh,* but I have none with me. I had none even before the fliers attacked."

"I'd like to try it sometime," Valentine said, looking around the cracked and peeled walls of the ranch, the stained ceiling and the musty furnishings.

"You told me about your people; I'm not sure what to say about mine. We used to classify ourselves by color and language, where we lived and what we did. Not anymore, though. To me there are only three groups left: the ones who help the Kurians, the ones who endure the Kurians, and the ones who resist. The ones who help them, I have no sympathy for, and I've found that there's very little I can do for the ones enduring. If I think about it too much, I despair. I'm in the group that fights the Kur.

"So was my father. I'm not certain about his reasons for quitting the Cause, but now that I've done it for a couple years, I can guess. I don't know if he met my mother before or after he stopped fighting. I think it was after. But he left. He tried to live quietly about three hundred miles north of here, like your One out of Ten who looked for a place where the winters were too long and harsh for the Kurians to live. My parents raised a family—I was the first, and I had a younger brother and sister. In northern Minnesota every summer the people retreat deep into the woods and return in the fall. During the summer, the Quislings—you know what a Quisling is, right? Anyway, we hid out in the summer from them, as well as from the Reapers. In the winter, we were cooped up in our houses. Getting firewood and ice fishing were probably the only times we went outside.

"I guess my father didn't go deep enough into the woods. A Quisling patrol came by—I was away gathering corn. They killed them all, more for fun than anything. Another man, an old priest who was a friend of my father's, brought me up and educated me.

"When I was seventeen going on eighteen, some soldiers came by, from the Ozark Free Territory."

"I have heard of this place," Ahn-Kha said. "You cause a great deal of problem to the Kur."

"Problems," Valentine corrected absently. "But you would probably want to say, 'You cause a great deal of trouble for the Kur.'"

"Not troubles?" Ahn-Kha asked.

"No," Valentine said, causing Ahn-Kha to shake his head in disgust.

Perhaps we are some kind of kindred spirits, Valentine

thought. *Who else, with death all around, would worry about grammar?*

"Go on with your tale," Ahn-Kha prompted.

"I went south with some other young people from Minnesota. I was curious about these men who fought alongside my father. I wanted to do something, avenge them in a way, or replace him. It was my way of learning who I was, by following in his footsteps. Or that's what I told myself then.

"I also wanted blood. Show the force behind all this that you might be able to kill the father and mother but the sons and daughters will take their place. A schoolmate of mine, a girl named Gabriella, came south with the group. I had . . . feelings for her."

"I see, my David. When do you humans mate, at that age?"

"The question is, 'When don't humans mate?' I think."

Ahn-Kha put his hands on his stomach—Valentine knew enough of him by now to know that the gesture showed quiet amusement.

Valentine continued: "The first year, they just worked us half to death in construction and farm labor. I think they were winnowing out the shirkers. We were toughened, learned to work together, and all the sweat helped the Free Territory. But that year Gabriella died—it had to do with those damned Harpies and a Reaper. We did manage to get the ones responsible. They made me a soldier after that, and I've been one ever since. But it didn't bring Gabby back."

"A strange soldier, who fights alone," Ahn-Kha observed.

Valentine did not want to say too much. "It's a long story. I guess you could say I'm a scout that went out a little too far."

"Now you go home?"

Valentine nodded. "Now I go home."

"I think we were meant to know each other, my David. We both have lost our clan. We both wander alone. You are half my years, but your feet have stepped where I have only ventured in thought. I read your eyes when I spoke of the

General's men, the Twisted Cross. Would you change your mind about going home if I were to tell you exactly where they could be found?"

As they talked, Valentine idly wondered if this all was not some kind of elaborate trap. He discarded the notion; the Grog probably could have killed him in his sleep last night. Unless Ahn-Kha fabricated his story out of the still night air, he had more reason to hate the Twisted Cross than Valentine.

Valentine wanted a chance to examine the Twisted Cross base, but Ahn-Kha insisted that they first come up with more supplies, as they could not afford to wander and hunt near the Twisted Cross headquarters. And Ahn-Kha wanted weapons to replace the ones he lost to the Harpies. They were still debating the issue on the eve of their departure, as they packed to move on that night.

"My David, I feel naked without a gun."

"I offered you my pistol."

"Ha! I should have said I feel naked without a real gun."

"Ahn-Kha, I'm already overdue to meet my comrade. Your idea to go into the part of the city where the Golden Ones live seems a little risky. Why not try at this human settlement on the river?"

"There are Quislings there. We would certainly be noticed. My face might be remembered there. Besides, we have nothing to trade for a gun save another gun. Although we could get two good rifles for your automatic weapon."

"It still doesn't get me to the Platte, and there we can—"

Valentine was never able to finish the sentence. His nose alerted him to a strange scent, coming at them from the lakeshore.

"Danger," he whispered.

The Grog had reflexes. Ahn-Kha went down on all fours by the window before Valentine chambered the first round in his PPD.

"From where?" the Grog asked.

"The lakeside, to the north. Let's check the front." Valentine crawled for the front window. He stayed out of the light and examined the new stand of woods and brush between the house and what was left of the suburban road. Yes, there were Grogs out there. One of Ahn-Kha's Gray Ones had his long rifle in the crotch of a tree, sighted on the front of the house.

He returned to the common room. Ahn-Kha threw wet sand from their toilet bucket into the fireplace, killing the light.

"It is the Wrist-Ring clan, perhaps," Ahn-Kha said. "One of their scouts may have seen us in the house or read our tracks. There are six approaching from the lake. They have ropes. Perhaps they mean to take me back and place a harness on my back. If so, they'll find this old horse can still kick."

"Did they see you?"

"No, I believe not, they would have charged—or taken cover."

Valentine checked to make sure he had put his map case away in his pack along with the rest of his possessions.

"The way I see it," he said, "we have three options. Fight it out from in here—"

The Grog shut and opened his eyes. "They will burn the house around us, my David."

"The second option is to try to talk or bargain our way out of here—"

This time Ahn-Kha remembered to shake his head side-to-side. "The Wrist-Ring would make the best deal they could, so we do not waste our bullets fighting them, and then kill us afterwards."

"Or we could just run like hell."

"Often the wisest choice," Ahn-Kha agreed. "But they will shoot us as we run."

"Follow me," Valentine said. He picked up his pack and led the Grog into the garage. Light glimmered down from a hole under the peak of the roof, where the broken edges of a porthole window stood festooned with bracken. The wooden door still stood in its rusted tracks.

"They'll probably rush the house," Valentine said. "They'll come noisy, with grenades if they have them."

"No, my David. Grenades are too valuable to waste on

drifters. There is always the chance that we have powerful friends, too. Perhaps you are a wandering Twisted Cross official. They would come in and shoot anyone not in a uniform they recognize. Why do we speak in this place? It has no exit, and it will take time to climb out of that hole."

"We're not climbing out the roof. You're making a new door."

Ahn-Kha gripped the submachine gun, cradling it tight to his body in his massive arms. When Valentine heard an unintelligible cry, and the breaking sounds of the Grogs crashing through doors and windows, he counted silently to five, and then nodded at Ahn-Kha.

The Golden One lowered one of his saddle-size shoulders and charged the closed garage door. He struck it with the force of a demolition charge going off, splintering the ancient wood.

Ahn-Kha spotted the sniper at the crotch-tree, just where Valentine described a moment ago, but now Ahn-Kha had a much better angle than he would have had shooting from the house. He loosed a burst that peppered tree and Grog alike, sending it reeling backwards. Ahn-Kha twisted to his right and fired another burst into the Grog covering the living room from outside as its clan-mates went in. The wounded Grog dropped the rifle it had just begun to aim in their direction.

As planned, his living battering ram turned and tossed the PPD to Valentine, who lay down with the gun pointed at the front door. Ahn-Kha loped out into the front yard, to the tree where the late sniper positioned himself. The fawn-colored Grog picked up where his distant relative left off, sighting on the doorway.

Valentine backed down the driveway, now pointing the gun at the corner leading to the backyard on the garage side. He heard something coming around that side. Half a face appeared, peeking around the corner. "Your eye ain't much good if it doesn't bring your gun along," a gruff old Wolf had told him once, and Valentine taught the Grog the same lesson by aiming a burst at the half-face. He missed, splintering the corner of the garage, and the face withdrew.

He turned to run, and heard Ahn-Kha fire the booming fifty-caliber at something in the doorway.

"Cover me!" Ahn-Kha urged, and Valentine slid to the ground again, this time with the gun pointed at the mid-point of the house. Valentine marveled at how he worked with this remarkable creature—a being that was technically an enemy he might have killed on sight until a few days ago. Ahn-Kha stripped the sniper Grog of a bandolier glinting with shells and reloaded the cumbersome—to a human—weapon. Valentine saw motion in the front window and gave the trigger a twitch. The bullets went in the window; whether they struck anything was a matter of luck. Hips never leaving the ground, he wiggled next to his companion and lay down behind the fallen Grog.

The dead Grog had a homemade "potato masher" grenade jutting out of its bag. He held the grenade up to Ahn-Kha. "Can you throw this over the house?"

"I can throw it over the lake."

Valentine pulled the fuse and handed it handle-first to the long-armed warrior. Ahn-Kha drew back an arm, putting the other forward in the classic javelin-throw pose, and sent the grenade spinning over the deadfall-covered roof.

They ran, Valentine in the lead, cutting away from the house at an angle in order to force their attackers to get them with a crossing shot. They went over a fallen log in the middle of the road, Valentine hurdling it and Ahn-Kha vaulting over it sideways, using his long left arm as a brace.

The grenade Ahn-Kha threw never went off; perhaps the fuse went out, the bomb malfunctioned, or some desperate Grog behind the house extinguished it in time. The pair sprinted southward. Shots thwacked into trees around them as they ran.

Six Grogs followed, loping into the young forest of the ruined suburban tracts. It became five when Ahn-Kha halted behind a tree while Valentine kept running and brought down the lead pursuer. After that, the chase proceeded with less speed and more caution, and when Valentine killed another from a rooftop Ahn-Kha had stirrup-lifted him onto, the pursuit broke off.

"We got away from them," Ahn-Kha said, breathing heavily and resting on all fours.

"You bet, old horse." Valentine marked the setting sun. "But they won't get away from us."

Ahn-Kha got his pick of weapons that night.

They swung around in a crescent, and Valentine left the exhausted Grog with his pack and gun well clear of the house while he went back to the brick ranch, approaching from the opposite direction from which they had fled. He took with him two grenades scavenged off the dead Gray Ones.

He crawled around the perimeter of the house in his black overcoat, listening to the grunts and barks within. The Grogs had gathered around their wounded, resting in the back room by the fireplace. He armed and activated the grenade as quietly as he could.

Gray Ones have good noses and better ears; one of them heard or smelled the fuse. It barked a warning, and Valentine let the fuse burn down two anxious seconds' worth before tossing the grenade through the window. While it was still in the air, he stuck his fingers in his ears.

At the explosion, he drew his sword and came in through the back door. It was a matter of killing everything that moved in the smoke-filled room that was not a part of him. The stunned and stricken Grogs might as well have played blindman's buff with a buzz saw—only one had the sense to run. It left a blood trail across the floor as it hurried to leap out of the gap where the front picture window had once been.

It didn't make the window. Valentine was after it like an arrow, opening it with a slash across the back.

Ahn-Kha returned to the house and ignored the carnage. He examined the various rifles and eventually selected one with a black-stained handle. The Grogs liked the butts of their weapons to be gnarled and burled and this one was no exception. "I must shape this before it truly suits me, but it is a good gun." He also pored over the finger-size bullets, sliding the formidable-looking rounds he selected into his bandolier.

Valentine lined up the Grog bodies according to Ahn-Kha's instructions, placing them on their backs with the left palm over the heart, the right palm across the nose and mouth, weapons laid to either side. Another patrol from the Wrist-Ring Clan, upon finding the bodies, might pause for the proper ceremonies. They would seed the bodies with the correct decomposing fungi, and perhaps be too busy mourning their dead to pursue.

"You men anger the Gray Ones when you just burn their corpses. They think you kill them not only in this world, but deny them the passage to the Hero's Woods their bravery merits. Better to leave them to lie on the battlefield untouched."

"Ever heard the expression 'When in Rome'? They wouldn't have their rites ignored if they weren't here in the first place."

"That's the fault of another generation."

Valentine thought of the wilds of western Missouri. Wolf teams could reach Omaha, find paths that more powerful forces could follow. "By working together, some of that generation's legacy might be wiped away."

"The Golden Ones have tasted the fruits of their alliance with Kur. We found them rotten. Then came the Twisted Cross. Many would be ready to join your fight."

"I wish we could find explosives more powerful than these grenades," Valentine said, rooting through the Gray Ones' equipment. "We could hit the Twisted Cross in their own backyard."

"I can help you in that," Ahn-Kha said. "There are men in the Old Market who can obtain anything you need."

To Valentine, anything pre-2022 was "old." But this part of the city, set against the river, was aged even by Old World standards as he understood them.

The closely packed, square brick buildings had new windows where they weren't simply closed by masonry. The west and south faces of many still showed burnt-black smudges, lingering evidence of the airbursts that had destroyed the city and the old air force base to the south.

They came to the district walking along the Missouri. The river rolled south past the city, redolent of silt and algae, with only a hint of the sewage that Valentine smelled from many of the old storm drains. In the distance, a rust-colored dredger worked between the pillars of the rail bridge, bringing up masses of mud. Just upriver from the dredger, a few barges rested against a wharf. There were overturned canoes and even a few small sailboats sharing the riverside with the trim barges, baby versions of the huge transports Valentine had seen from a distance on the Mississippi.

Ahn-Kha told him a little about the settlement. Though all of Omaha and its surroundings had been given to the Grogs, the Golden Ones and Gray Ones still needed to trade—especially for tools and weapons. They invited a few humans to set up house, giving them protection for activities that were outlawed elsewhere in the Kurian Zone, and a little patch of land next to the riverside fields and C-shaped lake. The black marketeers flourished, and as the Quisling society in Iowa and parts of Kansas grew, they became semilegitimate even in the eyes of the Kurians.

Old Omaha had no walls. Once past the reeking piles of trash and the masses of feral cats sleeping in the sunny blown-out doorways and windows north of the wharf, Ahn-Kha led him to clean cobblestone streets. Every windowsill and rooftop supported a garden. Goats and calves grazed in open lots. The animals were marked with splashes of dye.

"The traders here run 'houses.'" Ahn-Kha explained. "When I came here, there were three. I am told it has been that way for years. The three tolerate each other, but no more. They share the common land but mark their animals. The gardens on the land of the house are their own. They tell me there are groves across the river for apples and cherries and chestnuts, but I have not been there to see how they divide it."

Men, most of them armed with gun belts, lounged here and there on the corners. Some rose from benches and made a show of standing in the sidewalk so Ahn-Kha had to step into the street to pass.

"You just take that crap?" Valentine asked.

"It is easier to receive an insult than a bullet."

Valentine saw the wisdom in that, but it still irked him.

"Which house do you wish to try?"

"House Holt. For the most part, they were good friends with the Golden Ones. It is run by the Big Man."

"What's he like?" Valentine wondered what to expect. He hoped it wasn't an Omaha version of the Duke in Chicago, alternately bluff and frightening.

"He was always evenhanded to me, though not friendly. He looked always to the future; I admired him for thinking, and speaking, in terms of decades rather than days."

"Not many can afford to do that."

"Here is his insignia. It hangs outside his house, and his men carry it as his token."

Valentine looked at the sign. He'd seen broken versions of it here and there; it was circular, green and white and black, featuring a serene long-haired woman surrounded by stars. Above the projecting sign on the second story, fans set in the window turned behind inch-thick iron bars.

"Electricity here?" Valentine asked.

"Yes. The three houses share the maintenance of a coal generator. Long ago I tried to get them to put one in for the Golden Ones. I failed."

As they approached the door under the sign, a man next to the door rose from his seat on a wooden locker and put his hand on his pistol. He had long hair and a longer stare.

"What's your business?"

"A meeting with your Executive," Ahn-Kha said.

"You let your Grog do your talking for you, kid?" the door warden asked Valentine. "Usually with you Black Flag types, the man's the mouth and the Grog's the muscle."

"I'm the bodyguard," Valentine said.

"That so. Put your weapons in this box, and I'll let you in. Whether you see the Big Man or not will be up to him."

Ahn-Kha gave Valentine a nod. The warden opened the

box. Ahn-Kha leaned his captured rifle against the door-jamb; the gun was too long to fit inside. Valentine placed pistol, parang, sword, and claws within, and covered it with his bedroll and submachine gun.

The warden shook his head. "More iron doesn't make you more tough, kid. I've got to check your pockets and pat you down. Anything sticks me, we'll float you back to your General on crutches. Anything else?"

Valentine removed a short clasp knife and tossed it in with the rest. It wasn't much of a weapon anyway. "Clean now. Enjoy."

The warden searched both of them from head to foot. "Strangers call," he shouted into the door.

"Opening for strangers," came the response after a moment. An older man, white at the temples, wraparound sunglasses worn against the glare outside, lowered a shotgun when he saw Ahn-Kha.

"Ankle! It's been years."

Valentine was glad he looked genuinely pleased.

The man nodded to Valentine, then shook Ahn-Kha's hand. "Thought you bought it in the Big Burn."

"I've been in hiding, my Ian. Please to meet my new brother, David."

Ian shut the door and sent a thick bolt home.

"You no longer run your route?" Ahn-Kha asked.

"The routes are drying up. Even north. Those of us who still want to draw food work carrying guns now. The General's giving us the squeeze."

"Then perhaps we can do business. We wish to see the Big Man about the General."

"Lost cause. That rat's got muscle from here to KC. Keeps trying to get us to come on base, wear his damned cross. Doesn't sit right with me—lots of us—going down there just to salute and put new heels on Reaper boots. This is House talk only, but immyho, the Big Man says that's the only alternative to just pulling up and leaving for God knows where. He's down to trying to get us a good deal and keep us off base."

                    *   *   *

Within fifteen minutes, they were speaking to the Executive of House Holt.

The Big Man wasn't big, or even of average size. Valentine guessed him to be about four feet nine inches, and a bantamweight to boot. He had lush black hair falling back from the crown of his head to his thick beard. An open-necked shirt, silver-buckled belt, and cuffed pants over pointed-toe boots. He was bowlegged, pigeon-chested.

Valentine guessed his age to be mid-forties. When Valentine was training to be a Wolf, he heard a senior Wolf talk about a generation the veteran called the "children of chaos." In the years of what the Free Territory called the Overthrow, many babies were born underweight and malnourished as a rule, and in the tumultuous years that followed, they never had a chance to catch up. Valentine had known only a few from those hard years, compact-framed like the man before him, but generous spirits. Extreme hardship, it seemed to Valentine, had polarized that generation to extremes of magnanimity or selfishness.

Valentine hoped for magnanimity.

Their host stood at a window on the third floor, surveying Old Omaha from a floor-to-ceiling window, the layered panes somewhat distorting the view. He stood resting against a chair; the chair and its mate sat to either side of a wooden chess table with gold and silver pieces arranged on the board and beside it. The office was opulently furnished around an immense wooden desk and bookcase, but it seemed crammed—with everything from statues to rugs to paintings to vases and urns—rather than arranged, especially when compared with Roland Victor's in Kansas.

The corner nearest them, separated from the Big Man by a folding screen, was occupied by a squint-eyed assistant. She wrote in a ledger resting upon a drafting table. The Big Man's burled desk had nothing on the top except a lamp and a leather blotter.

"Ahn-Kha." The Big Man had a flat voice, a trifle reedy. "What brings you and your 'bodyguard' to my house?"

"My compliment on your promotion," Ahn-Kha said. "What became of the Big Man?"

"Ravies. Some rats they'd released, I suppose on the Ozarks to the south, made it into one of our barges. Bad luck; he was checking incoming cargoes and stuck his hand into a bag of rice without wearing gloves."

"You took the name along with the Executive title?"

"Sort of a joke. I don't mind."

The Big Man walked around to his desk and sat down. He moved stiff-leggedly, with the aid of a pair of canes. The canes disappeared as soon as he sat.

"Shall we leave right now?" Ahn-Kha asked.

"Without introducing your friend?" the Big Man asked.

"His name is David."

He swiveled his gaze to Valentine. "I should explain. Ahn-Kha and I have had our differences in the past. I didn't care for our house trading weapons with his kind." He returned to Ahn-Kha. "I accused you of eating human babies, as I recall. Ten years ago I . . . anger tended to get the better of me. Anger that had nothing to do with the Golden Ones."

"For my part, I challenged him to combat," Ahn-Kha added. "Aggravating insult with greater insult."

"Was there a duel?" Valentine said when neither offered an end to the story.

"No," the Big Man said. "Calmer heads interceded. Unless you wish to take up the challenge?"

Ahn-Kha closed his eyes, opened them. "No."

Valentine felt some of the tension seep away. "We need your help. House Holt's help."

"What do you offer? We're traders. Smugglers, to some. Quislings to others. I saw you take off a Wolf parang."

"My company was destroyed this spring," Valentine said. The truth, even shaded, was preferable to a plausible lie. "Our request is unusual."

"January, please get our guests some sandwiches and lemonade." The woman behind the screen slipped out.

"Lemonade?" Valentine asked, going over to the chess set.

"Thanks to the Kurians, they grow fine in some of the more sheltered parts of the Missouri Valley."

Valentine stared down at the pieces. The gold king was in trouble—nothing but a castle and a pawn protected him from a knight, two pawns, a bishop, and the silver king.

"Do you play?" the Big Man asked, turning his chair.

"A little. My dad taught me. I used to play it with my adopted father—neither of us were very good."

"Do you see a way out for the black king? I'm trying for a draw."

"*Black* meaning the gold one?"

"Yes. Sorry. Convention requires black and white no matter what the color of the pieces are."

Valentine looked, thought. "No. I think mate in three moves."

The Big Man sighed. "Two. The king can attack."

"How about a game? While we have the sandwiches."

Their host looked eager again and rocked his way back to the table. "You're the guest. White or black."

"Silver."

Valentine moved a pawn.

Eight moves later, behind leaping knights, the black queen came forth. "Checkmate," the Big Man said in his inflectionless voice.

Valentine shook his hand. "What's the General to you, Executive? An enemy bishop, or your king?"

The Big Man rested his chin on his cane. "An opposing king. I give him tribute, barges of food. He'd rather I were one of his pieces. My position isn't that different from the way the pieces were before our game. Though I don't have a castle. Just three floors of odds and ends."

The sandwiches arrived, pulling Ahn-Kha from an examination of oil paintings in dusty frames.

"January, I won't need you for a bit. You can go home for the afternoon if you wish," the Big Man said.

Valentine saw a look pass between them. "It's all right—I'm perfectly safe. They're not Twisted Cross." He began to put the pieces back in their starting positions. "Care to switch chairs for the next?"

This time the Big Man's silver bishops eviscerated him like a pair of dueling swords. Checkmate in eleven moves.

"What did you come here for?"

"Guns for the Golden Ones. Explosives," Ahn-Kha said, as Valentine and the Big Man switched chairs again. "My people would use them against the Twisted Cross."

"I'm only crippled physically, Ahn-Kha."

Valentine moved his queen, taking a knight. "Southern Command would help, too. Perhaps in a few months, we could have Bear teams up here. You know what they are, don't you?"

"A kiss and a promise. I'll believe it when I see the teams. Besides, I don't have that much time. The General has given me an ultimatum. Join, leave, or . . . be burnt. Your move."

Valentine saw it coming this time—the Big Man had sacrificed a knight to draw out his queen. He lost a bishop, and then it was, "Checkmate."

"Let's play again. No switching chairs, I like silver."

"Very well."

This time they were silent. Valentine lost a knight, and when the bishops came forward again, his pawns occupied them until his queen had space. She took a castle, a pawn, and a bishop before falling. Then his castles came forward. The Big Man let out a small noise, wrinkled his brows, moved a knight back. Valentine sent a bishop forward, took a pawn, lost his bishop, and brought out his last knight.

Valentine checked.

The Big Man moved his king, a smile on his face.

"Checkmate," Valentine said.

The Big Man offered his hand. "My compliments. I saw it two moves ago, but went through the motions. You deserved the gratification."

Valentine arranged the pieces the way they'd been when he first approached the table. "Sir, in your quest for a stalemate . . . suppose you could have gotten that pawn to the white side and converted it."

"Unlikely."

"Suppose the unlikely happened."

"Reliance on the improbable is a bad strategy."

"Even so," Valentine said.

Ahn-Kha's ears pointed forward, listening.

"The whole balance would change. I could get the draw. Depending on the white bishop, I might be able to squeeze a victory."

"If you got enough arms to the Golden Ones, in the ghetto, on the base, that lonely pawn could become a terrible weapon."

"No. I won't put my house's future in jeopardy."

Ahn-Kha's ears drooped as he stood. "Thank you for the sandwiches. I am glad we have put the past behind."

The Big Man nodded. "Good luck with your own future."

"What there is of it," Valentine said. "Thank you for your time."

"Thank you for the game. I haven't been beaten in years."

Valentine and Ahn-Kha went to the door. As they opened it, the Big Man spoke again. "David, a bit of advice: Practice the tried and true. You'll win more often. The intuitive player can be brilliant. Once in a while even beat the best. But most of the time, you'll lose."

The Cat nodded. The Big Man returned to his board. Valentine left a crack in the door and looked back through it. The Big Man wrinkled his brow in thought, then pushed his golden pawn forward.

"So much for explosives," Valentine said when they were in the street again.

Ahn-Kha looked at the sky. "There's one other place we could try. It's only a few blocks away."

"A different trading house?"

"None of the others deal in anything but hunting rifles."

"Then what?"

"The General's building where Khay-Hefle now rules. It lies behind the walls that imprison my people."

From what might have been a corner office within the skeleton of a high-rise, Valentine looked across central Omaha at the ghetto of the Golden Ones.

Flat on his stomach, he leisurely surveyed the quarter of

the city's ruins allocated to them. Behind the old library, now the residence of their usurping chief and his Twisted Cross shield, were the twin buildings Valentine knew to be home to the dank farms of heartroot of which Ahn-Kha rhapsodized and home to Omaha's captive Golden Ones. Ahn-Kha said the lower floors and stairways of the buildings were sound, though the walls and windows had been blasted out by the overpressure of nuclear explosions. Many Golden Ones lived on the structurally intact floors in a warren of partitions and rebuilt rooms, complete with a gravity plumbing system that Ahn-Kha claimed to be the wonder of Omaha.

The Twisted Cross added on some changes. Piles of rubble topped with cemented-in broken glass formed walls all around the Golden Ones' quarter. Their new Principal Elder insisted on this measure for the safety of his people. Ahn-Kha maintained that the wall did a better job of keeping Golden Ones in than their enemies out, a belief supported by the slapped-together wooden guard towers that stood both inside and outside the wall.

Valentine guessed the whole area to be well over a square mile, in what was once downtown Omaha. As Ahn-Kha described, there had been a thriving population of Grogs controlling the heart of the city, but even in their reduced space behind the walls, the ghetto appeared far from crowded.

"I don't see many of your people. A few working in the gardens, some more clearing that field of rubble to the northwest."

"Every day a train comes through the rail-gate in the south. My clan is great builders; your Twisted Cross need them in the old base south of the city. Those who wish to eat adequately get on the train. They serve soup and bread for those who work. They even keep some of my people in pens on his base."

"Hostage taking. The General likes the tried-and-true as much as the Big Man."

"Once the Golden One who traded profitably, or spun the best poem-chant, or threw the *sook* most accurately at sport was considered a Great One. Now it is the back that moves the most dirt."

"Have you been back inside since all this happened?"

"Yes, brief trips. It is dangerous. But I have met many times with those who sneak out for trade and to hunt. My people are good engineers; they open a new hole as soon as another is blocked. It is a dangerous business, especially at night. The Hooded Ones of the Twisted Cross see through walls, sometimes under the ground."

"*Seeing* isn't the right word. An energy that a sentient being creates, called an aura, is something they sense."

The Grog nodded. "I heard of this, but I thought it was a tale to frighten us. The General's men roam outside the walls at night. During the day, my people are under the eyes of the guards in the towers. Some are men, some are Gray Ones, some are Khay-Hefle's lickspittles."

Valentine, his eyes still to the binoculars, broke into a smile. "You are well read, Ahn-Kha. I don't think I've ever heard the word *lickspittle* spoken in my life."

"I grew to love your language, my David. It has little logic or music to it, but there are some fine phrases."

"Agreed. My engineer-sergeant, when I served in the labor regiment, he had some fine phrases. No logic or music in them, either, but he got his point across."

Ahn-Kha laughed. "Foremen are the same everywhere."

"You said you had a plan for getting us inside. What do you have in mind?"

"We cannot go over the wall. There are many obstacles, traps, and noisemakers. During the day we would be seen; at night, the Hooded Ones could sense us. That leaves only two other ways in. The first seems less risky on the face of it, but involves a good deal of luck. I know of two tunnels in, but my information is months old. As I said, they do find the tunnels. We may get below ground only to learn it is bricked up. Or it may appear clear, but have explosives placed all around to kill us and close the tunnel at the same time.

"The second way requires more daring. Both the rail gate and the city gate are guarded by humans, those in the lowest ranks of the Twisted Cross. To them, every Golden One looks alike. There is only rarely a Golden One on sentry duty; more often it is Gray Ones. I could march in as one of Khay-Hefle's lickspittles—as you like this word so much—with you under guard. We might get as far as the Clan Hall. There, however, Khay-Hefle's bodyguards do stand sentry duty, and they would recognize me."

"How big is his bodyguard?" Valentine asked.

"There are twelve or fifteen. Three always attend to him, standing outside his door day and night. Another stands at the Hall Doors, and those off-duty gather inside the Hall or near it. They are well armed, for they fear my people whom they have betrayed."

"The Great Hall has the weapons of the Twisted Cross?"

"Yes, the armory is there, under the supervision of this General's men. I understand they also have a small post on the other side of the river. They have done much work on the old base south of town. This General recruits artisans and technicians from many places. He covets more than just Omaha."

Valentine nodded. "That's what I'm afraid of. From what you said, he means to destroy the lands I come from. He could succeed, given what I've seen. Southern Command is only just hanging on as is."

You're just one man, he told himself. *Get back to the Ozarks with what you have.*

One man can't wreck the factory, but he can drop a wrench in the works, another, more confidant part of him answered. *Southern Command wouldn't get an expedition organized until next spring, if at all, and by then it could be too late.*

Valentine had done some brazen things in his life, but walking up to a guard post with a well-spoken blood enemy holding a gun to his spine was the crowning act of audacity in his career. He dragged his feet down the cleared road through the rubble of what was once a wide thoroughfare with his hands over his head.

At first he asked Ahn-Kha to move him along with the

submachine gun. "No, my David," the Golden One dis-
agreed, "it would be noticed. The lowliest gate warden
holds himself superior to my people, and would take your
weapon without thinking twice."

So they hid the PPD and Valentine's pack in the rubble
of the building they used to observe the Golden One zone.
Ahn-Kha carried Valentine's sword, parang, and pistol in
what had been Valentine's pack. The would-be prisoner's
only weapons were his fighting claws.

Evening shadows began to settle across the city while a
Twisted Cross noncom watched them approach with an
interested air. He carried himself with the impatience of
one who expects to be promoted to better duty. Valentine's
ears picked up their conversation. "One of our valiant
allies caught himself a real prize," the corporal with the
silvered swastikas on the sleeves of his gray overalls commented.

"Wish they'd bring in a woman for a change, Corp," the
private in an urban camouflage version of the same overall
commented.

"Wish for a promotion, then. The officers get the mis-
tresses, the sergeants get the whores, and the rest get the
shaft."

"Ain't it the truth, Corp."

As the pair drew up to the zigzag of barbed-wire fencing
blocking the gate in the daytime, the corporal stepped into
the sun. "That's far enough," he said, assault rifle cradled in
his elbow. One of his eyes was set higher in his face than
the other. As if to balance it, he kept the opposite corner of
his mouth turned down. "What's this, soldier?"

"Da-Khest, Railroad Security, sir!" Ahn-Kha barked. "I
caught this man just this side of the old interstate, on the
south line. He was armed, sir!"

The corporal turned back to the sentry. "Railroad Security," he said, sotto voce. "Three meals a day to sleep under
a bridge." He turned back to the Grog. "Good work, De-
test. We like to see results for a change. Usually we get stories from your *people* about bandits dragging their dead
away. Let's see that gun."

Ahn-Kha pulled out Valentine's revolver and handed it over. "It was empty, sir."

The corporal examined the weapon. He spun the cylinder. "I'm not surprised. Private Wilde, you have any use for a .357?"

"No, sir. I know Ackermann is looking for a spare nine-millimeter."

"Who wants a wheelgun anyway?" another sentry put in.

Wilde nodded. "Those Troopers are the only ones who carry that hardware. Dumb goat ropers."

"It's too scratched up," the corporal commented, spinning the cylinder and working the double action. "Be worth something if it were chrome, or at least stainless. This blued steel looks like hell after a few years."

Valentine spoke up. "There's been a mistake, sir. I'm just a courier, but I have friends on both sides of the river. Both sides, sir. It would be worth something to the Big Man in the Old Market if I got back to him."

The low eye squinted on the corporal. "Listen, mook: I'm not some hungry Trooper or a Marshal on the take. I'm chiseled out of stainless steel. Bullshit slides off me."

You're also so busy being superior, you're not asking the right questions, Valentine thought.

"This isn't worth the sweat I'm working up in this heat," the corporal decided. "De-test, this man's in pretty good shape. Running packs of contraband builds the muscles. He'll find them useful at the Cave. Throw him in the hold for now; he'll go out on tomorrow's train."

The corporal returned to the little shed and made a note on a clipboard. The sentry moved aside half the wire barricade, and Valentine led Ahn-Kha home.

"Think about it, sir," Valentine called over his shoulder. "Get in touch with the Big Man. Tell him Blackie's in the cuffs, he'll be grateful. And generous."

"He'll do what he always does," the corporal laughed. "He'll claim he's an honest businessman and say he's never heard of you."

Exactly what I'm counting on, Valentine thought.

Ahn-Kha marched Valentine into the Golden Ones'

ghetto and turned up a little lane that led up the hill to the library.

"About one more hour until the work train returns," Ahn-Kha whispered. "It will be dark then, and the Hooded Ones will be out to watch it unload. They always watch whenever great numbers of my people are together. We hide until then, my David."

They passed a row of houses built out of old cinder blocks and scrap metal. But these were no makeshift hovels—the Golden Ones worked with rubble like some artists did with broken glass, creating mosaics and patterns out of broken paving bricks and twisted structural steel.

Older Grogs—their fur had turned to gray white—lounged in front on wooden chaises, chatting in their rumbling tongue.

"In this door, quick!" Ahn-Kha said, and Valentine complied. He pulled the curtain aside, and they entered the rude home.

A white-haired Grog looked up from his evening meal. He blinked his eyes twice, and suddenly his ears shot up.

They spoke for several minutes in their native tongue, and the older one finally limped outside. Valentine watched out of the corner of the window, observing ghetto life from inside.

"He is an old friend of my parents," Ahn-Kha explained. "He goes now to tell the others to pretend they saw nothing; then he shall pay a call on another friend at the Clan Hall. Ahh, here, my David, taste this."

Ahn-Kha broke a tubular growth in half. It had a hole running down the center, as if it had grown around a spit. Valentine tasted it and found it pleasant, a little like pumpkin with the texture of half-cooked pasta. "We used to dip it in honey, but there's no honey to be had these days." Ahn-Kha opened up a locker and began searching through folded clothes, and he found a simple blue version of the robe-kimonos the Golden Ones preferred to wear.

"Not bad," Valentine said, taking another bite. "Tastes kind of like spoon bread. I'd like to try it with molasses. What is it?"

"Did I not tell you? This is heartroot, the staple of my people. From nothing but dead growth, night soil, mud, and time we get this. It grows year-round as long as the water does not freeze, although much more slowly in winter." He changed his torn and dirty old robe for the blue one he selected. They passed the time talking about the former library and the probable location of the armory within.

They waited until darkness and left at the banshee wail of the train whistle pulling into the ghetto. Valentine carried his revolver and sword, the former now loaded and in a holster at his hip, the latter strapped across his back under the black trench coat, with the hilt projecting out the loose collar behind his head. Ahn-Kha still bore the fifty caliber, the gun carried midbarrel in his right hand. The Grog had Valentine's parang tucked inside the fresh robe.

They traversed the common ground in the center of the ghetto, part cultivated garden and part parkland. Some sheep lay in the shade by a lily pad–filled pond.

Ahn-Kha stood very erect. "This way, my David."

The Grog took him to a little clearing bordered by another Grog shantytown. Valentine saw, and smelled, a latrine in the center of the field. Ahn-Kha halted and, using his rifle as a staff, gazed out onto the meadow.

"This is where they buried my people," Ahn-Kha said, slowly and quietly. "When Khay-Hefle took over, they dumped the bodies in a pit here. My parents were among the dead, along with the Principal Elder, and many of my people who fought back. Along with those who just got caught in the battle."

Ahn-Kha took off his mitten slippers and dug his long toes into the earth.

"My wife and sons are buried here. I wished them to go with the One in Ten to Canada, but she refused to leave her family. Two thousand of my people rest beneath this soil. They say if you are very silent, you can hear weeping.

"At first, after the custom of you humans, my people planted flowers here, I am told. Then one day, after the walls had risen, this General who accepts only submission or death came on an inspection. He saw the many beautiful

flowers and ordered them pulled up. In their place he dug
pit-toilets, and ordered all to use them. The first, of course,
was Khay-Hefle, who always seems to find new insults to
put upon those who had been his people. At one time they
would march the workers all the way from the train station
to here at the end of the day. Golden One workers are not
considered fit to use human toilets at the Cave this General
is building. They must go to the river bushes or wait until
they return here."

"I'm . . . sorry," Valentine said, choking on the second
word. It was inadequate. "Never said you were married."

"I play tricks on myself. When I do not speak of it or
think of it, the pain lessens for a time. She was very beautiful, both in the looking and in the knowing. You own my
apologies, I am speaking in English but my private voice
speaks in the Golden Tongue. Let me try again. She was
very beautiful to look at and to know."

"I'm sure she was," Valentine said, and meant it, although he did not have the first clue as to how a Grog measured physical beauty.

"My David, I am glad we could come here. I have only
seen this place from afar. But we must hurry—we have
business on the hill."

They moved among the wooded parkland up the hill to
the old library. From below, it loomed like a temple built to
the specifications of a fortress. Valentine sensed a Reaper
somewhere within. A coyote or feral dog crossed their path
ahead, head and tail both held close to the ground. A few
Golden One couples could be seen here and there among
the trees, the smaller females walking just behind the
males, touching the backs of their partners.

"Let's wait a moment, please," he asked Ahn-Kha. The
Grog knelt and followed Valentine's gaze to the building.

Valentine quieted his mind. He felt his body relax. The
Reaper came into focus. It was below ground.

"Are you all right, my David?" Ahn-Kha asked.

"Yes, now I am. One of your Hooded Ones is in there."

"You smell it?"

Valentine didn't have time to explain. "Something like that.

"You said you had a plan for getting in," Valentine reminded him, looking at the stoutly barred and shuttered windows around the first floor of the building.

"My father's old friend knows one of my people on Khay-Hefle's staff. She hates the new Principal and gives news to my people when she can. She has arranged to unlock the shutters on one of the windows on the second floor after the guard checks it. It is very dangerous for her; it means she must remain in the building all night. The windows on the second floor are not barred, for the climb is thought impossible."

"Then how are we going to get up there?"

The Grog pointed at a flagpole in front of a long low building, just to the right of the Great Hall.

"We shall use that."

Valentine looked up at the flag of the Twisted Cross hanging limp in the night sky.

"Don't tell me that's the barrack for the Twisted Cross soldiers."

"Yes, it is."

"That's quite a risk." Valentine checked the view of the guard at the Great Hall. Khay-Hefle's soldier wore padded leather at his shoulders, shins, and forearms, and a helmet cut to accommodate the flexible pointed ears. He could not see the barrack.

"There is no sentry in front of the barrack."

"No, the Twisted Cross close up tight in the evening."

They avoided the Golden One sentry standing outside the main doors of the ex-library, now the Golden One Great Hall, and moved around the side of the building. Valentine took a long look and listen. Satisfied, he slapped Ahn-Kha on the arm, and they dashed across the cracked cement sidewalk. The Grog made so much noise running, Valentine found himself wishing in vain for the absent Duvalier. Was she on her way back to the Free Territory? Waiting at the rendezvous, cursing him every hour on the hour?

"How many of these Hooded Ones are there in the ghetto?" Valentine asked.

"No one knows. The number seems to vary. On some days I've been told as many as thirty will be here. They use our lands for a base to operate elsewhere in the city, perhaps training, perhaps subjugating another clan."

The Reaper hadn't moved. Valentine hoped that whatever was occupying it would keep its attention for another few minutes. "Here goes." They jogged up to the flagpole.

"Put up by humans, not by the Golden Ones," Ahn-Kha said. He placed both hands around the pole. "Now to pretend this is the neck of Khay-Hefle." His muscles bulged and tightened as he first pushed the flagpole then pulled it. Valentine kept watch for a moment and then decided it was pointless. They were so in the open—if they were seen, it would be all over anyway, so a few seconds' warning would make little difference. He got on the opposite side of the flagpole and began working with Ahn-Kha, though he couldn't bring half the strength of the Grog's arms. When Ahn-Kha pushed, he pulled, and then they switched. Soon the pole was rocking in its dirt. Ahn-Kha wrapped his thick arms around the pole, hugging it as tightly as a constrictor taking a wild deer. With a mighty pull, he uprooted its concrete base.

The Grog took the heavy end, and Valentine the flag tip, and they managed to get it to the side of the building.

"It's a good thing the Twisted Cross don't garrison your people properly," Valentine observed, legs burning in protest of the load. "A few patrols in this area, and we could kiss this project good-bye."

"My people live in abject fear of the Hooded Ones and a return of the flamethrowers, my David. They are worked half to death for their daily soup. They need little policing." Ahn-Kha wasn't even breathing hard, though burdened by the heavy end. If anything, he looked energized.

They reached the base of the window, though not a crack of light showed from the supposedly unlocked shutters. The team managed a two-person raising of the Iwo Jima flag and carefully set the pole against the side of the building. Valentine winced at the *thunk*.

"Wait here," Valentine muttered, and began to shinny up the flagpole, wishing it were made of wood so he could use his claws.

The shutter pulled open silently. He hopped down the ledge into a dark office, smelling Golden Ones. Its shelves were lined with paint and cleaning supplies, and Valentine could understand why a roaming guard might check its window only once as the sun went down. Hardly worth stealing. Duvalier might want the turpentine to make—

—burn the place down!

It was a tempting thought, but he turned back to the window. "Get rid of the pole," he called down, sounding like a laryngitis patient in an effort to be heard without speaking loudly.

Ahn-Kha complied while Valentine wound and knotted a pair of canvas drop cloths. He soaked the canvas in a washtub—wet fabric would hold better at the knots and strenthen it. He wrapped the improvised line around his back, got a good grip, and sent his dripping line out the window for Ahn-Kha. The Grog grabbed it and began to climb. Valentine had all he could do, legs braced and quivering against the wall under the window, to hold up his end of the job by not letting go as what seemed like half a ton of Grog swarmed up the line.

The Grog made it through the window, his awkward rifle left outside. They opened the bag with Valentine's weapons. Valentine offered the Grog his choice of pistol or parang.

"It'll be knife-work if we have to fight in here," Ahn-Kha said, drawing the parang and passing it, blade out, between his lips. The Golden One's eyes blazed.

Valentine heard a step in the hallway on the other side of the door.

He put his fingers to his lips and pointed out the door. Ahn-Kha's ears went up and forward, listening for the tread.

"A Golden One," Ahn-Kha whispered.

There was a knock. Ahn-Kha gave Valentine a reassuring nod and opened the door to reveal a more petite version of himself, without the pronounced canines but with longer and more expressive ears. They gargled to each other. Valentine doubted he would even be able to generate the necessary sounds should Ahn-Kha decide to teach him the Golden One's language some day.

She passed two keys on a little metal ring to Ahn-Kha and left as quietly as she had come.

"She was hiding, waiting for us in the next room. Vihy has no business staying here after hours; she would be killed if caught. She asked for us to be sure to lock the shutters behind, just in case."

He showed Valentine the ring. "The keys are to an iron gate at the basement stairs. For our cleaning people to get in the basement, a Twisted Cross officer on duty must open it. She stole it from his office as he slept on duty. Not all are 'men of stainless steel,' it seems."

The bravery of some of the people who lived under the Kurians never failed to humble Valentine. Kur ruled through fear, intimidating their subjects into submission. But for some, after a certain point, even the threats of torture and death no longer work. These helpless people chose death, even welcomed it when it came, as long as they were able to strike some kind of blow against their oppressors. Not for the first time, he wondered if he had that kind of courage.

But such thoughts did not help mask his aura. Valentine brought his focus back within himself, until his worries were a hard little crystal locked in his brain.

"Ahn-Kha, there's still a Rea—a Hooded One to deal with. I think it's somewhere in the basement. I'm afraid it will sense or hear you coming. Would you be good enough to wait here while I deal with it, please?"

"Yes, my David. Whatever you ask of me. I would prefer if it were something other than waiting."

"You could get a bunch of rags together here, and open a can of turpentine. We may have to start a fire as a diversion."

Ahn-Kha nodded and began to pile some dirty towels in a janitor's bucket. "May your blade find your enemy's heart."

Valentine handed over his revolver. He half drew his sword, tested the edge with his thumb. "A Reaper has two hearts, one on each side of his body. I go for the neck; they have only one of those."

Ahn-Kha extended his fist, his long thumb up. Valentine smiled in recognition; the proportions were all wrong, but the thumbs-up nevertheless heartened him. He threw the sword's harness over his shoulder, tightened the straps.

He crept out of the storage room. A hall led down to a shadowed open area. Valentine could see a decorative rail looking out on the central atrium his companion described. Low-wattage electric lights cast patterns across the Golden Ones' renovated stone and woodwork overlaid on the older human design.

Keeping on his belly, Valentine crawled down the hall toward the atrium. He paused now and then to listen, but while there were sounds of activity on the floor above, he could hear nothing near him. He crawled out to the atrium and slithered to the staircase. Look. Listen. Smell. And then down.

On the first floor, he waited two full minutes in an alcove, feeling the rhythms of the sleeping building. The only sounds came from the guardroom just inside the main door, where the off-duty Golden One guards were eating and talking. He smelled heartroot, a rich smell like carrots pulled fresh from the earth. Following Ahn-Kha's instructions, he made it to the staircase down without encountering anything other than vague noises from somewhere below. As he moved down the stairs, listening and using his nose, he identified the sound and smell of machinery. A generator whined somewhere in the bowels of the building, and he picked up a faint medicinal odor, like disinfectant.

The Reaper definitely moved near him now. Life or death depended on the Cat continuing to sense it, and the Reaper being unable to read Valentine's lifesign until he was too close for it to matter. A silent contest, like the Old

World books of submarines hunting each other in cold darkness. He waited until the Reaper was somewhere far from the gate door at the base of the stairs before employing the keys.

Valentine noticed an alarm bell mounted on the wall just down the hall, next to a door with light and the sound of voices coming from it. A switch with a conduit pipe running up to the bell probably activated it. The door was wired, a detail perhaps none of the Grogs knew. He thought for a long minute, but could not come up with a decent plan. That Reaper would not stay in the opposite corner of the building forever.

It had to be done, and if it had to be done, it had best be done boldly. He unlocked both locks, his sword hidden against his leg.

"Yo!" he called. "I'm at the door. Wanna get the alarm for me?"

"Coming," a tired voice said after the echo faded. A human in a white lab coat appeared at the door and absently turned the switch. Valentine threw open the door and covered the ten feet of hallway in a single leap.

"Hey," the man in the lab coat said. Too late. He reached up to hit the red alarm push button, but Valentine's sword intercepted his arm, removing it from the elbow down. Mouth gaping, the man looked at the interesting phenomenon of his amputation as Valentine's sword point came up under his chin. Valentine withdrew the blade as he rushed around the corner and into the well-lit room. A woman, also in a white lab coat, had time to scream before he cut her down. When it was over, the only movement in the room was the slow spread of blood across the tiled floor. The remains of a meal sat on a table under dazzling spotlights. Stainless-steel counters and white cabinets marked the room as a dispensary or examination room. There were medical supplies, bandages and iodine-colored bottles and instrument trays available. Valentine saw machinery in the room beyond, but had no time to investigate.

The scream was nearly as effective as the alarm. The Reaper was coming. Valentine hurried to the gate and locked it again, then stepped back into the dispensary, dragging the dead man behind. He readied his blade, holding in his favorite stance, like a batter at the plate, just inside the door. He heard the Reaper's step in the hallway and listened to it pause as it saw the slain man's blood and the severed arm Valentine forgot to retrieve. Then it did something Valentine would not have believed of a Reaper. It turned and ran.

Valentine pursued. Cloak flying, the Reaper turned a corner, and Valentine had to slow in case it was waiting just around the corner. It wasn't—it was in a room off the hall. He heard the Reaper's odd, faint voice speaking urgently.

case red! post twelve calling a case red! it breathed, pressing the transmit button on the microphone of the tabletop radio. While the voice was that of a Reaper, something was wrong about the cadence, the urgency in the voice.

It sensed Valentine. Turned—slit pupils wide as screaming mouths reflected Valentine's blade flashing for its neck. It ducked, slowly for a Reaper—meaning it took a full blink of an eye to crouch instead of half of one.

Which was half a blink too slow. The Reaper's body crouched without its head—now spinning in the air sprinkling black blood on the painted cement walls.

A man in the urban camouflage of the Twisted Cross stood next to an overturned chair, frozen in shock at the site of the Reaper's death. The communications center man reached for his pistol, and Valentine opened his stomach with a right-to-left slash, then stood on the man's wrist and pulled the gun and pocketed it. The man lay on the floor, gasping out his pain and trying to hold his intestines in.

Valentine tore the microphone off the radio, ignoring the Twisted Cross man, who coughed out his final breath. He unplugged the radio and cut the power cord.

The swinging cord end reminded him of something. That something was connected with the woman in the lab coat he had killed. An item that she was holding. An IV bag. An IV bag just like the ones hanging above the machinery in the room behind the dispensary. Why did a machine need an IV bag? It all came together in a rush.

Valentine flew back to the dispensary and into the room beyond.

Twelve oversize metal coffins were lined up on either side of the room, quietly humming with electric power. A thirteenth stood in the aisle between the two rows. They were wider and deeper than coffins, however. More than anything they reminded Valentine of defunct tanning beds he had once found while sheltering in an Old World strip mall. They had mysterious, unlabeled knobs next to telltale lights flickering on the side.

He closed the metal door behind him and barred it, using a pivoting arm that swung into a receiver on the frame.

From the lights and noise, Valentine determined that seven of the oversize coffins were on and functioning; each also had an IV bag hanging from a T-shaped rack above the machinery. Valentine went to the humming, blinking center machine and circled it. His ears picked up the sound of water being cycled through some kind of plumbing. A cabinet-door-size hatch was fixed to the top at one end.

Not knowing what to expect, Valentine opened the hatch. Inside, floating in the water like a piece of wood, was a very pale, thin man with a bristling growth of beard. Wires were attached with little flesh-colored cups all over his body, concentrated on his shaven skull. A smell, both salty and rank, wafted out of the miniature pool.

The man's green eyes opened in surprise, and Valentine looked into the confused gaze of the man who until a moment ago was animating a Reaper. How many years' service did he have in? How many people had his avatar killed while under his control? Did he climb out of the tank desiring to tear the throats out of victims, like the Twisted Cross man he'd met in Chicago who'd been "in the tank" for weeks at a time?

This was the reason the Reapers spoke to each other, as Duvalier had observed. And killed with guns, wasting vital aura. The Twisted Cross were a weapon, combining the minds of human soldiers with the death-dealing bodies of Reapers.

Valentine grabbed the man's neck and shoved him underwater to the bottom of the tank. The Twisted Cross Master struggled against Valentine's grip, muscles that hadn't been used in days creaking, while a sensor of some sort on his water-filled coffin beeped. The man clawed against Valentine's face with long fingernails, and the Cat turned his head away. Bubbles. The thrashing finally ceased, and the sensor added an outraged, high-pitched whine to the beeping. Valentine looked back down at the dead figure. His electrodes had come loose during the struggle, and under each one was a tiny tattoo of a swastika.

Valentine turned off the annoying monitor-machine. In the fresh silence, the crash that always came after a fight hit like a delayed-fuse bomb, and it hit hard. Vomit made up of his heartroot dinner poured into the salty water of the tank. But there was more to do. He rinsed his mouth with a handful of the salty water from an unused tank and spat it back.

Finish this.

Minutes later, six more dead bodies lay in their individual tanks of now-bloody saline solution. Somewhere, seven Reapers were wandering in confusion, bereft of the controlling intelligence of their masters. Valentine cleaned his sword with a spare lab coat and checked each of the other capsules to make sure they did not contain further Twisted Cross. He wanted to scream, to howl, to lose himself in a burst of activity, anything to push the last few minutes out of his mind.

Forget it. What you killed were not men. Not anymore, the old voice inside him said. Valentine wondered in a half-amused fashion if he were going mad. Had id and superego decided to launch a psychic putsch? He did not really care—perhaps another symptom of insanity.

The alarm, a mind-numbing Klaxon, screamed.

He cocked the pistol and carefully opened the door. The basement was still empty as the tomb it had become. Valentine checked the main hall and saw Ahn-Kha tearing at the cage door. He turned off the alarm. It refused to die, so he did the next-best thing and shot out the speaker. Elsewhere in the building, it still brayed.

"Easy on the metal," Valentine said. "Twist it enough, and it won't open. I don't want to be stuck in here."

"I am thankful that you are well, my David. Did you find the armory?"

"The armory?" Valentine said, with the tone of someone who had forgotten to pick up a pound of sugar at the store. He went to the door and opened it, legs rubbery, trying not to stagger.

"Are you wounded, my friend?" Ahn-Kha said, ears pointed at him the like the horns of a charging bull. The Grog sniffed the nail-marks on his face.

"No. C'mon, let's find it—it has to be one of these doors."

They discovered the armory behind a steel door that was not even locked. The arsenal was not as well stocked as they had hoped: automatic rifles and pistols, a few shotguns, some boxes of grenades and mines, and two flamethrowers. Valentine found a case of satchel charges, and there was ample small-arms ammunition in cabinets and cases on the wall. Valentine looked in vain for bullets for his PPD and ended up arming himself with one of the Twisted Cross assault rifles. He filled his pockets with magazines.

Ahn-Kha selected a shotgun and a machine gun with a bipod at the front. He draped ammunition belts for it around his neck like a priest's vestments.

The pair moved out of the armory and to the basement gate. Valentine placed part of his load at the base of the stairs and crept up them with Kalashnikov at the ready. Ahn-Kha followed—only the slight *klink-klank* of the ammunition belts giving the Golden One away as he followed.

He could hear voices of Grogs at the balcony and stairs to the upper floors in the Great Hall.

"You cover the upstairs. I'm going try for the door," Valentine said.

The chattering sound of Ahn-Kha's machine gun behind him spurred him on as he made it to the entry vestibule. The Golden Ones who had been on guard had fled.

He slid open a wooden panel. In front of the hall, a group

of Golden Ones crouched on the hill just beyond the concrete sidewalk. They wore the simple smocks of common
laborers. Two more sheltered behind a defunct and over-
grown fountain, wearing stained overalls. They had improvised weapons: iron bars, sledgehammers, and lengths of
chain.

Valentine lifted the heavy bar fitted to the double doors
and unfastened the locks. He stepped out, tried to signal the
Golden Ones to approach. They crouched and looked at
him as if they expected him to open fire on them. A *zing-
pow* of a bullet chipping the doorpost got him out of the
entrance.

After waiting for another long burst from his partner's
machine gun to stop, Valentine called over his shoulder
"Ahn-Kha, there are some of your people out front. I think
they're ready for action, but don't know what to do. Let's
switch. Talk to them."

Valentine ran to the base of the stairs and sighted his gun
upward. "There's just one. You can't see him from the bottom of the stairs, but go halfway up and he shoots," Ahn-
Kha warned.

The Grog went to the door and threw both the portals
open wide. He began bellowing into the night, waving the
gun above his head.

Golden Ones rushed in, brandishing picks and mallets. It
appeared as though, without willing it, he and Ahn-Kha had
started a revolt.

"My David, show my people the armory, I beg of you. I
have business elsewhere," Ahn-Kha said, leaping up the
stairs three at a time. The example inspired some of his fellows to follow despite their lack of weapons. A shot splintered the banister, and the giant sprayed bullets up to the
third floor.

"Can you all understand me?" Valentine asked.

"Yes, sir," the growing mob said in various accents.

He led them down to the little room, wishing it had three
times as many guns. He handed over the automatic he had
taken off the dead radio operator. The Golden Ones just
took the guns and grenades and left the explosives, Valen-

tine was happy to see. Nothing saps the will to revolt like accidentally blowing up a dozen of your vanguard.

More and more Grogs gathered as the word spread. One of them, an oldster missing a hand, an eye, and with a pronounced limp, joined Valentine in handing out guns and the proper ammunition.

"My friend, was no-right at rail-gate," the elderly Golden One said in his halting, glottal English. "Own-eyes watched Hood-man drop dead. No-gun, no-hurt. Guard-mans watch their-eyes same-same, ranned away. Now my people done Hood-mans?"

"I hope so. I don't know," Valentine said.

The last guns left in the hands of their new owners. Valentine followed the flood of straw-tinted muscle to the door. He could hear shooting outside. The old Grog grabbed him by the arm as he went out the door.

"Careful-careful, sir!" he implored, and yelled something up the steps. "Or shoot you, maybe-maybe." The Grog led Valentine to the door.

In front of the old library, a bonfire had been constructed out of any wood the Grogs could lay their hands on, mostly in the form of railroad ties. Even now, pairs of what he recognized as females were carrying up more ties, adding to the blaze. Valentine heard shooting from the direction of the Twisted Cross Barrack, and saw further flames lighting the sky there. Guard towers on the other side of the wall were firing into the ghetto, but they were too far away for Valentine to tell whether they were achieving anything other than alerting every Grog in Omaha that something was seriously wrong in the Golden One quarter. Valentine, feeling that events were now well out of his control, just lugged his booty from the armory to outside the library and sat on the steps to watch. The old Grog barked orders this way and that to hurrying youngsters, but if they paid attention to his words, Valentine could not say. He could see the ears on the Grogs, twitching this way and that in excited confusion.

"My people were like that bonfire, my David," Ahn-Kha said, unexpectedly joining him. His machine gun was down to its last belt, and the Grog reeked like a sulfur pit as he kicked another of his kind, longer haired and fleshier, before him. "Sit, dog!" he told the prisoner. Then to Valentine: "The fuel was there. They just needed air and a spark. You provided both—"

"*We* provided both," Valentine corrected.

"*You* provided both," the Grog insisted, "when you destroyed the Hooded Ones. That was the air, allowing them to breathe. From what I am told, the Hooded Ones all dropped over unconscious at the same time. The spark came in this building."

"Interesting. When a Reaper's tie is severed with its Master, it acts on instinct. Dangerous, but not smart."

"Ah, but that is when the Master is still alive, is it not?"

"I don't know. Is this the esteemed Khay-Hefle?"

The wretch plucked at Valentine's pant cuff. "Sir, take me to—"

Ahn-Kha wrapped his long foot around the prisoner's neck. "Silence! Yes, my David. Though my dream of revenge is not to be. It is—well, it was—a law of the clan that none of my people may kill except in battle or duel of honor, and he was unarmed. With this pretender brought low, I believe the old laws will be restored. His fate will be for the new Elders to decide. Besides, he screamed for mercy. There is no triumph in killing such a One on his knees."

"That's so." Valentine doubted he would have been as charitable if his family had been buried under a latrine.

Other Grogs came and strung Khay-Hefle from the iron bars of his own palace, giving the General's surrogate a good view of events. He hung from his wrists, crying as Grogs came to shout what had to be abuse.

"He's right side up. Mussolini wasn't so lucky," Valentine said to Ahn-Kha. The mob surprised him with its restraint: it restricted itself to words, sometimes pointing and laughing. Humans probably would have set fire to him; he'd heard ugly stories from veteran Wolves about what happened when towns changed hands.

"This Mussolini, he once ruled your Free Territory?"

"Never mind."

Two more Grogs ran up to the bonfire, each with a huge
kettledrum on its back. They were beautifully fashioned,
carved so the different woods and metals looked as though
they'd grown together. A third Grog with a pair of club-size
drumsticks began to beat out a rapid-fire tattoo.

The pounding rhythm gave Valentine a welcome primal
thrill, heating the cold sour ache in his belly. The drumming
intensified until he felt the earth shake with the Golden
Ones' stamps. Even the muzzle flashes from the distant
watchtowers paused while the drums boomed. Then it
slowed to a steady, ominous beat.

The sound galvanized the Grogs. Without a word, they
knelt and rapped their weapons against the pavement, ears
pointed up and out like the horns on a Viking's helmet. The
drumbeat intensified, and its tempo increased as did the
clatter of rifle butts hitting concrete. As a people, they tilted
their heads back and began to bellow and howl to the stars.

Valentine took in the crescendo and he trembled for their
enemies.

Ten

The Cave: Strategic Air Command's old headquarters at Offutt Air Force Base has seen better, and worse, days. Better when it was a buzzing hive of planes and blue uniforms, jet exhaust in the air, and the camaraderie of men who know that they're the best in the world at what they do. Worse in the summer of '22, when the nukes came, thundering blossoms of thermonuclear heat that reshaped the landscape. They turned sand to glass and flattened anything that wasn't built to bunker specifications in a hurricane of wind, pushing first out from the blast and then rushing back toward the mushroom clouds of the MIRV warheads.

Now some of the great hangars have been rebuilt, SAC's old underground catacombs reoccupied. A new general has come, with men in strange uniforms; the swastika flag flies, its spiderish black-and-white design stark and forbidding against the blue of Omaha's skies.

Thirty-six hours after the bonfires died, Valentine, Ahn-Kha, and a strong young Grog named Khiz-Mem watched the shadows lengthen across the old base south of Bellevue.

Ahn-Kha selected Khiz-Mem after the flame-lit night in the ghetto.

Valentine remembered the rest of the revolt as little but a confused series of impressions. The Twisted Cross barracks aflame. Screams of Man and Grog. The endless drumming. Gunfire clattering in the distance, dying off, then starting up again. Fresh ash lifted skyward, turning the wind bitter.

Valentine had stayed out of the struggle at the request of his friend, who feared that in the confusion, some Golden

One would shoot him down as a one of their Twisted Cross overseers.

The killing did not stop until after dawn, when the last guards in the watchtowers outside the walls either fled or were brought down by snipers. The towers inside the walls unexpectedly revealed major structural faults as the revolt got going, and they came crashing down at a signal of one of the Golden One engineers. The Golden Ones shot as far and as well as their Gray One brethren, many of whom lay dead in the upper floors of the Great Hall and in the little barrack houses outside the two gates of the ghetto.

With a few hours' rest and some warm food inside him, Valentine decided to push on southward. He knew the Twisted Cross would not take the Golden One revolt lightly, and that they'd be back soon with everything the General had. Ahn-Kha shared Valentine's fear of the coming threat and refused to be parted from him.

"Ahn-Kha, your people need you more than I do."

"My David, here I am just one more set of hands. With you, I am half of the first alliance joining Golden Ones with the Freeholders, honored to stand at the side of a friend. In which role can I help my people more?"

Valentine wanted to go to the General's Cave and throw a little sand in the gears of the Twisted Cross war machine before it could return to Omaha and quash the Golden One rising. But now it would take more than blowing up a few hundred feet of bridge. In preparation, he and Ahn-Kha "liberated" flamethrowers and explosives from the Hall's armory.

Khiz-Mem made the pair a trio after Ahn-Kha drafted him to serve as packhorse and guide. Ahn-Kha assured Valentine that the young Grog knew every corner of the aboveground part of the old Strategic Air Command base. Khiz-Mem, in the full flush of his twenty-something strength, shouldered the weight of flamethrower, satchel charges, food, as well as his own pistol and rifle. Ahn-Kha carried the other flamethrower and a slightly lighter load. Valentine had an additional satchel full of grenades—white phosphorous incendiary grenades among the others.

Ahn-Kha examined one of the cylinders as they walked out of the ghetto. "With these, they burn the houses of those they would punish. I should like to give the Hooded Ones a sample of their own flame."

The Cave was a little more than a long day's walk south of the ghetto, but Valentine did not want to move straight down the rails connecting the base with the city center.

What was left of the Twisted Cross ghetto-police had taken that route; discarded equipment lay at the edge of the rail line like markers. They were probably holding some intermediary point, waiting for their own chance at vengeance.

So the trio took off west before turning south, retrieving Valentine's submachine gun and pack from the little cache. Picking its way south with Valentine scouting well ahead, sweeping the smugglers' trails of Omaha with his ears and nose, the party took its time. He wished he had another few days to look for Duvalier, they weren't very far from the rendezvous point.

The day had a hint of autumn to it; even the afternoon heat had a cool quality to it that the summer days had lacked.

They spotted a scout plane midday. If the little ship was not the ill-omened red-and-white one from the Dunes, it was its twin sister. It flew up from the south and circled the city above the Golden One ghetto. As they watched it from a halt, Valentine explained to Ahn-Kha the story of its use in the Dunes.

"So that means they will attack soon," Ahn-Kha said.

"Yes, they'll hit your people before the Golden Ones can get organized."

"Our people, my David, our people. From this day forward, you will always be accounted a member of our clan, and welcome in the Hall."

"I hope there'll be a Hall—and people to do the welcoming," Valentine said, studying the little plane.

At another break, in the roofless ruins of a warehouse, Ahn-Kha showed Valentine how to use the flamethrower. It consisted of three tanks on a backpack frame, a small one with compressed air and two larger tanks containing gasoline with a thickening agent. The mixture was fired by what amounted to a heavily built garden hose attached to a wide-mouthed insecticide sprayer. It fired the jellied gasoline a good thirty yards with a frightening roar of flame.

"I saw some burnt-out ruins in Wisconsin once where the Kurians had been doing some kind of training under the supervision of the Reapers. I wonder if they were teaching their men how to use these things? None of us could figure out how so much damage could be done without explosives."

"You must be careful with your trigger finger, my David," Ahn-Kha said. "This pack is half-empty now. You must use very short bursts, and even then you have only a few. Why do we carry these all this way?"

"I want to do the same thing at the Cave that I did at the Hall. Just on a bigger scale. The Hooded Ones are terrible, but the ones working them are vulnerable. Maybe more vulnerable than the General knows."

After a final hard march, they came up on the damaged areas outside the base in the late afternoon. The scouts shared a heartroot meal in a patch of tall grass at the old interstate, looking down at the outer edge of the camp. The perimeter fence consisted of two lines of fence topped with concertina wire. The main part of the base was hidden behind a lip of low hills; concrete observation bunkers set among them like teeth. A rail track ran along this, the western edge of the base.

Khiz-Mem talked in his native tongue and pointed to the wire and the area beyond.

Ahn-Kha patted the youngster on the head and turned to Valentine. "Between the wires are mines. You cannot see them, but there are guard posts well concealed behind the wire. Not all are manned all the time. The General still does not have all the men he wants, but he has plans for this place. He trains new soldiers always. Omaha was thought to be a good post to give recruits experience."

"They got an experience, all right," Valentine said, trailing his binoculars over the open prairie surrounding the base. It would be a nightmare to get in—there were probably trip wires within the concertina, if not Reapers prowling like guard dogs. "I don't think marching up to the gate is going to work for me here."

"I told you—our people are resourceful. There is a small tunnel, which stretches very far. It opens out on the far side of the old concrete road behind us. A few have used it to escape. We cannot go through it in great numbers, for the air goes bad within. Khiz-Mem says it is very tiring. You have to crawl the whole way. It opens within the base in a livestock barn, at the pigpen sluice."

"Fantastic," Valentine said. He was not sure if Ahn-Kha's knowledge of English extended as far as sarcasm.

"No, my David, this is to your advantage. They use dogs on the base, some running free, at night to find intruders. Pig odor may confuse them."

After the meal and rest, they swung around to the west in a final arc to the exit hole for the escape tunnel.

"Strange how things turn out. We dug this to let our people get out, but we will use it to get in."

"Not we," Valentine said. "I. I don't think we should all go in, especially at night."

Ahn-Kha opened his mouth to argue when the noise of engines caused them all to drop to the ground. Valentine and Ahn-Kha climbed up to the cracked and uneven remains of the old expressway and looked out at the western border of the base.

A column of trucks bumped along a road running alongside the rail line bordering the Cave, turning out from the main gate that Valentine could now see farther to the south. A four-by-four scout car led the column, followed by a genuine armored car on fat tires. Then came truck after smoke-belching truck, twenty-two in all, mostly old two-and-a-half-ton army jobs, restored and painted and towing trailers. A few of these carried machine guns mounted in a ring on the roof above the passenger seat. Double-axle pickup trucks towing cannon followed the army trucks, interspersed with camouflage-painted U-Hauls. In the beds of the pickups, uniformed figures sat facing each other.

Valentine plucked a piece of grass and chewed it as the procession of motorized military might passed by.

"I see some of our people still wish to serve the General," Ahn-Kha observed, as more utility trucks rolled by, their slat-sided beds filled with armed Golden Ones and Gray Ones.

"My species hasn't cornered the market on betrayal," Valentine said. "There's good and bad everywhere."

"I would have more good," Ahn-Kha said, lifting a mule's worth of gear.

"Someday, old horse," Valentine said, watching dust settle as the column bumped off to the north at a steady ten miles an hour.

The sun was setting, the Twisted Cross Reapers would be in Omaha soon, and he had a tunnel to crawl through.

They went back to the outlet, an old cement drainage pipe by the interstate, broken open by some force of war or nature.

"I believe you should let me come, be another set of eyes, if nothing else," Ahn-Kha insisted.

"Suppose we are crawling through your tunnel as a Reaper passes overhead. He might find it strange that lifesign is passing a few feet under his boots, don't you think?"

Valentine turned over the PPD and his remaining ammunition. "Here's my gun. If I'm not back by tomorrow morning, go to the meeting place at the river I told you about. There should be a human woman there—if not, look for a pile of four of anything: rocks, firewood, whatever. There may be a note in there, and you can act on it as you see fit. Or go back to yo—our people in Omaha."

He unwrapped his old nylon hammock, placed the flamethrower, his sword, and the satchel charge within its webbing, and then wrapped it all up in a blanket. He climbed into the tunnel, pulling the sack behind him.

"See you at sunup," he said, and backed into the hole.

The escape tunnel was a wonder of improvised engineering. Valentine had expected to have to wiggle through it like a mole in a garden tunnel, but forgot about the Grog shoulder span. Wood held it up in some places, corrugated aluminum in others, and beneath the road and rail line Valentine crawled through a real concrete tunnel. The building of this thing must be a fascinating story in itself; he promised himself to hear the whole tale from Khiz-Mem should he come out of this.

It grew pitch-dark as he left the opening behind. Valentine hated the abyss of absolute dark. The dark of the grave, of death. Even his newly sensitive eyes were useless; only the Reapers could hunt here. He imagined steel-like fingers reaching out of the darkness behind him and closing around his neck. He reached into a pocket for a leather tobacco pouch and brought out the diamond-shaped glow bulb that Ryu had given him as a parting gift. He had bound it in a little harness loop of leather, which he now hung around his neck. The comforting yellow glow was like a tiny little piece of the sun with him in the darkness, and he felt his fears shrink back to manageable size. He sniffed the damp air of the tunnel and smelled a faint piggy smell.

Dragging the burden behind him was an exhausting process; he had to stop every ten minutes to rest. He learned to do this under the too-infrequent air tubes the Grogs had poked through to the surface. Rats and field mice had taken up the tunnel as a convenient home; he smelled and heard them all around even if he couldn't see them.

With his back and shoulder muscles screaming, Valentine inched down the tunnel. It was kind of like rowing a boat, except for the absence of boat, fresh air, and water. He would scoot his buttocks a foot down the tube, which seemed to stretch endlessly through miles of midnight, then drag his improvised blanket-sled along behind with a pull at the nonexistent oar.

The piggy smell was his holy grail, his stink-at-the-end-of-the-tunnel. As it intensified to the point where he no longer needed his Wolf's nose, he pulled with renewed energy. When he felt his probing hand come away smeared with filth, he knew he was at the end.

He left the pack where it was. Fighting disgust, he smeared his face and hands with the soiled mud. He would have to remember to carry a can of Duvalier's greasepaint from now on.

Telling yourself you're going to survive this, eh? It's a one-way crawl, and you know it.

The tunnel bowed into an upward slope. Above, he saw a length of ten-inch pipe with a funnel at the end—running vertically through the tunnel. He put away his comforting light cube and let his eyes adjust. Hints of light could be seen around the edge of the funnel. He listened with hard ears, but heard only faint animal noises from above.

Valentine moved the funnel. The wide part covered a hole chipped in a concrete basin, just below dirty grating apparently set on the floor above. The smelly sluice pipe and funnel came out of the ground easily enough. He climbed up through the hole in the bottom of the space just below the grate.

He paused to listen again and then lifted the grate. He peered into the cement-floored pigpen of the barn. In one warm corner, a heap of porkers lay grunting in a pile. Across a low partition he could see another pigpen and its cluster of sleeping livestock.

He climbed out of the grating hole. One of the pigs woke up and gave him the once-over, but flopped back on its side when it saw he bore no slop pail. Valentine reconnoitered the lowest level of the unlit barn. It sounded and smelled as if cows were above on the main floor. The pigs shared the basement with a tractor and a horse-trailer on blocks, now filled with chickens.

He dropped back into the tunnel and began to transfer his equipment. He sensed a Reaper roaming somewhere as an unsettling tickle at the edges of his mind.

He lifted his arsenal out of the tunnel. The pigs took one look at the flamethrower and decided it looked like some kind new trough-filling device and began to gather around and oink in excitement. Valentine escaped to the garage area, listening for sounds of investigation.

He hid the satchel charge and flamethrower behind the tractor and climbed up a series of ladders to the hayloft. The smell of alfalfa and hay brought back a rush of memories of Molly and their first tryst. Keeping to the shadows, he surveyed the land as best he could.

The barn stood behind the apartments of the officers' residences. In the distance he could see a concrete tower at the restored airfield. As far as he knew, the Twisted Cross air force consisted of a single two-seat scout plane, but perhaps the General had plans to increase his fleet in the future. A bunker-flanked hummock of ground marked the entrance to what Khiz-Mem called the Cave, the nuclear-blast-hardened headquarters of the Twisted Cross.

The biggest aboveground structure on the post was the massive Train Hangar. Valentine could see the front of the building from the three-story-high loft of the barn. Built on the concrete foundations of a hardened airplane hangar, a network of rail lines ran parallel across the wide area in front of it before turning toward the main gate. It reminded Valentine of pictures he had seen of the German submarine pens in the Second World War. According to Khiz-Mem, they were in the process of adding enormous steel doors running down tracks in the concrete columns that held up the reinforced roof. Valentine could see sparks thrown by welders even now, in the dead of night, as work proceeded on the multiacre structure. They lit lines of boxcars inside, and Valentine could make out a few laboring figures within the machine shops and workbenches inside.

Somewhere deep within the Cave, a natural-gas power plant supplied electricity for the entire base, including for the electrified perimeter fence he knew to be in the works. He moved to the north end of the barn and watched the guards at the main gate. He wondered if the tracks were wired with explosives—if so, it might be feasible to assault the camp by running a train through the gate. More barracks stood behind the low ring of hills that sheltered the base from prying eyes, and two more looked like they were under construction. Valentine did not know if the hills were natural, man-made, or the remnants of crater rims caused by nuclear explosions in '22.

A Reaper lurked somewhere, near the entrance to the main gate. He sensed another near the Cave and possibly two near the hangar, though those last were at the edge of his range.

Valentine forced himself to rest in the hayloft for fifteen minutes. He was exhausted from the hike and the cramped crawl through the tunnel, and he needed to think now that he'd seen the hangar. He had a lot still to do this night.

The rational part of him wanted to get back to Southern Command with what he had learned. Certainly the Twisted Cross needed to be taken very seriously. Left untouched, the General would eventually have enough Reaper–human pairs to consume the Free Territory. Teams of Twisted Cross could destroy the border posts and principal bases as easily as they'd destroyed the Denverites at Fort Rowling. He knew Southern Command had some kind of emergency plan to fall back into the more rugged mountains, but how long could you feed hundreds of thousands of civilians in the hills?

The Twisted Cross had weaknesses hidden behind their black-and-white flag of terror. This General, whoever he was, seemed still to be in the process of recruiting and building his army, testing it against easy targets as he trained more men. If Southern Command could be convinced, he would guide as many Bear teams as they could afford to send up here, and this General's all-conquering army might be stillborn in the act of creation.

Valentine's mind kept returning to the Golden Ones, betrayed twice by Kur, and now in full revolt. Perhaps there were other Grogs elsewhere, equally mistreated and exploited, who would follow in their footsteps if just shown the way. Given time and training, the Cats could—

But the Golden Ones didn't have time. The attack was already being prepared, and Valentine knew that the Twisted Cross Reapers would hit the ghetto in the darkness. They'd go in to kill, not occupy, and leave daylight mopping up of any remaining strongpoints to the support troops. The threat to Southern Command might be years away—the Golden Ones woud die tonight.

If Valentine could use the demolition charge judiciously, the General might lose a few more of his precious Reapers.

Just the act of debating his course was an admission of surrender, in a way. If it was the fate of the Golden Ones against duty, duty would lose.

A few minutes after midnight, Valentine lurked outside the Train Hangar. He had found a blue jumpsuit hung up in the barn, and put it on along with a pair of muddy rubber galoshes. He piled the sword, flamethrower, and satchel charge in a wheelbarrow, threw the blanket over them, and headed for the gate to the officer's compound. He wheeled it slowly and tiredly toward the gate, and the sentry stepped out of the shadows and into the light, shotgun under his arm and collar turned up against the cool air.

"Sorry, that took way longer than I thought," he called to the sentry. "It turned out she had twin calves, and I just couldn't get the second out. I ended up having to pull it round by getting a piece of twine and drawing its head around," Valentine said, firing off the sum total of his calving knowledge in a single verbal broadside. But it got him ten feet farther toward the guard.

"Hold it, now—*now!*"

Valentine's arms were a blur, and his sword flashed. The guard fell over with a stunned look on his face, perhaps not believing that a human being could move that fast. Valentine put on the guard's jacket and hat and tossed the shotgun in the wheelbarrow.

He left his weaponry in a shallow depression in the middle of a field near the mountainous building, covered it with the blanket, and began scouting the Train Hangar. He found a four-wheeled pushcart, piled it with a few items of scrap metal, and began to push it around the pavement, looking busy. He counted twenty-eight boxcars in three rows in the Train Hangar, with guards and dogs protecting the cargo within. None of the workers approached the guards any nearer than they absolutely had to. Valentine looked in the open side door of one and discovered that the ordinary-looking boxcars contained more of the metal coffins, perhaps each with a Twisted Cross soldier floating inside and animating one of their Reapers.

E. E. Knight

Valentine let his hard ears roam, listened to the workers in the Train Hanger. The laborers were wondering what happened to the Golden One labor that usually was here to help them. Earlier that day, guards had come through and collected the Golden Ones. They had been placed in a special compound. Some thought they were being searched for weapons; others believed they had been taken as hostages to ensure the reliability of the General's puppet on the throne back in Omaha. There were rumors of a fight in the city. Then orders had come through to strip the base of anyone who could be trusted to use a rifle properly.

"The General's really lost it," one commented after Valentine had wandered away and he checked over his shoulder. Valentine's Wolf ears still picked up every disgruntled word. "First he tries to bite off more than he can chew out west and loses a big chunk of his best teams, and now it sounds like there's a trouble in Omaha. Instead of letting it cool down, he always demands scorched earth. He can't win a war because he refuses to ever lose a battle. He always talks about how patient he is, but—"

"Watch it, you. I don't want to be put on a list because I was talkin' treason."

"It's not treason to say there should be more carrot and less stick. I signed on to this for the carrot, a big stretch of land to call my own and a brass ring like my old man has. It's been four years of step and fetch, and still no ring, no land."

"I'd be happy if they just got the hair-backs working again. I'm breaking my back here."

A concrete control tower stood within in the center of the hangar. It sat on a base that Valentine saw housed a spiral staircase, going down as well as up. The tower widened out to a bowl above, and four Twisted Cross soldiers stood atop it. Machine gun muzzles projected out over the edge of the bowl. Valentine pushed his cart past bunkers standing outside the hangar at the corners. The strongpoints didn't worry him. Their firing slits were designed to cover the approaches to the yard, not the interior. He looked across the cavernous interior, trying to figure out where the satchel charge might do the most good and how to deploy it.

He brought his cart outside again, ostensibly heading for the junk pile. When he returned, the weapons were still hidden in plain sight in the wheelbarrow. He put them on his scrap cart and pulled it toward the center of the Train Hangar.

As he approached the whitewashed guard tower, a sentry challenged him.

"Just a sec, buddy—where do you think you're going with that shit? Nothing's allowed to be stored by the cars, even temporarily."

Valentine kept pulling the cart, and pointed across the yard to a line of workbenches against the far wall. He bumped over the last set of tracks, deeply recessed into the floor of the Train Hangar next to the tower, and an eight-foot-long metal rod rolled off his cart, helped by the tiniest nudge of his leg.

The guard stepped around in front of him. "You want to get over there, dumbass, you go around. Just because the lieutenant ain't here doesn't mean I can't take your number."

Valentine picked up the steel rod and moved to put it back on the cart. Suddenly he uncoiled his body, swinging it up and catching the guard under his armpit. Ribs and shoulder bones cracked. The guard's rifle flew away, batted by the steel rod as its owner tumbled to the ground.

A whistle blew from somewhere near the boxcars. Valentine pulled the cart to the door at the base of the tower and shouldered the flamethrower first, its nozzle clipped to the tanks. He put the satchel charge over the other arm and went up the spiral stairs with the shotgun in one hand and his sword in the other, the dangling nozzle of the flamethrower clanging on the metal.

A Twisted Cross guard was on the stairs above. Valentine could hear his rapid-fire breathing as if the man were panting in his ear. He put down the sword and heavy weapons.

He bent and jumped up five full steps, turning in the air

as he went. He fired the shotgun in the man's face, sending flesh and bone flying.

Nearly at the top, he could see the ceiling above. Valentine pulled the pin on one of the concussion grenades, counted two quick heartbeats, and tossed it up into the balcony.

"Grenade," someone yelled, too late to do any good. Valentine was already running back down the stairs to his other weapons when the explosion hit.

Even with concrete and two loops of the metal staircase to protect him, Valentine still felt the blast of the grenade. Everything seemed to slow down, and he felt closed off from the world, as though swimming underwater. Off balance, he lifted his gear and climbed up the stairs, bracing himself like a drunk.

The men in the tower had either jumped or been blown out of the fifteen-foot-diameter circle. Two machine guns still rested in their mounts, and a pair of shoes lay incongruously on the floor.

A flutter in the air, like bird wings beating against a window—

—the Reaper almost had him when it jumped into the tower. But this was no Kurian-operated killing machine, owner and avatar seasoned by long years of psychic symbiosis. The man in the unknown tank pulling the wires of his puppet was an apprentice, not a Master, and the Reaper tumbled as it landed.

Valentine had time to take up his sword as it rose. Before it could point its gun, he slashed downward, catching it at the knee. He jumped out of the way of the rising gun barrel, and the bullets tore through the empty air where he had stood an instant before. Now the Reaper was seriously off balance, and another whirlwind stroke by the Cat caught it across the neck. The head wasn't severed, but the central spinal cord was; the Reaper dropped to the ground, helpless. Its black teeth bit impotently at its own extruded syringe-tongue.

Valentine ignored it, unhooking one of the strap-ends of the demolition charge. He flipped open the satchel charge and pulled both starter fuses from the top. The heavy bag began to hiss and smoke. Valentine spun like an Olympic hammer-thrower with the single strap held in his hands and sent the bricks of plastic explosive arcing off toward the lined-up boxcars.

They may have been easier to guard packed together like that, but they made an unmissable target for Valentine's explosives. He heard the *thunk* of the charge bouncing off a wooden boxcar's roof, and he dropped behind the yard-thick concrete wall of the guard tower. The part of his mind that always drifted around himself in a fight wondered for a moment why the General would use wood for his boxcars, and the answer came as he opened his bag of grenades. Metal would be too hot in the sun—it could cook the men in the tanks inside. But wood had disadvantages, as well.

He picked up one of the white-phosphorous grenades and covered his ears and nostrils against what was coming.

The thick walls of the hangar magnified the tower-shaking *boom* from the explosives. With debris still in the air, Valentine pulled the pin and released the safety handle on the grenade. He pitched the hissing grenade into the destruction in the center of the boxcars. Shots from the hangar's few guards whipped through the air around him, and he dropped back down before they could improve their aim. As he continued to throw as fast as he could pull pins, he saw the first grenades explode. The phosphorous bombs scattered burning white particles into the splintered wood all around it. Fires devoured paint and wood in half a dozen places.

He heard the sound of footsteps at the bottom of the spiral staircase and sent his last grenade bouncing down the metal stairs. It went off somewhere below, eliciting cries that brought a savage satisfaction.

He turned on the pilot light of the flamethrower and came up over the edge of the parapet with the nozzle pointed at the boxcars.

Valentine loosed a long stream of fiery rain on the sentries aiming their guns at him among the line of boxcars nearest the tower, painting the roofs with orange and yellow flame. The jellied gasoline roared as it consumed paint and wood, splattering and running down the sides and filling the Train Hangar with black smoke. Fire, the most ancient of terror weapons, was as effective on the Twisted Cross as on the Golden Ones. The boiling flames silenced the shots from the men around the cars.

The Twisted Cross guards ran for their lives, some dropping their weapons as they escaped flame and smoke.

Looking down from his concrete nest, Valentine exulted at the havoc wreaked below. No wonder Ali enjoyed lighting fires; the results *were* spectacular. The flamethrower ceased its napalm ejaculation, empty of everything but harmless compressed air. Valentine dropped it and moved to one of the machine guns. With precise movements, he opened the ammunition box mounted on the side of the gun and slapped home the belt in the receiver. Teeth gritted and a snarl on his face, he pulled back the bolt and fired a burst at a group of guards running toward the boxcars. The gun chattered, steady as a rock in its mount, with less recoil than he would feel tapping a pool ball with the cue. Crouching, he concentrated on keeping anyone from fighting the fires now vigorously burning among the boxcars. He could feel the roaring heat almost painfully on his skin from thirty feet away. Nothing mattered but keeping those boxcars alight and the fire growing.

Two thin, nude figures staggered out from the cars on shaky legs, arms waving in front of them. He cut them down with the .50 and fired a burst into the cabin of a train engine being backed into the hangar to tow out some of the cars. Peppered by bullets strong enough to pierce the thin metal walls of their locomotive, the engineers jumped out of the engine and ran. Another nude Twisted Cross operator crawled from the wreckage, burned on his hands and feet. Valentine fired until the pale form ceased twitching.

Valentine heard orders shouted beneath the tower. He looked over the side and saw automatic rifles pointed up at him. He pulled back his head—not fast enough. A bullet grazed hot across his skin and he registered a hard tap, as if a doctor had taken his reflex hammer to the ridge of bone just below his eye, and then a second later the pain hit.

My God, I'm shot.

Not quite believing yet, he put a hand to his face, tracing the heat and feeling open skin with his fingertip. The bullet had torn a furrow up his face from his chin to the corner of his eye.

The burn that lasted a few seconds was just practice for what came next as his nerves revved up.

It was like a white-hot poker being held to his face. He felt himself scream, but there was just a ringing in his ears, lightning in his eyes as he viewed the world through a glittering curtain of diamonds. Somewhere outside the fog of pain and disorientation, he heard steps on the stairs. Concentrating like a drunk trying to get his house key into a lock, he picked up the shotgun, went to the stairs, and fired blindly down the spiral staircase. Blood poured out of his face. Dripped onto the storm-cloud-colored concrete and the metal stairs going down. Fell across his chest, warm rain. An apple dropped from the sky and into his concrete tree house. No, not an apple, a grenade.

There was nothing to do but jump. He launched himself out of the tower, spinning and pivoting —*wow! just like a cat*—to land hard on the surface below and run toward the darkness outside the hangar. Running had never been so easy; he hardly felt his feet touch the ground.

Though there was no one around, someone managed to kick him in his left leg as he ran. No matter, the foot on that side wasn't working that well anyway. He could hop into the darkness. But the darkness could not wait—it came rushing at him, greeting him in its comforting embrace like a long-lost love.

"It'll be all right, Molly," he said, lost in a strange new tunnel he had somehow floated into, an ever-lengthening passage of closing mists. "If you can't walk, I'll carry you."

He found the strength to turn his head, the darkness having decided to put him gently on the ground. He could see campfires in the distance. The fires burned brightly, meld-

ing into a single fire like the sun coming up. The fire was
what counted. The fire was all that mattered.

Too bad he was too tired to remember why.

David Valentine's body fought a hard war against waking
up. Every time consciousness charged up the hill, his exhausted, pained, exsanguinated body held the line and at
the last moment sent consciousness tumbling back into the
darkness of oblivion. It tried to return when he was picked
up and carried from where he fell, and tried again when he
was placed on a table. A bright light in his face and surgical
tape over his cheek brought other battles. Later, on a hospital bed, consciousness launched a series of sneak attacks.
He had vague dreams of speaking to Captain Le Havre,
then to his father.

Death never arrived to relieve his body from its war
against the pain, so Valentine eventually awoke. He was
disoriented; for some reason he wanted more than anything
to know how long it had been since he'd been taken.

As he spun back to the awful real world, he reached
up, but some kind of restraint frustrated his first instinct
to touch his face. In fact, he couldn't even turn his body.
The whole left side of his face throbbed in pain, and he
felt a tired empty nausea. There was cold dampness between his legs, as well as a warm, sticky, solid presence in
his undergarments. His left leg was missing its pantleg,
though the rest of his clothes were still on. The pain was
too much to deal with, so he sank back into a groggy
sleep.

He did not sleep deeply enough. A woman eventually cut
away the rest of his clothes and cleaned him up, a surpris-
ingly agonizing process, though she handled him as gently
as if he were a baby. When they changed the dressing on
his face, under the care of a man not nearly so gentle, it
hurt like the bullet cutting through his flesh a second time,
and he passed out again, unfortunately for only a minute.
He came round while they were applying more searing
iodine and another dressing.

The hours ticked by, and he tried playing games with the

pain, offering the pain thirty minutes of agony for just five minutes of relief, but pain would not agree to his terms.

He dropped into a fitful doze and came out of it a little further at a shake of his shoulder.

"Would you like some water?" a man in a lab coat asked.

"Yes, please," he croaked. There were more sensations now. The pain, always the pain, but he could also taste the air, and something about it told him he was underground.

The man brought the cup lower, and Valentine sucked cool water down through a surgical tubing straw.

"He can talk, that's good enough. Bring him."

Through the mists, he felt himself being lifted, carried down a hall to another room. They sat him up in a tube-steel chair with a hard wooden seat, the kind of chair that's been sitting in a neat row with five others just like it in some assistant principal's office since the school was built. They handcuffed his hands behind his back, which amused him. He was too weak to crawl, let alone fight. When they moved his leg to handcuff his ankle to one of the chair legs, the pain became so bad that warm urine flooded his pants. It felt like he was pissing nitric acid.

"Aw, Christ," one of the guards said, seeing the seat get wet and smelling the urine. "He pissed himself."

"So what."

Valentine's head lolled, and he looked at the pale green tiles on the floor. He tried to remember if he had ever seen such small tiles, so evenly laid out, when he again slipped into unconsciousness.

Later he had to wait. It felt like days, but perhaps it was only hours. His consciousness strengthened, and the haze began to fade. He realized that he desperately wanted to live, even if it was only for a few more hours. He wondered if they were just going to shoot him or if they had a more elaborate end in store.

They gave him more water. He was able to drink it, though it hurt his face to do so. The room was uninterest-ing, not even a desk or another chair decorated it. The little green tiles went from the floor about one third of the way up the wall. From there on up, it was unrelieved and undecorated concrete, marked only by a swirl or two of the mason's smoother. He smelled chalk somewhere and tried to remember if there was a chalkboard in the room from when he was brought in. The lone door to the room was also behind it, and he heard people passing in the hall at intervals.

When he heard a set of heavy steps in the hall, something inside him told him *This is it*. He tried to steel his mind, even if his body felt like worn-out rubber. But his mind was a slave to his body; intellect prostrated itself before the pain and fatigue just when he needed his wits most.

The door opened, and he was able to turn his head enough despite the pain in his cheek to see two tall Grogs enter. They were Golden Ones, dressed in black leather robes cut like a double-breasted trench coat of the Old World and shiny as a beetle's back. One stood to his right, the other to his left. Their fawn-colored hair was shorn down to stubble.

A dried-up husk of a man walked around in front of him. His skin had the waxy look of a cancer patient in the last stages of the disease; his lips chapped. Vigorous dark hair grew out from a widow's peak on his forehead and was brushed straight back across his head. His eyes could have been pale blue or pale green, depending on the opinion of the person looking into them. He wore a simple rust-colored uniform, and a Sam Browne belt very similar to Valentine's own. Red tabs with golden reverse-swastikas marked his collar. He wore no tunic, sidearm, or decorations.

"One of the best things about living so long," he said, in a vaguely European accent that Valentine was not experienced enough to place, "is that you get to see all the mistakes historians make, talking about something they don't really know.

"For example, the only history widely read since 2022 is that wretched pamphlet called *Fallen Gods* by that would-be Margaret Bourke-White named Kostos. She says the first of the new doors to Kur were opened in Haiti in the eighteenth century. She only missed by about a thousand years. How do I know? *I was there.* My eyes have looked on Charlemagne, young man. Kur had a door open in the Dark Ages, but they were not dark times for me—oh, no. During the Inquisition, we managed to get another open in Spain."

The General walked around behind Valentine and wheeled a cart into view. On it was his sword, his fighting claws, his little glow bulb, and a few other personal effects.

"So you joined long ago?" Valentine asked. "What did they offer for betraying a whole world?"

"What no price, no wisdom can buy. Time."

"So you feed."

"Yes. Long, long ago, I was given a gift, a revelation of biblical proportions, you might say. For my service, the scientists taught me how to achieve immortality."

"An immortality others pay the price for," Valentine said tightly.

"Don't cows, hogs, chickens pay the price for your life?"

"Not the same thing."

"That's where you and so many others are wrong. Cows and so on are eaten because they are tasty, certainly, but more important, because they aren't developed enough to keep themselves from being eaten. Mankind took a great leap forward when it learned to keep livestock, putting it ahead of all other creatures on the earth with a few bizarre exceptions like those honeypot ants that keep aphids. We were once no better than the cows, but we developed and the cows didn't. The cows pay the price, and we are better for it."

"Why are we talking about this?" Valentine asked.

"When you get to be my age, when you've seen people come and go over not just generations or centuries, but millennia, you become a good judge of men. In my days as a monk, before my awakening, I didn't think much of the human herd. No spark, no imagination, and misunderstanding even the simple concepts we tried to teach.

"As I've aged, I've found it harder and harder to suffer fools. Most people aren't much better than cattle. They've just inherited more complex stimulus-response routines. When you see men making the same mistakes, over and over and over again, you lose empathy and acknowledge only utility. That's what I tried to tell Kant when I lived in Prussia."

Valentine could hear someone outside the door asking for a message to be delivered to the General, and his aide accepting it.

"I think," the General said, "you are above the herd, a valuable piece of human capital. You, too, have been given gifts by the Lifeweavers. You have a talent I need badly. I'd like to have you on my side, rather than dead and in some Grog's stomach. If you found a tarnished bar of gold in the road, would you shine it up, or would you grind it up and toss it to the winds? I'm in a position to offer you what amounts to eternal life. A chance to grow your talent instead of wasting it."

"How can you have an opinion of me if you don't know me?" Valentine asked.

"When someone gets the better of me, I'd want to learn how they did it. I've done a little research, asked a few questions. A skilled man asked you some questions while you recovered. You were at the Eagle's Wings Brand out on those forsaken grassy dunes. Before that you were a promising officer, until you were sacrificed by an ambitious superior trying to keep his record clean. Yes, I have sources right in Southern Command. There are people you work for who want to live forever."

"You know me, then. Who are you?"

"Someone like you. A reader. A leader. More of a realist, but you are young, and idealism is the asylum of the young."

"I'm sorry you escaped the asylum."

The General ignored him. "I was, before my personal Enlightenment, a monk of the Dark Ages, one of those depressing, chanting celibates who claimed to be keeping culture alive after the fall of Western Rome, but were in fact dreaming up new ways to take advantage of the gullible. I was something of a historian, and I found hovering on the edges of certain ancient tracts pieces of a larger story. I convinced my superiors to let me go on a pilgrimage to the

Holy Land and beyond. I ended up going far beyond anything my order expected of me. I found the ruins of the Kurian City of Brass in Central Asia and met a smooth-skinned Chinaman who claimed to be two thousand years old. Thus began my education into the Arts of Kur. Later they sought us out. But the Chinaman—old Zhao—he was my savior, in a way.

"When I got my first infusion of vital aura, I was old and sick. It—you have to experience it, I can't put it in words. Where there had been weakness there was new strength. I'd forgotten what the flush of youth was; it's the finest feeling in the world. The opportunities it opened . . . I could live my life all over again. I lived dozens of lives all over again. The Golden Horde knew me. I saw the Turks come and fade, I rode with Cossacks as the Grand Armée retreated from Moscow. I invested and let time work for me over generations.

"My wealth bought power and influence, which I put to the bidding of Kur. I owned prime ministers and generals, diplomats and writers. Have you ever heard of major league baseball? Owners of teams used to buy, sell, and trade their players in an effort to get a team that would win the pennant. I was doing the same on a global scale, slowly and patiently. That is the great advantage of the Kurian scientists' immortality, Valentine. It gives you the luxury of patience."

Valentine looked at the dried-up old General. If anyone ever looked old and sick, except for his lush band of hair, it was the former monk.

"Where did you get the Twisted Cross?"

The General touched the reversed swastika on his collar tab. "This is an old symbol, a token of special status of those who are counted as a friend of Kur. You can find it on artifacts from prehistory almost the whole world over. I chose it to symbolize a reawakening of the old open alliance between Earth and Kur, men and their old gods. Men with the vision not just to accommodate the New Order, but to shape it for their own purposes, as well."

"So you're on a longer leash than most. It's still a leash." His croaking voice took some of the spite out of the words.

"Kur needs me, desperately, to do their fighting for them. They are too busy running their dominions, feuding and scheming amongst themselves. Now that they have won so much, they no longer want to risk their precious Reapers fighting with the pockets that are left. You've been troublesome in your obstinacy, unwilling to admit the war is over—like starving Japanese soldiers in an island bunker."

Valentine felt very tired, and began to wonder if he would remain conscious for the rest of the interview, or interrogation, or inquisition.

"General, I'm the one in handcuffs here. What's next for me?"

"You have a choice, a choice that you deserve, given your abilities and manifest intelligence, albeit talents wasted in the unrewarding service of the ungrateful. I am not just speaking of the pathetic Lifeweavers, either, I am referring to your so-called brethren who stay at home while you risk your life to protect their chicken-hearted existence.

"I will not insult you by asking you to join me. You need not say yes. All you have to do is ask for another week's life. And then another. And then another. I will show you visions, introduce you to possibilities that will fire your imagination, your belly, your loins. Someday you may be given touchstones and have knowledge at your disposal that Aristotle couldn't have dreamed of. The rewards are literally endless. What shall it be, son? The pistol—or another week's life?"

What'll it be, Cat? Die defending "the herd"? Or feed off it?

Valentine, hurt and tired, found an answer in his pain. Faces flashed through his memory. He saw Molly, the Carlsons, Sutton the generous pig farmer. Linda, who'd been Mrs. Poulos for a few hours, and the squalling baby from the Rigyard. Donna and her armoire-building son. The young Grogs gamboling with human children around the well of Steiner's little enclave. Ahn-Kha and the Golden Ones. Jocelyn Hendricks. Who would be sacrificed for whom?

His voice was strong this time. "Shoot me, Judas."

"A pointless end to the tale of the Valentines. You'll find your Golgotha lonely."

"How lonely is your bunker, General?"

The General struck the smirk from Valentine's face. Blood began to run out from under his bandage.

"You had defeated me in battle—well, defeated the men I trusted to fight my battles, which may mean the same thing. But that is a question for the philosophers. But what is a delay to me? Do you think you have really harmed me?" he asked, his eyes beginning to light up with angry fire. "Do you? Your pathetic little gesture was spittle in a hurricane. I can afford to think in terms of thousands of years. That is why this base is being built, not for one campaign in Nebraska, but for control of a continent. It takes years to select, grow, and train a fighting pair; I began this project before you were born and have seen it through setbacks worse than the fire you started.

"The science of Kur and my leadership has proved that this system works. Men can control Reapers, Reapers who fight like soldiers, without the weaknesses and desires of the Kurian from which they sprang. First principles, my son. I proved that I can do it with one, and if I can make one, I can make a thousand, and if I can make a thousand—"

The door opened again, and another shorn Golden One in the leather uniform of the bodyguard entered, almost dragging the protesting aide. The arrival said something to the other two in their own tongue. "I'm sorry, sir," the aide apologized. "There seems to be a disturbance outside in the Grog pen. We should go to the emergency shelter at once."

Valentine looked at the panting messenger, and his heart leapt.

The former monk let out a tired breath and nodded.

Valentine tried to stand, drawing the General's eye. "That may be true, sir, from a logical point of view. But I think someone is going to have to pick up where you left off. It appears you've fucked with the wrong species."

"Wha-*awk*," the General managed to get out, before

Ahn-Kha wrapped his viselike fingers around his throat. The angry titan picked up the General, swung him at the shocked aide.

Valentine's chair fell over in the struggle, but he still could see the unique sight of a man being beaten to death with another man used as the murder weapon. With six blows, Ahn-Kha reduced both the General and his aide to bloody pulp. The General proved to be a poor choice of club; he began to fall apart after the third swing.

The bodyguard Grogs shrank away from the twitching corpses, as though the General might rise again in demonic fury. But it was just reflex of muscle and broken bone making wet sounds against the floor. The bodyguards exchanged a few tremulous words with Ahn-Kha and then embraced him.

The Golden One breathed hard after his exertion. "You do not look yourself, my David. Let me help you."

The bearlike face hovered over his. As the world slipped, Valentine tried to stay conscious.

Back. Feel the pain. Smell the blood. Hear the—gunfire. There's gunfire?

"What did you say to the bodyguards?" Valentine asked weakly. A few shots sounded from the hall.

" 'If you do nothing, all is forgiven.' It is a little more poetic in my tongue. I hope this does not hurt you further." The Grog's arc of muscle at his arms and shoulders tensed, and the handcuffs snapped in two.

The door opened, and Alessa Duvalier stood silhouetted in the frame, encased in Twisted Cross assault armor. The gear made her look a little absurd, like a turtle in too big a shell. She held a rifle to her shoulder, covering the hallway, and her naked, blood-smeared sword stuck blade-up in her waistband. A sweat-soaked headband kept flame-colored hair out of wild and hungry eyes.

"No time for kiss and tell, boys. Heat's on."

Valentine wondered if he were in some wild dream brought on by loss of blood. "Ali?" he said, "What are you doing here?"

She reversed the magazine in her gun, quickly substituting the full one for the empty one taped to it. "I'm milking a male ostrich! What does it look like, Val? I'm taking point for your pointy-eared friend."

Ahn-Kha scooped Valentine up in his arms and followed the female Cat out the door and down the hall. At an intersection ahead, Valentine saw another Golden One with a machine gun at his hip, spraying the corridor with fire. They turned at the corner opposite to where the Grog was firing, and Valentine got a brief glimpse of a corridor littered with bodies. Valentine felt himself being carried up some stairs, thinking that perhaps it wasn't so bad to be partnered with a mentally disordered woman—sometimes. Then he passed out.

"The hardest part was figuring out where you were," Duvalier explained the next day.

Valentine lay in his hammock in some thick woods on the Missouri River well south of the Twisted Cross base. Ahn-Kha was sleeping soundly, Valentine's PPD cradled in his arms. Valentine sipped some willow-leaf tea to ease the pain. According to Duvalier, he had the blackest black eye she had ever seen.

"I caused a little trouble with the column that hit the Eagle's Wings, but I mostly wanted to learn where their base was. It was just a matter of getting into camp and keeping my ears open. The stunts you pull are the type of thing only Bears are stupid enough to try—I'd just as soon stay out of the way of bullets, thank you very much. Not that I don't admire your balls."

She kissed the bandage over the left side of his cheek.

"Maybe I can introduce you to the twins and their big brother when I can walk again," he suggested.

"Dream on, Valentine. So I go to the rendezvous and wait, and naturally you don't show. So I leave a note and come hunting around the south end of Omaha. I pretty much mapped out the base, got an idea of the numbers the Twisted Cross had, and found out that oversize perimeter wasn't too well guarded. The General was planning for the future, I suppose. But his present couldn't do the job.

"So one day I'm checking out the west side of the wall, and I see this ugly ape trying to move through the brush, real sneaky-like but making more noise than a bulldozer in a bottle factory. I'm about to do him in from ambush, when I see this ugly, drum-fed gun in his hands. It's just too much of a coincidence for there to be two of those in Nebraska, so I stick my blade to his throat and start asking questions."

Ahn-Kha opened an eye and snorted. But he didn't disagree.

"It turns out you've disappeared into the camp, they heard an explosion from a mile off, but then you were MIA the next day. He sent his buddy off for reinforcements and had just about decided to try to bust down the main gate to go looking for you when I showed up.

"That night I went into the Cave and acted like a *Cat*—instead of a one-man army, please make a note of that Valentine—just looking and listening and hearing what was being talked about. It turned out that you were in the basement medical center below this Train Hangar. I saw the General return from Omaha, with what was left of his force after his Reapers mysteriously started dropping in the middle of the assault on the Grogs. He said something about wanting to meet the man they captured, and I knew you were still alive. I also found out you were going to be interrogated the next day.

"I got back to your big friend here, and he has a hundred armed-to-the-ears Grogs, wanting Twisted Cross blood. And you. And then more blood."

Ahn-Kha carried on the story. "The Big Man came to our aid after all. He hid a few pistols and grenades in the food going to the Golden Ones the General had hostage on the base. It was not much. But it got them out of their pen.

"I told them to start tearing the place down. After that, it was just a matter of sneaking in with your uncle over there and waiting for our chance to get you and the General both."

"What happened at the base?"

"They still had a lot of firepower. There were losses. It

was really two rescue missions, a little one for you and a big one for the Grogs still on the base. I don't think we'll have to worry about the Twisted Cross for a while. They don't have many of those Reapers left. Maybe they can put the operation back together, but it'll take some time. Their underground is intact. We couldn't even get near that Cave of theirs. We'll need to get Bear teams up here to blow that."

Ahn-Kha yawned, showing off his tusklike teeth. "Ha! Not if the Golden Ones had anything to do with it. Whatever we built, we know how to destroy. Even now we use the great construction machines to build a cairn for our dead. On top of the Twisted Cross bunker, of course."

"Old horse," Valentine said, "I think the balance of gratitude has shifted back in your favor. Now I am in your debt."

The Grog's eyes were closed in his dozing, so Ahn-Kha settled for the human gesture of shaking his head. "I told you there could be no talk of debts between brothers, my David. I always wanted to see the wider world."

"We could learn from you, too. That heartroot could be grown on every farm in the Ozarks. Wherever people are, there's moisture and, uh, fertilizer. The idea might take some getting used to, though."

"I have pieces of spore-pod in my pack. No Golden One travels without it. This I can do."

"What about it, Ali, shall we go home?"

"You need to rest a little. Why do you always have to rush things?"

Valentine smiled. "Because life is short. Thank God."

She furrowed her eyebrows at him and went back to re-bandaging his leg.

He felt sleep coming on him again, and he looked over at Ahn-Kha. He wondered what would have happened if the Cat and the Grog had not shown up. His conscience pained him more than his face. Did they rescue him from a quick death—or endless life? He remembered the knot in his stomach, fearing his life had run its course. His words had been brave enough, but they were just words, stiffened by pain. When he felt the cold barrel of the pistol at the back of his head, what would have been his choice? *A question for the philosophers,* as the General said.

Eight weeks later, in the rich colors of autumn in the Ozarks, Valentine limped right into an ambush. Of course, since he saw the men watching and waiting, it could hardly be called an ambush, but the young Wolves were clearly proud of their work, hallooing to each other once they had the trio dead-bang. He, Ahn-Kha, and Duvalier put up their hands.

"Where the hell do you think you're going, Groglicker?" the leader of the close fire-team asked, squinting at them from under woolly eyebrows and a notched felt hat. Valentine would have handled the ambush differently were he in charge, letting the far fire-team make contact and keeping the close team hidden to provide a nasty surprise in case things got hostile.

"My code name is Smoke," Duvalier said, stepping forward. "This is my partner, Ghost. Verification November: five-oh-three. Take us to the nearest post—we're coming in with a priority report for Southern Command."

The sergeant in charge of the patrol pushed his coonskin cap back on his head. "That so? Well, Cats or no, we'll have to put you under guard. Unload your weapons and sling them, and we'll oblige right quick. What's that with you, a prisoner? Don't think I've ever seen a Grog like that before. Where'd you capture long-legs?"

"That's not a prisoner," Valentine corrected, leaning on his walking stick. "He's my brother."

"Hell's bells," one of the Wolves in the background said to his comrade out of the corner of his mouth, "what was his old man thinking? I've heard of a guy being desperate, but there are some things that just ain't right."

The Wolves, pointing their weapons away from the three, gathered around their charges, positioned to guard as well as to guide. The Hunters turned and headed home.

Read on
for an excerpt from another
exciting tale of E. E. Knight's
Vampire Earth . . .

TALE OF THE THUNDERBOLT

Available from Roc!

"Tea and rum, if you've got either," David Valentine said, dripping from head to foot on the sawdust-sprinkled floor. His coat trapped the wet of his shirt better than it kept the rain out.

"Got both, Coastie."

"The hotter the better," he said, pulling his hand through his slick hair to get it out of his eyes. A silent mental alarm had tripped a switch in his nervous system, warming him better than any fire. Details stood out: the meshed ranks of gray hair on the barman's arms, a blemish on a prostitute's neck, footsteps muffled by the sawdust scattered on the floor, the smell of a rancid spittoon.

The officer in the corner spoke to his men, and from their intent attitudes Valentine knew orders were being issued.

"You cold, Captain?" a whore asked, attracted by the Coastal Marine officer's uniform. She brushed a wet lock of hair behind his ear. "I got a way . . ."

"Some other time, perhaps. Sorry, I have to be somewhere," Valentine said, turning away from the girl.

Goddamn rain! Goddamn bar! Goddamn me! The voice inside his head recited, as if repeating some kind of blasphemous penance. Over a year's worth of preparation about to be flushed with the objective in sight. All because he felt like coming in out of the weather.

Valentine racked his brain for the name, picturing the hawkish face in the hammock that summer in the Yazoo Delta. Lewand Alistar, a freshly invoked Wolf six years ago and posted missing, presumed dead. So the Reapers hadn't killed him after all. Perhaps he had been captured and turned, perhaps he had been planted in Southern Command as a spy who saw his chance to get away clean. Whatever put him in a Carbineer's uniform in New Orleans was immaterial—the fact remained that mutual recognition occurred.

And act he did. Valentine remembered Alistar as a quick-witted, active comrade whose only fault was the prediction to give orders through a sublime belief in his own superiority. A steaming mug of spiked tea arrived, and Alistar chose that moment to rise and take up his coat. Valentine concentrated on blowing into the crockery in front of him. Alistar's companions shifted their chairs around, pretending to watch the barmaids and working girls, but in fact eyeing Valentine.

Valentine feigned nonchalance, hearing rather than seeing Alistar move behind him. He readied himself to turn and fight, should the footsteps approach. But the Quisling left the Easy Street in a hurry. Very typical of Alistar: not heroic but smart. No wonder he wore a major's cluster in the Kurian Zone. Valentine needed to get out of the bar too, without being impeded by Alistar's comrades, who he guessed had been ordered to keep him from leaving. He reached into his pocket and wadded a ball of money in his hand. He turned to the whore who had approached him.

"Interested in a little fun and a lot of money?" he asked, his rough voice low.

"Always" she said, smiling at him with a decent, if tobacco stained, set of teeth behind compound layers of lipstick.

Valentine thrust the money into her shirt, pretending to feel her up. "There's a hundred and then some. I want you to start a fight."

"And that's all I gotta do?"

"Yes."

"Shit, Marine, I'd do that for free."

Valentine turned away from her and moved to the other woman, a Hispanic with a thick fall of waist-length hair.

"I've heard you're quite a woman," Valentine said, raising an eyebrow suggestively. The whore cocked her head and smiled welcomingly.

"That's my up, you bitch!" his paid prostitute shrieked. The new girl reacted with a speed that would have done credit to many of Valentine's former comrades in the Wolves. She planted herself, lowered her hips, and spread her arms to receive charging fury.

The two women fell to the floor, spitting and hissing like two fighting bobcats; a ring of hooting barflies formed around the combatants. Valentine backed through the crowd, snatched a hat off of an unattended table, and moved out the door before any of Alistar's soldiers had a chance to push through the crowd to guard the exit.

The conditions could hardly be worse for tracking a smart man in the crowded city with a two-minute head start. Night, rain, and the cluttered streets all conspired to hide his quarry. Visibility was nil; the big bosses never bothered much with public lighting. Most men would not have had a chance.

Alistar would not just run to the nearest phone. He had no idea if Valentine was working alone, or with others who might have picked up a surreptitious signal and followed him out of the bar. Valentine remembered him as a man who liked to be in command. It was quite possible that he would get a posse of his own Carbineers together, to better take the credit for his coup in capturing or killing one of Southern Command's "terrorists."

The barracks of the Carbineers would mean a long walk, too much time wasted. But Valentine knew from months of working the port that a contingent of them guarded their supply warehouse by the docks. Some of Alistar's men would be there.

It was only a guess, but as good a guess as he could make. Valentine ducked through an alleyway and broke into a sprint down a road parallel to the one Alistar probably took. Even if Valentine had guessed wrong, the farther he got from the Easy Street the better.

He loosened his coat to run better. If anyone saw him, pounding down the center of the near-empty street, splashing through puddles, they might mistake him in the wet and darkness for a Reaper and give him a wide berth. His sprint did not end at the hundred-yard mark; he called on his reserves and they answered, propelling him through the night with legs and lungs of flame. Astonishingly, at least to anyone who did not know what a Hunter was capable of, his speed increased.

The warehouse he sought was in an old, brick-paved part of town. Garbage lay in heaps in every corner, and better than half the buildings were fire-gutted shells. Empty, glassless windows gaped out at the street like skulls' eyes. He pulled up at a noisome alley, partially blocked at one end by a stripped car turned on its side. Its gutters served as the local populace's aboveground latrine, judging from the smell. Valentine used it to cut back to the main thoroughfare. Alistar was a former Wolf, and there was every possibility of him scenting Valentine before seeing him without some kind of masking odor.

He paused in a deep well of darkness under a fire escape and drew a pointed knife from his boot, nerving himself for what he had to do. Killing in battle, with bullets cracking the air all around and explosions numbing your senses, was one thing. Premeditated murder required an entirely different side of his persona. It was a version of himself who had killed helpless men in their Control Tanks in Omaha, blew a bound policeman's head off with a shotgun in Wisconsin, and knifed lonely, frightened sentries on isolated bridges. Cold-blooded need provoked those killings, but his sense of exultation in the deeds bothered his conscience more than the acts themselves.

Valentine heard footsteps over the steady patter of rain, coming from the direction from which he expected Alistar. Two people hove into view in the middle of the street, walking together under some kind of tarpaulin sheltering both from the weather. Not his quarry then, but . . .

One was definitely pulling the other along. The insistent guide was about the right size and shape. Clever. Trusting his hunch, Valentine collected himself for a spring. As he crouched, the analytical side of his brain appreciated the irony of Alistar also using a woman as camouflage, paralleling his own subterfuge in the bar. The tarpaulin provided just the right touch of shape-concealing cover. He probably grabbed her out of a doorway, tucking himself under the improvised umbrella with her and ordering her to accompany him. Alistar had always shown cool in a crisis.

As they passed, not seeing him in the rain and dark, Valentine leapt. His standing broad jump covered five meters, ending in a body blow catching Alistar in the small of the back. The two tumbled down, the man he was now sure was Alistar ensnared in the wet canvas.

The girl screamed out her fright, and Valentine heard her stumble and right herself. He paid no attention, concentrating on getting his knife to the Quisling's throat. The man struggled in the folds of the tarry material like a netted fish.

Valentine straddled Alistar, pinning his chest and arms with the full force of his body weight and muscle as he cut open the tarp. The stiletto dug into his former comrade's neck, eliciting a squeal. "No, no, Dave! Wait!"

Valentine paused, not moving the knife either farther in or back. He had not been called Dave since his days as a recruit.

"Dave, it's not what you think," Alistar said, his face colorless with fear. "You think I wanted this? You remember how it was—we separated, with the Reapers coming after us. One got me, picked me up. They took me all the way back to Mississippi. Had the choice to join or die. They wanted to know more about the Wolves. I fed them a bunch of bullshit with just enough truth mixed in to be convincing. Never really joined though, never really joined. That's why I ended up in this rear-area hole—didn't want to fight against y'all. You have to believe me. I met a girl, got married. We've talked about running. Every chance we get alone, we discuss it."

"You could have contacted me in the bar, then. Quietly. What did you run for?"

"I . . . I got scared."

"Looked to me like you were running for help."

"I didn't tell the guys you were with Southern Command. I said we fought over a job once, and you threatened you'd kill me if you ever got the chance. I ducked out to go get my wife. I was going to have her go in there and talk to you. Make you see our way. She's honest—you can tell just by talking to her. I knew you could always read people, Dave. You'd be able to get us out."

Valentine listened with hard ears for anyone approaching to investigate. He let Alistar speak.

"We can be ready in an hour. Hide out wherever you tell us. I dunno why you're here, but maybe you need some advice about how to get away." Alistar looked up at his captor calculatingly, and Valentine wondered if he was worried he had overplayed his hand. "Or not. We'll do whatever you say. Any way you want it. Just tell us where you want us to be, we'll meet you. My men got a good look at you: I turn up dead, and they'll be on the hunt for a Coastal Marine or a man of your description. This is a big city, but it's got six thousand militia and as many paid informers. You let me go, and if I'm lying you're no worse off; they're still looking for a Coastal Marine of your description. But if you believe me, Val, you'll be saving my life and my wife's. Maybe I can help on your job, from the inside or outside. Just trust me, give me a chance to prove it."

Valentine put himself in Alistar's shoes. The summer of his eighteenth year, had their roles been reversed, could he honestly say he would not have followed Alistar's path, given a choice of death or grudging service? But how grudging? Alistar wore a major's cluster, after all. Perhaps he wore other insignia.

Valentine shifted the knife and used his right hand to pull open Alistar's raincoat. On his old comrade's breast was a row of little silver studs projecting out of the green uniform and set over a shining five-year badge. Valentine knew that each stud represented five confirmed kills of enemies bearing arms, and the badge had probably been gained through turning over friends, neighbors, or comrades to the Reapers.

Alistar read his fate in Valentine's eyes and opened his mouth to scream for help. Valentine shot his hand up to

Alistar's throat, crushing cartilage and blood vessels in a granite grip. A sound like a candy wrapper crinkling and an airy wheeze were all that came out of the Quisling's collapsing throat.

"Would've let you go another time," Valentine said, staring into the bulging eyes. "But what I'm here to do is just too damn important."

Valentine got up off the corpse of his former friend. Emptying his mind, quieting his thoughts with the aura-hiding discipline of the Lifeweavers, had a succoring side effect: it kept him from thinking about what he had just done. He carried the corpse off to the stinking alley and placed it in the gutter. He went to work with quick, precise motions. Using his knife, he tore a ragged hole just below Alistar's Adam's apple, then picked up the twitching body and held it inverted. The warmth of the draining corpse upset him somehow. He watched the blood mix with the rain on the cracked and filthy pavement, shivering from cold, wet and nerves.

Between the injury and the confused girl's story, assuming she was brave enough to go to the Authorities, there was a chance that whoever found Alistar's body would conclude a prowling Reaper had taken him, draining him of blood with its syringelike tongue.

A whistle blew somewhere in the night, perhaps connected with his murder. He stuffed the body in a debris-filled window well. For some reason the Reapers usually concealed their kills. Too slender a thread on which to hang the success of his mission.

It would have to start now. He was in for a very long night.

THE NOVELS OF THE VAMPIRE EARTH

by

E.E. Knight

Louisiana, 2065. A lot has changed in the 43rd year of the Kurian Order. Possessed of an unnatural hunger, the bloodthirsty Reapers have come to Earth to establish a New Order built on the harvesting of human souls. They rule the planet. And if it is night, as sure as darkness, they will come.

This is the Vampire Earth.

WAY OF THE WOLF

CHOICE OF THE CAT

TALE OF THE THUNDERBOLT

VALENTINE'S RISING

VALENTINE'S RESOLVE

VALENTINE'S EXILE

FALL WITH HONOR

WINTER DUTY

Available wherever books are sold or at penguin.com